D

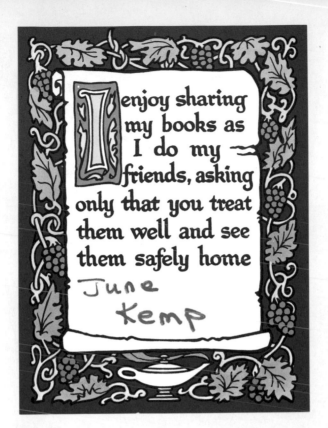

I enjoy sharing my books as I do my friends, asking only that you treat them well and see them safely home

June Kemp

D0358840

DOMINION

DOMINION

PAMELA FERGUSON

CASSELL
LONDON

CASSELL LTD
35 Red Lion Square, London WC1R 4SG
and at Sydney, Auckland, Toronto, Johannesburg,
an affiliate of
Macmillan Publishing Co., Inc.,
New York

First published in Great Britain 1979

ISBN 0 304 30469 7

Typeset by Inforum Ltd., Portsmouth
Printed in Great Britain at
the Camelot Press Ltd, Southampton

To Jocelyn
for enduring

ACKNOWLEDGEMENTS

Although Dominion is the story of a fictional dynasty and a fictional company, it draws on much of the historical material that established the multinational tobacco combines, and consciously reflects many of the controversies surrounding the industry today.

I would like to acknowledge a few of the books that helped deepen an insight I gained into the industry during my days in journalism and advertising in London: *Trust in Tobacco*, Maurice Corina (Michael Joseph 1975): *The American Cigarette Industry*, Richard B. Tennant (Archon Books 1971): *Cigarette Country*, Susan Wagner (Praeger Publishers 1971): *WD & HO Wills and the development of the UK tobacco industry 1786–1965*, W.E. Alford (Methuen & Co 1973): *The Story of Tobacco in America*, Joseph C. Robert (University of North Carolina Press 1967): *Sold American—the first Fifty Years. 1904–54* (The American Tobacco Company 1954): *The Sacred Pipe—Black Elk's account of the seven rites of the Oglala Sioux*, recorded and edited by Joseph Epes Brown (University of Oklahoma Pess 1953): *A Treasury of American Indian Herbs*, Virginia Scully (Crown Publishers, 1971): *Red Man's Land/White Man's Law*, Wilcomb E. Washburn (Charles Scribner 1971): *The Superlawyers*, Joseph C. Goulden (Dell 1973): *Subliminal Seduction*, Wilson Bryan Key (Signet 1973): *Man and his Symbols*, Carl Cl Jung (Doubleday 1964): *A Dictionary of Symbols*, J.E. Cirlot (Philosophical Library 1962): *The Gentle Art of Smoking*, Alfred H. Dunhill (Max Reinhardt, 5th impression, 1973).

On the health issue, I'd like to mention: the three

successive reports issued by the Royal College of Physicians in London (*Smoking and Health* 1962: *Smoking and Health Now* 1971: *Smoking Or Health* 1977), *Smoking and Health—Report of the advisory committee to the Surgeon General (1964): Public Policy and the Smoking, Health Controversy*, Kenneth Michael Friedman (Lexington Books 1975): *Tobacco and your Health—the Smoking Controversy*, Harold S. Diehl (McGraw Hill 1969), *Smoking and Its Effects on Health*, World Health Organisation (Geneva 1975): *Work is Dangerous to your Health*, Jeanne M. Stellman and Susan M. Daum (Pantheon Books 1973).

In addition, my sincerest thanks go to the various heart and lung surgeons, pathologists, immunologists and cancer researchers in both Britain and North America who were so generous with their time and expertise in both supplying information and double checking my material. I would also like to thank the solicitors and barristers in London who took such care going through relevant scenes in the book.

Pamela Ferguson
San Francisco 1977

PROLOGUE

When Queen Victoria died, men were no longer required to puff cigars up chimneys, away from the disapproving eyes and noses of their womenfolk. The Prince of Wales had made smoking popular. Now, as King Edward, his tastes and habits were being followed openly and eagerly.

But a subtle shifting in social attitudes wasn't the sole reason why the heads of Britain's tobacco families came together to create Dominion.

The fastidious Mace twins, who headed the largest tobacco company, were alarmed when a tall copper-haired American in a brocade waistcoat, flamboyant suit, and bearskin cloak, swept into their offices one morning with the words, 'Hello, boys. Harmer from North Carolina. Come to buy your business.'

Stirling Harmer was, even then, no stranger to anyone associated with tobacco. The son of a poor Southern farmer turned manufacturer, he was to set a style that established the modern tobacco combines on both sides of the Atlantic. His was the era of the self-made buccaneer. Although his boyhood had been spent in the backbreaking cultivation of tobacco, he was a born salesman and soon learned that any man who lived by growing tobacco deserved to die starving.

As a young boy, he'd set off at dawn in his mule wagon to sell plug and twist by the roadside. Then he dreamed up names like *Gold Rush, Bronco, Strike,* and peddled his products in the nearest towns. Still later he paid salesmen to dress up in gaudy frockcoats and matching top hats to ride new fontiers, selling Harmer tobaccos. He even had salesmen on the dockside handing out free tocacco when the immigrant boats touched shore.

He saw the quick profits that could be made by making smoking popular. He strengthened his own manufacturing base

1

from time to time by moving into a new county and risking a month's profits to sell his goods at half the price of a close rival, until the rival buckled and was forced to sell out. Or he indulged in the modern art of industrial sabotage. He'd plant a man at the head of a rival's sales team for the sole purpose of directing their efforts into unprofitable areas. When profits slumped, the company was only too willing to sell to Harmer.

But building a solid manufacturing base and acquiring new companies wasn't enough for a man like him. His father had seen the effect the Civil War had had on the smoking habits of the Yankee and Confederate troops when their paths crossed at Durham, North Carolina. Each soldier who survived the war would spread the habit of cigarette smoking when he returned to his home town. So Harmer senior raised his son in the belief that 'it's the cigarette boy, the cigarette.' The cigar-puffing and plug-chewing tobacco diehards didn't agree at all. They dismissed the cigarette as a passing fancy or a fad fit for dandies. Cigarettes threatened the virility of the cigar, they argued. So the market was open for Stirling Harmer. And for him, that meant a rolling machine. To find just the inventive, uncluttered, and hungry young mind he needed for his invention, he held an open competition for engineering students and offered $75,000 plus a token cut of royalties for the winning design.

One young student from Boston came up with a contraption that looked like a series of forming tubes running down a staircase. Noisy, ungainly, but it could roll two hundred cigarettes a minute. The best one handroller could do was fifteen hundred a day. So Harmer fired his handrollers and employed the young student full time to build a series of machines and run the workshops.

Later he moved to New York, took a two-dollar room on the Bowery and prowled the streets at night looking for crumpled cigarette packets to teach himself about brand preferences. He signed up the best printers. He was the first man to introduce cigarette cards and promotional gimmicks. He launched a series of cards showing actresses in different stages of nudity and advertised them lavishly through window displays. That stunt

2

earned him the New York *Mercury's* label 'perverter of morals.' He laughed all the way to the bank.

By the end of the nineteenth century, he was in the grand position of being able to call his rivals together, suggest they lay down arms and create a mighty combine to dominate the American tobacco industry. That combine was to be known at U.S. Tobacco.

But Stirling Harmer wasn't a man to be content with one goal. He wanted more. America's tobacco industry was his. It was time to cast an eye across the Atlantic.

The tobacco families in Britain were a different breed. Their thoughts about tobacco were more traditional, less cutthroat. Their packaging and image were less concerned with frontier towns, gold rushes, or conquering the West: more concerned with the early colonial era of tobacco, when the grand plantations of Virginia were established by several leading families. Those days had long since gone, but they were part of a tradition to which men like Harmer didn't belong. The British tobacco families were aware of his flamboyant way of doing business and shocked by his methods and nerve. He had sent emissaries to prepare the way, offering licenses to chemists to stock U.S. Tobacco brands along with their drugs. This wasn't the British way of doing things at all.

When Stirling Harmer arrived at the offices of the Mace twins with a multimillion-dollar bank draft in his pocket, the twins had him promptly shown to the door. With their fundamentalist, nonsmoking, nondrinking background, they were horrified by the unruly American with his untidy hair and loud clothes.

Within a week they had arranged for the heads of all the British tobacco companies to meet. The idea of an amalgamation wasn't new, of course, but it took a buccaneer like Harmer arriving unannounced on their doorstep to hasten the men into their horsedrawn carriages late one December evening in 1903. The man, Harmer, was uppermost in their minds as they drew up one by one in the snow outside London's Tabac Club.

3

The Tabac was, and still is, exclusive. Because pipe smokers were barred from London's best-known clubs, the Tabac was established at the turn of the nineteenth century to enable gentlemen to smoke what they pleased, where they pleased But even given that freedom, many members still preferred to frequent the more exotic cigar dives by night.

The club was austerely furnished. Crests of the leading families adorned the entrance hall. A visitor then, and a visitor now, would face the same view. New members had to be approved by the leading tobacco families, a tradition still upheld by the club.

One room upstairs was maintained for the exclusive use of the leading families, and it was here that the Mace twins had arranged to meet their fellow tobacco men.

Oswald Mace took the chair, black frock coat, white wing collar and cravat meticulously pressed for the occasion. His brother Harold was dressed identically. He took the seat at the foot of the table.

The others gathered on either side of the large old oak table. There was the blustery Hamish McNab, whose father, a former paymaster to the toops during the Crimean War, had returned to Britain to set up the first cigarette factory. Just as the Civil War spread cigarette smoking in America, the Crimean War introduced the short, squat Turkish cigarette with its cane mouthpiece to British soldiers.

Sacha Penthman sat next to McNab. A Russian émigré, Penthman brought skills to Britain that had been in his family for generations. He made a fortune out of a shop front in Regent Street, filling the window with Russian cutters and rollers making cigars and cigarettes. He was shrewd enough to know that this was the best way for a newcomer to capture the imagination of the London public.

The youngest men at the table were Hugh de Balagne and Paul Lombard. De Balagne was the son of the Corsican pipe maker who first introduced briar pipes to Britain. He was the mystic of the group, a dreamy-eyed Cambridge history graduate who often made his poet and musician friends think up names

4

and descriptive phrases for his pipes and tobaccos. Paul Lombard was his more severely dressed accountant partner. Lombard was a fast-talking, City of London banker's son who converted de Balagne's poetry into profits. Lombard was to be Dominion's first financial director, to be followed by his son, and his son after him. His was to be the only direct blood link with the modern board.

Facing them, Willy Boscawen watched the shifting expressions with a bemused air. The Mace twins bobbed up and down importantly with their carefully prepared notes, urging the men to think in patriotic terms about the future of British tobacco. It had to be protected from the brigand American with his medicine man ways.

Boscawen chuckled inwardly. A cartoon from *Punch* hung on the wall behind Oswald Mace's head, mocking. Boscawen smiled and caught a fleeting wink from Sacha Penthman. He and Penthman appreciated one another as the two outsiders in the group. Members of the other families gathered there that evening came from backgrounds similar to the Mace twins'. They rumbled their disapproval of Stirling Harmer, agreed with the chair with shouts of 'Hear, Hear,' and bowed their heads respectfully when the name of the late Queen was mentioned.

Boscawen was the only Cornishman present. The talk of patriotism meant little to him. He wasn't even a dyed-in-the-wool tobacco man. Son of a bootmaker, he had acquired a chain of tobacco shops in a poker marathon during his early twenties and built them up with a retailer's flair. Tobacco was a religion to the Mace twins. It was a profitable business to him.

Dominion was established as an appropriately patriotic name for the new group. Within a few days of the conference, Boscawen joined forces with Stirling Harmer against the group. He sensed the mischief ahead, and that it would be more profitable to side with Harmer. The American offered him six hundred thousand pounds for half his business, double the amount suggested by the Mace twins. But Boscawen was more intrigued by the scent of jousting in the air. He wasn't to be disappointed.

5

As soon as Dominion was officially formed, Harmer set about wooing the tobacco retailers. He urged the head of the association to stock up on U.S. Tobacco products, and 'if y'all slash prices to the bone, we'll make up your losses'.

The Dominion board soon found itself in the midst of a long and bitter price war, with each side offering the retailers incentives to stock one side's brands rather than those of the other. As the bidding intensified, Harmer made it known that he would share his first four years' profits with the retailers. *The Times* wrote, 'There is no parallel to his magnanimity, except perhaps in the case of that friend of country yokels who sells sovereigns for sixpences'.

The retailers were now in a position to put pressure on Dominion. When Dominion rallied, Harmer introduced coupons that could earn the smoker anything from a haircut to a new bicycle.

Paul Lombard was the first to suggest a shrewd compromise. The price war had to stop. Why not give the retailers the right to sell what they wanted, as long as they didn't display Harmer and Boscawen products in their windows?

His suggestion threatened to split the board. Backing down was seen, by some, as a sign of weakness. Well, the more farsighted members of the board reasoned, perhaps the time had come to call a truce and invite Harmer and Boscawen to join the board.

A second meeting was called at the Tabac Club, where the warring factions agreed to lay down their arms and work together for mutual profit. Harmer and Boscawen sold a third of their company stock to Dominion and were automatically elected to the fledgling board of directors.

Harmer got what he had wanted all along and what the price-cutting war had been all about. He now had a base within the British Empire and access to the hungry markets of the Commonwealth.

But with men like Harmer, there comes a time when society calls to collect. In his long, acquisitive climb to the top, he had grown immune to his roots. The tobacco farmer had become merely a supplier to feed his machine. With the power of U.S. Tobacco behind him Harmer was able to dictate prices and cut the farmers down to size.

The farmers rallied against him by forming associations and pools. But they weren't strong enough. And when many farmers discovered that they were forced to sell at a loss, they resorted to violence. The era of the Night Riders was born. Any man who sold to Harmer direct and refused to join the pool was in danger of seeing his crops and barns go up in a blaze of fire. The masked, gowned figures rode by night, and continued quietly cultivating tobacco by day. Public sympathy was with them and eventually the government.

Stirling Harmer was served an antitrust suit which succeeded in dismantling U.S. Tobacco. The year it happened, the Trust sold over six billion cigarettes in the U.S., in spite of their prohibition by twelve states.

The various hearings succeeded in uncovering countless companies within the Trust, which the public had always thought to be independent rivals. Harmer had built an empire out of a combination of boot-strap and giant. The revelations drove him out of America. Like the farmers, he had been cut down to size.

Subdued and somewhat humbled, he returned to Britain, intent on serving out his business life as a member of the Dominion board. Hell, he thought bitterly, they knight men like me in Britain.

It was in London that he met his match in Amy, the illegitimate daughter of Willy Boscawen. Estranged from her father for some years, Amy had been raised by an aunt on a small farm in Cornwall until she left home to work with Sylvia Pankhurst, organizing political and social centres in the East End of London.

Any industry that exploited female labour became Amy's recruiting ground. Cigarette factories were an obvious target. It was on a makeshift platform outside one of Dominion's factories that Stirling Harmer first encountered Amy. She was a tough-minded fighter, a belligerent contrast to the delicate ladies of the day. She spoke with a strongly resonant West Country accent, in a language that Harmer could understand. She was a new challenge to him.

In spite of the difference in their ages, he fell in love with her almost immediately. Her abrasiveness appealed to him. So, in an odd way, did her unmasked disapproval of his capitalist attitudes.

Like many of her fellow suffragettes, she was arrested on several occasions and force-fed in prison. She became a victim of the 'Cat and Mouse' Act and was forced to go into hiding. On one occasion, fearing her near death, Harmer asked her to marry him. She agreed to do so, but only when women got the vote.

He sensed the unlikelihood of this. It was her way of saying 'when hell freezes over'.

When the first World War broke out, Harmer returned, with some reluctance, to America. The war was extremely profitable for tobacco companies, and Harmer paid handsome wages to the captains who would ship his leaf across the Atlantic. Dominion signed up exclusive contracts with the War Office.

Even Willy Boscawen, who wasn't immune to the wealth the company brought him, questioned the morality of the industry with its gleeful enthusiasm for supplying the War Machine. Unlike many industries, tobacco, which was heavily dependent on female labour, didn't suffer from the exodus of male factory workers, and profits soared during the war.

Boscawen found his thinking drawing closer and closer to that of his daughter. The war appalled him but during it he died.

When the war ended, it seemed inevitable that Harmer and Amy should marry. At least that was uppermost in his mind when he heard that women had got the vote.

Although she openly disapproved of his politics, Amy liked Harmer's earthy ways and the shocking effect he had on the Dominion board. He was as much a challenge to her as she was to him. They had both been born poor and raised on small farms. But where a fear and hatred of poverty had made him acquisitive and hungry for power, it had made Amy into a radical. The fight for women's rights wasn't an end in itself, but the beginning of a class war that would see vast political change.

Harmer's private fortune financed many of her projects, and she saw no conflict in this. It was her private way of distributing wealth to the many who had earned it for the few.

In the early twenties, a daughter, Daphne, was born to Stirling and Amy. She inherited her mother's stocky physique and her father's flamboyant copper hair. She was a bright, cheerful little girl with a vivid imagination that her mother was careful to nurture.

But being the product of two such extremes had a strangely maturing effect on the young child. Her father filled her with tales of tobacco. Her mother talked at her about revolutionary politics. Where other children grew up on fairy stories and tales from the Bible, Daphne was weaned on a mixed and not altogether compatible diet of tobacco and Trotsky.

Instead of opting for one or the other, she retreated from both into a silent, imaginative little world of her own.

Stirling Harmer died when his daughter was very young. She discovered him early one morning, and the image of his still, white face and busy copper hair and side whiskers remained with her throughout her life. She felt abandoned by his death.

Escape came during the second World War in the form of a handsome young army officer from a crack British regiment. His name was Charles Courtland. He had descended from a long line of eminent generals dating back to the American War of Independence. Daphne prepared herself to be a army wife, but Courtland had other plans. After the war, and after he had served time in Palestine prior to the dismantling of the Mandate, he told Daphne he believed he had a future at Dominion.

When Courtland joined Dominion's management training programme he and Daphne had two children, a daughter, Tessa, and a son, Harmer. The children were markedly different and Courtland couldn't hide his disappointment that his first child wasn't a son, and that his second child wasn't the son he wanted.

He and Amy could never see eye to eye. He couldn't abide

9

her abrasive tongue and outspoken criticism of him. His strongest weapon against both his wife and her mother was his social background and famous family name. Nor did he see the need to hide his feelings from his children. 'With my breeding and your mother's money,' he was fond of telling them, 'you children lack nothing.'

When Amy died in the early sixties, Daphne and her descendants became the sole heirs to the Harmer Trust. This had been established by Stirling Harmer a few years before he died to prevent his headstrong young wife from squandering his personal fortune and investments on her various political causes. A condition of the Trust was that its recipients could not sell Dominion shares.

Daphne was secretive about the Trust. She never discussed it, or its contents, with her husband. If there was one thing her mother had made her understand, it was the need to maintain a certain aloofness about her personal money matters. It was her weapon against Charles, the only one she had to combat the Courtland family name.

Charles Courtland rose within the company and held various executive positions. He was made chairman of the Dominion Group during the sixties. He was subsequently knighted for his contribution to British industry.

He was bitterly disappointed when his son Harmer rejected the idea of an army career, thus breaking a tradition reaching back across several generations of Courtlands. And to make matters worse, the boy had no interest in tobacco.

Courtland felt partially compensated when his son joined a company parachute team.

Dominion had invested heavily in sports promotion following the banning of cigarette commercials from the TV screens, and parachuting proved to be one of the more popular sporting activities. Courtland never missed an opportunity to watch his son jump. It was second-best to seeing him enlist as a paratrooper.

1

On the morning of her forty-eighth birthday Daphne Harmer-Courtland looked up and watched the plane carrying her son and the *Mace 8* parachute team climb higher and higher. It hovered like a tropical bird over the crowds waiting expectantly below. The day was piercingly clear. Daphne felt very alone.

'Everything all right, my dear?' Dominion chairman Sir Charles Courtland glanced quickly from left to right. He hoped some TV cameraman wasn't planning to film her anxiety.

Dammit thought Courtland. The hostesses dressed up like walking *Mace 8* advertisements were supposed to catch the camera's eye, not his wife! He touched Daphne's arm and wished their daughter were beside them to complete the family picture. But Tessa hated public appearances, and nothing he could say made the least difference. Sir Charles snapped his fingers irritably and a chair appeared behind him.

'Daphne, my dear, if the sun's too much for you, why don't you sit down?'

She shook her head and stared with hypnotic fascination at the plane circling above them.

Music shrieked out from loudspeakers scattered through the crowds. There was a crackling noise followed by a tap-tap-tapping.

The announcer, sporting a red-and-white striped blazer and cream slacks to match the *Mace* house colors, pulled the mike free of the wires at his feet. The loudspeaker protested and whined. 'Hello, hello, hello—testing, testing, one-two-three-four. *Yeeeeeowwwl.* Can you hear me up there, Tom?'

The crowd looked up, expecting to see a voice materialize in the sky.

The announcer made a swooping gesture with his arm.

11

'Tom says we look wonderful down here, ladies and gentlemen, and the first parachutists are juuuuuust about ready to jump. Those of you who do not know our team will be interested to hear they won the European cup last year. They're wearing *Mace* colours so you'll have no trouble telling them apart from punk elephants, those of you who were at the *Mace* ball last night.' He chortled at his own joke.

Daphne wanted to run to the mike and scream a warning, but something told her to stop being so ridiculous. She sensed her husband's disapproval and smiled brightly waving her hand at no one in particular.

'... and here come the first to jump, ladies and gentlemen, Peter and Paul Stevenson; a graceful twosome. When the others jump the four of them will form a circle above you in the sky, so have your binoculars ready. Harmer *Courtland* will be the next to jump, uh, Mr. chairman, are you watching your son? To digress into history for a minute, young Harmer's grandfather, Stirling Harmer, founded the company in America that first used aerial chirography, ah, skywriting, to advertise its leading cigarette brand in the early twenties. So you are about to see his grandson continuing a fine tradition.'

The crowds cheered spontaneously. Courtland acknow-ledged the applause and squinted up at the sky. Nice to have the odd touch of family history thrown in. Went down well with the press.

'...and there go Bobbie Toledo and young Courtland. Whoops, there go the Stevenson parachutes. Perfect timing, lovely sense of timing.'

Two red chutes flashed brilliantly in the sky.

'. . . and there's the third to open, Toledo's. Wonderfully clear day we have for this, don't we? Feel I could *touch* our blue sky. Oh, don't worry about that fourth chute ladies and gentle-men, that's young Courtland playing his usual game with us, keeping us on tenterhooks till the veeeeery last second. Experi-enced jumpers all of them, and they take turns doing this. Keeps the old adrenalin working, doesn't it? Phew!'

Daphne stared at the shape falling in the sky. *Open it.* Don't

12

do this to me, Harmer. Open it. Jesus, open it.

The crowds, believing it all to be part of the thrills, cheered wildly. The announcer laughed nervously. Suddenly everyone stopped laughing and cheering.

The shape hurtled to the ground.

Running. Sirens. Ambulances. Someone dragging her by the elbow. Terrible screaming. TV cameras. Blackness. *My son.*

'She seems to need to relive it every year on her birthday.' Charles Courtland stared out of the french window and gestured toward his wife.

Tessa Courtland looked up from her book and frowned. 'Do you mean this has been going on for ten years, and you havn't told me before?'

Courtland nodded.

Daphne Harmer-Courtland stood alone in a muddy field at the bottom of their garden. She was a short figure in a motheaten brown fur coat, dark corduroy slacks, and rubber boots. A gray cat lay across her shoulders, nuzzling her face.

'Does she talk about him to you?' Tessa stretched in her chair to peer across the garden.

'Never.'

'Have you tried?'

'No.'

Courtland reached self-consciously for his pipe. He avoided his daughter's eyes by relighting it carefully. After puffing vigorously for a few seconds he asked, 'Does she ever talk to you?'

'She did at first,' said Tessa, closing her book. 'But not now. I had no idea this happened every year. Why on earth didn't you tell me?' She stood up and joined him at the french window.

Courtland grunted impatiently and blew out a pungent cloud of smoke. 'No point in indulging her. Not healthly. I had to learn to live with it, why couldn't she? I'll go and make some tea.' He turned abruptly and left the room.

Tessa didn't bother to reply. She opened the french window and reached for an old dufflecoat lying draped over a chair outside.

Daphne knew she was dealing with things better each year. Harmer's death had released her. Yes, that was it. Was she being selfish, admitting it to herself? All her married life she had played at being an appendage to her husband's career, latterly nothing more than a hostess and entertainer for his ghastly business friends. Before that she had been trapped in a world of political extremes. The memory of her father on one side and the unrelenting round of political activities pursued by her mother on the other. In the middle of it, a child, bewildered, unable to resolve anything. And in the distance a faint memory of parents so fiercely independent, it was as if they needed one another to enforce their differences.

The child had escaped into a dreamy private little world, and that was where the adult had returned. Now she could be what she really had been all along, primitive, eccentric, reclusive.

Charles called it symptoms of withdrawal. But that wasn't it at all. This was Daphne being Daphne.

The cat looked up, startled. It sprung from her shoulders to the ground and scampered off through the long wet grass to the house.

Daphne turned. 'Oh, it's you, Tessa, you frightened me.'

'It's getting so cold, Mother.' Tessa squinted up at the sky. A heavy gray cloud was moving menacingly toward a lone patch of blue, winter reminding spring not to push its luck.

Mother and daughter looked at one another intently. Tessa saw the tranquillity in her mother's eyes and some of her anxiety lifted. She smiled and linked Daphne's arm with her own, turning her toward the house.

From behind, the two looked curiously different, except for their hair. Tessa was tall, angular, a Harmer. Daphne was short, stocky, a Boscawen. But the copper curls piled high on their heads were identically styled. Harmer hair.

Daphne was secretly pleased she saw more of her parents

14

than her own husband in her daughter. If only Amy had lived long enough to see Tessa mature from a gangly schoolgirl into a poised barrister, heir to her grandmother's uncompromising campaigning spirit.

Daphne sensed a streak of the hustler in Tessa too, and that came from both Stirling and Amy. She looked up at her daughter and admired the strength in her profile and high cheekbones. Her skin seemed translucent in the afternoon light.

Tessa flushed and smiled down at her. 'What's the matter?'

Daphne shook her head, and the two continued to walk on slowly, listening to the grass squeak under their boots. She wished she could have had the same undemanding relationship with Amy, instead of growing up knowing she was a disappointment to her mother, but eventually she sought her own liberation by making a hasty exit from a home filled with Marx, Trotsky, Sylvia Pankhurst, and Jane Addams into an early marriage.

Unsurprisingly, Amy was dismissive of Charles, then a young Dominion trainee. 'Fortune-seeking schemer, Daphne, after you father's money. No doubt you were bloody fool enough to tell him you were rich.'

Oh God, thought Daphne, Charles was *my* choice, mine. Why speculate on what might have happened had I followed Amy's advice? I didn't. 'That was what was important,' she said out loud.

'What was, Mother?' Tessa glanced at her anxiously.

'Hmm? Oh.' Daphne turned and stared at the field.

'Do you want to talk about Harmer?' Tessa sopke quietly but firmly.

'No, dear. If I did, I would.'

Tessa sensed that this was true. She decided not to say anything more. She was open to her mother's needs, but careful never to press her. For all her mother's feyness and gentleness, she was self-protective to a point where innocent probing could provoke a sudden flash of anger. Tessa was accustomed to it. She knew how to avoid it.

Daphne sensed the unspoken in her daughter and relinked

15

their arms. She returned to her own thoughts. Like many people who had inherited wealth, she was indifferent to it. Unlike Charles. She'd heard him vehemently denying that his present wealth and position had anything to do with her. 'Nonsense,' he'd scoff. 'Got drafted into Dominion after the war like many young army officers. Their chances were as good as mine. Fact I'd married Daphne Harmer didn't make any difference. No difference at all. Public companies can't afford to be sentimental about family ties.'

Daphne wondered if Charles would have been different married to someone else. She always believed he wouldn't have been so obsessed with the need to become chairman of Dominion. Somehow, that was his only means of dominating her. Not that she ever saw herself as a threat. How could Daphne ever threaten anyone? No. It wasn't *Daphne*, but what Daphne represented, a germinal fuck between two powerful people.

She'd given up apologizing for not being what was expected of her. She withdrew.

She lived simply, in a ramshackle sort of way, and let Charles go his own way, allowing their separate lives and interests to become reflected in their home. Once, when he was a nervous young army officer recovering from the onslaught of war, and she was a quiet attractively plump young woman with large searching eyes, they couldn't stand separation. They owned, or rather she owned, a five-room early Victorian terrace house, but they lived, ate and slept together in one room as though afraid the walls would deny them even five minutes of togetherness.

But all that had died long ago. She watched him shelve his lifetime collection of stamps and fill their Tudor home of some twenty years with ice-cold jade. His gleaming, silver Rolls-Royce stood importantly in their twin garage; next to it stood her own defiantly shabby 1950 Prefect. She filled her part of the house with voluminiously comfortable sofas, rocking chairs, her mother's book collection, and half a dozen cats. Courtland filled the 'show' part of the house with antiques.

The effect was clean and sedate, like rooms in some vast

16

stately home, roped off during public viewing time, and used only on formal occasions.

The cats stayed out of it voluntarily.

Courtland's own room and dressing room were strictly functional. Bed, military chest of drawers, large wardrobe, rolltop desk, orderly bookshelf. Long, oval mirror on a stand, silverbacked brush set. Quarters awaiting the arrival of a general from another regiment perhaps. The pipe rack, whisky decanter, and framed box of war medals could easily have been left by a previous tenant. The eye searched for signs of daily use: crumpled pair of pajamas dropped on the floor, dirty ashtray, wrinkled holiday photo. But such details were painfully absent.

Daphne was as uncomfortable in her husband's rooms as he was in the chaos and clutter of her own. Neither of them displayed a photograph of their son, a point that wasn't missed by either but was never discussed.

The only room that sustained some kind of family warmth lay behind the french windows. It was dominated by a heavy monklike trestle table, flanked by sturdy wheel-back chairs. A couple of chintzy armchairs and the Boscawen rocker surrounded the fireplace.

The room was compact, attractively uneven, and still had its original sloping beamed ceiling and oak-panelled walls.

Courtland was happiest here, but would never have admitted it. Now, as he peered out of the windows at Daphne and Tessa meandering across the lawn toward the house, he gave a satisfied grunt and leaned down to place another log on the fire, kicking it into position with his foot. Three sleeping cats protested and glared up at him. He ignored them, stretching over their heads to warm his hands. Courtland and the cats had long since agreed to respect their mutual distance. They never trotted to him for the brisk ruffling they got from Daphne. He never reached out to them for company or warmth.

They slept on Daphne's quilted bed, and that sealed the final separation between man and wife.

Courtland studied the two women approaching him and felt saddened and a little envious of their closeness. He might

17

have had that once with his son, and now there was no one. Harmer's room had been cleared out, completely, and as each year passed he regretted that more and more. All his possessions disappeared one day in a row of crates and tea chests. Courtland wanted that at the time, but now he secretly longed to sit in the room as it had been and feel his son's presence around him.

Why was it Daphne had that in the field, in *public* and he couldn't find it anywhere?.

He had to look elsewhere for something to fill the emptiness. Courtland sighed. His thoughts drifted toward Ted Mallett, Dominion's young American product development director and something of his protégé. Not that Mallett ever suspected Courtland was subconsciously moulding him like a son, and not that Mallett resembled Harmer in any way. Mallett was as tempestuous as Harmer was tranquil. Courtland had never believed in hiding the hurt and disappointment he felt when Harmer scorned the army and a career in tobacco for a job teaching music at a scruffy school in South London. Courtland felt a sudden twingle of guilt, a fleeting echo of the arguments he used to have with his son. The guilt turned to pain. Some of the pain he could ease by concentrating on Mallett's meteoric career. It was stimulating to study the way Mallett, a former football pro, treated business developments like a series of Super Bowls.

Courtland watched his wife and daughter pause by the honeysuckle border. He had been brought up to expect everything from a son and nothing from a daughter except respect and love. So he couldn't really understand Tessa's career. Why wasn't she *married* to a successful barrister and raising a family, *his* grandchildren, instead of creating a formidable reputation for herself at the Bar?

Secretly he envied her lack of inhibitions. He refused to admit she had more guts than his dead son, although he knew Harmer had taken up parachuting solely to please him. After the accident, cruel tongues suggested Courtland had driven him into parachuting, but Courtland dismissed such talk.

His son was a poet, and parachuting was a sport for poets.

18

One thing did please him. Whatever Daphne may have thought, he believed both their children had inherited from him their tall, slender physique.

Courtland turned from the window and quickly examined the table. It was the housekeeper's day off. If he had his way he would keep a permanent butler and cook, but his wife flatly refused, allowing the housekeeper to bring in professional caterers and helpers when business functions demanded it.

But sometimes, only sometimes, he enjoyed being alone with his family. This particular day he wanted everything to look nice. A Large pot of tea was keeping warm under a red velvet cozy. A dark, rich fruitcake waited to be sliced next to a plateload of honey-colored scones, dishes of home-made blackberry jam, and freshly whipped cream. Milk, sugar, and three of the best cups.

Three.

He glanced away. How long would it take for the hurt to stop, the sight of three cups, three plates, three everything, whenever Tessa visited them? Courtland ran his fingers through his wavy silver hair and wished he could tell Tessa about it.

He also wished there was some solution to his wife's withdrawn behavior; he saw his inability to deal with it as a sign of weakness that he wasn't prepared to expose.

Courtland looked up. Daphne and Tessa were a few feet away from the house. He stepped over the cats to open the french windows. 'Hello, my dears. Just in time,' he said, rubbing his hands briskly, pipe clenched firmly between his teeth. He glanced at the sky and pulled a face, 'Ugly old cloud. Might be foreced to spend the afternoon playing Scrabble.'

Tessa peeled off her dufflecoat.

Courtland stared at her washed-out blue overalls crisscrossed at the back over a collarless shirt. 'Tessa, darling,' he asked his thirty-seven-year-old daughter, 'why must you always dress like a workman when you come home?'

She turned and eyed his cashmere cardigan, checked Viyella shirt, and thickly woven tie. 'Dad,' she replied. 'Why must you always dress like an advertisement in *Country Life*? '

19

He laughed good-humoredly. 'Touché. Dammit where's your mother disappeared to now? I'm famished!'

'I'm here,' came a singsong voice. Daphne kicked off her boots outside and appeared at the door in her stockinged feet. She smiled at her husband and knelt down beside the cats.

Tessa switched on the radio and Bach's B Minor Mass boomed into the room. She turned it down to a more soothing level and reached for the tea pot.

Daphne removed her fur coat and draped it over a chair, rolled back her sleeves, and started to butter some scones.

Courtland placed his dead pipe in a glass ashtray on the mantelpiece and hummed with the choir in a pleasing baritone.

The tea was poured, plates filled with scones and cake, and the three of them sat down around the fire which hissed lazily in the grate.

Courtland was the first to speak. 'Daphne, have you made a decision about the opera tomorrow night?' He rose to refill the cups. 'After all, it is the opening of the Dominion season and I'd like you to be there. I do need you on these occasions.'

There was an awkward silence.

'Oh, all right, Charles,' Daphne said with resignation, stretching out a foot to stroke one of the cats. 'As long as I don't have to stand around exchanging mindless drivel with everyone afterwards.'

'Of course not,' said Courtland shortly, trying hard not to sound irritated. 'Carruthers will drive you straight home from Covent Garden.'

'No, I don't think so, dear.' Daphne looked fondly at her daughter. 'Perhaps I'll stay with Tessa for a few days.'

'What, in her canal warehouse? You'll freeze to death. We'll stay in the flat.'

Daphne shuddered. She hated his London base, used for formal occasions, or whenever he worked too late to drive home to the country.

Tessa smiled. 'Why don't you both stay with me for a change! Long as you don't mind sharing space with an Irish girl whose husband lingers in Brixton jail waiting to be charged with something, or two black kids whose parents have disappeared in Johannesburg.'

Courtland moved defensively and glared at his daughter. Dominion had subsidiaries in Ulster and South Africa. 'I thought we agreed never to discuss politics here,' he said, stabbing viciously at the fire with a poker. A shower of sparks hurtled up the chimney.

'I'm not,' Tessa said honestly. 'I think it would be a good idea if mother came up to London with you. If I'm not in court we could all lunch together.' She paused to sip some tea and waited for the fire to recover. 'Good excuse to introduce you to an excellent brasserie opposite the Old Bailey.' She grinned and stood up to brush crumbs off her dungarees. 'Someone mention something about Scrabble?'

Daphne brightened visibly and started to clear away the dishes.

For the sake of his wife's birthday, Courtland decided to ignore Tessa's bait. He laughed affably and rose to get the Oxford Dictionary.

2

Dominion House stood out, tall, spare, and uncompromising on the south bank of the Thames.

Its seventeen stories of sandstone and glass had been built in an area transformed by the property boom from a windswept hodgepodge of decaying warehouses into a prime site.

The world's largest tobacco combine and one of Britain's leading industrial groups, Dominion lived in sight of the buildings across the river that could reflect or direct the mood in the executive suite for the day. To Dominion's east, the Stock Exchange soared into the sky beyond the dome of St. Paul's in the heart of the City. To Dominion's west, Fleet Street ribboned its way between the nation's newspaper empires. And beyond that, the towers of parliament sat upstream at Westminster.

Ted Mallett was oblivious to the semicircle of landmarks facing his office window. His world of product development drew more from Madison Avenue than from anything remotely British.

Today he was disturbed by the laboratory report lying in front of him. Whichever way he looked at it, it told him his career was at stake.

He felt something he hadn't experienced during his ten years away from professional football. Panic. As one of the highest paid quarterbacks on the field he remembered how it felt to misjudge the game, and to hear the disapproving roar from the stands. He was *their* Super Bowl hero. And there was one thing a star could never do in the public eye, be human, make a mistake.

Now he was holed up in a cedar-paneled office far away from forces of adrenalin, muscle, and sweat. He could sit there all day and stare at the report. The play would continue around him. But the feeling was the same, and so was the pressure.

Ted touched the button of his intercom.

'Yes, Ted?' Manna Henderson, his assistant. Brisk, cheerful, reassuring.

'Could you buzz Lawrence in the lab and ask him to come up in about twenty minutes?'

There was a pause. 'Don't forget your meeting with the chairman later this morning.'

'Oh, I'll be through by then.' Ted released the button and smiled. Henderson had him nailed to a precise timetable. He saw himself as an ideal man and was often irritated when a creative session was cut short by some company ritual. Left on his own he'd be a hopeless manager of time. He needed Henderson. He knew that, but sensed he was the only executive who didn't consider himself part of the formally stratified group structure. He was the corporation man directing the nerve centre of the eighties and nineties.

He had been wooed away from Harmer Brands, Dominion's American subsidiary, to do a specific job. Develop new products. When this included spearheading the search for tobacco substitutes to neutralize the antismoking controversy, the reason for the transfer from New York to London became highly political.

Political? Ted stared at the lab report. It held data on a project he believed could solve the tobacco problem in both the United States and Britain. It was too damned important to be stalled at this stage by the results of poor lab tests.

When he had started working on tobacco substitutes everyone was thinking in terms of synthetics, which is why Britain led the research. To conduct such studies in America was to invite open confrontation with the tobacco states. The American end of the industry used the tobacco farmers' contribution to the Southern economy as one of its major lobbying tactics. How could it suddenly dynamite this argument by developing alternatives?

In the beginning, he had thought in terms of synthetics too. Alternative smoking substances that could be developed in the

23

lab. Fibrous compounds that drew the tobacco companies closer to the chemical combines in research. But Dominion's introductory step into the era of new smoking materials had been a disaster.

Ted recalled the colourful launching of *Catch*, in a lemon sherbet pack, with a tide of posters and advertisements in the glossy magazines. The public responded instantly to the novelty. Then without warning sales began to plummet. All it had taken was a columnist in a mass circulation daily to say: 'Smoking *Catch* is like smoking *Tampax*.'

The lesson taught him something profound. In the expensive rush to find alternatives to tobacco, Dominion had missed the obvious. Smokers found tobacco sensuous. It was as simple as that. They couldn't respond to a synthetic in the same way.

No lab could compete with that.

Which is why he had delved into history for a solution. Perhaps the answer lay in an alternative plant.

The solution had to offer tobacco's appeal and marijuana's mystique. It also had to cool the medical objections to smoking. These requirements were never openly admitted by the industry, but were nevertheless fundamental to his research.

The trail led him back to the origins of smoking. Tobacco wasn't the only plant to be smoked or chewed by the aboriginal peoples of the Americas. He delved into the lore of American Indian herbs. Of all the plants that had been smoked for medicinal or pleasurable reasons, one stood out for development and study in a modern context. Even the name was poetic. Yerba sacra. The sacred herb.

Ted relived the moment of intense excitement at the revelation after months of field study. To think everyone had gone running to the test tube for a solution, while the answer lay right there in history. Unlike tobacco, yerba sacra had almost passed into extinction. Bushes of it could be found scattered amidst the sagebrush in the Northwestern states. But it was only certain elders of the various reservations in the area who still dried the leaves in the sun to mix with tobacco and spice up their smoking.

Yerba sacra was one of various substances used for centuries to highlight or subdue the effects of tobacco, or to produce a special fragrance. There was the bark of the red willow, kinnikinnick, red-osier dogwood and magnolia bark, sandwort and the quinine bush, mullein and ceanothus leaves. Everyone in his division had tried them, mixed them together or smoked them on their own, pressed into pipe bowls, or rolled like joints. But yerba sacra scored the highest points on taste and acceptability. It was also best suited to the needs of the mass-produced cigarette.

It had taken them a few years to develop an ideal hybrid and an exotic cigarette that appealed to successive consumer test panels, all of whom believed they were sampling some new, rare tobacco mixture.

The novelty and aboriginal source of the product was a gift for any advertising man. Unlike tobacco, yerba sacra had never been adopted by explorers and transported over the seas to the courts of Europe to be spread by the decades into a daily habit. Which left it fresh, romantic, authentic.

Ted visualized the product's instant appeal to youth. There was enough sensuality to suggest a trip, but not enough to make it illegal. It was made for the back-to-earth, alternative lifestyle generation.

Most important of all, it could eventually be grown in the tobacco states.

The experimental station and farms he had set up on and off reservation land in areas where the yerba sacra bush was indigenous was only the first phase. He wanted a hybrid that, like tobacco, could eventually be grown from Florida to Ontario.

But, however much he tried to boost and justify the product in his own mind, Ted couldn't escape the report staring at him from his desk. Argue with it as he might, it threatened yerba sacra.

The results from the skin painting experiments on mice were self-evident. They had a potentially dangerous product on their hands. They were back to square one.

25

Ted saw his hopes and dreams of being the man who revolutionized the industry at the end of the seventies swirl into nothingness.

Perhaps he was just being morbid.

Ted stood up and walked into his bathroom. If he didn't shave twice during the course of the day his five o'clock shadow felt like sandpaper by midafternoon. But this morning he was shaving for diversion. He needed time to think.

He eyed his wiry black hair tamed to a suitable executive length, thick but not unruly. It made a change from the days when little more than a crewcut had his coach screaming for a barber. Now, in his early forties, Ted knew that if he weren't a Dominion director he'd let beard and hair do exactly as they pleased.

He was trapped, goddamn it. Football or business. They decided what his image should be. He never seemed to have any choice in the matter. There had been a time when he considered his handsome features and body a liability because no one would take him or his master's degree in economics seriously. What had he achieved since then?

He left professional football at the height of his career, fearful of becoming the has-been everyone laughed at on the side. He had always vowed he would never succumb to the classic alternatives, sports commentating or movies. But advertising and marketing? He would have laughed that one off too. *Mallett leaves the Vikings for Madison Avenue.* How the hell did that happen? Chance. Not choice.

When one of the top five New York agencies asked him to appear in a sportsmen's shampoo commercial, he told them they could damn well use his ass instead of his face unless they allowed him to change their lousy product. They said go ahead and try. He told them to tear up their research data and send teams into locker rooms all over the States to find out exactly what sportsmen wanted in a shampoo. When the computer processed the data, it pinpointed a gap in the market no one had noticed. A need for a conditioner shampoo that could stand up to the athlete's daily hairwashing ritual, a container that could be kicked around a shower, and a product with sufficient macho to convince sportsmen to stop washing hair and body with the same harsh deodorant soap.

Mallet named it Head Up and the agency made him tell the story of its development in the commercials. The product broke the first year's sales target within two months. The client moved swiftly on to Head Up colognes, aftershave, deodorants, and soap and promised to double the account if the agency could entice Mallet away from football full-time. Mallett admitted he was turned on by Head Up's surprising success. If he could call the shots, there was no reason why he couldn't be as good in advertising as he was on the field.

His time in pro football had turned him into a skilled tactician. Strength, he knew, depended on knowing your opponent's weaknesses and on your ability to fool him and exploit the breaks.

The business world was no different. The individual was only as good as his team. Working out new products in tandem with a client's marketing forces gave him the chance to exercise his skills in a highly creative way.

When Harmer Brands took over the Head Up company Mallett waited for the knock on his door.

Tobacco companies were wooing sportsmen with a vengeance to help promote smoking as a healthy activity. He didn't smoke, but there was something else. He was from Florida, and no kid grew up in the South without knowing about the colourful role tobacco had played in American history. Hell, it was the crop that helped build the first colony at Jamestown. He lost count of the number of times tobacco was used as currency. During the American Revolution, Virginia leaf paid for war materials. George Washington's plea to the people was, 'If you can't send money, send tobacco.'

Washington's namesake, George Washington Hill of American Tobacco, introduced slogans and compaigns over some three decades, that were still an inspiration. Ted saw Hill's classic 'Reach for a Luck instead of a sweet' slogan of the late twenties winking at him from behind modern advertisements for *Silva Thins* and *Virginia Slims*. But his knowledge of economic history had also shown him how the original companies had moved from their flamboyant origins into a surprisingly small number of vast multinationals.

The secrecy of those mutinationals puzzled and intrigued him. Not until he had joined Harmer Brands, the company he considered the epitome of the American capitalist dream, the empire that had grown out of a log cabin, did he discover that it had become a subsidiary of the London-based Dominion group after Stirling Harmer's death.

Once inside the company he was determined not to let that stop him from creating a product that would reflect modern American history as much as Harmer reflected the past. He hallmarked his arrival with a brand called *Peace* to be kept on ice until the end of the war in Vietnam. Advertising men later called it a model of concept and timing. *Peace* captivated the exalted mood of the American people and rose quickly to top the sales charts in its division.

Dominion invited him to London to become their youngest board member at thirty-eight, on the strength of his track record. But the label, Ted recalled, wasn't nearly as important to him as the chance to leave his football image behind. People didn't gape at him in London's streets, and there he was judged solely as an innovator. He was even losing his Southern accent.

He put down his electric razor and reached for a bottle of Head Up aftershave, smacking it on his cheeks and sniffing the gingery tang in the air indulgently.

He returned to his office, reached for a pencil and memo pad and began trying to view yerba sacra in perspective. Ted believed in capitalizing on popular fads with cigarette brands. It was one way of bucking the restrictions on tobacco advertising. When denim became more than a fly-by-night fashion fancy he worked on its essential youth acceptability and classlessness by launching a French-style cigarette with a pungent smell and called it *Denim*. The brand shook Gauloises within a year, backed by provocative posters and a strongly youth-angled choice of media outlets.

And now yerba sacra. Very acceptable to the consumer in the limited terms of their test panels. Launch date into test market scheduled for the following spring. And now some *mice* could ruin everything. A smoker would have to puff away at thousands of cigarettes a day to be exposed to the same amount of smoke condensates painted on the back of mice. But if too many mice developed too many tumours from the substance that was enough to stall the project.

For God's sake, we're not intending to sell the brand to *mice.* . . .

His intercom was purring gently.

Ted pressed the button. 'Mm hmm?'

'Dr. Lawrence is here,' Henderson announced.

'Ask him to come in, Manna, and keep on holding my calls.' Ted released the button and crumpled the top sheet of the memo pad into a tight ball.

The door swung open to admit Dr. Chris Lawrence. The young biochemist's plump body looked ready to burst out of his skintight jeans. He wore a see-through white muslin shirt open down to the last two buttons.

Ted had once believed researchers were middle-aged men with thinning hair and starched white coats, but business had taught him otherwise. He ran his division like an informal cross between an agency and a football team, but on this day he found the biochemist's appearance annoying. Lawrence's thick blue black hair cascaded over his shoulders, and his own bushy version of a Fu Manchu moustache looked untidier than ever.

Lawrence was oblivious to Ted's reaction. He dropped casually into a swivel-bucket chair opposite the director.

'Lawrence, I need more details on your mouse theory.'

'Not theory, it's fact,' said Lawrence tartly through his slightly protruding teeth. 'Three out of the four strains of black mice we're required to use in the skin painting experiments develop malignant tumours from the condensation of yerba sacra mixed with tobacco. The rate of development is roughly twice that of mice exposed solely to tobacco, or solely to YS.'

'That doesn't mean smokers will react in the same way.'

'Ah!' The young biochemist removed a crumpled pack from his pocket. 'Ah,' he repeated, rolling himself a cigarette in liquorice paper. 'The nonscientist has pinpointed the total inadequacy of the laboratory in its relation to the human condition.'

'Don't be sarcastic Lawrence.'

Lawrence struck a match casually on the heel of his boot. 'Faced with this problem of inadequacy,' he continued, lighting up, 'we are nonetheless confronted by a larger problem, namely, to have the product cleared by the Tait Committee and approved by the stringent standard of no less than Sir Heath Tait, fellow of respected medical institutions, vice chancellor of Edinburgh University, and formerly dean of its medical school.'

Mallet sensed Lawrence was trying to needle him. He wasn't going to be needled. 'All the previous tests seemed satisfactory. Why should the committee get excited about this one?'

'Viewed in isolation these tests don't seem all that dramatic. Viewed in conjunction with the results from the smoking dogs and baboons, however, they take on a different perspective. If you recall, animals trained to smoke the new substance develop a quick addiction to it.' A tiny puff of smoke escaped from Lawrence's moustache.

Mallett was irritated by the biochemist's smugness. 'The human test studies didn't show acute signs of addiction,' he reminded him. 'The committee was more impressed by those results than the results from the dogs and baboons.'

Lawrence clucked impatiently. 'The human studies are necessarily limited. We can't control and monitor them twenty-four hours a day and examine their reaction to a choice between food and a cigarette. We can with baboons, and they are a close second-best. My set of baboons became so addicted they showed fewer signs of stress when exposed to an electric current and then rewarded with a cigarette than when they were withdrawn from smoking altogether.'

Mallet stared at him. '*Electric* currents? Who the hell asked you to do that? Tait doesn't require you to go that far.'

Lawrence laughed at him. 'Nothing I do in this lab is anywhere *near* what is done by medical and psychology students in labs all over the bloody country, not to mention the countless tests done by other commercial labs. We're the lads who have to make your products work, remember that.'

'By using electric shocks?'

'Well, what would you prefer, a terminal cancer ward?'

'I don't share your logic, Lawrence. The rate of addiction isn't necessarily related to disease.'

'Oh? The more a person smokes the more likely he is to contact something from it.'

'We're getting away from the point of this conversation, Lawrence.'

'Not really. No addiction means no sales.'

'I'll choose to ignore that.'

Lawrence shrugged.

Ted glanced down at the report. 'To get back to the mice. I'm not convinced your experiments are conclusive.'

Lawrence shifted his position aggressively. 'Reread the tables and you'll see how many months and how many different experiments it has taken me to reach these conclusions.'

'I'm still not convinced.'

'Very well, I'll prove it to you. Why not give us the rare pleasure of your company in the lab?'

Ted hesitated.

The biochemist watched him closely and rolled his cigarette between his fingertips like a genuine Havana. 'What about this evening?'

Ted shook his head. 'I have to make an appearance at the opera.' The *opera?* God, he thought. My project is at stake and I have to stall everything for an opera?

Lawrence raised his eyebrows. 'Tomorrow evening? I can spend more time with you at the end of the day.'

There was a long pause. Ted thought about the report and fingered the security seal. He wondered why Lawrence hadn't discussed the matter with the research director Noel Sorensen. Or perhaps he had. 'I'm surprised Noel didn't raise this with me before he flew to New York.'

31

The biochemist inhaled quickly and blew out a puff of smoke. 'Because he doesn't know about it. We work in our own little worlds down in the lab. No one knows about this. Yet.'

Mallett studied him. The sarcasm had dropped abruptly from Lawrence's voice. Both he and Lawrence knew the enormous expense involved in making a discovery during the final research stages. Millions of new seedlings at the experimental farms were about to be transplanted. A delay now for a re-examination of the hybrid could result in wiping out existing stocks and the year's new crop and restarting the laborious process of lab tests. If it had taken them over three years to get this far, it could take another three years. . . . He dismissed the thought quickly and stood up. 'Okay, Lawrence, tomorrow evening. I'll call down at seven, seven-thirty before I leave the floor.'

Lawrence confirmed the arrangement with a wave of his hand, climbed out of the chair and walked out.

Ted stared at the empty doorway.

Still disconcerted by his earlier meeting with Lawrence, Ted Mallett postponed his session with the chairman and decided to cut the day short. His chauffeur drove him home. Like Dominion, he lived south of the river, but unlike many of his colleagues he didn't live in the country. The hours they wasted in commuting to and from the office each day, he spent jogging around the nearest common, or working out with weights.

He had invested part of his football earnings in a Georgian house in a remarkably quiet cobbled crescent situated a few streets away from one of the main arterial roads linking London with Kent and the southern counties. Avoid the stock market, invest in property, everyone told him when he first arrived. But it was Colette his sculptor wife who had taught him to stop stapling dollar signs to the house and start loving its harmonious lines, floor-to-ceiling windows, and air of spaciousness and privacy.

He agreed with her every time he unlocked the front door. The afternoon had turned bitterly cold outside, but his home felt evenly warm and welcoming. Easy strains of John Coltrane's saxophone met him as he stepped inside and slipped off his shoes. Colette was nowhere to be seen, but there were rare sensitive moments like these when he could close his eyes and tell which rooms she had been in within the last hour. He paused, flexing his toes in the chocolate-brown deep-pile rug, and tiptoed down to the basement.

Colette's north-facing conservatorylike studio overlooked a wall garden. She stood with her back to him, silhouetted against the dying light from the sloping glass roof. A hammer in one hand and a chisel in the other, she was chipping away gently at a block of marble and didn't hear his step. Mallett could just make out the slow, careful beginnings of a spherical form where days before there had been nothing.

He watched as she paused every now and then to touch the stone with her fingertips as though it spoke to her, guiding her chisel. Ted felt soothed and humbled by the rhythmic movement of her hands. The sense of wonder he experienced when he first saw her at work had not diminished with time. He was reluctant to intrude.

'Hello,' she said, not turning.

'I might be a burglar.'

She shook her head and her hands continued to work on the stone. After several moments she put the tools down and smiled at him over her shoulder.

Ted made no move toward her. Her face and oatmeal smock were covered with a fine white dust. She removed a kerchief from her hair and shook it. Her eyes were shining and she radiated beauty. Ted could tell the day had been good for her, and even his own feelings of anxiety seemed to evaporate in the studio.

Colette moved around the marble slowly to view her work in the last moments of clear, natural light. Satisfied, she draped a cloth over it and held out her hand to him.

Her petite but perfectly rounded body looked minute next to his. Together they left the studio in silence. He longed to make love to her but found himself reluctant to impose on the privacy of her thoughts at that moment.

Moving away from him she walked upstairs to the shower. She tingled with creativity, but this was a block of marble that couldn't be rushed. Two months to the next exhibition and she was almost there. Almost. Time. Temptation to look at previous works for inspiration. No. Not with this one. She wanted it in the exhibition, but not at the expense of spoiling it for a deadline.

She didn't have to compromise any more. For the first time in her life her creations were her own, not just commercial objects commissioned by an architect's office. So what was wrong? She opened the shower door, turned on the taps and let the water run a while. The noise was clean, uninterrupted. She had been in the studio since six that morning. She was still high from it. Come down, come down. Had Ted disrupted things by arriving home early? No. Not really. Easy to blame others. Too easy. Time to stop.

She tested the water, stepped out of her clothes and into the shower. She was creating something entirely new, and that was a slow, painful process. There was nothing outside herself she could draw on, nothing. How was it possible to feel the form so strongly within and find it so hard to make it assume physical shape? What was missing? Conflict?

The oyster created a pearl around an abrasive grain of sand. No abrasion, no pearl. No conflict, no art.

But her life was full of conflict. *Was.* What had happened to the little girl who saw her rebel father being shot by the French in Hanoi? Six men with machine guns. A four-year-old child cowering under the bed. A large fan clicking somewhere above in the heat. Enough rounds of fire to kill an army. Blood spurting in all directions. Glass exploding into the street. A mass of pulp lying in the centre of the floor.

Colette raised her face to the water and trembled. No memory after that. Try. French mother tortured by the authorities to divulge her Vietnamese lover's hiding place. Papa one dead, and papa two. Hanoi, Paris. Little girl growing up. Poor. Mother insane most of the time. Seated at a window

34

staring at the street.

'*Maman? Maman?*'

'*Oui, ma petite?*'

'What are you thinking?'

'*Rien.* Nothing.'

Mother's family no help. A cheque each month to keep them alive and far away. Hiding. All the time hiding. From what? Memories. School was no escape. Convent. Navy serge uniforms. Girls laughing at her almond-shaped eyes. Nuns making sure everyone knew she was illegitimate. *La bâtarde.* Peace and solitude found in the Louvre. Scholarships to art schools, Paris then London. Mother dying in an asylum. Release. Phases of Manet, Monet, then van Gogh, Munch. Much conflict in the last two. Can't paint my own conflict. Start meditating. Peace. Start working with wood, stone. Linear, global forms easy on the eye, easy to sell. That's no good. Art must reflect the inner self, not the public need for decoration.

Conflict. Ted was full of it, but she had softened much of that in him. She needed his conflict now. Not too much. Little by little.

Ted draped his jacket and tie over the bannister downstairs and walked into the kitchen for some chilled vermouth. He took the ice tray out of the freezer, twisted the frame and shook a couple of cubes into two glasses. He sliced lemon peel over the ice, poured out the vermouth, and emptied a jar of black olives into a dish.

Love was new to him, this kind of love. He treated it like a delicate vase, not wanting to crowd or rush in for fear of smashing it, yet sometimes finding himself unable to hold back.

During his years in pro football women had crowded him. He was caught in a vicious circle, disturbed by feelings of inadequacy and too afraid of exposing his weakness to do anything about it.

But with Colette? She didn't see him as a pin-up. He sometimes doubted if she noticed him at all. But he was as captivated by her now as he had been the day he first saw her, when she come to Dominion to design a fountain for the foyer. How he had haunted her. A lovesick boy running from galleries to studios, studios to galleries. For some strange reason he could never understand, she had found his semivirginity charming. She said it was more creative for her. She liked its contrast with his supermacho image as much as he liked the contrast between her outer remoteness and passionate sexual expertise. Each found the other original.

If this was love fulfilled, he was glad it had happened now. Adolescence with none of the pain.

Ted walked upstairs with the vermouth and olives and opened the bathroom door. Her body was a blur or movement and steam behind the opaque glass, and her smock lay in a crumpled heap on the carpet next to a potted palm. Two freshly laundered bath towels hung over a wicker basket.

He settled himself on the carpet and quietly sipped his drink, waiting until the shower was turned off. The stillness in the air was broken by stray drops of water on the tiles when she emerged. He rose and shook out a bath towel, waiting until she stepped forward before enveloping her in it and holding her against him.

Colette looked up at him. 'What's wrong, Teddy?' Her voice sounded low and concerned.

'Nothing,' he said, resting his cheek against her short damp hair.

'Hmm mm? You don't hold me like this unless something is wrong.'

'Like what?' He avoided her eyes and moved his lips against her ear.

She clenched her fists against his chest. 'As if you're trying to hide.'

He moved away from her and reached for his drink. 'Oh hell, I come home to forget it. Small technical problem that could delay the yerba sacra project.'

'So it's small, so fix it?' She shrugged philosophically and reached for her vermouth.

'Yuh,' he said tightly.

36

'Come, Teddy, tell me about it.' The towel dropped from her shoulders.

He watched with mingled feelings of sadness and longing as she stepped into a silk petticoat.

He wanted to tell her, but couldn't bring himself to talk about tumours on mice in a setting so tranquil and lovely. 'Let it go, honey. I need to work it out in my mind for a couple of days.'

She studied him intently, sensing his unease. He would tell her when he was ready. She stook on tiptoe to kiss him and moved out of the room. 'M'sieur Coltrane has stopped playing his saxophone,' she called from the bedroom.

Ted was thankful she wasn't going to probe. 'I'll turn it over,' he said, moving toward the door.

'Teddy?'

'Uh huh?'

'Put on some Sibelius.'

Ted hesitated. He was uncomfortable away from jazz. 'Would you settle for Cleo Laine?'

'I don't see the connection.'

'There isn't one.' He smiled and checked the time on his way downstairs to the stereo. They were expected at the opera in a couple of hours.

3

'Find us a cab, Stan.'

'Certainly, Mr. Mallett.'

The chauffeur glanced disapprovingly in his mirror. The American director had no sense of occasion, he thought suddenly. He tried to ignore the intimate whisperings on the back seat, and edged the mink-colored Mercedes out of the evening traffic. If Mr. Mallett didn't know how to behave, it was up to Mrs. Mallett to set some kind of example. But she was foreign and an artist, so it was pointless expecting anything from her. He drew up facing Trafalgar Square and got out to flag down a roving cab.

'You've embarrassed him, Ted. That's unlike you. Whatever bothers you, chéri, it shows.' Colette wound herself elegantly in a wrap.

'Opera isn't my scene. You know that.'

'The opera doesn't make you nervous like this.'

Ted's jaw tightened angrily. 'Sometimes, just sometimes, I would like to be a mystery to you.' He knew that this sudden need he had for her had come partly because he felt inhibited in his own home earlier, and partly because he had to clear his mind of office anxieties. He invariably craved Colette at the least opportune moment. His cravings reflected a need for the fulfillment of his fantasies.

A set of knuckles rattled against the tinted window. The chauffeur pointed a gloved finger at a yellow light inching through the traffic.

Mallett jumped out and sprinted nimbly toward the cab. 'Thanks, Stan,' he shouted over the noisy *tak-tak-tak* of the engine.

The chauffeur nodded and pointedly held the door open for Colette.

38

A pair of legs in a clinging, flamingo-tinted cashmere dress emerged slowly from the Mercedes. Colette smiled and accepted the chauffeur's hand. 'Thank you, Stan. I hope you enjoy your evening.'

He touched his cap. 'I will Mrs. Mallett.'

Ted thumped impatiently on the side of the cab door. 'Move it, honey, move it!'

Colette made no effort to rush.

The chauffer waited patiently until she had disappeared into the anonymity of the cab before easing the Mercedes away from the curb.

Ted reached for her wrap and began winding it around his hand. 'Jesus, Colette. You could kill a man this way.'

She ruffled his frilly shirt affectionately and leaned forward to hand the driver a £20 note. 'Please, drive along the Embankment. Take the longest route to Covent Garden.'

The driver slid the glass panel between them and pocketed the note without comment. He waited for a break in the traffic and did a quick U-turn.

Colette nestled into the corner. 'You'll never learn the art of waiting, will you, my love?'

Ted dropped to his knees and grinned happily. 'You know, I don't think I want to learn.' Like an eager schoolboy never tiring of a new game, he began to unbutton her dress.

Covent Garden was ablaze with light. Passers by could tell from the number of expensive cars blocking the narrow street between the TV vans that this was no ordinary evening.

Deep inside the opera house, Sir Charles Courtland watched the TV cameras pan leisurely around the celebrities in the foyer and mezzanine. Good cross-section, he thought approvingly. Really must congratulate Hughes in PR for an excellent guest list: several actors, a few cricketers, that toothy comedian whatsisname disappearing into the gents, finalists from last year's Wimbledon, couple of those lunatic dress designers who keep appearing in the headlines, and a few token avantgarde playwrights. Very nice, too. All of them helped contribute to the philanthropic air of the occasion, and why shouldn't they? Dominion was doing more to support the arts than any other industrial group.

What a splendid idea it was to use the corporate image for the occasion. Certainly, he had to admit, the group was better known under its dozens of different brand names, but somehow none of them alone were adequate for an evening like this.

Courtland excused himself from his private party and mingled freely with the guests, reaching over heads to clasp hands, waving across the floor, leaning over to peck a cheek, standing back to admire a dress.

Outwardly, he was the perfect host. Inwardly, he continued to review Dominion within the context of the occasion. A chairman needed to do this. It was so easy to become swamped by corporate responsibilities. Covent Garden, for example, was being used as part of a public-minded campaign to help enhance the image of the tobacco division and raise public awareness of the group's other activities. Courtland felt sceptical about the latter. How aware, really, was the public of Dominion's rapid diversification in the sixties into areas like packaged foods, farming, drinks, hotels, confectionery, and cosmetics? Now they were negotiating terms to acquire a supermarket chain, a logical step considering the number of household goods produced within the group. Dominion hotels and pubs were already proving to be highly profitable outlets for their tobaccos, drinks, and foods.

But, no matter how much they diversified, tobacco still accounted for a steady sixty percent of their turnover. And considering the anticonglomerate atmosphere of the day, perhaps it was wise not to overstress their varied activities. After all, reasoned Courtland, that was the art of the multinational. Let the holding company convey size and a quiet power, but allow the subsidiaries to retain their individual characteristics.

That was one of Dominion's founding principles, he reflected. How faithfully it had been retained within the vastly different companies in the tobacco division supplying the smoking needs of princes and paupers.

And how that principle had metamorphosed during the era of acquisitions when he was financial director.

Companies were examined under the headings of positive and negatives in terms of profit and popularity. Emotive phrases like 'Established since 1770,' or 'Napoleon's favorite drink' were retained, while behind the scenes computers were put to work to help isolate and strip down areas of slack or waste and the personnel that went with them.

Courtland's eye followed the logic of his mind and quickly scanned the Dominion products being served at the bar. The wine came from the Burgundy estates of successive generations of St.-Michels. Dominion highlighted the family dynasty in a series of advertisements in glossy magazines, while the group's hatchet men quietly removed several cousins and in-laws from the vineyards' payroll. The smoked salmon, caviare, and pâté came from a venerable firm that had once supplied only Harrod's food halls and a few exclusive clubs. Dominion saved it from bankruptcy by retaining its traditional image and placing experts in fast-moving grocery products at the helm to quadruple output and distribution within a few months.

All good business. All highly creative. The chairman watched the hostesses hand out white and gold presentation packets of cigars, cigarettes, and perfumes. When Dominion acquired the famous house of *Madame d'Anjou* cosmetics, it had quickly launched a spouse in *Monsieur d'Anjou* cosmetics for men. Today even the boxes were made by Dominion-owned companies.

Yet, watching the guests handle their presents and refill their glasses at the bar, Courtland sensed that few of them knew of the group connection. Whatever his PR men said, he preferred it that way. It was subtle, unstated, and didn't clutter the image of the holding company.

Courtland shifted his gaze to three well-known music critics who sat hunched around an ice bucket supporting a large champagne bottle. A young press officer armed with bulky press kits approached the table hopefully, but was briskly waved away.

Courtland supressed a smile. A hand fluttered in the air to catch his eye. The last of his personal guests were being ushered across the floor toward him. Behind them he noticed a TV camera swing around to film four members of the British Lions rugby team.

The Lions?

Dammit. Ted Mallett should be in front of that camera. Where the bloody hell was he? Courtland made eye contact with his personal assistant, Henry Peach, poised obediently on the wide stairway. The young man shook his head and shrugged. Courtland flushed with annoyance. One shot of Mallett's sportsman's physique and fresh face did more to endorse the group's tobaccos than a million pounds' worth of press advertising.

'Good evening, Charlie.'

Courtland turned. 'Hal. Delighted you could make it.' He stretched out his hand toward Hal Burnaby, Chief executive of Harmer Brands.

Burnaby was in London for the week. 'It's good to be here,' he said clasping Courtland's forearm with his spare hand, while his eye searched out Daphne.

Courtland noticed this and resented it, along with the brotherly hug that followed it. He was envious of Burnaby's easy, freewheeling style and the confidence portrayed in his curly, muttonchop whiskers. He had once tried to dent Burnaby's self-assurance by wooing Ted Mallet away from Harmer Brands to join the London head office. But it was like denting water in a pail.

Damn Ted. Where the hell was he?

A hostess swathed in white and gold appeared at his elbow, carrying a tray of drinks. She smiled at him warmly. She knew he didn't like champagne and nodded at his glass of Irish whiskey and Perrier.

Someone, somewhere, was babbling into a microphone, shattering his thoughts.

'Dominion is known worldwide for its four hundred different cigarette brands, and about half as many pipes, tobaccos, cigars . . .'

Reluctantly, Courtland looked past the girl in the direction of the voice. He recognized a young marketing executive and peered over the heads of the crowd to see who was with him. A radio journalist, tape recorder hanging from her shoulder, looked unimpressed. 'I can get all that from the press kit,' Courtland heard her say tartly. 'I want to know how much a jamboree like this costs you, and what you hope to achieve by it.'

Her words tailed off into the first warning bell.

Courtland glanced once more at his assistant to see if the Malletts had arrived. Peach shook his head. Courtland cursed swiftly under his breath.

People began to break up into groups and leave the bar. Courtland stepped toward Daphne to take her arm, and smiled warmly at his guest.

The cameras turned from a fleeting glimpse of the chairman and his wife to look into the clear blue eyes of TV's best-known music commentator. Several moments before the royal crested curtains were due to part, he took the viewers rapidly through an outline of the *Marriage of Figaro*.

The Dominion Opera Season was about to begin.

A cacophony of tuning rose from the orchestra pit. One by one, the executive board members led their guests into the boxes on either side of the auditorium.

The Courtlands appeared first, flanked by the Conservative shadow chancellor of the exchequer, the head of the Arts Council, Hal Burnaby, and the American ambassador.

Deputy chairman and head of the tobacco division Jolyon Williams stepped into the box next to the Courtlands. A reedy man with thinning sandy hair and a nicotine-stained moustache, Williams glanced nervously at the camera and moved to block its view of his wife. A florid-faced bosomy woman seated herself at the back of the box. Williams barely glanced at her while pointing out his guests, the chairman of a large publishing house and a well-known heart surgeon dressed flamboyantly in emerald-green velvet.

Financial director Paul Lombard, grandson of Dominion's first financial director and the only direct descendant of the original board on the executive committee, walked confidently into his box between the governor of the Bank of England and a senior vice president from Chase Manhattan. Compared with Williams, Lombard looked relaxed and happy, well bronzed from a recent skiing holiday, eyes twinkling behind square-rimmed spectacles. Lombard faced the royal circle and waved energetically to someone in the front row before sitting down.

Fitzgerald, the group's craggy, bald-headed director of overseas subsidiaries, sat between the ambassadors of Brazil and Iran, and a senior official from the Foreign Office. Fitzgerald always looked as though he was wearing his dead uncle's hand-me-downs.

The Malletts were missing from their box, a point that wasn't missed by a single member of the executive committee. The head of public relations, Alun Hughes, tried to ease the situation by showing Ted's guests to their seats and personally arranging champagne in a long-legged ice bucket. One of the guests, Tony McKay of advertising agency Kestner McKay, tried to keep out of view but wasn't finding it easy. His deep-purple suit and ice-blue dress shirt had a way of catching the eye.

The cameras darted indiscriminately from the boxes to the main body of the opera house, defying the strict order of priority in which senior and junior management filled up the tiers of seats. Guests poured in from the back and fanned out like flocks of colorful geese.

Daphne Courtland watched it all with an amused smile. She hung over the edge of the box and fanned herself non-chalantly with a programme. If only my father could see this, she thought. He'd be hollering for someone to move their ass with his bourbon and get the goddamn show on the road. And my mother? Daphne's eyes rose thoughtfully to the Malletts' box on the opposite side of the house. Over seventy years ago Amy had stood up in that same box to bellow abuse at the royal box during a glittering gala performance of *Jeanne d'Arc*. How like Amy to use such an oppropriate event to shout for women's rights.

Daphne visualized her mother, magnificently dressed for the occasion, leaning out of the box to litter the audience with leaflets. More than seventy years ago. Little evidence of Amy's militance here tonight, she thought, eyeing the directors' wives. Helen Lombard is the only one who looks as though she is enjoying herself. Pretty woman, nice face. But still just an appendage to Paul's career. Sheila Williams is considered an embarrassment to Jolyon because she drinks too much gin, an embarrassment to him, note, not to herself. And poor Verity Fitzgerald. Totally diminished by life. Like a little sparrow perched there between Fitz and his friends. God, Fitz is funny-looking.

Daphne started to giggle. She crossed her arms on the edge of the box and quickly buried her face.

'Chairman's wife is gold, pure gold,' chuckled the TV director in the control room. 'Zoom in for a closeup, Peter.'

His assistant glanced anxiously at the clock. 'It's time for the leader of the orch–'

'Oh, fuck the leader of the orchestra.' The director kept the zoom lens on Daphne as long as possible, switched reluctantly to the cameras facing the stage and gave the necessary signals. He connected himself with the cameras at the back of the auditorium. 'Someone's bound to fall asleep in those boxes during the show, so let's see it. Remember this isn't your average opera-loving public.' He waited for the applause to fade and signalled for the conductor to take the stand.

Behind the curtains, final calls were made for Susanna and Figaro.

The first notes of the overture sounded.

The TV director stretched comfortably and reached for his glass of champagne. But his trained eye never left the panel of TV screens in front of him for a second. A quick movement in the corner of the screen scanning the foyer made him sit up abruptly. 'Jesus, who do we have here? Anyone recognize this gorilla with the svelte lady in pink?'

Feverish excitement. 'What guerrilla?'

'As in baboon, you idiot. Alert the cameraman on the

45

mezzanine.' What TV man could resist this? 'Beautiful timing, beautiful,' murmured the director, beaming the scurrying couple out to the TV viewing millions.

Ted Mallett swept Colette into his arms, sprinted up the main stairway with her and across the mezzanine. There was a frantic moment of wondering whether their box was on the left of the right. They reached it seconds after the curtains parted on Act 1.

Dr. Chris Lawrence set up two transitor radios facing one another on either side of his office. He twiddled the dials to Radio three and adjusted the balance to get the benefit of a full stereo-phonic effect from Covent Garden. He was passionately fond of opera but didn't have the ten quid to spare to sit in the gods on opening night.

He found opera on TV far too static, and anyway, the acoustics were surprisingly good in his small, narrow office. He liked being on the lab floor alone in the evenings. It gave him time to iron out the day. And he could turn up the heat without worrying about an exorbitant fuel bill at the end of the quarter. He reached into a cupboard, pulled out a quart bottle of pure alcohol, and patted around behind a box of test tubes for a can of tomato juice and a paper cup. He suched the liquid up through a pipette and released a sizeable tot into the cup. It was years since he'd bought liquor. One of the advantages of being a research scientist was access to unlimited supplies of pure grain alcohol. No bill and no hangover.

A strong tenor voice filled the room. Lawrence felt himself relax in the resonant cavern of sound and stood still for a few minutes to enjoy it. When the pace quickened he reached for the tomato juice and prepared a strong Bloody Mary. Shoving a stack of folders to one side he sat down with the drink and tipped his chair against the wall, using one booted foot against the desk to rock himself to and fro. The music was rich and beautiful. He sipped the Bloody Mary and closed his eyes. This was the night he had set aside to study the tests that had been done on different cigarette papers for yerba sacra, but what the hell.

46

Yerba sacra.

Lawrence stopped rocking and contemplated his bulging stomach with dismay. The sort of hours he worked each day on the product prevented him from taking more exercise than a brisk walk over the bridge from the bus stop. And during the weekends he felt too tired to do anything but collapse with a book or listen to music.

The girl who shared his two-room flat on a noisy street didn't mean so much any more, but their relationship was one of convenience and habit. Jesus. If he felt like this at twenty-eight, how was he going to feel at forty?

The sort of work he was doing on tobacco alternatives wasn't being done anywhere else in the world. Big deal, It meant he was specializing himself deeper and deeper into the company. That was how Dominion held on to young researchers. Help them get their doctorates with generous grants, then direct their eagerly creative minds to an area where the work was a few years ahead of anything being undertaken by a rival. That got them hooked. It also stopped them looking around too soon for another job. And the salary? Lawrence swished the drink around his mouth. He couldn't afford a car, eating out was a luxury. Once the mortgage was taken care of, he had to choose between adding to his record collection or getting some fresh air in the country twice a month.

Music was a blissful, purifying escape.

Once upon a time he thought a 'doctor' in front of his name would lift him above the humdrum. He was born a pudgy replica of his father. Now, from the depths of their grey life in suburbia, his parents resented it.

His doctorate symbolized his ability to escape from the lower middle-class existence they had accepted as their lot. Escape? Superficially they were right, of course. He earned as much now as his father earned after some thirty years with the Post Office. And he didn't share his father's grovelling gratitude for being in a steady job. But he had seriously believed his generation to be free of the declining class system—until he joined Dominion.

47

Men from all kinds of backgrounds were making their way up through the ranks, yes. But it took a complete outsider, an American like Mallett, to reach the top in the seventies without the right political or social connections, an acceptable public school or regiment behind him. The best a woman could expect to achieve was middle management, and the same was true of a non-white executive. To Lawrence, Dominion embodied and preserved the sort of pre-war attitudes everyone believed had disappeared with the death of the Empire. Token departmental adjustments were made to accommodate modern movements like worker participation in management decisions, but it would be many years before this was reflected at board level. Compared with the motor industry, tobacco had a tame, obedient union. And the Age of Consumerism drowned in the Thames at the foot of Dominion House.

A sudden burst of laughter from the audience at Covent Garden made him sit forward with a start. He looked from one transistor to the other. *Marriage of Figaro*, he thought cynically. What an ironic choice from Dominion. Whisk the froth off the opera and you're left with a stringent satire. Underneath the masquerading and frolicking lay a scathing social attack on the aristocracy.

In a modern context, the company made *him* feel patronized. It had helped him get a Ph.D. in the seventies in the same way it would have handed his grandfather a bowl of soup in the twenties. Patronage with a price tag.

Why did he feel so bitter about it? The secretaries who fluttered in and out of the building each day with their colorful Cockney slang were freer than he was. They owed the company nothing and could leave tomorrow.

He couldn't. His contract didn't run out for another three years, and he needed one good success under his belt before he could move up or out. Gone were the days when British-trained scientists could land plum jobs in America without something startling to their credit. It was irrating to have to work with fat cats like Mallett, a handsome hulking *Playgirl* centerfold type all the women swooned over. But Mallett was Courtland's

48

blue-eyed boy, and many believed he was being groomed to succeed the chairman.

If that were so, then Lawrence was determined to ascend with him. In a strange way they had something in common. Both were outsiders, Mallett because he was an American import, Lawrence because he chose to remain aloof and bury himself in his work. Both were involved in products of the future. I can make myself indispensable to Mallett, he thought, tapping the cup against his lip. Not by genius alone, that isn't enough. I have discovered the Achilles heel of this giant—his obsession with winning.

Lawrence sensed the power of holding another man's weakness in the palm of his hand. Not any man's, but Mallett's.

The thought suddenly reversed itself to mirror his own weakness. Music was a solace and provided a sort of quick, spiritual repair job. The day he stopped listening to music he would know that the desensitizing process was complete.

He contemplated and resumed rocking to a fro in his chair.

Back in his first year at university he had screamed 'Nazi' at lecturers who did the sort of experiments on animals that were now commonplace in his life.

The others had laughed at him, told him to toughen up. He watched dogs being injected with thirty different drugs to test the after-effects any student could read about in books. He saw baby monkeys clinging to simulated mother-machines that moments before had subjected them to a series of electric shocks. He knew how to train or produce certain responses in dogs with different forms of torture. Far from being in the 'interests on science' many lab experiments, he knew, merely duplicated work that had already been well documented world-wide. The belief that these experiments were related strictly to man's fight against disease was hopelessly naïve.

But yes, he had become hardened to it all after seven years at university. He knew that by a curious twist of the law they could do things in the labs that were prosecutable in the street. Feed animals toxic substances and record the slow dying process, or subject paws and genitals to electric currents. He lost count of the number of beagles and baboons they had strapped into machines forcing them to smoke, or the number of cancerous lungs he had dissected afterward. Lawrence drained his drink. The company spokesmen might skirt around the smoking/lung cancer connection, but the evidence was there, in his lab, and in buckets of preserved lungs in every teaching hospital in Britain. Weird, this. Trying to disprove something they already knew. The denying publicly what they knew and denying they were trying to disprove what they knew.

Oh, to hell with it.

Lawrence tipped his chair forward and reached for the pipette. He sucked up more alcohol and plunged it into the cup, swilling the liquid around to mix in the clinging remnants of tomato juice.

The second act of *Figaro* over, he consciously blocked out the filler discussion on *King Lear* and scratched around under his papers for a half-eaten packet of gingerbread. Several hours had gone by since lunch-time. He nibbled a piece and then flung the remains into the waste-paper basket. It was no wonder he couldn't keep his weight down. He picked up the Bloody Mary and rinsed his mouth with it to clear the taste of ginger, feeling the liquid burn its way down to his stomach.

God, he felt exhausted. A good few years had drifted by since animal experiments last bothered him. Lawrence, you're being ridiculous. Old Kit what-ever-his-name-was in Dominion's cosmetics division did far worse things to animals. He tested substances on the eyes of rabbits and cats and used special devices to keep their lids open for twenty-four hours. You see, rapid blinking could wash out the substance and ruin the experiment. The cosmetics industry killed about a million animals a year in its British labs. At least the work *he* did was connected with health and not with narcissism.

But even dwelling on that didn't make him feel any better. Why should he carry such a burden? Such anxiety? The research director Noel Sorensen was lazy as hell. He left everything to the men in the lab and they could have been preparing the next atom bomb for all Sorensen cared.

Here I am, thought Lawrence bitterly, making the first great break-through into tobacco alternatives actually *work*. And the men who juggle the projects between airy marketing terms, computer printouts, and flashes of colour on drawing boards streak by me in sport cars as I stand waiting for a bus in the pouring rain. Finks like Mallett don't leave the building with these clothes stinking of ether.

From now on, Mallett is going to share some of that burden with me. Both our careers depend on the success of yerba sacra. Fine. Both of us are going to make it work.

Act 3 was in progress. Lawrence returned to his chair and stretched out, mentally conjuring up the scene on the stage to match the voices in his office. He regretted not bringing the libretto, and then decided it was more relaxing perhaps to close his eyes and let the music take over completely. The aria *'Dove Sono'* was being sung with such compassion it made him tremble.

The Malletts' late arrival at the opera was uppermost in the minds of the members of Courtland's political think-tank as they gathered in the chairman's walnut-panelled office the following evening.

None of them knew that Mallett was at the moment dialling Lawrence in the lab and about to become involved in something that would make his breach of company protocol seem minimal in retrospect.

But for those who had served Dominion over a number of years, protocol was no minimal matter. It was a long-established and intergral part of company ritual. You did not question it, neither did you slight it. For some, like the deputy chairman Jolyon Williams, abusing it in public was second only to committing a capital offence.

'Mallett should be reprimanded in front of the entire board,' he said, sweeping the air with his hands. Williams, a one-time district commissioner in the colonial service, had the air of a man who knew he once cut a dashing figure in regulation khaki. He had stuck to brown or faintly tweedy suits ever since, defying the variations on the pinstripe theme worn by the chairman and several board members. He was surprised and peeved when Coutland started to laugh at him.

'Come come, Jolyon, don't get carried away by something so trivial,' said the chairman patting him on the shoulder.

Williams flushed angrily. 'Trivial? You call running with his wife along the corridors of Covent Garden on TV trivial? Didn't you read the headlines in the *Mirror* and *Sun* today?'

'Well, my department is pleased.'

All heads turned toward Alun Hughes, director of public relations. A cheerful-looking Welshman in his early forties, Hughes was a strong Mallett supporter. He delayed the moment by lighting up a panatela. 'It made us look *human*,' he said liltingly. 'You know how we're constantly being criticized for our lack of humanity, profits before public health and all that. Any criticism we expected for staging the opera last night was pre-empted by Ted's sprint. We couldn't have stage-managed it better.'

Williams looked appalled. 'What do we have in store for us next time? A line of chorus girls kicking their heels in the foyer?'

Hughes chuckled approvingly.

'Calm down, gentlemen,' said Courtland, deciding it was time to step in. He was relieved when a waitress appeared to serve coffee.

While the men helped themselves to cream and sugar, he rose from the round table, walked over to his desk, and selected a favourite meerschaum from the pipe rack.

Believing the atmosphere in the room needed a few more minutes to settle down, the chariman paused to fill his pipe. He realized that the fourth man in their midst, Nigel Swan, one of the two Conservative MPs on the board, had stayed out of the argument. It wasn't the first time Swan had refused to take sides in company infighting.

Williams and Hughes represented the split on the board between the tobacco diehards, sprinkled with ex-colonial administrators and army officers, and the younger progressive elements. Hughes was a business school graduate who cut his political teeth during a stint as secretary to a junior minister in the Commons. The heads of the nontobacco divisions fell evenly on either side of the split, and it had taken a majority of one to get Mallett, the outsider, elected to the executive committee.

Courtland enjoyed the split. He saw it as an abrasive and a necessary part of keeping the board on its toes. He heard the three men laughing behind him and sensed his opening. He returned to the table, pipe in hand, and sat down between Williams and Hughes.

Courtland brought the meeting to order.

With the general election only a few months away, he told them this was a good opportunity to rethink their political strategy. The general mood of the country, according to recent polls, predicted a Conservative victory, but this was no time to be smug.

'We've been through four of our toughest years gentlemen,' said the chairman. 'But unless the Conservatives win with an overwhelming majority, which I doubt, we can't afford to let up for one minute.'

There was a murmer of agreement. The Labour government had passed various forms of restrictive legislation on the industry. But everyone knew this wasn't only legislation inspired by socialism. It was a response to the increasing restrictions being imposed on the industry by one Western country after another. Legislation had stopped short of imposing an all-out ban on tobacco advertising, such as had been done in Norway.

The industry knew it could no longer rely on arguing its defence in terms of its tax contributions to the nation's coffers. The amount had dropped from ten percent in 1970 to under five percent of Britain's total tax revenue. And highlighting the company's philanthropic side by diverting funds from sports sponsorship into the arts simply wasn't enough to push back the public's increasing hostility to smoking.

MP Nigel Swan was less pessimistic on this point than the others. 'It's a fashionable fad, gentlemen,' he said loosening his cuffs. 'It's soon going to be fashionable to remind virulent nonsmokers that smokers have rights, too. We've seen evidence of that in the columns of our cigar-smoking friends in the press.'

'Hear, hear,' said Williams.

'We have something better in our quiver than that,' said the chairman. 'The next health minister.'

Swan looked at him with interest.

Courtland smiled back. 'I know who you think it will be, Nigel, but I have it on higher authority that we are in for a surprise. The Department of Health and Social Security is in for massive budget cuts. And we aren't going to have a health minister gunning for us with the missionarylike zeal we have just experienced under Labour.'

'Well, obviously,' said Swan tightly.

'What I mean,' Courtland explained, 'is that the minister selected will be a hatchet man first and a social services man second, but I shall say no more.'

There was a pensive moment while Courtland relit his pipe.

'How can we utilize the twilight period following the election? Should be a whole batch of new MPs in the house. Any ideas on how we can harness them?'

'Yes,' said Hughes brightly. 'I feel we should involve the newcomers in our tobacco substitute project. Talk to them about yerba sacra.'

There was a stunned silence. Courtland removed the pipe from his mouth and studies the public relations director. Tobacco alternatives were the company's most closely guarded secrets.

Jolyon Williams was the first to speak. 'By doing that you are implying there is something wrong with tobacco.'

'Oh, what nonsense, Jolyon,' Hughes sounded exasperated. The same argument had been used in the fifties when the industry believed the development of filter tips suggested there was something harmful about untipped cigarettes. It had been used again in the early to mid-seventies with the development of low-tar, low-nicotine brands. Hughes felt the argument was paranoic and retrogressive, but a warning glance from the chairman stopped him from saying so.

54

'What do you have in mind, Alun,' said Nigel Swan.

'Frankly I'm tired of apologizing all the time, being on the defensive. The substitute programme is positive, fresh, unique. It should appeal to the new MPs. Obviously we can't tell them everything, but we can made them feel involved. People respond well if you take them into your confidence, sound out their reactions, seek their advice and so on.'

Courtland watched Williams's reaction. He could understand Hughes's reasoning, but they were walking mined land as far as the tobacco division was concerned.

'Look,' Hughes persisted, 'after the last election we flew the new MPs to our cigar factory in Amsterdam. They loved it, and we used flying and meal times for informal briefing sessions. What happened? The press suggested we were trying to "bribe" them.'

Williams nodded grimly.

Courtland sighed and waited for the public relations director to continue.

'I don't mean we should open our yerba sacra files to them, gentlemen,' said Hughes, eyeing each man in turn. 'But let's lift some of the mystique out of the subject. Talk generally about policy and philosophy. All right, we're still stinging from the *Catch* mishap, but let's give the impression we've gone way beyond that.'

Williams's jaw tightened visibly. After the *Catch* affair, a decision had been made to move the new products division out from under his wing and create a separate entity, allowing Mallett a freer hand. Williams saw the move as a threat and a personal insult. It was fundamental to his hostility toward Mallett.

Courtland knew this. To ease the situation, he had personally decided not to involve Mallett in the political think-tank. He had used the excuse that Mallett was an American and alien to the industry's lobbying tactics in Britain, which differed vastly from those used in the States. But now they would have to involve him. Williams was just going to have to get used to it.

Swan seemed to read his thoughts. 'We need Ted from now

55

on,' he said. 'He's the best person to talk to the new MPs. It's an excellent proposal, Alun. By concentrating on tobacco alternatives we might also win over a few dissenting MPs.

Courtland nodded approvingly. 'Jolyon, we'll need all the back-up we can get from your division of course,' he said to his deputy. 'We'll be limited in the amount we can divulge on yerba sacra, so have something up your sleeve, old boy. I propose we all mull over Alun's suggestion and pool our thoughts at the next meeting. Ted can then brief us on exactly how much he is prepared to say.'

There was a general murmur of agreement. Williams seemed more or less resigned to the inevitable.

The meeting adjourned on time.

4

Ted Mallett heard the sound of loughter. He looked up and smiled. Acoustics were weird. It took a laugh to find its way through the expensive wood panelling that divided the offices on the executive floor. And then only when the building had emptied itself for the day.

He felt reassured. Before leaving for the lab, he dialled home, swivelling around in his chair with the receiver to face the river. He could tell from the skyline which parts of London were dead or alive at night. A colourful glow hovered over Piccadilly Circus while to his right, light from the slablike office blocks in the City marked the beginning of a working day for armies of cleaners.

A soft voice said, 'Hello.'

He cradled the phone against his face. 'I'm going to be late.'

'Late hmmmmmm?'

His eardrum vibrated deliciously. He leaned back. The sensation started to move slowly through his body. 'Don't stop, baby, please don't stop.'

Colette took a deep breath. Her humming sent pins and needles to the tips of his toes. 'All right,' she whispered eventually, 'I'll sit here and hummm until you come home.'

'Couldn't you save it all for me?'

'Teddy, you're very selfish.'

'Hungry, not selfish.'

'That too.'

'Is the lady complaining?' Ted twisted the telephone wire around his fingers.

'Complaint? No, ah swear,' she said, mocking his Southern accent. Ted smiled and released the wire. 'I'll only be a couple of hours.'

57

'Try for less?'

'I will,' he murmured, and reluctantly replaced the received. The humming stopped, but the tingling sensation didn't.

He spun the chair away from the window and sat bolt upright. No sense delaying the meeting with Lawrence any longer. He phoned down as he had said he would, and descended the four flights of stairs to the lab.

The section devoted to yerba sacra and other top-secret experiments was guarded around the clock, both manually and electronically. He waved his security pass under the guard's nose and walked along the corridor to meet Dr. Lawrence.

Ted disliked labs. They represented an alien world to him. He liked to control each and every stage of input that went into his products, but where the lab side was concerned he felt out of place. He resented pipsqueak Ph.Ds like Chris Lawrence having that edge over him. He resented a bunch of *mice* having an edge over him.

The biochemist was waiting for him, a pudgy figure in a tattered lab coat, working away at eight mice strung out on a board. 'Colleague of mine has been doing some skin grafts,' he said chattily, glancing up from the formica-topped counter when the director walked in.

Ted stared down at the twitching figures and wrinkled his nose at the stench of ether.

Lawrence smiled. He reached for a pair of surgical gloves and pulled them on, flexing his sausagelike fingers until the material was taut against his skin. The exercise was slow and meticulous, deliberately. The scientist was in his own domain. Mallett wasn't.

He turned toward the mice and began to untie them, working nimbly and expertly.

Then, placing the mice gently in a box with a wire-mesh cover, he said, 'I'd like you to look at these.' He began toying with the clasp all the time watching the expression on Mallett's face.

The biochemist's stomach pushed through his shirt and

peered out of the skimpy lab coat. Ted stared at it in disgust and forced himself to study the mice. 'They all look the same to me,' he said sullenly.

'Excellent!' Lawrence promptly picked up the box and turned toward the door. 'Now come with me.'

Ted was puzzled, wondering what he was supposed to be seeing. He followed the biochemist across corridor.

Lawrence jangled a set of keys and opened the door facing them. He reached inside to turn on the light.

It wasn't the first time Mallett had been in this room. Cages of mice lined the walls from floor to ceiling, jumping, leaping, frantic. The walls seemed to slope toward one another and spiral together in a dancing frenzy of wild spueakings and the incessant *tic-tic-tic-tic* of tiny claws against wire mesh.

'This shouldn't take long,' said Lawrence. He crouched down on the floor, his fat thighs sticking out on either side of him, checked the tags on four cages and placed two mice in each. 'Curious to know why I'm separating them?' he asked chattily. 'Because they belong to different strains.'

Ted frowned. The mice looked identical.

There was a moment of silence. The biochemist continued, 'The reason I showed you those mice on the board close up, is because they match the strains of mice in that block of cages over there.' He pointed toward the corner. A block of twenty-four cages stood apart from the others, four abreast, six down. 'Now, see if you can tell them apart.'

A neatly printed card above the cages read: CARCINOGEN-ICITY STUDIES IN ANIMALS, STAGES II

Some of the mice had what appeared to be recent skin paintings and kept up a running circle inside their cages. But those with sizeable or multiple tumours on their backs crouched and huddled together away from the light.

Apart from that, they looked identical.

Lawrence explained. 'The four different strains are arranged horizontally, a strain to each line of six cages. So, reading across, we have strains B10.A, B10.Br, B10.D2, B10.'

Mallett watched as the biochemist pointed out each strain

59

in turn. Up till now they had been statistics on a chart.

'The skin-painting experiments are arranged vertically,' the biochemist continued, 'two for each set. So, we have mice painted with yerba sacra tars at the top, yerba sacra and tobacco tars combined in the middle, and tobacco tars only at the bottom. The skin paintings were all done on the same day, but compare the different results in those cages.' Lawrence stood back to give the director a better view.

He concentrated on the tumours. Now he could see for himself. They were far more numerous in the middle block of cages where the mice had been painted with yerba sacra and tobacco tars combined. He double checked the labels and frowned. The tumours appeared to be concentrated on the backs of the first three strains of mice but could only pick out one or two afflicted animals in the cages with the B10 strain. He questioned Lawrence about it.

'Simple,' said the biochemist. 'Yerba sacra compounds the effects of tobacco. It's a clear-cut case of synergy. The very latest we can study. We can find a useful analogy in the industrial field. The asbestos worker who smokes is far more likely to contract lung diseases than the asbestos worker who *doesn't* smoke.'

'Right,' said Mallett turning from the cages. 'Then explain to me why only three out of four strains of mice are producing tumours.'

'Different genetic mechanisms in the strains determine whether or not the mouse will develop a tumour. We're required to run a series of experiments over a number of months on dozens of mice to make sure the differences are consistent within the strain, not merely peculiar to one batch. And they're consistent all right.'

Ted shrugged. 'But they all look the same to me.'

Lawrence grinned at him.

'What's so damned funny? I know I'm no scientist.'

The biochemist laughed. 'Those mice look the same to you as they do to every researcher in these labs, from the director down to the little girl who washes out test tubes. They differ only in their histocompatability complex. That determines the number of tumours that you can see, and whether they will be benign or malignant. Now watch me.'

Ted stood back.

Lawrence unhinged the B10 cage and reached inside for a handful of mice. He withdrew his hand, unhinged the cage marked B10.D2 and placed the B10 mice inside. He took out a handful of B10.D2 mice and placed them in the B10 cage. He glanced at Mallett and rubbed his gloved hands on the lab coat. Then he turned back and began swapping around mice between the B10 and B10.A cages, and repeated the exercise between the B10 and B10.Br cages.

Mallett couldn't believe it. He watched the hairy forearms dart back and forth between the cages, opening, closing, opening, swapping. Graceful movements. Not a falter or moment's hesitation anywhere.

The biochemist fastened the last cage and turned. Without commenting on what he had just done, he pointed at the top and the bottom cages.

Mallett knew he hadn't touched them during the exercise.

'Mice painted solely with tobacco tars, or solely with yerba sacra tars, produce roughly the same number of tumours so we're on safe ground there. Remember all we have to prove is that yerba sacra is no *more* harmful than tobacco. But YS and tobacco tars combined? Lethal.'

Mallet gazed at the cages. Lawrence's balletic exercise had successfully redistributed the tumour-free B10 strain, visually reducing the former concentration of tumours.

'Simple, isn't it?' said Lawrence flexing his fingers. 'From now on, all I need to do is *start* the skin paintings with a few more B10 mice scattered throughout the other cages, to reduce the total number of tumours produced. And that's what the Tait committee will see when they trail through the labs checking our various experiments. You said yourself the mice look identical.'

'Lawrence, are you out of your mind?' Mallett stared at him. The purpose of the exercise was now crystal clear. 'Put those goddamn mice back in their proper cages.'

61

'You do it.'

The biochemist folded his arms and stared at the director.

Mallett stood frozen to the spot, then found himself backing out ot the room into the corridor.

Lawrence followed and locked the door.

The two men stood silent in the lift. Ted felt a curious mixture of panic and relief. Everything seemed so goddamn *simple*. Too simple.

The doors parted and they walked together toward the biochemist's office.

It reeked of strong tobacco. Ted relaxed visibly. The combination of ether and the strong, oaty smell of mice was beginning to nauseate him.

Neither man spoke. Conspirators, but tense with one another, they needed to delay words on what had just happened.

Lawrence peeled off his gloves and dropped then in an empty box before scrubbing his fingers with a nail brush. He then dried his hands vigorously and reached for the winchester of alcohol, the pipette, and a couple of clean cups. 'It's not the Dorchester,' he apologized, flinging away the empty tin of tomato juice from the night before, 'but I do have fresh orange juice.'

'Anything'll do,' Ted said quickly.

Lawrence pulled open a drawer and two small oranges rolled to the front. He stripped the foil off a plastic scalpel and halved the fruit in two shift movements.

Mallett watched the fingers that had switched the mice prepare the drinks with the same assurance and dexterity. The pipette moved from the bottle to the cups. The oranges were squeezed into the liquid, pips and all. He accepted one of the cups with a curt nod and drank deeply. Then he sat back and fixed the biochemist with a level gaze. 'I could have you kicked out for what you did to those mice.'

Lawrence shook his head disparagingly. 'The Nobel Prize has gone to men who've done things that make me look like an amateur. Yes, Mallett, cribbing someone else's research, often a student's or rigging experiments to prove some thesis. I'm positively Christlike by comparison!'

'Dance around the facts whatever way you want, Lawrence. It still stinks.'

'Stinks?' Lawrence raised the cup to his lips. 'You said yourself we can't draw hard and fast conclusions from lab experiments, but a project stands or falls by them. All those tests show is the *possibility* that existing smokers who switch to yerba sacra stand a greater change of developing a disease from it. I say, *possibility*. But new smokers are in no more or less danger than with tobacco.'

'Possibility, huh,' said Ted bitterly.

'Right. So why destroy months of work because of a possibility?'

Ted stared into his cup. Lawrence's aggression was overwhelming. He got up and walked to the window. 'Why didn't you discuss this with Sorensen?'

Lawrence pulled a face at the sound of the research director's name. 'Because his involvement with our projects is minimal. He prefers playing politics upstairs. Besides he's a Williams man. He thinks, lives, and breathes tobacco and doesn't relate well to what we're doing here.'

Mallett knew what he meant. He turned from the window as Lawrence propped himself on the edge of his desk. The two men looked at one another. Each knew the importance of the yerba sacra project's success to the other. Both had been badly stung by *Catch*. Neither could risk two failures in a row.

Both believed their careers depended on it. Lawrence, because he saw it as a springboard out of obscurity, Mallett, because he saw it revolutionizing the history of smoking.

'Well?' Lawrence asked.

'What's in if for you,' Ted said, not looking up.

Lawrence clenched his fists. 'I need to get out from under Sorensen's feet. It's like a school lab down here. Requisitions for test tubes sometimes lie unsigned on his bloody desk for weeks while he frigs around the world. I nearly go crazy when things get held up because of petty pink slips trying to shuffle their triplicate way through the system. I'm supposed to be part of

63

your division, but I'm controlled by Sorensen's civil service mentality.'

Lawrence took the bull by the horns. 'I want to advance my research,' he continued. 'Sorensen isn't the least bit interested in experimenting beyond the exact demands of the project in hand. It's bloody well stifling me.' He moved away from the desk and ran his fingers through his hair with exasperation. 'Once yerba sacra is on its own I want funds for a special lab and a couple of assistants under me. There are reasons why those B10 mice don't develop tumours, from either tobacco or yerba sacra, or *Catch,* for that matter. But there's nothing on file to tell me why. No one has been imaginative enough to find out. I'd like to do that as soon as possible. It might help us in future studies on tobacco substitutes.'

'You talk like an immunologist.'

Lawrence picked up his empty cup and tapped it thoughtfully.

'I also want to make comparative studies between the toxic and carcinogenic compounds of tobacco tars and our two substitutes, *Catch* and yerba sacra.' Lawrence started to roll himself a cigarette. 'We don't know nearly enough about the common denominators,' he added, lighting up. 'There's no question in my mind that any substance smoked in large quantities will cause cell changes in the body. Once I start isolating things, our research into substitutes will make more sense. At the moment we're simply duplicating tobacco and calling it something else.'

Ted frowned. 'You're a weird guy, Lawrence. One minute you're switching mice to get a potentially dangerous product cleared. The next minute you want the freedom to research new ways to make smoking less harmful. I don't get it.'

The biochemist blew out a puff of smoke. 'If yerba sacra fails, I'm out. What kind of job can I get with two failures to my name and millions of pounds' worth of research work down the drain? A Ph.D. is judged solely on his postdoctoral research successes and written papers. I'm prepared to cut corners once to achieve my aim.' He deliberated this and added, 'I also need to safeguard myself.'

Ted looked baffled. 'Against what?'

'A young researcher like myself first isolated one of the most significant of the carcinogens in tobacco smoke, namely, 3,4-benzpyrene. He was funded partly by Harmer Brands in New York. When he presented them with the findings, well, the Harmer funds suddenly dried up.'

'Jesus, Lawrence. That was nearly twenty years ago.'

Lawrence toyed with his cigarette. 'If I isolate the carcinogens and co-carcinogens in yerba sacra tar, I won't be very popular either.'

'So you're asking me to close my eyes short term so you can hang yerba sacra in a couple of years? That doesn't make sense.'

'Yerba sacra won't hang; that's ridiculous. Tobacco is still on sale, isn't it?'

The logic was complex, but unquestionable.

'All I'm asking,' Lawrence presisted, 'is that you look on yerba sacra as *part* of the groundwork in the long-term research into a safter cigarette, a means to an end.'

Mallett wasn't going to be backed into a corner. 'Why the hell didn't you talk to me like this before? Why go to such lengths?'

Lawrence slapped his thigh noisily. 'I had to do something extreme to get your undivided attention for nearly two hours. Two minutes is the most you generally give me. And you would have kicked me out of your office if I spouted off about Sorensen like that upstairs.'

'What's to stop me repeating all this to the chairman tomorrow?'

'The risk of losing yerba sacra,' he said simply.

Lawrence felt under his papers for a packet of *Denim*. Like most members of the new products division, he knew this was Mallett's last success before the *Catch* episode. He twirled the blue packet in his fingers. 'Your statisticians tell me this has the fastest sales record of any new brand to hit the market in the last few years.'

Ted acknowledged the fact with a nod.

Lawrence examined the packet at arm's length. 'High tar

brand, this, very high. In my mind far more dangerous than yerba sacra, but it's out there, selling faster than we can spell its name. Ironic, isn't it. Government has less control over *Denim* than it has over a tobacco alternative.'

'That doesn't mitigate our problem, Lawrence.'

'No, it doesn't.' The biochemist stared into space. 'And that's not the point. Success in your world is the same as it is in mine. If you don't keep on beating your own past brilliance, people are all too eager to dismiss you as a one-night stand.' He paused and threw the pack of *Denim* over his shoulder. It landed in the wastepaper basket with a loud plop.

Mallet had had enough. He got up to go. 'Let's talk again tomorrow evening.'

Lawrence nodded and removed his lab coat. He'd made his point.

5

Ted finished telling Colette about the Lawrence incident, and she lay in his arms for several moments without speaking. Their windows were opened wide to the bracing night air. Bits of moon peeped out from behind the clouds as they chased one another restlessly across the sky. The room was bathed in silvery light one minute and plunged into total dark the next.

'Ted?'

'Uh?'

'You have to make a choice. You want to hear the alternatives?'

'You think I don't know them?'

Colette propped herself on one elbow and began to caress his chest, tracing the taut line of muscle with her fingertips. 'Tomorrow,' she said, 'you can go to Charles and tell him what happened. Everything.'

'And sabotage the project?'

'No, just listen to what he advises.'

'He'll talk to that idiot Williams, who'll strut around the board-room like a cock to see me put down.'

'So, it's pride more than anything else? Losing face is more important than your conscience?'

Ted dwarfed her hand with his.

'Okay,' he said bitterly. 'Pride, dedication to a project's success. The feeling I've gone so far with it I can't back down now. My responsibility to the boys in the division.'

'Etcetera, etcetera, etcetera,' she replied, pulling her hand from under his. 'I can build a ladder to the moon with your excuses. Why don't you talk to Charles and then resign?'

'*Resign?*' He moved away from her angrily and climbed out of bed.

His powerful body was outlined by the half-light for less than a minute. She lay back in the dark and listened to his feet move swiftly across the carpet and down the stairs.

The refrigerator door opened and closed. Ice cubes clunked heavily into a glass. One glass. The sound of liquid being poured. The footsteps didn't return.

Ted walked into the living room and sprawled out on a heap of cushions on the floor.

His intestines felt as though they were strangling one another. He lifted the glass of *Old Grand Dad* to his nostrils. Something about a good bourbon you could get you teeth into—not like Scotch. He knocked half the drink back in a gulp. The knot in his stomach protested violently.

He lay back and groaned. His stomach used to do this when as a young boy, he had been subject to frequent moments of panic, feeling doomed to an existence in his small Florida home town twenty-odd miles from the Alabama border. The town had nothing to keep it going but the county seat and a vehement Confederate spirit. The people, even the young, looked old, pinched, unyielding, hardened by successive generations of interbreeding, isolation, and fundamentalism. Anyone who had even faintly crinkly hair like his was regarded with suspicion. His father used to stare at him through slit eyes, glance at his mother, and sneer, 'There's a plantation nigger in y'all, yeas ma'm!'

Oh God, thought Ted. He used to gaze at the football heroes pinned to his wall and ache to be like them. With the help of a Charles Atlas body-building kit and a dedicated high school coach, he began to see football as a one-way ticket out of hell city. Without football, what was he? *Nothing!* But now, the tides had changed. Without Dominion what was he? *Nothing!* He couldn't survive alone. He needed a group, needed to mastermind the winning team. Football or business, it made no difference.

Yerba sacra had to win.

Colette appeared at the door in a close-fitting velvet robe. Ted sat bolt upright and said nothing.

She came over and sat down cross-legged on the carpet in front of him. Her short dark hair was tousled from bed. She looked more delicate than an elf. She reached inside his robe and began to caress him, more to comfort than to arouse.

Ted touched her cheek tenderly. 'Sometimes I wonder if I'm weakened by my love for you.'

'No chéri,' she said, then, as if sensing his thoughts, 'a man is weak only when he must win, win, win.'

'Honey, I'm over forty. I can't live on philosophy.'

'Your soul is not owned by Dominion.'

'That's not it. I can't live with myself if I resign and run.'

'Teddy,' she said gently, reaching for his bourbon, 'tobacco kills.'

But people *choose* to smoke he reminded her irritably.

'Ah, choice. The advertising man who walks with the tools of persuasion but talks to me of choice.'

'I'm too tired to fight with you Colette.'

She sipped his drink quietly. 'Come. I'll fix you more bourbon. Then you must sleep. Give yourself time, Ted. A day, two days. Don't fight with yourself. The answer will come to you.'

He stared glumly at the carpet. He wished he shared her calm. She touched the worry lines on his face. Slow, rhythmic movements along his forehead and around his mouth. Then she stood up and tiptoed away.

The clouds parted and the moon cast long angled shadows on the floor from the Georgian windows.

Mallett rose from the cushions. There was a smell of peonies in the air. He hadn't noticed it before. Give yourself time Ted, a day, two days. Maybe she was right. He turned and walked upstairs, leaving the bourbon alone on the floor.

The chairman stood at his plateglass window and fixed his gaze on a fully-laden barge as it floated by on the Thames below. It helped him fill a few contemplative moments as he puffed contentedly on a mellow briar pipe. The tobacco was his personal mixture for the morning, finely cut to burn evenly and steadily.

Selecting a good executive was a little like blending different tobaccos together, he mused. Just the right amount of strong Latakia made for a robust smoke. Too much, and you could destroy the blend. Ted Mallett was the Latakia on the board, and so far the blend had been just right. But now? With the possibility of yerba sacra being used to spearhead their new political drive?

Courtland weighed up the situation very carefully. Alun Hughes's suggestion made good sense. Now by bringing alternatives to the fore-front he was inviting open confrontation with the Jolyon Williams faction. It was inevitable. Williams was a jealous man, insecure, afraid of change. There wasn't a thing he didn't know about tobacco, and he was an astute director. Best man available to run the tobacco division and a model company man. It had always been taken for granted that Williams would succeed him as chairman in four years.

But now? Courtland caressed the pipe bowl. With the industry facing such revolutionary changes, surely men like Williams belonged in the past? With the financial division bringing in more and more non-tobacco interests? The group needed radicals like Hughes and Mallett at the helm, younger men with a sense of the consumer's pulse.

The barge disappeared from view. Courtland turned from the window and reconsidered the meeting of the previous evening. He knew Williams lived with the fear that Mallett would be voted into the chair over his head, and certainly the future concentration on substitutes brought that prospect closer.

Abrasive differences of opinion and outlook on the executive committee were good, but too much friction could be destructive. Somehow, he was going to have to find a way to ease the tension between Williams and Mallett, make them each consider the other's viewpoint. That meant telling Mallett he could benefit from seeking Williams's advice from time to time, draw on the man's considerable experience of the tobacco business. That was easier than telling Williams to modernize his thinking.

He'd find a way. Courtland pondered this and walked over

70

to his desk to consult his diary. Didn't he and Daphne have an anniversary coming up soon? He checked the dates. Yes. Six weeks. Good God. Thirty-nine years together. He shuddered inwardly. Still, it made a good excuse to arrange a dinner party: Williams and his wife, Ted and Colette. Could include Tessa too, to liven things up, although the Lord only knew who she'd bring with her. Last person she brought home was covered in hair. Couldn't tell if it was man or beast, male of female. Ah well. Do Williams good to be shaken up a little.

Courtland made a note of it on his memo pad. Corporate gear-changing was a slow and difficult process, but why not make it as pleasant at possible? He sat down and placed his pipe in the ashtray to cool. It was time Mallet acquainted himself more closely with the British political system, although perhaps it was a good thing he came in without the tobacco shroud. That made him freer, less complicated.

Courtland's thoughts were interrupted by the gentle hum of his intercom. He leaned over to press the button. 'Yes?'

A male voice replied, 'Mr. Mallett has been delayed, Sir Charles. He says, would you be good enough to give him ten minutes?'

The chairman checked his watch. Heavens. Daydreaming was far too time-consuming to be healthy. 'Yes, of course,' he said, releasing the button.

Along the corridor, Ted was studying two objects on his desk. Lawrence's lab report lay on his left. A telex from their Washington lawyer, Art Templeton, lay on his right.

At any other time the telex message would have annoyed him intensely. Now, somehow, it placed the Lawrence problem in a better perspective. Both problems threatened yerba sacra. He wasn't going to allow that.

He picked up the lab report and walked over to his private safe. He'd delay making a final decision until he sorted out the other problem with Templeton. He slid back the concealing wood panel and twisted the combination lock. Five turns to the left, two to the right, three to the left, four to the right. The door opened. He placed the report inside, twirled the knob, and slid

71

the panel back into place.

Ted returned to his desk and pocketed the telex message. Everything looked so bleak around him as he stepped into the buzz of a new day.

'Morning, Henry,' he said briskly to the chairman's assistant. Henry Peach was an ex-short-term commissioned officer selected by Courtland from his former regiment to head the chairman's personal staff. Normally just the sight of the neatly suited young man irritated Mallett. He symbolized everything Mallett saw as retrogressive in company.

Peach looked up. The feelings of distance were mutual. 'Good morning, sir. Sir Charles is expecting you.' He leaned over the intercom. 'Mr. Mallett is on his way in, Sir Charles.'

'Thank you, Henry. See we're not disturbed,' said the chairman's voice.

'Sir.'

Mallett opened the door.

'Ah, Ted.' The chairman beamed and gestured at the chair opposite his desk. He cast an approving eye over Mallett's dark-gray double-breasted suit and crisp white shirt. It made him look more traditional somehow. 'New tailor?' he asked.

'No,' Mallett grinned. 'St. Laurent, believe it or not.'

Mallett folded his arms. The chairman never mentioned clothes unless something was bothering him. Had Lawrence been to see him?

Courtland relit his pipe. 'I don't wish to dwell on this, Ted, but your sprint through Covent Garden is causing a rumpus on the board. Alun Hughes is delighted, but Jolyon believes a serious reprimand is in order.'

Mallett stared at him in amazement. After the anxiety of the night before, this was unbelievable. He laughed out loud.

Courtland wasn't amused.

'I realize some of our traditions make you impatient, Ted. I'm the first to admit that we can overstress our public image at times.' He paused. 'But I'm sure it's not asking too much of you to curb your impulsiveness.'

Courtland's tone was chilling.

Mallett found himself apologizing. 'I didn't know the cameras were live.'

'Ah, that's not the point. One's actions must not depend on whether or not one is on view. In a sense, one is always on view.'

Mallett recalled the evening with Lawrence and his pulse quickened. Did the chairman know? Was he waiting for him to discuss the matter?

'And this brings me to another point, Ted. You and Dominion.'

Mallett started to say something but the chairman raised his hand.

'The chair is for the taking when I retire,' Courtland continued meaningfully. 'I don't take sides, but I believe it's fair to offer you some advice. No man reaches my position unless he respects this group and has a sense of its history. Even hotheads like Alun Hughes recognize that. I don't mean slavishly toe the line, but it wouldn't harm your own image if you took corporate activities a little more seriously and involved yourself from time to time. I note, for example, that you are rarely, if ever, seen at the Tabac Club. Only four or five times since you joined us here in London. If you feel the company of too many tobacco men after hours to be overwhelming, I can personally get you into the Reform.'

'This is incredible,' said Mallett angrily.

Courtland sat back and waited.

'What you're saying, is that I'm not being judged on my work and my profit value to the group, but on how I spend my spare time, my choice of tailor, and the number of windbags who see me in the right places. Well, get one thing straight, here and now. If that's what is required to be elected chairman, you can take the position and shove it up your ass.'

Courtland smiled. 'Totally predictable response, Ted. Totally predictable. I wouldn't talk to you like this if I didn't think the group needed you more than you need it.'

Mallett looked away. Courtland never damn well failed. Never a word out of place. Everything carefully considered. Shove a man's face in donkey shit one minute and make him feel indispensable the next. Well, it wouldn't work this time. He wondered what Courtland would say if he told him about Lawrence. This was certainly not the occasion to find out. Protocol, tradition, image. Almighty *Christ*.

The chairman moved his pipe to the other side of his mouth. He flipped open a file and leaned over to reread the notes he had jotted down the previous evening. No harm in giving Mallett a few moments to cool off. He looked up and smiled.

Mallett wasn't going to be placated so easily.

Courtland continued as though nothing had happened. 'Ted, you'll be interested to hear that we're contemplating using tobacco substitutes in our new political drive after the election. I'm involving you in the political think-tank from now on.'

Mallett looked at him in amazement. He listened as Courtland repeated the discussion that had taken place and the response to Alun Hughes's proposal.

'What we need for our next meeting, Ted,' the chairman explained, 'is guidance on the amount of information we can divulge on substitutes—and when. Clearly timing is all important, and we wouldn't want to pre-empt your launch publicity. So perhaps you could think of a way around that.'

'I can't make such decisions about yerba sacra at the moment,' Mallett said tightly.

'Oh?' The chairman looked concerned. 'Problems?'

Go on, tell him. Talk to him about Lawrence. This is as good a moment as any. Mallett withdrew the telex from his pocket. 'We've had some worrying news in from Washington, Charles. The land we leased from the government for our experimental station in Washington State is being contested by the neighboring Columbia reservation council. They've filed a claim at the Indian Claims Commission.'

Courtland frowned. 'On what grounds?'

Mallett handed him the telex. 'They maintain the land belongs to them by treaty, and was only temporarily leased to the government for homestead.'

'How inconvenient. Surely this should have been gone into when we signed the lease?'

Mallett smiled. 'Where tribal land is concerned, the Indians have been cheated out of so much over the years that it often takes time to get at the truth. We're going to be dealing with two conflicting deeds.'

Courtland looked annoyed. 'I still don't see why this should hold up our political projections for yerba sacra here in London. Surely this will only effect a small proportion of the total land under cultivation?'

Mallett nodded. 'That's true. But that's not the point. We're cultivating land both on and off the Columbia reservation and on reservations across the Northern states, and I don't see this claim as an isolated move. They've gone to the heart of our operation and I want to know why. I believe the claim is a protest and a warning, and the way it is handled could effect all our reservation projects.'

'Meaning what?'

If we're not careful they could take the protest a bit further. Long drawn-out court case. Another James Bay. Think of the adverse publicity we'd get. Or they could go even further. Who knows? Modern Night Riders burning the station and fields?'

'Good God, Ted. Double the security budget. If that's not enough, surely the national guard can protect the property.'

Mallett shook his head. 'We need co-operation from the Indians. That was my intention all along. I am not going to have our experimental station turned into an army camp.'

The chairman made a dismissive gesture with his pipe.

It had been Ted's idea to cultivate Indian land in different states, using the Columbia reservation as a base model. The scheme generated various government grants and cut the initial Dominion investment to the bone. They had barely tapped the land potential or the labour pools on the reservations. This would be a good moment to remind the chairman of the economics involved. 'Dollar for dollar Charles, the yerba sacra project can be one of the most profitable this group has ever seen.'

'Hm,' said the chairman acidly. 'Until the tobacco states start cultivating the plant, of course.'

'Oh, come on, Charles, come on. That won't happen for a

long long time. Yerba sacra isn't any threat to tobacco at the moment. When the time comes for the farmers to switch over, the government will step in with generous subsidies. You know that.'

Courtland scratched his head. 'I was uncertain about your reservation projects from the start,' he said, reviving a past gripe. 'We could have had excellent returns from any of our considerable land holdings in the underdeveloped countries, but you scratched that idea. Too much risk involved, you insisted. What happens if there is a sudden change of government and we're nationalized overnight? Well, what in God's name have you got us into now?'

Mallett was silent for a few seconds. The chairman had a point, of course, he had to admit that. But he still believed that the American base was a far better proposition in the long run. He had deliberately avoided Dominion's estates in Brazil, not wanting to become involved with military dictatorship.

'This is all so damned inefficient,' Courtland said crossly.

'Unpredictable,' snapped Mallett, 'but not inefficient. The American government's to blame. Not us. When we drew up our leasing arrangements with them, there wasn't a word mentioned about the land having been part of the reservation.'

'So let Art Templeton get on with it in Washington.'

Ted made an impatient gesture with his hand. 'He's too damned East Coast when it comes to tackling problems like this.'

Courtland exhaled noisily. Their Washington lawyer was a brilliant strategist when it came to approaching the relevant Senators and bureaucrats to get legislation and grants moving. Now all of a sudden he was 'too damned East Coast'. Mallett was beginning to push things too far.

In fact, Mallett wasn't. But he wanted Courtland to think he was. He had every intention of letting Templeton handle the matter in his own way. But he earned the reputation of a pink rebel on the board, and it suited him now to play up the image. The more radical and contrary he appeared, the better he felt about the conspiracy with Lawrence. Complicity with Courtland and other stalwarts on the board wasn't his style at all. He enjoyed agitating them.

'It's wise to respect the grass roots,' he stressed. 'If this project's going to make sense, we have to work *with* the Indians. Not against them.'

'You're beginning to sound like my daughter,' Courtland remarked dryly.

'I take that as a compliment, but she wouldn't. Profit's at stake here, Charles. Not politics.'

Courtland studied him. True, no one could call Mallett a *convinced* radical. Naïve and idealistic, perhaps, but no activist. Still, something was eating him. Why this fervour? Casually he asked, 'Everything all right at home, Ted?'

Mallett looked at him in surprise. 'What's that got to do with anything?'

Courtland smiled. 'Merely enquiring.'

'Everything is perfect.' Mallett sounded emphatic.

Courtland raised his eyebrow. 'When is Colette's next exhibition?'

'Couple of months. Why?'

The chairman referred to his memo pad. 'Because I'd like to invite you both to our anniversary dinner in six weeks. It could be a joint celebration. Would you ask your secretary to confirm the date with mine?'

Mallet nodded curtly. He had too much on his mind to worry about anything as trivial as a dinner.

'I'll be inviting the Jolyon Williamses as well,' added Courtland.

Ted glanced up. The dinner was no longer a social occasion but a company obligation. He groaned inwardly. 'I'll check the date with Colette,' he said dryly.

There was a long pause. Eventually Ted rose and looked at his watch. 'I'll give Templeton a couple of hours to get to his office,' he said.

'One word of advice, Ted,' the chairman warned quietly. 'Don't cross Art. An angry lawyer in the capital is far more dangerous than an angry reservation on the banks of the Columbia River.'

77

'I doubt that.' Ted shrugged. Tactfully he paused by the door and smiled at the chairman. 'Trust me, Charles.'

Courtland watched him go. What a time for this to happen. He felt uneasy when the group got entangled with too many hot spots at once. They had come under a lot of criticism for helping Rhodesian tobacco farmers resettle in Argentina and Brazil. They didn't need the press to pick up on their activities on reservation land in the Northern states of America. Radical agitators linked up such issues and accused multinationals like Dominion of abusing native land rights, and of perpetuating the status of the white settler. Rothmans was subject to wide criticism because of its South African connections. Once the press got something into its head about a conglomerate, it didn't let go, anywhere. Look at the mess ITT got itself involved in over Chile, and the way that incident prompted investigative reporters to delve into the bowels of the group worldwide.

The reservation thing in America must not get out of hand. Too pressworthy. No point in blunting Ted's approach. But he had to make sure Dominion's interests were served before Ted's.

The chairman glanced thoughtfully at his watch. He pressed his intercom.

'Yes, Sir Charles?'

'Henry, dear boy. Get me Art Templeton in Washington will you? Doubt if he's left for the office yet. Probably still enjoying a quiet breakfast at home.'

'Certainly, Sir Charles.'

By the time Ted got through to Washington, the chairman had given the lawyer the green light to do whatever was necessary, and if necessary, to withhold information from Ted.

Templeton's voice sounded calm and reassuring across the transatlantic wires.

'I didn't mean to alarm you, Ted,' said the lawyer. 'We can take care of the reservation council without too many problems. We might need to make a few contractual adjustments.' He paused and continued, 'We'll probably settle on a compromise.

78

Release some of the land that's closest to the boundary and open it up for Indian cultivation.'

Ted listened and scribbled some notes on his memo pad. A vision of the lawyer seated at his expansive uncluttered desk gazing across Lafayette square crossed his mind. He could see Templeton's long, tapering fingers, forever fondling a slim, rolled-gold pen. He didn't like the lawyer's faintly patronizing tone. With very little effort, Templeton managed to make him feel like a dumb jock from the Deep South. No one in London made him feel like that. In Britain he was simply 'an American'. He knew what the lawyer was saying. *Stay out of this one, Mallett, it's not your ballgame!*

'All right, Art,' he said, barely concealing the irritation in his voice. 'Do what you have to. But I expect you to involve more Indian farmers in the cultivation of yerba sacra. Hell. We can't forget that we learned about the plant from the Indians. A little more respect for their feelings wouldn't do us any harm,' Ted snapped.

The lawyer agreed. The two men cut their conversation short. Ted had said, tacitly, 'Do what you have to.'

Templeton did.

Company personnel near the reservation were quietly told to look away. Within a week or so, a taxi driver would be mysteriously murdered on the reservation, and militant activists would be systematically rounded up, held in custody, and denied bail. Templeton, of course, wasn't involved. The authorities and the multinational had quietly helped one another set something up to eliminate a potentially violent situation. Nothing was put down on paper. Everything would be carried out quickly, efficiently, clinically. Which was how Templeton liked to work.

6

Daphne Courtland lay awake and listened to Tessa typing. She reached wearily for her watch. It was 5 A.M.

She pushed back the bedclothes and pulled on a dressing gown. The scene wasn't new to her. She had grown up listening to Amy work at a typewriter until all hours. Then it was political speeches, articles for newspapers, strategy plans, angry letters to *The Times*. Now, with Tessa, the output wasn't all that different. Except it was channelled through a different medium. The courts.

Daphne sat on the edge of the bed and shivered. Charles was right. Tessa's warehouse was bloody freezing. One corner of the main room had been partitioned off into a spare room and bathroom, but the bed may as well have been standing outside in the cold. She put on a pair of thick woollen socks and rubbed her hands together vigorously before leaving the tiny room.

The 'warehouse' was in a line of deserted factories left to run down beside the canal in Islington. The borough itself had alternated from chic to slum, slum to chic, ever since early Georgian days. Tessa lived in one of those last blind spots of Victorian industrial wasteland between Islington and the City. No one really knew what to do with the area. Clear it and turn it over to the drawing boards of the urban district planners. Or leave it to rot. Borough finances dictated the latter.

If it wasn't for being with her daughter, Daphne would have described visiting the warehouse as some kind of penance. She had to stumble through an old scrapyard from the road to get to it. The 'view' across the canal was a sprawling factory even the vandals had deserted. Every pane of glass was smashed from the ground floor to the third story. When the canal was low, the factory wall glowed a vivid green.

Yet, less than half a mile away, a series of Georgian squares had been restored to their original harmony and elegance by the march of the middle classes back to the area.

The canal seemed to take its cue from the dwellings on its banks. Where the stately, three and four-story houses had been expensively restored, the canal looked neat and clean. Pretty gardens faced one another across the water. Brightly painted houseboats and converted barges were moored on its bank.

But where the area was poor, the canal grew foul-smelling and ugly. Old bicycle wheels and dead dogs floated by on a permanent mat of slime. Winos collected under the bridges at night.

Tessa lived in a no-man's-land between the squalor and the splendour, a site the local estate agents would sniffingly call 'uninhabitable.' Certain friends suggested she only lived there because she didn't have to, but she ignored such cracks. She went where there was no danger of ever becoming complacent, or where she would feel compromised by neighbours, either looking up, or down at her.

She bought the old warehouse for a song, and spent as much again stripping and scrubbing the interior down to its original iron and woodwork, scaling years of grime of the tall windows facing the canal. She had an extra floor put in to break the height and built a couple of rooms upstairs. Her own bedroom was half bared to the sky by a wide, sloping skylight. The other room was used by a steady stream of transients.

Downstairs, she left the canal-front space open, furnishing it with items salvaged from demolition sites and the canal banks.

A large potbellied stove stood in one corner, surrounded by a wooden framework seating arrangement covered with soft cushions. The area doubled as a formal meeting corner, or a place to sprawl out and relax with a book, facing the canal. It was separated from the kitchen at the back by a long, bowsprit bar lined with old wooden barrels for seats.

Bookshelves built from an assortment of planks and bricks lined the opposite wall. The shelves followed the angle of the warehouse and did a quick ninety-degree turn into Tessa's work nook. This was just large enough to house a scrubbed farmhouse table and chair, and volumes of law books.

The floor was covered with old Persian carpets, passed down by Amy from her father's house. Leafy ivy trailed around the windows. A tall avocado plant stretched several feet in the air next to a palm growing out of an old chimney pot.

Depending on Tessa's mood or workload, the warehouse looked stark and orderly, or as though a whirlwind had passed through during the night. Daphne could live amongst her own clutter, but not anyone else's. So when she moved in for a few days, the whirlwind moved out.

This time it had scuttled into Tessa's work nook like someone looking for shelter. Her table was piled high with papers and hefty law books, overflowing wire-mesh trays and a stack of dusty buff folders bound with pink tape. All in direct contrast to her room in chambers, which was kept in order by a fastidious clerk. Three cats, offspring of Daphne's collection, housed themselves in this precarious mountain of work, two curled up in a mesh tray, another stretched out on back copies of the *Modern Law Review*.

Tessa sat wrapped in a grubby blanket with her back to the room. Her hair stood out around her head as though she had been attacked. She was haunched over the typewriter. An angle poise lamp hung over her like a vulture, creating a lone pool of light in the grainy dawn.

When the potbellied stove wasn't lit, the sole source of heat in the room was a collection of old gas heaters salvaged from a brewery. They hissed together loudly, giving off far more noise than heat.

Daphne turned on the lights over the bar. 'Would you like some tea, dear?'

The typing stopped. Tessa turned around and peered vaguely at her mother over square, gold rimmed spectacles. 'Hell. Did I wake you?'

Daphne laughed and stretched her hands toward the nearest heater. 'No, not really. Shall I put the kettle on?'

Tessa nodded and flexed her shoulders.

'I thought you said the PVC case was winding up this morning,' said Daphne, tossing mildewed bread into a plastic bag to feed the birds.

'It is. Suppose I'm suffering from prejudgment nerves.' Tessa watched her mother hunt the cupboards for something to toast. 'Try the one on the left, Ma.' She turned back to the typewriter. If she was honest with herself she was going through the case to prepare for an appeal, should the judge's decision go against her. She hadn't handled many industrial compensation cases like this one and was unsure of herself. It wasn't a clear-cut political thing like defending members of the IRA. Compensation cases required more than a superlative grasp of the industry and the medical facts. She had had to scour the company for evidence of negligence. That meant digging up similar cases occurring in the same industry elsewhere in the world, building up a mound of evidence to disprove the company's claim that it was unaware such and such a danger existed on the shop floor.

This was a union case, supporting the claims of widows against one of Britain's largest chemical combines. Three workers had died within a year of one another from a rare liver cancer, allegedly caused by PVC gas. It was the first case of its kind to reach the courts.

As usual, Tessa had discussed only the barest outline of the case in progress with her mother. Daphne knew the issues, but that was it. The newspapers told her little more. So it surprised her when Tessa asked, 'Does Dad ever discuss my cases with you?'

Daphne shook her head. She swilled boiling water around in a large brown tea pot. 'He was a little embarrassed last year when you defended the IRA of course,' she laughed, emptying out the water and reaching for the tea cannister.

Tessa walked over to the bar, trailing the blanket. 'I know,' she said dryly. 'Embarrassed for himself or for his pompous bloody friends at the club?'

'He didn't discuss it with me dear. He knows it would end in an awful row.' Daphne bustled around the stove, buttering buns.

'Hmm. Sometimes I wish we could have it out in one almighty row. Mediterranean style, clear the air.'

'He'd consider that ungentlemanly.'

'Bollocks. I ask about his work. He never asks about mine.' Tessa poured the tea into mugs and pulled up a barrel.

Daphne didn't reply.

Mother and daughter sat in silence and sipped their tea.

Tessa had always believed that her father had given up on her the day she was expelled from school at fifteen. She'd started a window-smashing campaign as a protest against the unfair dismissal of a popular teacher. Charles was deputy managing director of Dominion's retail division at the time, and vowed the incident delayed his promotion by several years. He had never forgiven her for making headlines in the *Mirror*.

The teacher in question had been caught cavorting with the school electrician. Tessa said no one would have minded if the teacher had been caught with some chinless wonder with a double-barrelled name.

Charles claimed the incident was the beginning of her 'downfall' because it meant she had to move in with Amy—then over seventy—in London, and attend a crammer. For Tessa, that was the start of her political education. It was the year of Suez and the Hungarian revolt. Amy taught her how to go about analyzing the events, reading between the facts, criticizing most of what she read in the newspapers. She introduced her to people who thought differently from the mainstream.

Daphne suddenly announced, 'He's jealous of you, you should know that by now.'

'But why?' said Tessa. 'If Harmer had been called to the Bar, he'd be boasting all over London about the future judge in the family. It's not just my politics he doesn't like?'

'No, dear.' Daphne looked away and thought back to the week when Tessa, nearing graduation from the London School of Economics, announced she was going on to the Bar. Charles thought it was a ridiculous waste of time. The girl was entering a strongly male domain. No self respecting solicitor would ever seek her representation on a case. Anyway it was so damned unfeminine, he'd said. If she was interested in the law, why didn't she become a solicitor, handle divorces and property transactions and so on? This is all Amy's influence, filling the girl's head with nonsense.

His antagonism had fired Tessa's enthusiasm all the more. Not so much the challenge of cracking a strongly male domain but the need to get inside and niggle one of the final bastions of the class system. She knew where she could make her impact.

Few really dedictated radicals got inside the system. Few could afford to pay the fare. Tessa was one who could, and her money helped others to get inside. She had been raised on Amy's political diet. Sting them where it hurts most, where the ranks are tightest. And sting them she did. She was no outsider, she knew their rules. She played them and manipulated them, turning each case into a political case. And yet, it hurt her that her own father couldn't admit she had proved him wrong, couldn't bring himself to acknowledge her work.

Tessa leaned over and flung the dregs from her cup into the sink. Daphne sat in silence and listened to the steady hissing of the brewery heaters. It was comforting and lulling, and the room was gradually warming up. The grey light began to lift outside. 'Think you'll finish court in time to meet us for lunch?'

'I don't know. Play it by ear. Let's make it half-past one,' said Tessa tersely, her mind whirring back to the notes on her typewriter. 'I have to be in chambers at nine. Do you want to come with me or go back to sleep?'

Her mother smiled. 'I'll stay here.'

Tessa nodded abstractedly and returned to her typewriter.

'Lawrence?'

Chris Lawrence paused on the steps of Dominion House and turned around.

Ted was in his Mercedes, engine running, heading for the underground car park.

The biochemist walked toward him slowly.

'Do you have time for a quick talk?' Ted asked.

Lawrence shrugged and climbed in beside him.

Ted reversed, turned away from Dominion House and drove toward the bridge. The Embankment was virtually clear. The early morning rush hour traffic was only starting. It didn't take them long to reach Battersea Bridge.

Ted said nothing and neither did Lawrence. This was hardly a social occasion for either of them. He drove along the bridge and parked next to a tea van that operated around the clock, mainly for the benefit of shift workers from the Battersea power station. A few of them hung around puffing on cigarette butts, coat lapels turned up against the biting wind from the Thames.

Ted climbed out and smiled. It was the safest place in London for a private talk. He bought two teas in plastic cups and gestured at Lawrence to join him at the wall. Both men stood gazing down at the wide, grey river.

'Well,' said Lawrence, 'what do you want? You didn't bring me here like someone planning a bank robbery just to study the view!'

Ted turned away. The wind was so penetrating, it was difficult to talk. 'I need to know something, Lawrence.'

The biochemist watched a tug emerge from under the bridge and chug purposefully downstream.

'Have you switched mice before?' Ted asked quickly.

Lawrence didn't reply.

'Lawrence?'

'What difference does it make? Actually, I haven't. But cutting corners and speeding up experiments isn't *all that* different. And that's standard practice.'

Ted deliberated this.

'If we didn't do that,' Lawrence continued, 'do you think we'd ever get everything done on our tight schedule?' He laughed suddenly. It sounded more like a choke in the wind. 'As I said the other evening. There's no room for the dreamy, creative scientist going off on a tangent in our labs.'

Ted nodded. In a highly competitive, fast-moving consumer business like theirs, the lab research boys took their orders from the marketing department. And that meant keeping

86

in step with a cost-effective timetable. With new brands or relaunches coming on and rundown brands going off the market every few weeks or so, there wasn't room for some nut down in the lab to delay the programme because he wanted extra time to play around with some new ingredient. With a million pounds tied up in each major brand launch, and the need for a new brand to attain average monthly sales of over a hundred million cigarettes, or under one percent of the British market, to stay in national distribution, they walked a thin tightrope each time. Sure, Dominion controlled over half the market, and its two leading cigarette brands accounted for one in three of every packet sold. But that meant each and every brand had to work like hell to earn its right to stay alive.

And yerba sacra wasn't simply another brand waiting to hit the marketplace. It was a whole new concept. With so much capital tied up in it, it had to do more than spin sales of over five million packs of twenty each month. It wasn't merely one new brand finding a niche amidst Britain's ninety-odd major advertised brands.

Yerba sacra had to set a whole new style in smoking.

With the stakes running that high, who the hell cared about a bunch of mice?

Really, who cared? Who could afford the luxury of caring?

Ted drained his tea and pulled a face. Anything was better than English coffee. But this powerfully strong brew was enough to bust a man's gut.

Lawrence crumpled his own cup and tossed it into the Thames, leaning over like a small boy to watch it sway downward in the wind and bob away on the water. The wind teased his hair. From behind, the biochemist began to look like the wild man of Borneo.

'Okay, Lawrence,' said Ted. 'Do whatever you like to the mice. Don't involve me more than necessary. And for Christ's sake keep your nose clean where Sorensen's concerned.'

The biochemist smiled. 'Sorensen's no problem. Long as I keep the pink recky forms moving in triplicate through his "in" tray, he's happy,' he said hunching his back to the wind. He had known Mallett would go along with him. What choice did the director have? What choice did either of them have? He waited for Mallett to say something about his part in the arrangement. Fixing things in the lab to give him more freedom, getting him out from under the research director's bloody feet.

Ted could hardly move his lips with the cold. 'Come on', he said, jaw clenched against the wind.

The two men returned to the warmth of the car, and spent the first few minutes blowing on their hands. Ted nodded toward the glove compartment. 'Couple of bottles of *Chivas Regal* in there for you,' he said, switching on the engine.

Lawrence shook his head. 'I won't touch a drop of your grog until I know the precise details of what you can get going for me in the lab. I'm not looking for gifts,' he added sourly.

Ted turned the car and headed back across the bridge. 'I'll talk to Sorensen and the financial director,' he promised.

'Talking isn't enough,' said Lawrence. 'I want an assurance, now. Or the mice go back to their right cages.'

Ted glanced at him. Arms folded defiantly across his balloon like chest. Face buried somewhere inside his hair. Lawrence would make a good advertisement for the Stone Age. Ted couldn't take him seriously any more. He felt the urge to laugh, but managed, with some difficulty, to restrain himself. Lawrence wasn't easily humoured. No point in upsetting him deliberately. Too dangerous.

'Well?' the biochemist said, impatient for an answer.

'You'll get what you want.' Ted turned into the Embankment and automatically began tossing some figures around in his mind. 'Write down exactly what you require. With rough budgets,' he said, panning over areas in his division he could trim back to accommodate the extra expense.

Lawrence removed an envelope from his coat pocket and slapped it on the dashboard. 'There it is,' he said. 'Costed down to the last frigging bunsen burner.' He felt insulted. What sort of a scientist did Mallett think he was?

Ted began to find the biochemist less and less amusing. He pocketed the envelope and turned off the Embankment onto

Blackfriars Bridge.

'You'll get what you goddamn want, Lawrence,' he said suddenly. *'Now quit bugging me.'*

Ted drove into the car park and climbed out of the Mercedes. 'I'll talk to you soon,' he said briskly, and turned on his heel.

'Charles, I think it's high time we talked about exposing Ted more systematically to the press.'

The chairman looked at his public relations director and smiled. Hughes, ruddy-cheeked in a new dark-blue suit and candy-striped tie, was more like an enthusiastic headmaster of a public school than one of the shrewdest members of the board. But he sensed a new restlessness in the man. 'I thought you made your thoughts pretty clear at the meeting a few nights ago,' he told him.

Hughes shook his head. 'Not really. Involving Ted with the new MPs is a fraction of what I have in mind.' He paused and referred to his notes. He hadn't elaborated at the political meeting because timing wasn't right. He knew how touchy Jolyon Williams was about Mallett. So he had purposely saved his thoughts for the weekly PR briefing session with the chairman.

The two men had long since agreed to be perfectly frank and open with one another about board members and personnel. The meetings would have made little sense otherwise. The formal memo circulated around the board and PR division afterwards reflected the bare bones of the discussion. Private views stopped at the chairman's door. Courtland enjoyed the sessions. They gave him a chance to speak his mind. But this time he was doubly pleased. The PR director's proposal mirrored some of his own recent thinking.

'We've kept Ted out of the limelight during the last year or so,' said Hughes, 'because of the secrecy of his work. Nothing a journalist hates more than to be invited in to interview an evasive director.'

Courtland nodded in agreement.

'I wasn't being flippant when I said Ted's sprint through

Covent Garden did us the world of good. What a debut!' Alun raised both hands in the air. 'Alerted the media to him in a way no one expected. Wham. Colette was a hit too. Nothing like a beautiful and unusual-looking woman to catch the eye and focus attention on the lucky devil of a husband!'

Courtland laughed approvingly.

Hughes's eyes crinkled at the corners. 'I thought we might offer to do the publicity for the next exhibition. Friendly basis. Nothing too formal.'

The chairman frowned. 'She's sufficiently well-known in the art world not to need us, Alun.'

'I know. But we'd be there to impress everyone that Ted has an exciting, talented, and liberated wife. I could alert some of my contacts in the glossies, suggest and exclusive feature on her. *Cosmopolitan. Good Housekeeping.* You know the sort of thing. Double-page spread with pictures. Could even get her tantalizing wardrobe featured in *Vogue.* She'd make a super model. Photographer could have a field day selecting different outfits to go with her exhibits,' he added enthusiastically.

Courtland scratched his head dubiously. 'Colette and Ted have always been very firm about maintaining separate identities. Remember how she flatly refused to become involved in our arts sponsorship programme? Even as an advisor?'

Hughes agreed. 'I'm suggesting something very low-key from us, a word here, a word there. I don't mean a plug for Mrs. Ted Mallett. All we are trying to establish in the public eye is a pair of successful and glamorous individuals. People respond well to that, especially the younger generation. The executive wife has come in for a lot of scrutiny recently. Who or what she is, how she feels, taking the back seat and so on. And the days when she was just expected to be a decorative hostess are going.'

'Yes,' said Courtland ruefully, remembering many a row with Daphne on the subject.

'It says a lot for Ted if he is seen to have an independent wife. Her talent speaks for itself. But we want more than the art collector to know about it. Remember we have a whole new breed of investor out there—The "new woman." I don't think

90

the City is doing nearly enough to entice her to be more creative about her investments.'

'And you think we can appeal to her by pushing Colette into the spotlight? How?'

'Appeal? Who knows? But we can certainly show her a different view of the corporate wife. Colette Sable, successful sculptress, wife of Ted Mallett, director of Dominion.' He paused and leaned forward to make the point. 'Charles, through Ted and Colette, our group name is linked with progressive activities that have nothing whatsoever to do with tobacco. A mere mention of the name is enough. Very subtle.'

Both men knew the industry had suffered a severe blow when the government decided to ban sports sponsorship by the tobacco companies. The multimillion pound investment dated from the 1965 ban on TV cigarette advertising and was a clever way around it. Brands found their way back to the TV screens through the massive media coverage of popular sporting events like motor racing and cricket. In public, the industry hotly denied it was using sport as another advertising medium. Behind the scenes it invested heavily in programme linking brand names with popular sports personalities, and directing brands at desired target audiences via different sports. Associating healthy outdoor activities with the industry was a necessary plus.

The arts sponsorship programme only partially offset the ban on sports. The audiences weren't as huge. The media coverage nowhere near as wide. But Hughes was fed up with the sighing that went on about governement restrictions on promotions and advertising, and what they could do if only. He wasn't paid to sit around and moan about the bans. He was impatient to make breakthroughs with a new approach.

'We need to involve more individuals, more personalities,' the PR director stressed. 'Chaps in market research keep telling us this. Consumers resent the large combines because they're faceless and alienating. That's even before the consumer starts reacting to the various products marketed. So for God's sake, let's build up some star qualities within the group. Give the public someone it can relate to with a feeling of goodwill.'

Courtland sat back in his swivel chair and contemplated this, fingers steepled against his lips. Their 'public' had to be viewed on so many different levels. Decision-makers, especially politicians and doctors, the consumers, and the potential investors. True, Alum had a point. They needed to do a lot more about going after the young investor, especially the increasing earning power of the female work force. His classic image of their noncorporate investor was the wealthy dowager, or the retired Colonel, travelling up to London by train from Guildford for the annual general meeting. But those days were going, speeded on by inflation. Their new investors ranged from scrap metal merchants to hairdressers, laundrette owners to fashion designers.

Hughes studied the chairman's furrowed brow, silver hair glinting in the light from his window. Distinguished-looking man, he thought. Pity the PR division couldn't have done something with the Harmer-Courtland family, give the feeling of Dominion being a nice, wholesome extention of it. But what with a son killed at a group-sponsored sporting event, a dotty wife who looked as though she dressed in Salvation Army handouts, and a daughter who made her name defending terrorists, the chairman hardly had a promotable family.

'You may be right, Alun,' said the chairman, breaking the silence. 'Schweppes and Kelloggs both had their splendid father figures at the helm. So of course did the tobacco companies in the early days. My late father-in-law, for example. Everyone who bought the products felt they knew these characters, or, more important, that the men knew *them*.'

'The folksy thing has had its day,' said Hughes hastily, wondering if the chairman had read his thoughts. 'It's important now for the consumer to relate to strong individuals who aren't part of the central family, so there's no hint of nepotism in the air. Ted is very much the outsider. Being American and good-looking helps. And he doesn't give the impression of being a yes man. People respond well to that. Remember, this is the age of the rebel.'

'So my daughter keeps telling me,' Courtland said tightly. 'Very well. See what mileage you can get out of Colette's exhibition. But it would be prudent not to let either of them sense your motives in any way.'

'I won't,' Hughes reassured him. 'One other thing, Charles. Can I make a suggestion? Go to the opening of the exhibition. If you buy something, we can make a story out of it. Better still, why not select one of the pieces for our new building in Paris? It would give you an excuse to invite both Ted and Colette to the opening in September. Make a difference wouldn't it? We'd get good coverage in the European media too, Colette being part French and Parisian-trained.'

'Hmmm. I'll mull over that one. What immediate plans do you have for Ted?'

Hughes crossed a number of items off his list and turned the page. 'Well, fortunately for Ted, he's not directly associated with the *Catch* disaster of last year. Jolyon took the full brunt at the time. Makes my role easier. No dirty linen to bleach for Ted. Far as the management press is concerned, he's still largely unexplored. That makes them curious.'

'They wrote about him when *Denim* was launched.'

'That's not enough. Single items like that make news one day and become fish and chips wrapping the next. I mean something more comprehensive.'

The chairman pursed his lips thoughtfully and scribbled a few notes on a memo pad. Hughes wasn't simply concerned with new image building. He wanted to use Ted as a battering ram to break down the wall of silence surrounding the industry.

'I want to invite a mixed group of business journalists to lunch with Ted,' said Hughes. 'Let him talk freely about tobacco substitutes, review the *Catch* failure and what he learned from it. We have a good news peg—the launch of the *Harold Mace* extralong king-size. There's also a new packet design coming out for *Pentham* panatelas in the next month. Ted and his boys can talk about them and do a quick review of *Denim's* first years, discuss the new media schedule planned for the spring. There's plenty of meat. I'll ask Ted to set a suitable date.'

'Who do you have lined up for this "mixed group"?' asked the chairman tentatively.

'Marketing correspondents from the *Financial Times, Times, Management Today,* and *Marketing.* Couple of people from radio.' Hughes ran a pencil down his list. 'Oh, and that girl who's giving us so much trouble in the advertising press. One with the uncombed hair and ink-stained face.'

'Good grief, Alun. We don't want Ted involved in a flaming row!'

'No, but he's at his best when he's provoked. He doesn't scurry away like Jolyon. He fights. Comes out with controversial statements. He's excellent profile material, and that's what I want to establish in media right now. By the time yerba sacra is launched I want the media to be fighting over him.'

'You'll be at these lunches of course,' said Courtland, searching in his drawer for a new tin of tobacco.

'No,' said Hughes emphatically. 'The handholding has got to stop. I'm confident Ted can do this on his own.'

The chairman sat up straight. It was always strict company policy to have a PR executive present at any meeting with the media. He was trained to ward off the body blows, keep the meeting on company tracks. He also made tapes of every topic discussed, even the small talk. The group had learned to cover its back.

Courtland shook his head. 'I want a senior man from your division to be there.'

The PR director moved impatiently in his chair. 'We're always so bloody defensive. You should hear what the press say about PR men, hired mouths as they call us, sitting in on meetings. They hate it. And it reeks of a bad conscience.'

'Surely you're not suggesting Ted should take an independent line on the medical issue?'

'I think that's something we should start discussing very seriously.'

'Can't make a decision like that without clearing it with the executive committee.'

'Fair enough. We'll discuss it at the next meeting.'

94

Courtland sighed deeply. To date the industry as a whole, on both sides of the Atlantic, had agreed to do one of three things on the medical issue. Maintain that the argument against smoking was based on statistical, thus inconclusive evidence. Pay independent journalists or individuals in the medical field to write reports or newspaper articles to discredit or belittle the medical evidence against cigarettes. Or, as a last resort, state that the company was not qualified to make medical judgments. And now Hughes was suggesting something radically different, and from a nontobacco director like Mallett! The chairman felt uneasy. He'd have to think this one through very carefully.

Alun Hughes was smiling. 'I have something else that should appeal to Ted, and to you,' he said, flipping over another page.

'Something we can agree on here and now, I hope?'

'Oh, why not, it's very innocent. I'm going to meet the headmaster of the American school next week for a drink.' He glanced up. 'You know, the school by Regent's Park. I'll suggest he invite Ted to coach a few games of football. Get the media along. Good story for the tabloids. American football is a novelty here—most people haven't seen it. I'm aiming for a plug on TV news. Peak viewing time.'

'Ted coaching young boys? You'll have the antismoking forces down our throats in no time, suggesting we're trying to corrupt youth,' the chairman warned. 'You know how agitated they get on the issue.'

Hughes laughed out loud. 'They won't have a leg to stand on. There won't be a tobacco advertisement in sight. We'll get someone from the American embassy along to talk about the importance of sport in building friendship between nations, etcetera, etcetera. Suggest one of the London schools comes along to watch.'

Courtland glanced at the ceiling. 'Could be a nice story. How are you going to persuade Ted to agree to it? You know how touchy he gets about football.'

'Oh, that's simple, Charles. I'll ask the headmaster to extend the invitation. I'll say Ted's very modest and doesn't like

95

the company pushing his football past at people. It's good publicity for the school, after all.'

The chairman looked at him. 'I approve, finally. But give me time to think over your other suggestions. Let's talk about the nitty-gritty. What press releases are going out next week?'

7

Tessa Courtland made her way between the tightly packed rows of tables crowding the brasserie floor. Several people glanced up. Some smiled in recognition. Others were simply curious. She had a way of sticking out in a crowd. Unlike most tall girls who stooped apologetically, she walked tall, with an air of dignity. She was wearing her 'court look,' as she described it. But this was a far cry from the staple black skirt and white blouse adopted by many of her female colleagues. True, the copper curls were rerouted to the back of her head and held in a demure bun to sit under a barrister's wig, but her dark culotte-styled skirt and cream stock tie blouse were effectively stylish.

Daphne and Charles sat in a far corner, heads bent on separate menus. An empty chair waited between them.

Courtland rose and glanced at his watch.

'Sorry to keep you waiting,' Tessa apologized.

Daphne looked up and raised both hands toward her daughter. 'You won, didn't you?'

Tessa nodded and clasped her mother's hands warmly, before sitting down.

Courtland leaned over to peck her on the cheek. 'Congratulations, darling. Who do we have back on the streets this time? Mass murderer? Bomb maniac?'

The two women ignored him. 'Did you get what you expected?' Daphne asked.

'Oh, even more,' said Tessa, smiling broadly. 'A quarter of a million quid for the three widows, and a trust fund for future victims. It's what I hoped for, not dreaming we'd get it.'

Courtland snorted. 'Those PVC workers had been in the industry a couple of decades. Liver cancer? Probably drank themselves to death.'

His daughter looked at him. So he knew about the case after all. That made a pleasant change. She shook her head. 'No, Dad. The victims died from angiosarcoma. Not cirrhosis. Two of them had worked with PVC for a long time, you're right. But the third hadn't. He was exposed to PVC gas for only five years.'

'Still don't see why the company should take the rap,' said Courtland briskly. 'Majority of workers leave the shop floor unscathed, no doubt. Why should the company be held responsible because a couple of bloody fools refuse to wear masks? Anyway. All this is so recent.'

'It isn't,' Tessa stressed. 'Similar liver anomalies were discovered among Russian PVC workers over thirty years ago.'

'Oh? And did the widows sue the company? Would have been sent to Siberia if they'd dared!'

Daphne stepped in hastily. 'What do you think won the case for you, Tessa?'

Her daughter pondered this for a moment. 'Last week I paraded twenty widows through the witness box, five minutes at a time, one after the other. Maybe that was it. They were all married to PVC workers who'd died from liver complaints. Of course, most of the doctors weren't sufficiently informed fifteen, twenty-five years ago to pin-point PVC gas as the cause. But I discovered all of them had been exposed more than the average worker to gas. Most of them were pipe-fitters, fixing gas leaks and so on.'

'Trust you to resort to emotional blackmail,' Courtland snapped, eyeing the floor for a waitress.

'Hardly,' Tessa snapped back. 'I had records of union officials who tried to get the company to improve safety precautions in the early fifties.'

'Early fifties? Good God, darling. Company wasn't even part of the chemical combine then. I'm surprised that evidence stood up.'

'Why? If you acquire a company you acquire its union recommendations, surely. You don't invest millions and then profess ignorance about the shop floor a decade later. Shop stewards tried to get the new management to do something in the sixties, but inadequate measures were taken. Plant manager thought the union was making a fuss about nothing.' She paused. 'I still don't understand why a strike wasn't called.'

'Well, there you are, couldn't have been all that important,' said Courtland, reaching for the wine list. 'If you changed machinery on the shop floor every time some stroppy steward made a noise, you'd never get any work done. Probably find this was one of *scores* of different complaints. Just jolly bad luck the company settled the others and dragged its feet on this one.'

'What utter shit, Dad. They ignored the warning signals. You should have seen their counsel's face when I produced color photos of the dissected livers in court.'

Tessa winked at her mother. Daphne raised her eyebrows and turned to gaze vaguely around the noisy interior of the brasserie. The terrazzo floor created general din that drowned most private conversations, although the tables were jammed together, cheek by jowl. Situated across the road from the Old Bailey, a stone's throw from Fleet Street, and a brisk walk from the Royal Courts of Justice, it was a popular haunt for barristers and journalists alike. Snatches of shop talk fought for space between the tables.

'Oh, Daphne,' Charles said, trying to catch her attention. 'I thought we might arrange a little dinner party for our anniversary.'

She looked at him distantly. 'Party?'

'Nothing elaborate, my dear. Just a few friends. Jolyon and Sheila Williams. Ted and Colette. You needn't be involved in the arrangements,' he added quickly. 'We can have it at the Tabac Club. Dammit, it's so long since we entertained a few friends.'

'Friends? Honestly, Dad. Can't you think of someone who doesn't belong to Dominion?'

Courtland could, of course, but that wasn't the purpose of the dinner party. He wanted Williams and Mallett together, outside the company walls. He ignored his daughter and looked across at Daphne. 'We've been married nearly thirty-nine years,' he said, softening his voice.

99

Daphne said nothing.

Tessa glanced sympathetically at her mother. 'What are your plans for this afternoon, Mum?'

Daphne shrugged. 'I really should get back to the country, I suppose. My pussycats will think I've abandoned them.'

'Another day won't hurt! Come to an early show with me,' she suggested. 'There's a festival of Garbo films at the Curzon, or we could go to a play. Something frivolous perhaps. Or would you prefer a concert? I'm behind in everything at the moment, so you choose. Why don't you join us, Dad?'

'Adore to darling,' he said, 'but some other time perhaps. I have a director's meeting planned for six. Shall we order another carafe?'

Colette sat crosslegged on a velvet sofa in her studio. A large bowl of fresias stood on the floor beside her, filling the air with a sharp and exquisite perfume.

Rain pitter-pattered above her on the conservatory roof. Two spherical marble shapes faced her on a pedestal. She had been studying them for a long time. They belonged together, these shapes. Gentle curves, compatible, yet not touching. The art was in the viewer's eye. The viewer had to be drawn by the silent words passing between the forms. The magnetism was there, yes, but the artist felt the work was incomplete.

She closed her eyes and lay her hands, palms upward, on her knees. By inhaling and exhaling deeply and slowly, she was able to imagine her breath travelling down her arms and into her hands. Her hands moved up, palms turning inward to face one another.

They remained in the air. She focused on the center of each palm, imagining these to be the outlets for her breath. After a few minutes, she sensed a line of energy drawing back and forth between them. She moved her hands, turning them gently, moving the beam between them. They came together, not to touch but to concentrate the energy. She held them still, turning her fingers in unison, holding the position, and turning back, one hand clockwise, the other against it.

100

She practiced the exercise over and over, strengthening the beam, trying different angles, drawing her hands apart, moving them close together, but never touching.

Then her hands became still, a taut, hot line linking the palms.

Colette opened her eyes.

She studies her hands. Fingers turned inward, drawing together. Thumbs reaching out to one another.

She measured the space between her palms, examined the angle of each hand, poised in the air.

Then she looked up at the marble shapes, her eyes moving between the pedestal and her hands.

Her legs uncrossed themselves and she rose, moving slowly toward the marble forms.

She measured the distance and angles of her hands against the stone, edging the shapes apart with with forearms.

Standing back, she studies the perspective, her hands in the air, the works of art in front of them. The energy beam moved between her hands. It moved between the marble forms.

Colette relaxed, shoulders dropping, hands by her side, head down. She looked up. The beam was still there, moving back and forth.

The artist's cheeks flushed with happiness. Weeks and weeks to get here, feel this. Purity of form. No strain. But no milky innocence, either. Strength and restraint. Anticipation. Forms touching, yet never touching.

It was time to work on.

8

Ted opened his front door to the shrill of a sander. Tonight he could have done without it. Normally he could blot out the noise. He walked into the sitting room. A glass of cloudy bourbon dregs still lay on the carpet from two nights before. The sight of it irritated him.

For a fleeting moment, he yearned for something else. The welcoming smell of a meal. A smiling, loving wife, waiting at the front door, face upturned for a kiss. 'Hello, sweetheart. Would you like a drink? Dinner won't be long. Have a good day?'

He ran upstairs, three at a time. Whole house seemed to be vibrating with the noise. Jesus Christ! Goddamn army could move in and she wouldn't hear it. These old houses were great, but oh man, did they carry sound. Two floors above, yet the sander was inside his eardrums. He got out of his clothes and kicked them viciously in the air before climbing into a tracksuit.

Damn her. At least she should know I'm here in case she's wondering. Which I doubt.

He ran all the way down to the basement. 'Colette, I'm home!' he bellowed.

The studio looked as though it had been victimized by a desert wind. The only thing distinguishing artist from stone was the movement of the sander, round plate shafting fine dust high in the air.

Ted leaned down and yanked the plug from the wall.

Silence.

'*Merde.*' Colette shook the sander irritably and struck it with the flat of her hand. A cloud of dust rose in the air like an apparition.

'I'm going out to jog,' Ted yelled. 'Can't stand that noise.'

She turned slowly and raised her goggles, pulling down the

handkerchief covering the lower half of her face. She stared at him and wiped her mouth. Another dust apparition escaped into the air. 'Ted,' she said quietly, 'plug the sander in.'

Ted started to say something but decided against it. She was taut with anger. He hated her like this. He plugged in the machine and walked out of the studio.

The sander followed him down the street. It had started to rain. English rain, like no other he had experienced anywhere in the world. Cold and dispiriting, penetrating deep into the marrow.

If it was going to rain, let it rain like in Florida. Rain thrashing out of the shuddering skies. Feel of a hurricane always in the air.

He crossed the busy highway and sprinted five blocks to the common, listening to his sneakers go smack, smack, smack against the wet pavement.

The peak hour traffic had subsided into a monotonous drone. It was music compared with the sander.

Ted felt the sweat building up inside his tracksuit. He plotted his route via a system of landmarks, judging his fitness by the time taken between each one. Tonight he was slow, puffing too early. Weary, for Christ's sake. Shouldn't use the body like this to work out irritation and resentment, he thought. No good starting out tense. Muscles sensed it and they didn't like it. Not one bit.

Deep into the common, he slowed down, stopped by a tall oak tree and hung over from the waist. His body felt cumbersome, like a big dog who didn't want to be dragged out into the rain. Above him the sky glowed a sulphurous yellow from the street lights. Pubs across the road began to fill up gradually. A piano was busy murdering 'The Sound of Music'.

Ted regretted not bringing some cash with him, just enough to forget everything over a pint of companiable draft *Guinness*. Oh, what the hell. He had to get back some time.

Hands on hips, he turned toward home. He took a long route back, half walking, half slow trotting.

The meeting with Lawrence slipped back into his mind. It

didn't really bug him any more. Sort of adjusted itself into a slot. What concerned him now was trying to find the budget Lawrence had requested. He had spent the latter part of the afternoon tapping away at his calculator. Not much slack anywhere in the division, and what there was would soon evaporate with inflation. The marketing and advertising budget for yerba sacra couldn't be touched. Not one penny. Spending on *Denim* was going up. There was no other way out. Someone in his division would have to go. But who? New product division was lean and quick as it was, moved faster than any other area in the group. Marketing men working under him were stretched to their limits. Maybe a couple of secretaries could go. Donkey work could be passed on to the typing pool. He didn't like the idea of dismissing anyone. But what alternative was there?

The Lawrence thing reminded him of the few times he'd been asked to fix a football game, and he didn't like being reminded of that. Oh sure, nobody got hurt then, and nobody got fired, either. If he thought about it long enough, it sort of rationalized itself in his mind. All he had to do then was eat the ball and allow himself to get sacked when he could easily have passed it on. Delay things a little. Bruised his ego when the fellas bawled him out for it, but he soon made up for that. Hell, he didn't own the game. With a couple of hundred million dollars at stake for the owners, half that at stake for the networks and Jesus only knew how many millions running around with syndicate bookmakers, you played the game by their rules.

And once the game was over, that was it. Clear-cut. Not like this mice thing. This was going to go on and on. Adjusting budgets was only the beginning.

Ted slowed down just before he came to his crescent. The rain pelted on undaunted. People scurried home from the bus stop with newspapers covering their heads. All he could think of was a long, hot shower.

Silence met him as he turned the corner. The house looked dark and forlorn. Maybe she'd walked out? She'd done that once before when he yelled at her. Just disappeared for a couple of days. Had him walking the streets, frantic for her.

He unlocked the front door quickly. 'Colette?'

The kitchen light was on.

She stood in front of the stove emptying a bag of apricots into a saucepan, and didn't turn when he walked in. A grey flannel shirt billowed around her body. Her bare legs were pink from the shower.

'Colette, I'm sorry.'

'Sorry? You selfish bastard! Two nights you keep me awake till dawn to discuss your problems. Okay,' she said, gesturing with her hands. 'I prefer to share these things. But I get tired. Then my work sticks inside, and it makes me unhappy. This afternoon, slowly it began to happen, and it was *beautiful.*'

'And I blew it?'

'No! If my work is so fragile a plug coming out of the wall can fracture it, then I must put my chisel away for good.'

Ted took hold of her shoulders and turned her to face him.

She shook free and eyed his damp tracksuit and mattered hair.

'Okay,' he said, dropping his hands. 'I get the message. Hey. You want to eat out?'

'No. *Vraiment.*' She turned to stir the apricots.

Ted watched her. Apricots? Was that all they were going to eat? 'I know,' he said. 'Give me ten minutes to clean up. Then how about if I throw some chops on the grill and toss up one of my special salads?' He tried to sound lighthearted.

She shrugged as if she didn't really care, one way or the other.

Ted quickly mixed her a Compari and soda and led her into the lounge. He puffed up the big cushions on the carpet and switched on the TV news.

She promptly switched it off and reached for a sketch pad.

'Oh, go to hell,' he said and ran upstairs.

Later, freshly showered and more relaxed, he put on a bright red shirt and matching slacks to help cheer things up, and returned to the kitchen to prepare their meal.

He placed a bottle of burgundy on the table and seasoned

the chops with thyme and lemon juice.

Then he left the chops to do by themselves and poured himself a Scotch.

Colette lay stretched out on the carpet, legs bent at the knees, feet twirling in the air. She moved a piece of charcoal in wide, squeaky arcs across the sketch pad.

Ted put on some jazz flute and turned it up just loud enough to hear. He watched the charcoal for a few minutes, then put down his drink. Leaning over, he cupped Colette's feet in his hands and massaged them gently from the instep up, rotating his thumbs wherever the muscles felt tense. 'Remember when you first taught me how to do this?' he said.

'Do I,' she murmered, moving her hand freely and easily across the paper.

He looked wistfully at the back of her head. Hell, they needed more time together. He raised the subject tentatively.

'Maybe, chéri, I need solitude for a while,' she said simply.

Ted nodded and lowered her feet to the carpet. She rolled over onto her back. He sat down, hands on the floor, and pressed his feet against hers, right against left, left against right.

After several moments, they changed positions, Colette leaning on her hands, head well back.

'Colette?'

'Mmm?'

'Don't be cross with me any more.'

'Cross? You piece of shit!' She moved her feet away. 'You throw yourself into my studio like a hand grenade. What do you want me to say?'

'Aw, honey. All I wanted was to say hello.'

It was hopeless. She drew her knees up protectively, arms clasped around them. 'There's a way of saying hello, and a way of saying hello,' she said wearily.

Ted rose and picked her up like a bundle from the carpet, reaching under the flannel shirt to touch her warm skin.

'Ted,' she said. 'The chops are burning.'

9

Ted arose well before six and jogged to work through the grey, damp, early morning air. His routine meeting with the Kestner McKay agency was scheduled for 8.30 A.M. and the team was ready to present him with the final plan for yerba sacra.

He could have done without the irritable Colette for a curtain-raiser. He hoped the brisk jog would help clear his mind.

The road was virtually deserted apart from a few whirring electric milkcarts and the occasional lorry. The long, flat-fronted blocks of terraced houses were still heavy-lidded with sleep. Ted envied them. Any other time he would have spent the extra hour curled around his lovely Colette.

He felt a sudden pang of regret. Dominion had certainly encroached on their early carefree sex life together. Or no. Perhaps it had as much to do with Colette's increasing involvement in her own work. What had happened to the days when he arrived home from work and they would start before the front door was closed?

Now, snatches of those early days returned only rarely. And it just wasn't the same any more, although it frightened him to admit that. He was beginning to feel that perhaps Colette was indulging him, that her mind was really elsewhere. It bothered him. He was reluctant to talk about it in case he was imagining things, allowing office anxieties to make him paranoid. He even resented confiding in her about Lawrence. He made a pact with himself not to discuss it, or his complicity with the biochemist, again. There had to be a limit to the number of weaknesses he revealed to her. It gave her an edge over him, and he was beginning to find that unsettling.

Ted paused by the traffic lights to catch his breath, feeling his thoughts ribbon on up the road. Jogging helped to clear his head. That was essential if he was going to judge the morning's presentation free of doubts or misgivings.

The lights changed. He jogged on.

At a certain point in the agency workshop sessions he always backed down to let the team have its head, run with the ball without him. Reluctant as he was to do this, he recognized a stage in the proceedings when his pace setting and play calling became inhibiting to the team. This was when the quarterback dropped out and the clever adman took over. There was another advantage. By temporarily removing himself from the action, he gave himself the necessary distance to be able to review the results with a fresh eye.

Which was essential in the complicated world of cigarette advertising. Each advertisement had to work twice as hard as it did in the past. Political trends had dictated the swing to filter tips, low-tar brands and tobacco substitutes. Yet the consumer must be reassured that all was well on the smoking front. There was a special art in that. The image also had to fulfill its basic role, cutting through the jungle of the consumer's real and fantasy needs, peeling back the layers of repressed feelings and hankerings. The adman was trained to know the consumer better than the average consumer was ever likely to know himself.

Ted believed that executives from poor or deprived backgrounds like his own usually made the best admen.

They knew the power of fantasy.

They understood the subtle fuelling process that drove the acquisition machine. Advertising was geared to accommodate both emotional and material inadequacies. The ability to tell the consumer what his subconscious wanted to hear or see must be sufficiently powerful yet sufficiently subtle to supersede conscious awareness.

There was a cigarette brand pinned to each corner of the complex psychological maze of reasons that prompted people to smoke. Some brand images suggested peer group acceptability, others suggested rugged individualism. Some brands implied poise, others suggested hyperactivy. Some images were kept deliberately low-key and humdrum to imply that smoking was a normal, everyday habit. Others suggested romance, intense sexuality, adventure. Some advertisements were provocative and exciting, others plainly reassuring. Via sophisticated design techniques, each brand image reflected an exact composite of the desired target audience.

Stirling Harmer's pioneering work in the mass production of cigarettes was inspired partly because he knew this was where the real tobacco millions were to be made. Not in handrolled cigars for gentlemen, but in competitively priced, appealing promoted cigarettes for the common man.

Ted liked to inspire his marketing team with stories about Harmer. It brought them back to earth. The buccaneer didn't have opinion polls and market research teams and computer printouts to play around with. The street taught him about brand popularity. Because he was born poor, Harmer knew firsthand the power tobacco had to give a few brief moments of pleasure, and his whole marketing policy was built on this knowledge.

Ted slowed down by Waterloo Station, and walked the last half mile to Dominion House, not wanting to arrive steaming and sweating. The grey light was beginning to clear. He felt rejuvenated from the concentration of physical and mental energy over the past forty-five minutes. He trotted up the wide stone steps and waved to the night security officer whose shift was just about over. The usually busy foyer was quiet except for the steady *hishhhh-hishhhh* from the fountain. Colette's fountain.

Ted took the lift to the executive floor, quickly showered and changed.

Artwork for the proposed spring and summer campaigns for *Denim* were lying on his desk, awaiting approval.

Ted smiled. One of his ban buckers, so named for the way they bucked restrictions on cigarette ads, must have left the material in his office the night before. They wanted him to clear it before his thoughts were swamped with yerba sacra.

Both *Denim* and the yerba sacra cigarettes were aimed at a stongly youth-orientated market. There were bound to be overlaps and a certain amount of crisscrossing between the two brands before smokers decided on preferences. Promotional success would depend on the creation of two distinctly separate brand images. There was no point launching an entirely new product onto the market only to see it drain sales from a highly successful existing brand.

Denim's proposed magazine and poster campaign developed subtle variations on a lazy summer idyll. In the popular 'theft' theme of the previous summer, thieving fingers had moved cautiously toward a pack of *Denim* stuck in a back or shirt pocket.

The sexual overtones and interchangeability of the male and female hand were highlighted by catchy 'keep your cotton pickin' fingers off my *Denim*' taglines. It had been voted one of the best campaigns of the year by the design and advertising magazines.

And that was precisely why Ted insisted on a new campaign now. He lived with the belief that an advertising team should start worrying when themes and taglines hit the top of the popularity stakes, not when things began to slough off. The temptation to milk a popular campaign dry could prompt a backlash.

A theme should be replaced when it was at its peak, leaving the consumer with positive and nostalgic feelings about the campaign.

The new theme came in on an entirely different beat, but with obvious links to the previous one. The composition suggested that the same models were retained and that the conversion to *Denim* as a result of the previous campaign had released all inhibitions.

This time, instead of shirt or ass pockets, one saw only the models' feet, clad in a colourful assortment of demin sneakers.

In one advertisement, four pairs of feet hung over the edge of a hammock, all squashed together like kids lined up for a holiday photo. The catch-line—'Now try for a *Denim*'—was provocatively suggestive if the eye stopped after 'for.' The ads would run consecutively for four weeks though the late spring, and then, as the weather grew warmer, the sneakers would be shed for an appropriate 'smoking feet' campaign to run through the summer. These advertisements showed bare feet sticking over the hammock. Cigarettes gripped between the toes alternatively pointed up or down, under the line, 'Look what happens when you smoke *Denim!*'

The average consumer would see merely a zany jumble of feet. But click, click, whirr, his subconscious would pick up the implant. Every advertisement was a combination of messages aimed at the conscious and subconscious. What the consumer saw, consciously, he could choose to accept or reject. He had no such selective powers over the things he didn't consciously preceive but stored indiscriminately.

The art of advertising was to find devices that would make an impact on the consumer's subconscious. Taboo subjects linked with sex or death and related symbols were the frequent tools of this subliminal science. The subtle embedding of seeds to stimulate or scare the subconscious was the adman's key to turning the consumer's fears, phobias, desires and fantasies into buying motivations. Tobacco admen were well versed in the art. The mounting objections to the industry, coupled with increasing government restrictions, had sharpened the wits and tools of the creative genii who put the finishing touches to the advertisements.

It wasn't unusual for an agency chairman to appear on a TV program with a hurt and pained expression saying pathetically, 'But in most cigarette advertisements, all you see are straight packet shots.' What he didn't talk about was the sexual overtones embedded in the taglines.

It also wasn't unusual for cigarette advertisers to utilize death or cancer toboos. The paradox of the death wish and the desire to cheat death was inherent in man, and most visibly expressed in dangerous spectator sports.

Government health warnings were cleverly designed to appear innocuous. Exiled to the base of the advertisement or primly boxed in, the health warnings were deliberately designed to conjure up the image of some minor civil servant. Those advertisements containing laughing or sociable couples mocked the bureaucratic content of the health warning. Everyone wanted, somehow, to circumvent bureaucratic intrusion. Thus the government health warning achieved the exact opposite of its proposed intention.

Who, thought Ted, could possibly take the government health warning seriously when it was printed under a bunch of silly feet?

He was more than pleased with the team effort on the *Denim* campaign. It had the right balance and feel somehow. It was also appropriately unisex, which meant it would be used in both women's and men's magazines, and the general media too.

Ted judged the value of a new campaign on its ability to adapt and spawn other ideas. There was a lot of mileage of be gained in stimulating and sustaining public awareness. The smoking feet theme would do that all right. Within a few weeks they would be running and jumping across posters on the sides of London buses, and doing similarly crazy things across billboards in prime sites near busy stations and subways.

Wall posters and T shirts would hit the streets in time for the tourist season.

Even if the message of the new *Denim* campaign was pretty clear to most people, and more provocative than other brands in the same category, it still wasn't blatant. The company could easily block objections from the antismoking lobby. What on earth are you talking about, sir, accusing us of violating the advertising code? How can *feet* possibly make smoking appear romantic, daring, or sexy? We can't help it if you're some kind of a foot fetishist.

But with yerba sacra, the launch theme couldn't be quite so relaxed and cheeky. It would have a lot more work, and a lot more convincing, to do.

Yerba sacra was different, he thought, as he flung his empty coffee cup away and left the office. First of all, they were launching something entirely new. Secondly, they had a lot of reassuring to do after the disaster with *Catch*. They were up against a cynical public and a vociferous antismoking lobby. The government was impatient to get more and more 'safe' cigarettes on the market to silence the protesters' howl.

The critical eye of the competition was upon them. Not even a minor mistake would go unnoticed.

Everything depended on the brand image.

During his years at Dominion, Ted had defied the normal company policy of using a selection of the top eight advertising agencies in London for different brands, reshuffling brands between agencies when necessary.

He had opted instead for the small 'hotshop' agency. Most of the hotshops were run by creative or product development teams that had decided to break away from the big name agencies and set up on their own. Many of the individuals had had their fill of big name agency experience in New York as well as London. The hotshops offered a tight concentration of talent and brought in extra services or help where necessary.

Ted liked the closeness, the informal workshop sessions. He also liked working with men who were working for themselves. That, tended to sharpen creative instincts. A large agency could afford to lose a million pound account. A small agency like Kestner McKay couldn't.

He liked McKay's style. No bullshit or flannel.

Weekly progress meetings were held gathered around the table in Tony McKay's office at precisely 8.30 A.M. The popular myth about the English working day starting around 11.30 A.M. didn't exist here. If people didn't like McKay's penchant for early starts, they didn't last very long. Like Ted, he was at his desk before anyone else in the building and maintained he could complete a full morning's work before the phones went mad.

You got the feeling that Tony didn't pander to fashion. It pandered to him. Ted had met the ex-creative director in New York and sought him out when the Londoner returned home to set up his hotshop.

Tony's office was papered with awards for winning designs. The previous year's campaign for *Denim* was among

113

them. But Ted wasn't dazzled by his artistic ability as much as by his ability to handpick and retain an excellent staff. Coupled with the marketing boys from Ted's division, they made an ideal team of 'ban buckers'.

To keep overheads down, Kestner McKay operated from a converted butterscotch factory half a mile away from Dominion House. All surfaces were painted the color of the syrup. Furnishings were basic and functional and walls were decorated solely with the group's products. Clients knew their money went into work and not wall-sized op art paintings. The bustling atmosphere, encouraged by the ex-factory setting, contrasted vividly with the smooth carpeting, chrome and leather furnishings of the larger agencies.

When Ted arrived, two of his young marketing executives were waiting for him. The meeting forged ahead with the freshness and spark of an agency pitching for a new account.

Months of work had been carefully sifted and processed. A tight programme had evolved out of the endless arguments, the late night brain-storming sessions, the grind, and the inspirational flashes.

The average consumer had little idea of the time and science that went into the creation of a brand image.

Tony McKay paced Ted through the proposals, hands working expressively in various descriptive movements to prove a point.

Aided by a back-up of market research reports, he had eventually swung the team in favor of retaining yerba sacra as a brand name. Dozens of possibilities ranging from *Cube* to *Yes* had been scratched. Yerba sacra became *Yerba Sacra*.

Research executive Andy Pound elaborated, relating everything he said to a series of tabulated charts on the pinboard. Consumer test panels had come up with a consistent series of positives for the name *Yerba Sacra*. Telephone interviews in key areas around the country confirmed the panels' response.

Those questioned were given a series of names and asked to list various adjectives in order of priority. Initially, they were

114

not told that the proposed names were associated with smoking, but only that they were being considered for a mass-produced product with which they were familiar.

Any misgivings the agency team had about the effect of the foreign name were quickly dispelled. Several people thought yerba sacra was a herbal tea, and they were asked for associations. Herbal teas were consistently linked with health and vitality, and that presented a huge plus for the name.

Even when people subsequently learned the product was tobacco substitute and not a tea, something, Pound explained, of that positive initial response would remain.

Sacra evoked a similarly sound reaction. The panels reasoned that if something was sacred, it had to be good, pure.

Other descriptions favoured 'exotic', 'poetic', a hint of 'faraway lands', something 'Spanish', something to do with 'Spanish explorers', proving that the name was working, in a curiously paradoxical way. The association with tea inspired trust and familiarity. But the ring of the name was also capable of evoking fantasies of exotic lands and voyages of discovery. That was a double bonus. It revived the stories of the explorers who brought smoking from the Americas to the courts of Europe. It also suggested a modern 'trip'.

Copywriter Felicity Klein reminded everyone of their own immediate reactions to the name. 'Familiarity has caused us to think of yerba sacra as a generic name, like tobacco. We have to make ourselves rediscover it. Relive it through the test panels' eyes.'

The support was there, but the agency team had to overcome its own subjectivity to see it clearly.

Graphic designer Sam Schenk quickly summed up the various inputs that determined the image. The product had to reassure and excite at the same time. The name did that. It also had to establish itself as something entirely new, without being flashy. The image had to do that.

Their prime target audience was in the sixteen to twenty-five age group, their second largest from twenty-five to thirty-five. But they couldn't afford simply to pander to a pop image.

The impact had to be more serious, more lasting. By comparison, *Denim* was a relatively transitory product.

Everyone in the room knew the importance of catching smokers young and promiscuous when important brand preferences were being established. They also knew that the younger the smoker the greater the desire for a stronger-tasting brand.

The brand was going to be test marketed initially in the London area, and then systematically introduced into the areas that had the highest percentages of sixteen to twenty-fives and twenty-five to thirty-fives, with a concentrated target on the major university towns.

'After the cock-up with *Catch*,' McKay pointed out, 'everyone is going to be highly suspicious of *Yerba Sacra*, wondering if it is another tasteless fibroid wonder from the company lab. With the name, we've established the irritial work of rooting the product in the soil—there's no mistaking the significance of the word *Yerba*. Now the image has to back that up.'

The team's packaging expert, Bill Gopsill, took over at this point. The increasing restrictions on cigarette advertising emphasised the importance of the packaging. Packaging experts knew the power of their art to direct taste, attitude, likes and dislikes. Gopsill used a series of videos, taped secretly during consumer test panel sessions, to emphasize the effect of packaging on clients. A single brand of cigarette would be packed in a plain brown wrapper and in an expensive-looking silver wrapper. The unsuspecting test smoker would give two distinctly different responses. Similarly opposing responses could be evoked from a single variety of wine or a brand of sugar, all depending on their 'packaging'.

Equally important was the power of display in boosting purchases at point-of-sale.

Gopsill had categorized the various sales outlets in terms of super-markets, corner stores, and licensed outlets like pubs or wine merchants. Colour photographs from a random sample in each category established the prime visual requirements for packet graphics. It was pointless coming up with a dazzling packet in the studio if it was going to be visually slaughtered on the shelves by rival brands, or lose definition under the artificial lighting of the sales outlet.

So the *Yerba Sacra* packet had to stand out under the stark lighting of supermarkets, in the reddish light of pubs, in the unsophisticated and often uncluttered atmosphere of many corner shops, and in the usually grainy light of the tobacco and confectionery hutches of street, station, or subway.

Visual requirements quickly whittled down the list of colours to possibles and probables. These were pitted against the necessary image requirements and the name. Everything had to be multifunctional in the selling game. The packet had to be a whole team of salesmen.

When the list was whittled down, brown and gold stood out.

Tony McKay lifted the tracing paper off the proposed logo, and slid it along the table to Ted.

Ted held it aloft. There was an immediate hush in the room. He studied it for several long moments, and said, simply, 'Perfect.'

The table relaxed and smiled.

The squat, soft packet was a basic earth-brown. The focal point was a vivid gold zigzag Y, slightly off centre, encircled by a gold ring.

Ted looked at it, thinking back to the original planning meetings. 'So you finally decided on lightning,' he said. 'Effective and appropriate. Works beautifully. Terrific!'

Following Ted's initial instructions, the team had imbued itself with Indian mythology and design, especially where this related to smoking. The zigzag motif occurred frequently in Indian graphics, in basketry, weaving, beadwork, among tribes from the North and to the South. The zigzag was an elemental symbol. If signified fire, lightning.

Admen worked, talked, and thought in terms of archetypal symbols. Once the mind accepted that man was a symbolizing animal, a window opened on a lingo that linked cultures, mythologies, and religions. Even the sceptics had to admit that certain shapes, forms, angles, geometric combinations and

117

colours would evoke similar responses in people of widely differing backgrounds. Archetypal symbolism was fundamental to the stimuli used in advertising.

'Come on, Ted,' said research man Pound impatiently. 'What else do you see there?'

Ted folded his arms and shook his head.

'There's something else there *none* of us actually planned,' Pound said excitedly. 'It came out of the test panel. Concentrate on that zigzag Y in the circle. Delete all thoughts of lightning.'

Ted, slowly, said, 'I'll be damned. It's an egg, cracking open?'

Everyone smiled and nodded.

Designer Sam Schenk, blue-tinted glasses on the edge of his nose, leaned forward like a college mathematician about to deliver a lecture. 'The egg is a cosmic life-giving symbol,' he said. 'An emblem of immortality in several prehistoric cultures, not forgetting its Christian significance in that respect. The Easter egg cult reflects this, though how many of us ever stop to think about it? We follow rituals all the time without ever questioning their origin.'

The team lapsed into silence and gazed down at the design. Spiritual and religious overtones aside, everything was done with a strong commercial purpose in mind. There was no point producing some geometric wonder if it didn't do a cold, hard, selling job up there on the shelf. The art of making one logo stand out among thousands was to achieve maximum effect with a minimum of visible effort. Power had to be generated by total simplicity and restraint.

The life-giving message of the lightning motif was compounded by the cracking egg. Gold wasn't only appropriate for the lightning motif, it was also a primitive symbol of spiritual superiority.

The primal qualities of the design were literally rooted in the earthy brown background of the pack, suitably textured to create the desired effect of freshly ploughed soil. The multiple significance was necessary to reassure consumers that the product was truly nature's own, and not, as McKay had pointed out, some fibroid invention from the labs.

So, the various sales messages rang loud and clear. Test panels confirmed the pack as 'eye-catching', 'exciting', 'dramatic,' and 'reassuring,' and that was the desired response.

The proposed squat, untipped appearance of the cigarette, and the careful selection of a roughish, off-white paper, would complement the earthy, back-to-basics image. There was also a conscious effort to offer something that looked like a refined joint.

Yerba Sacra was truly years ahead of its closest rivals.

Ted returned to the office feeling buoyant. *Yerba Sacra* was beginning to develop a personality of its own. It was no longer a research project dismembered under subject headings in the filing cabinets. It was a flesh and blood brand. The name really meant something. The brown and gold image was terrific. Nothing could stop it now.

The budget had, of course, been established well in advance, with inflationary adjustments made at regular intervals. But when Ted presented the logo to the board a few weeks later, he made a few adjustments of his own. He was in the rare position of telling his fellow directors that, remarkably, they were running slightly under budget.

The logo proved extremely popular, and few exceptions. The budget news was most popular, without exception.

Ted had planned this carefully as a tactical device. He would have to ask for additonal funds to set Chris Lawrence up in a lab of his own. Winning board approval at this point prepared the way.

He timed his request most carefully.

He and financial director Paul Lombard attended the same gym and sauna in the city, and their workout sessions coincided regularly. Ted admired Lombard. The director was in his fifties, and, like Ted, a fanatic about physical fitness. They respected that in one another on a board largely dominated by ulcers, liver complaints, and heart murmurs.

So, the sauna seemed an appropriate place to sound Paul

out on a separate budget for Lawrence. Ted talked informally, seeking his advice. Part of the proposed budget could come out of the money saved on the advertising budget. He could dismiss a secretary in the new products division, and his two marketing executives could share one, with excess work being passed to the typing pool.

Ted casually tossed figures around the steamy, cedar-panelled sauna. Paul lay stretched out on the slats beneath him, listening, deliberating. He liked it when Ted used him as a sounding board before presenting new ideas and proposals to the executive. Being grandson of Dominion's first financial director. Lombard was the only blood link with the original board. Unlike Courtland, he wasn't self-conscious about the family connection. He was the architect of Dominion's recent acquisition policy, and had a lively, creative mind.

He liked what Ted was saying to him. It sounded progressive. He was always in favour of encouraging restless talent among the younger employees but had learned that it wasn't always easy to convince the old guard. He felt flattered when men like Ted and Alun Hughes considered him to be on their side. But he was shrewd enough to know that Ted's proposals had to be handled delicately where research director Noel Sorensen was concerned. It wasn't simply a matter of the budget. Ted was presenting him with roughly half the desired amount and requesting the other half. Paul didn't foresee any major problems, except the need for extreme tact with Sorensen.

Ted was equally aware of this. Before approaching the research director, he had a separate meeting with Alun Hughes. As he expected, the public relations director jumped at the idea. The company was constantly taking so much flack that any additional expenditure on tobacco substitutes was always seen as a good source of publicity.

When Sorensen returned to London, Ted arranged a meeting and invited Lombard and Hughes along. The idea was tactfully but encouragingly presented to Sorensen for his seal of approval. The research director was a little put out, but he was aware that his reaction could be misread as sour grapes.

So he agreed, tacitly, and left it to the board to make the final decision.

The idea and the budget were both approved by a sound majority. The plan seemed so logical that even the chairman wondered why it hadn't been set in motion before. It was just the sort of information that he liked shareholders to hear at the annual general meeting. He agreed with Hughes that snippets like that went over well with the press.

It had taken Ted nearly four weeks to achieve his objective, timing his requests and meetings with care and skill. He was more determined than ever now that nothing would stand between him and the successful launching of *Yerba Sacra*.

Chris Lawrence was stretched out on his carpet listening to Beethoven violin sonatas the night Ted telephoned to tell him the budget had been approved. The biochemist was wearing earphones. He didn't hear the ringing.

Ted tried at half hourly intervals, cursed out loud and hung up. The next morning, he waited until the biochemist arrived at Dominion House and drove him to their usual meeting place on Battersea Bridge.

Lawrence didn't seem surprised at the news. Ted, who had expected some sort of reaction, got nothing more than a brief nod.

The two men couldn't seem to look at one another. They stood together, leaning over the bridge, staring down into the grey waters of the Thames. They were reticent, monosyllabic almost, unwilling to spell out more than was totally necessary.

Ted told Lawrence when he could expect to get a new research assistant and the necessary lab equipment, and advised him, tactfully, to be guided by Sorensen wherever possible.

Lawrence agreed. He confirmed that fresh experiments were being set up with mice rearranged as he had suggested, and with the results adjusted accordingly. As this was his domain within the project, no one even bothered to check what he was doing.

The two men stood there in silence. Conspirators, uneasy,

yet both wondering why everything seemed so simple. Ted put it down to the years in professional football that had maximized his skilful talents as a master planner and tactician. He knew how to get the best out of people.

The biochemist wondered why he didn't feel more excited about the news. Any other young scientist in industry would have been doing handstands on the bridge with such an opportunity offered to him. But for Lawrence is was merely another grey, flat London day. The prospect of the additional workload didn't seem all that appealing. He felt in need of a holiday. That cheered him up a little. At least now he could afford a decent fortnight in the sun.

The two men turned, walked to Ted's Mercedes, and rode back to Dominion House in silence.

As soon as Ted was secluded in his office, he unlocked his safe and removed the biochemist's original and incriminating report. Without giving it a second thought, he fed it quietly and unceremoniously into the shredder, page by page.

He told none of this to Colette. She had an insight into too many of his insecurities, and he had to hold something back.

10

The chairman's quiet grooming of Ted developed slowly. Ted attended his first political think-tank, and was tactful enough not to say or do anything to cross Jolyon Williams, even when he disagreed with the man. He enjoyed the energy the team was putting into *Yerba Sacra*, and the proposed use of the brand to spearhead a new political campaign following the election.

But Courtland was equally concerned with refining a few of Ted's rough edges. The political think-tank wasn't enough. The product development director needed to spend more time, socially, with tobacco diehards like Williams. It wasn't enough just to meet them at the head office.

The Courtlands' anniversary dinner at the Tabac Club was arranged with this purpose in mind. It wouldn't do Ted any harm, the chairman reasoned, to be reminded of the solid traditions that had built the industry in Britain. And it would be good for Ted to become more closely acquainted with the family connections within an informal setting. For all Ted's brilliant business creativity, the chairman was still bothered by his lack of mellowness. He appreciated the effect Colette had had on him in a year or so of marriage. But Courtland was still far from satisfied. There was a lot of grooming to be done before he could retire with an easy mind.

What the chairman couldn't have predicted was the effect his own daughter might have on the dinner party.

The Tabac Club in London had changed little from that evening at the turn of the century when the heads of the various tobacco companies drew up one by one in their carriages to become the founding directors of a group that had dominated the tobacco industry ever since.

Crests of the leading tobacco families still adorned the

123

entrance hall. Those families who had no crests quickly created them to gain immortal display on the wall. But it wasn't the various coats of arms and Latin mottos that caught the visitor's eye. It was the large outline of a spittoon embossed in fine silver, hanging on a block of polished walnut. Stirling Harmer had had it designed before his death. He knew of no better way to leave his mark on a club that doggedly refused to supply a spittoon for him during his lifetime. It was also a final tribute to what he called the 'dyin' craft of plug chawin''.

The room in which the group had been created, since renamed the Dominion Room, was reserved for the exclusive use of the executive committee. By tradition, successive chairmen also used the room for their formal entertaining.

The Dominion Room was still dominated by the dark oak table around which the tobacco men had gathered on that historic November evening. The 1850 caricature from *Punch*, of the army officer smoking a cigar on horseback, still hung on the wall behind the chairman's seat. A large, colour tinted photograph of the Dominion board dated 1910 hung on the opposite wall. Stirling Harmer's bright copper hair and gaudy brocade waistcoat stood out amidst the sombre attire of the men surrounding him. Willy Boscawen sat next to him, rotund, in a neatly tailored brown suit. Both men were smiling, sharing some private joke in the midst of the stiffly formal mood of the photograph.

Daphne had often gazed at the pair of them. Her father was no more than a vague memory of a large man with a booming voice who laughed a lot and swung her high in the air. She had never known her mother's father.

On this anniversary night, she caught glimpses of the photograph through the open door of a small adjoining study which had been carefully prepared for the guests. A fire burned cheerfully in the iron grate. Bowls of full-headed chrysanthemum adorned the tables. The atmosphere was expensively contrived to give the appearance of the host's own home.

The Malletts had been the last to arrive that evening.

Colette drifted between the early nineteenth-century landscape and hunting paintings lining the walls. In one corner, Ted talked animatedly to Charles and Jolyon Williams.

Tessa Courtland stood by the fire, elbow resting on the mantelpiece. Ciaran McGannm, an Irish solicitor and friend of many years, sat on the edge of the sofa near her. They were arguing some delicate legal point that excluded everyone else in the room.

Sheila Williams sat beside Ciaran, eyeing him from head to foot. Except for him, all the men wore dark suits, subdued ties and crisp white shirts. He was in deep crimson velvet with a matching dress shirt. But the elegance stopped dead at his ankles. A pair of navy socks were last seen running for cover into his shoes and didn't reappear all evening. His shoulder-length grey hair had been suitably styled for the occasion but didn't quite match the craggy face. He looked more like a stunt man, dressed up as the hero in a gothic novel, waiting around for his cue to plunge headfirst from the attic window of the burning mansion.

Tessa was in a grey-green Edwardian lace blouse and long, slim velvet skirt. The eye might have mistaken her for the heroine, until the ear caught the saltiness of her tongue.

Colette continued to drift between the paintings. She wore a long black dress, soft, collarless. The neck was cut in a deep V, accentuating her cleavage and the dramatic design of her wide silver choker. She watched Tessa out of the corner of her eye, her gaze idling between the girl, her copper hair, the amber glow from the fire, and the vivid autumnal shades in the hunting scenes.

Colette shifted her attention to Sheila Williams.

Sheila moved restlessly on the sofa, tired of being excluded from the central figure, she said tightly. 'How do you have the living gall to defend IRA thugs?'

There was an immediate hush in the room. Everyone turned.

'I don't discuss my work in public, Sheila. It's most unprofessional.'

'Nonsense,' Courtland scoffed, reaching for a decanter of

whisky. 'Don't let her get away with that, Sheila. She's perfectly happy to argue with me in public. Jolyon, did you want some ice, old boy?'

Williams jumped hastily into the gap. He accepted the ice, took his drink and glared at his wife.

But Sheila wasn't silenced so easily. She had arrived well-oiled and was into her second double gin. 'I'm interested,' she insisted peevishly, 'how can you defend those terrorists?'

'Did you follow the trial in the press, Sheila?'

'Well . . . yes.'

'And what did you learn?'

Sheila fidgetted, embarrassed. She eyed the faces in the study for support. 'Those thugs blew up a busload of people.'

'It was an *army* bus,' said Tessa, 'and all the soldiers had recently returned from Belfast.'

'What difference does that make?'

Tessa tapped her glass thoughtfully. 'You must answer that for yourself. You can't start applying moral standards to war to suit your own convenience.'

'I don't see that at all,' said Sheila crossly. 'Those madmen who come over here and disrupt the lives of innocent people don't have any moral standards. They blow up half of Oxford Street, throw bombs into restaurants.'

'Sheila's right,' Jolyon blurted protectively. 'Members of the IRA deserve to be put against a wall and shot.'

'War doesn't breed gentlemen,' Tessa reminded everyone, cautiously shifting the discussion away from the various bomb attacks.

Both she and Ciaran were accustomed to the emotional hysteria generated by the war in Ulster. The suppressive hand of Britain and the class struggle involved were issues too explosive and too blood splattered to be studied objectively. A predinner discussion at the Tabac Club was hardly the place to launch into a serious talk about the historic war in Ireland. So Tessa philosophized about war in general, quoting Seneca: 'A man cannot be a good general and a good man at the same time.'

Jolyon Williams reacted haughtily. 'Poetic nonsense,' he

said. 'The British army is renowned for producing officers of impeccable conduct.'

It was Courtland's turn to look uncomfortable. 'Oh, come along Jolyon,' he said, trying to sound affable. 'Even I wouldn't agree with you on that one. We play our own terrorist game when we have to. Good Lord. I soon learned that in Palestine in forty-seven!'

Tessa raised her eyebrows. It took a lot for her father to admit such things. But far from defending her, she realized he was doing it because both Sheila and Jolyon were embarrassing him.

Ted was growing acutely aware of Ciaran sitting quietly by the fire. If there was anything Ted despised about the Court-lands and the Williamses, it was their tendency to discuss embarrassing subjects as though no one else were present. They frequently made scathing remarks about Americans when he was around. During a brief lull in the conversation he turned to Ciaran and said, 'What do you think about all this?'

Ciaran looked up at him and smiled. 'I think it better that in times like these, a poet's mouth be silent.'

Ted frowned, uncertain.

Courtland glanced down at the Irishman with interest. 'Yeats,' he said approvingly. 'Tessa tells me you were up at Oxford. Balliol I believe.'

'Ah,' Ciaran said gently, 'but I didn't have to go to *Oxford* to study Yeats!'

Courtland cleared his throat awkwardly. 'No, of course not,' he apologized hastily. 'I didn't mean that at all. Can I pour you another drink? Colette, my dear, why don't you come out of the corner? Join us by the fire?'

Colette moved to the centre of the room, and sat down next to Daphne on the sofa. The conversation broke up again into its previous cliques: Ted, Charles, and Jolyon in one corner, Tessa and Ciaran by the fire, and Sheila, adjusting herself on the sofa to talk to Colette and Daphne.

'I still say the soft packet is essential if you want to hit and hold the youth market,' Ted insisted, reaching for a fistful of cashew nuts. 'It fits neatly into a back or shirt pocket and looks informal. That's the *Demin* image. Lines it up with *Lucky Strike* or *Gauloises*. We'd commit suicide if we tried marketing *Demin* in a flip top.'

'Maybe so,' said Jolyon, not totally convinced. 'But don't under-estimate the growing demand for the luxury accessory packet. The *Benson and Hedges* gold packets are a classic example. Have you ever tried to assess your soft packets sales losses over the weekend, when smokers switch to upmarket brands?'

'That doesn't happen with *Denim*,' Ted said firmly. 'A *Mace 8* premium brand smoker will move upmarket at the weekends to one of your extralong king-size varieties. Pack looks good at parties, expecially if the guy is trying to impress a girlfriend. But a *Denim* smoker doesn't switch. He's hooked on the smoke and the image. A *Gauloises* smoker is the same.'

'Hmm,' said Jolyon. 'But I still believe there's room to introduce a box of *Denim* fifty, costing the same as two packets of twenty. What sales do you make at cinema outlets during the weekends?'

'Jolyon, that's such a small proportion of total sales,' said Ted, moving toward the tray of drinks to help himself to more Scotch.

'Ah, but an excellent barometer to test the accuracy of my argument,' Jolyon stressed, pointing a finger defiantly in the air.

Ted knew he was right and made a quick mental note to check the figures with one of his marketing executives on Monday morning. Cinema audiences had risen steeply since the recession, and over eighty-six percent of all cinemagoers were aged between eighteen and thirty, *Denim's* prime target group. Ted was annoyed at himself for not making a recent check on sales at cinema outlets to see if there was room for introducing a pack of fifty. Somehow all his thinking lately had been devoted to *Yerba Sacra*, and he left nitty marketing details to his team.

Courtland listened with interest, placed an arm across the shoulder of each of his directors and turned them away from the others in the study. 'Wanted to ask your advice about something,' he said quietly. 'One of the major poultry suppliers to the retail and hotel division is in difficulties. Paul Lombard believes we should move in, make an offer. Good addition to the agricultural division. Modest outlay, low risk, and excellent returns I'm told. Business requires a minimum of management. What are your immediate reactions?'

Colette watched Tessa throw a brass shovel of coals into the fire, and turned to Daphne. 'Your daughter is not like you, and very different from Charles,' she said, laughing.

Daphne smiled. 'She's inherited Charles's arrogance. But in looks, she's more like my father. Have you seen the photograph in the other room?'

Colette nodded. 'This red hair in the family. It's very strong. Undiluted from one generation to the next.'

Daphne patted her own curls, now salt and peppery compared with her daughter's coloring. 'Yes, curious, isn't it,' she said. 'My own mother was dark. Do you and Ted intend to have children?'

Colette glanced over at Ted deep in conversation in the corner and she shook her head.

Daphne studied her thoughtfully. 'In my day if a woman *didn't* have children she was called selfish or peculiar.'

Courtland moved toward his daughter. 'I forgot to thank you for the port,' he said, touching her cheek. 'Wherever did you find it? Can't make out the date, but it must be at least fifty years old!'

She smiled at him. 'I don't think you're meant to drink it.'

He leaned towards her. 'You look beautiful tonight. And I like your friend,' he said approvingly.

Tessa caught the end of the conversation between Daphne and Colette and moved toward them, curious. 'Do you regret being obliged to have children.'

'Obliged?' said her mother. 'I never even considered that I might have a choice.'

Tessa frowned. 'What do you mean?'

'Furthering the dynasty didn't mean anything to me. It was

your father who wanted a son.'

Tessa looked at her. She turned from the sofa, placed the glasses on the tray and moved quietly out of the study.

She sat down at the dining room table. Son. Dynasty. If only the two of them knew what the 'dynasty' had done to their son! For the sake of family appearances she had kept quiet about her brother's suicide. Why? Who was she protecting?

His letter had reached her two days after he plummetted to his death. Silly, stupid, unnecessary. And all because he felt he couldn't live up to the family ideal. What ideal? His father made him feel a musical career was a weak and inferior alternative to the industrial achievement of the Harmers, and the military achievements of several successive generations of Courtlands. He wanted neither. *Please*, he wrote. *I can't live with their disappointment and I can't die with it. It will cause such a public scandal, father's position and all that. Let them think it was an accident.* So he made a grotesque spectacle of his death to prove some superhuman strength, to save the family 'honour'.

There was something so ridiculous about it all. What was she doing? Ten years of being protective, attentive, loving. For what? To be made to feel guilty because she had survived and their 'son' hadn't?

There was a gentle rustling beside her. Tessa glanced up.

Colette, smiling, moved on to the other side of the white damask tablecloth. 'It's only a dinner party,' she said philosophically. 'People make these comments without thought.'

The 'people' bustled into the dining room, filling the air with shrill voices, forced laughter.

Ciaran noticed the brief exchange between the two women and smiled, pulling out a chair beside Tessa. Ted noticed too, and sat down next to his wife.

The Williamses sat apart, and so did the Courtlands, Charles at the head of the table, Daphne facing him.

A waiter in fawn livery and snow white gloves appeared through the double doors bearing a silver tray of shrimp cocktails. Tessa faced a sliced grapefruit in vegetarian solitude.

A second waiter hovered, pouring out a delicate white wine from the cellars of Dominion's estates in France.

Tessa sat in silence, dimly aware of the snippets of conversation drifting to and fro. Ted regaling everyone with stories of Indian peace pipe rituals. Then: 'We should revive the Victorian cigar dive,' he announced grandly, 'Luxuriously decorated dens where connoisseurs could learn about ancient smoking rituals. Share a pipe. Try a new cigar, perhaps.'

Jolyon Williams looked doubtful, but the chairman seemed intrigued. He also liked Ted's descriptive flow.

'I'm serious,' Ted insisted, believing the silence spelled disapproval. 'The dens could have controlled membership. We could employ experts to do the blending and mixing on the spot. Offer the greatest variety of tobaccos and cigars in the world.'

The chairman chuckled. 'And a few hubble-bubbles thrown in.' Glancing quickly at the women he added. 'Water pipes my dears. The Turkish word is *nar-gi-leh*. Any old soldier who's done service in the Near East knows about such delights, eh Jolyon? The young whipper snappers today think they know it all with their ounce of grass hidden under the mattress.'

Ted quickly brought the topic to heel. 'We could collect traditional pipes from all over the world.'

'Hmm,' the chairman agreed. 'I'm all for reviving the dying *art* of smoking.' He moved the subject on, not out of politeness, but because he was aware of the noncorporate ears at the table. A chance remark here, passed on at another dinner party, to be overheard at a third, and before they knew where they were, a rival could pick up the idea. He winked discreetly at Ted and asked if anyone had seen the Velásquez auctioned recently at Sotheby's.

'Which Velásquez?' asked Colette, but the chairman couldn't remember.

The first course done, the dishes were removed from sight silently and efficiently.

The second course was ceremoniously wheeled in. A long carving knife was raised in the air and sharpened briskly, expertly, to slice thick helpings of beef.

Tessa glanced at her mushroom casserole and pushed it to one side. Even the innocent could seem obscene.

The conversation skipped from subject to subject. Should Dominion contribute 'X thousand' to the Canterbury Cathedral restoration fund? Had anyone been wise enough to invest in French paperweights? Someone someone knew in Manchester had seen his collection appreciate a thousand precent in ten years.

Ciaran listened, half expecting Peter Sellers to leap out of the orchids. Did people still talk like this? Beyond the walls of the club, most Londoners were anxiously worrying about their quarterly electricity and phone bills, and busily reheating last night's leftovers. French *paperweights?*

Colette caught his expression across the table and smiled. Ted made the appropriate noises. Daphne's thoughts wafted into space. Jolyon talked nonstop.

Tessa kept quiet until someone asked about her vegetarianism. 'It's the one solution to world starvation,' she said softly. 'It restores the balance between need and resources. Fifteen pounds of protein-rich grain are required to produce a pound of meat. All that grain can be consumed by humans. Yet think how much of it now leaves the third world to feed livestock in the West.' She was aware of sounding like an advertisement for Oxfam, but didn't see why she should be apologetic.

'Think of the poor cattle ranchers who'd go out of business if everyone thought like you,' said Courtland irritably, signalling the waiter to slice more beef. He sensed his daughter was just trying to make everyone feel uncomfortable, and he wasn't going to put up with it. He thought Ted was bad enough, but Ted was an arch-conservative next to Tessa.

Colette asked politely if she followed an Eastern religion. Tessa shook her head.

Sheila leaned forward crossly, a sprig of broccoli stuck to her cheek. 'How *dreadfully* boring you are,' she said, delighted to find a chink in Tessa's armour at last. 'You don't smoke, you don't eat meat, you don't appear to be drinking much. I mean,' she said, laughing, 'what on earth *do* you do?'

132

Tessa smiled graciously. 'I fuck beautiful women.'

There was a stunned silence.

Courtland had had enough. 'For all the wealth Stirling Harmer acquired,' he began, toying with his knife, 'he was nothing but a crude, poor-white American who married a loud-mouthed peasant. Clearly, the stock lives on.'

The guests looked away, embarrassed, shuffling in their seats.

'*Charles,*' Daphne pleaded. Courtland ignored her and continued to eat.

Tessa rose.

Ciaran rose at the same time, forking the last of his beef into his mouth. 'I'll go with you,' he mumbled.

'You don't have to.'

'I know,' he said, wiping his lips. 'But I think I'd like to.'

11

Ciaran kicked off his shoes and spread himself on the cushions beside the window. He thought about the abandoned beef and sighed wistfully. 'It must be years since I've tasted beef like that. Why didn't you save your act for the liqueur?'

Tessa shrugged and wrenched open a window. An icy blast flew in from the canal, followed by three cats in brisk succession. They enveloped themselves in her skirt and nudged her toward the kitchen.

'Had my nice suit specially cleaned,' he said, trying to make light of everything, watching her scratch around in cupboards for cat food. 'Mind you, I was glad to get away from that big Williams woman. God bless her.'

Tessa said nothing. She was angrier with herself than with her father. It was so pointless, all this silly dressing up and buying vintage port and trailing dutifully along to the Tabac Club. Like children forced into their Sunday best to visit some awful great aunt. Why did she put up with it?

She and Ciaran knew one another well enough not to have to discuss something that was painfully obvious. He took it all with a sort of bemused air. The club was pure comic relief for him. He worked at a downbeat local solicitor's office, and gave time to the local law centre, handling the sorts of cases that typified the borough, like wife and child-battering, unfair evictions, and young offenders with a knack for getting into trouble.

The borough also held a large Irish community. So it was solicitors like Ciaran who were often called out in the middle of the night by fellow countrymen hauled in for questioning by the Special Branch. It was Ciaran who had asked Tessa to represent his clients on the army bus bomb case. But of course he saw no point in informing the group at the Tabac Club of this.

He had known Tessa for a very long time. They had curled up together on the occasional rainy Sunday afternoon after a few bottles of Chianti. But this had never placed any sort of strain on their friendship or working relationship.

He had observed her performance in the club that evening with a twinge of professional interest. He wanted to talk to her about a client, seek her advice on something that could develop into an important test case. But she could be maddeningly aloof and dismissive unless consulted at precisely the right moment.

He watched her prepare coffee, aware of her anger, 'what you did in the club was eccentric. Your class accepts that from its own.'

'*My* class? Poor-white farming stock?'

Ciaran waved this away. In his book it didn't make much difference what one set of grandparents had been. She was born into wealth and privilege and that was that. He knew it wasn't the first time Courtland had let loose on his wife and daughter in public. But both Ciaran and Tessa knew what he meant about the class thing. Almost anything a member of the privileged classes did was acceptable, provided the sacred institutions weren't mocked or abused. Murder, swindling, cheating on one's spouse, all that was acceptable, so long as it was carried out with a certain discretion and style.

And they both knew how this worked in the court system. An old-age pensioner could end up in prison if he couldn't afford to pay his rates. But a smooth-talking financier from some well-known City firm could cheat the inland revenue of millions through various fraudulent transactions, and wind up with a suspended sentence.

It was class and the right school tie—not always money—that won a special privilege in the courts, simply because the majority of barristers and judges came from the same group.

Tessa and Ciaran had had long and sometimes bitter discussions on the subject. He often criticized her for shielding herself behind the family name, walking the middle road, never sticking her neck out too far. It wasn't enough to live in a broken

135

down warehouse. She only did that because she had never been destitute. Self-denial wasn't going to change the system.

'You're still far too much of a revisionist,' he said, knowing how she hated to be called that.

She argued back, saying he could call her anything he wanted. She behaved the way she had to in court to win a case. It was all a matter of technique.

'Aha, technique!' he said triumphantly. 'But it prevents you from handling the cases that *really* matter, that later raise hell in Parliament.'

'I defended the IRA, didn't I? Look at the stink that case raised in Parliament!' As a result of it, a commission of inquiry had been set up to examine police interrogation methods, and the manhandling of political detainees by prison warders.

But Ciaran was dismissive. 'Whitewash, pure sop. Tell me if it made any difference. Have things changed?'

She poured their coffee and joined him by the window. He was only trying to rattle her, so she ignored him.

He helped himself to cream and sugar.

She watched Ciaran sip some coffee. His craggy face was a mask of innocence.

'You devious sod,' she said, rising for a bottle of *Cointreau* and two glasses. 'You've got a brief up your sleeve. You think I won't handle it, am I right?'

He grinned up at her and held out his hand for the glass. 'You might well be. But it's not for you,' he said, shaking his head and sniffing the liqueur approvingly.

'Try me.'

'Too hot. Far too hot.'

'Come on,' she said, 'you've been leading up to this for days. Why were you so eager to go tonight?'

He sighed and stared at the ceiling. 'This would be the test case to begin and end all tests cases,' he said.

He studied her closely and suddenly became very serious, lowering his glass to the floor.

She sat on a stool facing him, swirling *Cointreau* between her cupped hands.

He felt torn about involving her. If she accepted, she would become totally committed to the case as was her style. But where would that leave her? Did he have the right to throw such a challenge at her? Well, why not, he reasoned silently. Why make exceptions simply because she was a Courtland? If he made concessions for Tessa, he was guilty of the same sort of selective attitudes for which he had criticized her in the past.

Eventually he rose, plucking cat hair off his velvet suit. 'There isn't a barrister in London with your inside knowledge on this one,' he said slowly.

Tessa smiled. 'I can always say no.'

He looked away. 'Brigid Anderson, a young Irish woman in the borough. Came to see me at the law centre recently. Her husband's dying. Lung cancer,' he added almost casually, gazing out at the canal. 'Month to go, maybe less. He's only thirty-four.'

'Hmmm,' she replied thoughtfully. 'How can I help?'

'I want to move on this one,' he said quickly. 'Make a lot of noise. He's worked for Dominion all his life.' He paused and turned to look at her. 'I'm advising them to ask the company for compensation.'

'Pity Tessa and her friend left,' said Ted, watching Colette undress. 'Evening fell apart after they went.'

'Jesus, Charles can be vicious,' he added, climbing into bed. 'Imagine calling one of the greatest American industrialists a poor-white.' He shook his head. 'Jolyon's boring, isn't he?'

Colette listened to him rattling on watching him throughout the evening had confirmed her suspicion that he had merely been going through the motions. He'd been like that ever since the problem with the yerba sacra experiments, and wouldn't talk about it. She knew better than to probe.

Her exhibition opened in a week. Perhaps she'd been too remote and lost in her own thoughts to give him the attention he needed. Oh God, she thought silently. Am I being selfish or is he? I can be his wife, mother, sister, lover, but I can't be his conscience, too.

137

'Jolyon's boring, isn't he,' Ted repeated loudly, waiting for an answer.

'Hmm? Oh I didn't really talk to him,' Colette said lightly. 'Is his wife always like that?'

'Sheila? I guess so. She looked pretty bombed when we arrived. Jolyon's spent a fortune trailing her around to various specialists. Nothing seems to work.'

Colette stepped into a silk nightgown. 'I wonder if they've tried talking to one another.'

'What?' Ted glanced up and frowned, shrugged, and started hunting through a mound of paperbacks piled next to the bed. 'Poor guy,' he continued, 'much as I dislike Jolyon I feel sorry for him. Some people say he hasn't a hope in hell of becoming chairman with a wife like Sheila.'

Colette turned. Board gossip didn't interest her. Normally it didn't interest Ted, either. 'Do you want to be chairman?' she asked.

He'd always insisted that he was no diplomat and hated excessive administrative responsibilities. But there was something about his tone that made her ask.

Ted didn't answer immediately. He selected an Ed McBain thriller and leafed through it. 'No,' he said eventually. 'Although I wouldn't mind heading Harmer Brands in New York.'

She looked at him in surprise. 'Ted, I thought you hated New York.'

'Maybe I do. Maybe I don't.'

She gave up, walked into the bathroom and started running water into the sink.

The Williamses argued all the way home from the Tabac Club, Jolyon accusing his wife of being a cow.

The Courtlands didn't say a word to one another, beyond a polite good night as they went to separate bedrooms in the chairman's London flat.

Daphne rose early the next morning and took a train home to the country.

The anniversary dinner was never mentioned again.

12

Tessa, Ciaran, and the Anderson family lived within a two-mile radius of one another in Islington.

In many ways, the borough was a microcosm of London's political and social extremes. It was still fiercely working class, in spite of the growing number of middle-class ghettos. The restoration of elegant Georgian squares and early Victorian houses, did little more than offer a few brief moments of visual relief in a borough dominated by squalor and homelessness, squatters and exploitative landlords.

Corner grocery shops, bookmaker's betting shops, and cafés reflected pockets of Cypriot, Pakistani, West Indian, and Italian communities. The Irish showed themselves in graffiti: *Troops out of Ireland Now, End Force Feeding of political prisoners.*

The compression of contrasts had turned Islington into a hotbed of conflict. Local injustices over housing or civil rights were rife. It wasn't by accident that the borough housed some of the most active community-action and experimental theatre groups in London. Or that the area attracted an above average quota of politicos, writers, playwrights.

Council housing in the borough also reflected the extremes. Sheer chance and the luck of the draw directed needy families to Dickensian tenements or new developments in neat brick.

Tessa lived in a no-man's land between the extremes.

Like most relative newcomers to the borough, Ciaran lived where he could find space. He rented the converted basement of an old house owned by a teacher, his musician wife, and an assortment of noisy children. Ciaran, divorced and struggling to keep up the maintenance, was determined to maintain an atmosphere carefully balanced between monastic solitude and debauchery. He succeeded.

The Anderson family lived in a bleak Edwardian council estate next to the railway line. It had been earmarked for demolition to make way for another arterial road, but in the curious way of urban planning, people had been talking about it for years, never really expecting anything to happen. Rumours of plans alternately shelved or revived with each new council election swept from corner to corner like an old cardboard box rolled by the wind.

The gloomy, tunnel-like entrance to the block smelled of burned fat and antiseptic. The metal plaque on the wall originally inscribed LONDON BOROUGH OF ISLINGTON had been scratched and scraped to read LOO BOROUGH OF CUNT.

Tessa and Ciaran walked up five flights of stairs in silence. A group of girls aged eleven or twelve clattered past them on platform shoes. One of the girls had her hair streaked like a rainbow. She pouted suggestively at Ciaran.

On the top floor, a few families had made a determined effort to spruce up the soot-blackened bricks with pots of geranium and pretty lace curtains. Ciaran knocked at a door flanked on either side by red windowboxes. It opened a few inches.

'It's Ciaran, Brigid. With a colleague.'

The door opened wide. Brigid Anderson was small, with an open, moon-shaped face, dark wavy hair and large hyacinth blue eyes.

She stared questioningly at Tessa. 'Is your friend a social worker,' she asked in a strong Dublin accent, much broader than Ciaran's own softly rhythmic voice.

He shook his head. 'No. This is Tessa, she helps at the law centre.'

Brigid led them through the sitting room. Three young children sat lined up on a couch eating fish fingers and watching cartoons on TV.

'Turn it down a little, Maureen,' she said to the eldest. 'Come in the kitchen, Ciaran.'

She closed the door behind them and gestured toward the table, turning abruptly to light all four gas burners on the stove and the pilot in the oven to keep the room warm.

Brigid Anderson was barely thirty. She gave the appearance of being practical and capable, a woman who had long since discarded the luxury of dreaming as an unnecessary waste of time. She had come to London from Ireland before the age of twenty to look for work, served in a factory cafeteria and married a young man of twenty-one who had been born and brought up in the borough. Three children later, she faced an early widowhood.

'Jimmy's sleeping at the moment,' she explained gesturing toward the door. 'Weight is draining off him, like his flesh is melting before my eyes.'

'Wouldn't it be better if he was in hospital?' asked Tessa.

Brigid shook her head. 'He was in the Royal Free, up at Hampstead Heath. But with three young children I couldn't get away to see him every day. It's better he should go here with us.'

'Isn't it upsetting for your children?'

'Of course it is,' Brigid snapped back. 'But I'm thinking all the time, if they see their father die like this, so young, maybe they won't smoke. My eldest, Maureen, is nearly eleven and half her school friends smoke. Terrible it is, to see them run from the school gate to light up.'

Brigid moved around the kitchen while she spoke, clearing away dishes, swilling out glasses under a tap, sweeping crumbs off the table. Every question seemed to open a different floodgate. Of how Jimmy had started to smoke early, hooked by the time he was fourteen, and went to work as a packer for Mace Tobacco, where he got free cigarettes. When they heard he had lung cancer, they took him off the payroll.

Ciaran and Tessa glanced at one another.

'Didn't they give him sick pay?' asked Tessa.

'No,' said Brigid. 'Cut him off the day he told them what was wrong. We've been on sickness benefit since them. I can't work, what with the three children, and taking care of him.'

'Does you husband belong to the union?' Tessa asked.

141

Brigid nodded. 'Oh yes, dues up to date. But they're no good. Said there was nothing they could do. Jimmy's been working for the company for nineteen years, but neither his boss nor the union would do anything. Sort of wiped their hands of him.'

There was no surprise in Brigid's voice, nor was there a hint of subservience. She spoke about the past months, the careful preparation of them all for the inevitable, and the company's attitude with the same matter-of-fact tone.

It was only her inability to sit down and talk to them instead of constantly moving around the kitchen, clattering saucepans and dishes, that gave her away.

Finally she turned and looked at them both, wiping her hands on her apron. 'Do you know what upsets me most?' she said. 'My friends have stopped coming round. Almost like Jimmy has the plague or typhoid.' She looked at Tessa. 'People can't talk about cancer. Can't sit her like the three of us and just talk. Sometimes a neighbour drops in during the evening for a cup of tea, but they'll talk about the telly or soccer or the price of bacon or what their children are doing or whose daughter is pregnant on the estate. Everything but what's happening here,' she said, rapping her knuckles on the table.

'They're afraid, Brigid,' said Ciaran. 'Feel they have to keep you cheerful. Do they bring you anything stronger than tea now?'

She smiled and shook her head. 'The company used to give Jimmy a bottle of whisky or two when he did those tests, along with money of course. But all that's gone now.'

There was an awkward silence in the kitchen.

Tessa frowned. 'What tests?'

Brigid glanced nervously toward the door.

Ciaran took her by the arm and made her sit down. 'You've never said anything about tests to me. What are you on about?'

'They made Jimmy sign a paper, swearing him to secrecy.'

'To hell with that,' said Ciaran.

Brigid looked from one to the other. 'The doctors said it wouldn't have made any difference, Jimmy smoking all these

142

years. But last year the company was working on some new brands. Funny smelling cigarettes, strong like.' She pulled a face. 'Jim and the others smoked forty a day, then they would be asked questions about the taste.'

'Did he bring any of these cigarettes home?' asked Tessa.

Brigid looked down at her hands. 'He wasn't supposed to, but he did. He liked them,' she shrugged. She stopped talking.

A small child was at the door, looking up at them with Brigid's eyes. 'Dad wants you, Mum.'

Brigid nodded and left the kitchen quickly.

'Do you know anything about these tests?' Ciaran asked.

Tessa shook her head. 'But I'll soon find out,' she said grimly. 'Last year, so he must have had cancer when they were doing them.'

Ciaran scratched his head doubtfully.

Brigid returned and led them to her husband's bed.

James Anderson looked more like a grandfather than a man of thirty-four. His face and head seemed recently chiselled out of a yellowish stone. He legs moved like pointed swords in combat underneath the bed covers.

Tessa and Ciaran sat down on either side of him.

Anderson groped around beside his bed for a packet of cigarettes and matches and lit up, blowing a gust of smoke in the air. 'This lady your assistant, Ciaran?' he said, nodding toward Tessa.

'Sort of. She agrees with me that we should get damages from the company for you.'

Anderson stared at her. 'No one in his right bleeding state of mind sues Dominion. They're above the law,' he said bluntly.

Tessa shook her head. 'No one is above the law.'

'Look,' he said bitterly, 'I worked there nearly twenty years and I know, m'girl.' He glanced at Ciaran. 'Can we talk in private? I don't think the lady understands.'

Ciaran started to say something, but Tessa silenced him and quietly left the room, gesturing for him to follow. 'I'll go home. It's better. Get as much information as you can about the tests, who did them, what they were, where and when and so on.

143

Milk him.'

'Does that mean you'll work with me on this one?' he whispered.

She looked at him. 'I'll go and say goodbye to Brigid.'

13

Tessa awoke early the next morning with the sun pouring on her through the skylight. The cats lay stretched out deliriously in the warmth. She uncurled herself carefully from their slipping bodies and walked downstairs, picking up the *Observer* and *Sunday Times* from the door mat en route to the coffee percolator.

The canal gleamed and twinkled in the spring sun outside. All over the borough, families were emerging like animals from hibernation. Some strolled to the various parks, other dragged chairs out to the pavement in front of their homes. The practically-minded rushed washing outside to dry. The gloom and dampness that clung to poverty like a parasite had lifted for a few precious hours.

Tessa sat crosslegged by the window and idled through the newspapers. But found it difficult to concentrate. She had dropped off to sleep thinking about the Andersons and reawakened with the same thoughts. Like most barristers, she had learned to view tragedy from a dispassionate distance. Any personal sense of outrage was, by necessity, tempered and kept in check until all the relevant evidence was scrutinized. But the Anderson case wasn't slotting itself so easily into a neat pigeonhole.

In many ways, her involvement in such a case was inevitable. She couldn't escape a certain feeling of destiny. A primitive, Celtic sense of fate flourished inside her soul, far from the reaches of a stringent mind. The two elements frequently clashed head on.

But today, the stormy elements were of one rare accord. Twelve years at the Bar had been preparing her for this moment. Deep down she knew that sooner or later something had to happen to force a final showdown with Dominion and the family. She couldn't go on indefinitely resolving the conflict between the source of her wealth and her politics simply by rerouting the bulk of her income into worthy causes inside or outside the courts.

She didn't completely share her grandmother's personal view of how the individual could activate the 'redistribution of wealth'. 'Don't waste time and energy grieving over the source of your money, my girl,' she'd say crisply. 'Hurry up and use it properly. Make sure every penny you earn from the company works twice as hard in the street to wear down the establishment.'

But money was only part of it. Certainly it gave her the freedom to handle only those cases that matched her politics, and enabled her to handle many of them *pro bono publico*, especially those that didn't qualify for legal aid. Other funds helped some radical colleagues through their first impoverished years at the bar.

She gazed across the canal. The smashed windows of the deserted factory opposite stared back at her like rows of eyesockets in a heap of skulls. The view was so familiar she had become blinded to it. In some ways, she reasoned, her relationship with Dominion was depressingly similar. Unresolved feelings had been too conveniently locked away in a trunk in the attic of her conscience.

It was high time she swept away the dust and cobwebs. The vast development of Dominion had dimished the significance of the central family, yes. But however much she tried to justify her own differences, she had been born into the industrial elite. She could denounce it, but never undo it. She could indulge herself in self-denial, live in a decadent landscape, and drive a rattletrap Daf, solely because she enjoyed the luxury of choice. She never had to join the ranks of the homeless, would never be housed on some faceless housing estate, had never been subjected to the indignities of sharing a toilet with fifty other people, or living in a dank basement with whining children.

Some girls born into families similar to her own had opted

for violence as a way of exorcising their backgrounds. A few went to other extremes. She knew of girls who believed that being one of 'the people' meant swapping their plummy public school accents for a local dialect and shacking up with a brute. Preferably someone who'd abuse them socially and sexually, kick his boots into the corner of the kitchen and beat them silly when he got drunk. At the same time they would march the streets shouting feminist slogans and demanding human rights for all.

Far from eradicating the class system, they were merely enforcing it. The times had simply flipped the coin. In an earlier era girls from modest backgrounds swapped *their* regional accents for modulated uppity tones and contrived family settings, trappings they believed were necessary for social acceptability. These days everyone highlighted working class origins for acceptability.

The role played by sex in all this class shimmy-shammy had been immortalized by D. H. Lawrence and others. Former public school girls who took brutish lovers were no different from the young men of a previous era who went 'below stairs' for their sexual kicks. Such behaviour found its modern equivalent in the tabloid scandals of well-known members of the aristocracy revealed in various sado-masochistic poses with whores. But again, Tessa reasoned, all the various sexual hijinks merely enforced the double standard that went hand in hand with the class system, because the protagonists rarely indulged in such activities with their own kind.

Anyway, she thought wryly, who the hell ever exorcised heritage through sex?

From all accounts, Amy and Stirling Harmer combined so much positivism, that they blew the fuse with Daphne. Her mother was ethereal if anything, not really there at all. Once prepared to function as a shadow to Charles, she had since cut herself completely adrift. In fact, the very act of cutting herself off had made her a saner entity, despite the fact that society might label Daphne 'unbalanced'.

As for her father, well, it didn't take much to see how the

147

regimentation of his early life had suppressed one side of his character. During his formative years men were imbued with a sense of authority, leadership, and unquestioning service to King and country. Any inner poetry or sensitivity was quickly stamped out, or, as in her father's case, found a thwarted outlet in a scathing tongue.

And her brother? So much like his mother that he thought something was wrong, not helped by his father calling him a sissy. To develop his father's characteristics for the sake of being somebody in his father's eyes, he went to extremes with the skydiving. And when that didn't work he had to kill himself to achieve status.

Throughout the endless rows at home between her father and herself, Charles would ultimately resort to sexual sniping. She could hear him now. Why the hell weren't you born a boy and Harmer a girl? Harmer doesn't shout at me and abuse my values the way you do. If you were a boy I'd put you in the bloody army. That would soon break your damnable arrogance. No discipline, that's your problem. No discipline whatsoever.

Tessa couldn't help blaming Charles for Harmer's death, even though she knew that in fact up bringing was to blame. Convention was the dictator. But everything she loathed about convention and its various trappings within the class system seemed to be summed up in Charles Courtland. What he didn't find in his son he seemed to construct in the men who were closest to him. Young Henry Peach, impeccable product of his own regiment. And Ted Mallett, who walked like an advertisement for the original steroidal male. Not merely son-substitutes, she rationalized, but reassuring trappings. Court-land knew a man was judged by those closest to him. His own insecurities and shortcomings could be comouflaged by the exaggerated qualities of ex-army officer Peach and ex-footballer Mallett.

Perhaps she was equally guilty, but in a different way. Crowding her life with work and causes prevented her from indulging in self-scrutiny. Unless something happened that demanded a quiet hour in front of a window. Once she was sufficiently mature to recognize the power of her own duality she could do things to satisfy both sides. Taking this to sexual extremes had involved various encounters with both men and women during her twenties. But Tessa had a tendency for seeking out people with whom there was no prospect of a lasting relationship. Why? For the sake of independence or for family appearances?

There was no point in advocating sexual liberation, preaching the rights of people to live openly with whomsoever they pleased, or alone, without fear of label or stigma, if she herself indulged in the privileged art of 'mistressing'.

But there again, there was no reason why she should be blatant and overt for the sake of proving some political lifestyle. In a way, she reasoned, hiding her affairs from public view was a little like hiding her true political conscience for the sake of the family. Going so far and no further. Still, there should be no conflict between belief and lifestyle, no convenient selectivity. And clearly there was with her.

Tessa allowed her thoughts to wing on. But all paths seemed to lead back to Dominion and the Anderson family.

All the causes she truly believed in were direct conflict with Dominion. Unless she made a public stand against the company instead of merely directing the interest from her shares against the system of which Dominion was one part, she wasn't worth a thing in political terms. She was merely marking time.

As for considering her family, what did that mean? What family had the right to blackmail its members? To obligate them to compromise their political conscience? Were any of her father's actions ever tempered by her politics? Did he ever hesitate during a board meeting to deliberate whether or not the matter in hand would embarrass or upset his daughter? As for Daphne, well, she was so out of it most of the time that something like this wouldn't really touch her.

Tessa knew in her heart that if she didn't handle the Anderson case, she might as well hang up her wig and gown for good. At the same time she had to ask herself why she felt so strongly about this particular case. What was her true motivation? Exposing the tobacco industry for disassociating itself from a moral public duty, or using the case to disassociate herself publicly from Dominion, the Harmers, and the Courtlands?

Tessa rose from the window. She couldn't really separate the components. A man was dying of lung cancer a few miles away. She couldn't loiter on the sidelines any longer. He was merely one of thousands who would die or suffer from chronic and disabling ailments.

She had compromised herself on the issue for the sake of her family. She had traded a heritage and a handful of comfortable people for thousands of afflicted families. The ratio was chilling.

Now, she thought, reviewing her various briefs, it was no longer enough to defend political activists, or saboteurs, or army deserters, or immigrants, tenants suffering from unfair evictions, battered wives, or families harmed by industrial diseases. It wasn't enough to represent rape victims and work behind the scenes with MPs concerned with changing the rape laws. It wasn't enough to feel satisfied that she won most of the cases she fought in court, stirred a few headlines for the week, had questions raised in Parliament, or enlightened a few people. She had to admit, finally, that all she did was produce superficial ripples of interest. She had never really plunged downward to shake the roots of a complacent system.

Tessa paused for a moment and listened to the coffee perking gently behind her. The sound emphasized the solitude of her thoughts. She ached for Amy. Amy would understand. Her grandmother had never compromised herself. Amy had died the year Tessa was called to the Bar and nothing had ever quite filled that void in her life. Everything Amy believed in, fought for, and grieved over made more sense now than it had done in the past.

Tessa poured herself some coffee and returned to the window. Spiritually, she refuelled herself by thinking about Amy, relating her work and convictions to her grandmother's.

In spite of the superficial appearance of classlessness in

150

Britain, the institutions still reigned supreme. Politicians made a name for themselves by their cunning ability to divert working class anger away from the system and toward the immigrant population. It was useful to stir up a race war to blur the edges of the unresolved class war.

The privileged public schools continued to provide over two-thirds of the men who ruled the major institutions. Land was still in the hands of the few.

Revolution? Hah! Tessa thought cynically. Britain would shift to the extreme right before it moved to the extreme left. The class structure was most obviously entrenched at the Bar. What had she done to shake that? *Nothing.* And activists weren't worth their salt unless they activated change. During her student days she'd done her share of political marching, scuffling with mounted police, sloganeering, and protesting. But it was still largely window dressing. So the lone anarchist in her chose the Bar, the inner sanctum of the establishment. If that wasn't agitated and changed, nothing else could be. But she hadn't changed it: it had changed her.

If she stirred up a lot of dirt with this brief, she would be attacking the sanctified unwritten code of the profession that ruled what was done and what wasn't. She would also be attacking one of Britain's major institutions. She wasn't so immune to the group that she didn't recognize its strictly establishment structure. Like the legal system, Dominion was ritual and tradition bound.

There were so many different aspects of the Anderson case to scrutinize, if this was going to make an impact that reached beyond the medical implications. She had to stop wasting so much time. Twelve years' preparation at the Bar was quite long enough.

14

Later in the week, Tessa was surprised to open her mailbox and discover an invitation to the opening of Colette's exhibition.

She had been applying an abrasive to her soul and conscience for days, cocooning herself in work. The idea of an hour or so at an art gallery promised some welcome relief.

Colette's exhibition was held in a small, select gallery off Bond Street, owned and managed with loving care and efficiency by art connoisseurs. It was carpeted throughout in slate grey and smelled pleasingly of fresh paint. The various exhibits were arranged on pedestals of appropriate height, expertly lit by the gallery owner under Colette's watchful eye and guidance.

There were over thirty works in all, done in bronze, marble, and wood. Colette had placed them in careful progression to give the sensitive viewer an insight into the evolution of her style. That was the essence of the exhibition.

The pure, easy forms, sinewy and sensuous, were upstairs, bared to the street through plateglass windows.

But, at the back of the gallery and in the room below, the works became more disturbing, less easy to define. Raw sections of wood or stone gaped out of the highly polished or sanded surfaces for which Colette was best known. The brutal contrast between the raw and treated material had the technically-minded spellbound. Other viewers found the work offensive. Some guests felt annoyed and cheated. The artist was known for her exquisite good taste and impeccable work. What was she trying to do to her reputation with these seemingly cracked surfaces and open sores? Critics who believed they knew her work were baffled.

Tessa was intrigued. She had never really taken Colette seriously, pigeonholing both the artist and her art as merely decorative. But now, she was aware of something more in this remote and beautiful woman. Her works revealed an intense sensuality, sometimes contained and distant, sometimes almost savage.

Guests clustered in small groups downstairs. The work that attracted most attention was the study of two coarse marble forms invisibly linked by a beam of energy. People encircled it, fascinated, bobbing down to view it from below, twisting their heads to see it sideways.

'Colette, my dear,' said Charles Courtland whimsically. 'I'm reminded of soft white clouds on a summer day.'

A young art critic, a fringe of long fine hair encircling his bald head, listened to Courtland and frowned doubtfully. 'Nothing quite so virginal I believe,' he said gently, but moved on without elaborating.

Upstairs, Ted idled between groups of guests, beaming like a cheshire cat. He always enjoyed Colette's exhibitions. There was something clean and ordered about them. After living with her moods, putting up with the scream and dust from the sander for months on end, he found something very satisfying about seeing the final products emerge, phoenixlike. It was equally satsifying to see Colette out of a smock, quietly elegant, the centre of attention. He felt an enormous pride in being the one man in the room who knew how she looked and felt under the soft, chamois leather jumpsuit and black silk scarf.

She was still living in something of a world of her own, now given to going off on long solitary walks, involved in little but her private thoughts. It bewildered Ted, but at the same time, the remoteness made it easier for him not to feel the urge to confide in her.

Tessa was as surprised to see her father there as he was to see her. Working on the advice of his PR director, Alun Hughes, Courtland had put his name to a lilylike bronze figurine. After the exhibition it would be sent to Paris to adorn the foyer of Dominion's new offices there. The chairman posed next to it for the photographer from the *Financial Times*. He turned around to see Tessa watching him.

They greeted one another coldly but politely. Neither had contacted the other since the night of the anniversary dinner. Tessa's decision to take on the Anderson case made her feel even more aloof. Between now and the time she openly challenged Dominion, she wanted nothing to do with her father. 'Is Mother with you?' she asked. Something simple to say.

Charles shook his head.

'I thought I might drive down to see her before the weekend.'

'Why don't you? Honeysuckle looks glorious at the moment. Must be weeks since you were down. Do your mother good to see you.' He turned from her to wave at a familiar face.

Absentmindedly, Tessa edged past her father toward the stairs, not wanting to become entangled in a further round of platitudes. Something caught her eye. Colette, smiling.

She hadn't had a chance to speak to the artist yet. Colette had seemed to be permanently engulfed by admirers.

Now, for the first time, she appeared to be alone.

'I'm looking for a carved bust for my patio,' Tessa said softly. 'Aquamarine, to go with my decor.'

Colette laughed at her. 'It's not so funny. It's what people ask for all the time!'

'You mean you have problems getting rid of these beautiful objects?'

'Ah no.' She paused and eyed the guests thoughtfully. 'But I know what will go this evening, and what will still be unsold in three weeks.'

'And your true creations are so private you hide them in the grotto below?'

The two women gazed at one another. 'Will you be here tomorrow?' Tessa asked.

Colette nodded. 'Until noon.'

'Then I will be here at three minutes to noon.' Tessa smiled and moved away, edging through the guests to the top of the stairs.

Ciaran was pacing up and down at the corner of Piccadilly and the Haymarket, all hunched up against the bitter night air.

'You're twenty minutes late,' he snapped angrily, climbing in beside her. 'Where the hell have you been, all tarted up?'

She glanced at him, smiled and released the Daf into the line of traffic.

'The devil weaves evil thoughts in the looms of your mind,' he said darkly, reaching into his briefcase.

She told him about the exhibition. Ciaran sat silently for a few minutes, watching the traffic edge by them in the Charing Cross Road. 'People with all that time to waste,' he said tightly. 'What did your father spend on the piece of trivia?'

'About two thousand pounds.'

'Mother of God. A little less than James Anderson's basic salary.'

Tessa was in no mood to indulge in the polemics of a subject that was plainly self-evident. 'Come on—what have you found out?'

The solicitor sorted through some notes on his lap. 'Anderson was used as a guinea pig during clinical tests on a new brand,' he said.

'What do you mean by "guinea pig"? All industries use consumer test panels for the development of their new products.'

Ciaran shook his head. 'No. The clinical tests were done exclusively on company personnel. These were quite separate from the consumer acceptability tests that involved some twenty thousand people all over the country. In the labs Anderson and his fellow workers smoked so many cigarettes a day. Then they were subjected to respiratory tests. And I was right. He must have had lung cancer at the time, undetected of course.'

What Ciaran said was bizarre but possible. All the various tests carried out by clinicians to determine the function of the small and large airways in the lung, cough frequency, and so on were hardly aimed at determining lung cancer. And unless the subject was coughing up blood, the clinicians would have no reason to suspect it.

Ciaran explained. 'I had a word with a chest surgeon at Guys hospital today. The reason why lung cancer is such a big

155

killer is because by the time it is detected, it's usually too late. By the time you see it on the X-ray, the fellow's usually had it.'

Tessa slowed down for a light. When Ciaran first approached her on the case she knew they would have to go for more than straight compensation. The fact that Anderson was a company employee and had free access to as many packets of cigarettes a day as he liked, and the fact that he stuck to one brand, *Mace 8*, for nearly twenty years weighed in their favour. But they were still up against the element of 'free will' in the act of smoking, the element that had lost all similar cases that had found their way into American courts. Dominion didn't force Anderson to smoke. But, if they could prove some element of negligence on the part of the company during the execution of the tests, well, that would make the case.

Negligence? At Dominion? Tessa wondered if any company would be so stupid. It was one thing to expose workers to poisonous gas or harmful dust for decades and deny all responsibility, but quite another to subject them casually to specific tests. She asked Ciaran how he managed to wheedle the information out of Anderson.

'Irish luck and a lot of time. Company made him sign a paper swearing secrecy. It also made him sign something confirming he was under no pressure to participate in the tests and would accept full responsibility.'

'Shit. How can any layman possibly know if he's going to suffer ill effects?' she said irritably.

Ciaran shrugged. 'Certainly he wasn't under any pressure, but the prizes were appealing enough. Twenty extra tax-free quid in his pay packet each week, couple of bottles of whisky thrown in.'

'Hell. So recruits came largely from the shop floor. Any women involved?'

'Apparently not.'

Tessa turned left at King's Cross. 'Did you manage to get hold of a packet of the test cigarettes?'

Ciaran withdrew something from his briefcase and held it at arm's length. 'No name. White packet. Looks like tobacco but it isn't.' He added, sniffing the pack, 'It's some new leaf they're playing around with. Funny Spanish name. Yerba sacra.'

Tessa frowned. The name rang a few bells. She recalled odd snippets of conversation, her father on the phone behind a half-closed door. But he rattled off so many brand names in so many different contexts that she had assumed this was some exotic new cigar. It hadn't occurred to her that this might be a new smoking material. She had more or less assumed those were being developed from synthetic substances. Ted headed new products. Ted? She could hardly expect him to co-operate. But Colette? Tessa gazed thoughtfully at the road.

It was crucial to gather as much information as possible before the company was legally approached for compensation, certainly before it had time to scare potential witnesses or feed vital documents or memoranda into the shredder. She could go only so far with her father before finally confronting him, and she had no intention of doing that just yet. Timing was all important. It was up to Ciaran to do the dirt-digging, obtaining as much as he could from James Anderson and his workmates without arousing suspicion.

Strategy had to be worked out very carefully. Impatient with the usually slow workings of the legal system, she was determined to cut corners on this one.

Company appointed solicitors and legal advisors too often utilized the to-ing and fro-ing of letters and meetings as a subtle tactic to wear down their opponent. The prospect of mounting legal costs often prompted the lone individual to back down.

But not this time.

Solicitors who consulted Tessa were aware of her penchant for hastening matters into court. No one approached her if all they wanted was a few carefully selected words of wisdom. She was there to act, not to pontificate.

She turned into her own road and pulled up beside the junk yard. As the sound of the car, cats appeared from nowhere and came running toward her, fur bristling with night static.

'Some sustenance, my dear,' she said to Ciaran. 'A light

Parmesan omelet and a few brown ales, perhaps. I can see we'll be working till midnight.'

Ted sat down with Tony McKay and his team at 7.45 A.M. The purpose of the dawn workshop was to formulate a tighter profile of the *Yerba Sacra* smoker and to discuss the proposed creative strategy for the media.

It was the point in the creative proceedings when the brand image not only reflected the market and consumer requirements formulated from the original input, but started to generate ideas of its own. The team had worked for the image, now the image was working for the team. The two-way process was the sign of a truly active logo.

Designer Sam Schenk, looking a bit bedraggled and hung over, busied himself by pinning up artwork on the boards behind Tony McKay's head.

Within minutes, the office radiated *Yerba Sacra* and the smell of freshly brewed coffee.

Tony McKay sat at the head of the table, Ted at the bottom, and the team on either side between them. McKay started the ball rolling. When he set up the agency he spent the first few months working with an outside market research consultancy on a more accurate method of defining consumer groups than the accustomed socio-economic grouping into dry 'ABs or C2s.' His models were defined by type, attitude, political views, cultural tastes, reading habits, lifestyles. The close definition of consumer types presented both agency and client with a more graphic description of people and motivations than could be otherwise visualized. In short, he put faces and feelings to statistics. By the time a new campaign left Kestner McKay, both the account handlers and the client were as familiar with their target audience as they were with one another. McKay felt that one of the ironic short-comings of advertising was the enormous creative effort and money spent on encouraging usually faceless people to buy the advertised product. He stopped anyone who spoke glibly about 'the housewife' and asked them to reconsider the concept in the light of modern developments:

158

single-parent families, the increasing number of male shoppers, and the child shopper.

It was a policy that Ted had found useful when coming into the business cold, straight from football. He kept thinking up nicknames for target audiences to help himself relate to them. If he was working on a new shampoo for sportsmen, he dubbed the target audience 'Chuck'. Admen like McKay who'd been in the business all their lives were first amused by the habit and then, seeing how it worked on clients, began to take it more seriously.

There was also something in making a creative team feel they were designing for flesh and blood, working like a tailor with a bolt of cloth for a specific client, and not for the faceless masses. When inflation bit savagely into the agency world, McKay's philosophy paid handsome dividents. Trimmed budgets forced marketing teams to work twice as hard, requiring a tighter difinition of target audiences, and often a complete rejigging of media schedules. That had been the McKay/Mallett philosophy all along.

So, as soon as the circumference lines were drawn around a target audience in terms of age and background, the team pitched in with research-backed descriptive material. Statistics provided the skelton. Like police pathologists, the team gradually built up the profile and personality.

'The *Yerba Sacra* smoker is discerning, radical, a constructive cynic,' said McKay, 'anti-hypocrisy, anti-bourgeois, an advocate of alternative lifestyles.'

'Not a street fighter or squatter per se,' added copywriter Felicity, 'but a *leader* of street fighters, the sort of person who sets up a centre for squatters' rights.'

'The sort of person who works for a political pressure group or studies at or teaches at progressive institutions, possibly a new university or polytechnic,' added marketing executive Jonathan.

'Professional and dropout. All backgrounds. A classless group,' added designer Sam. 'People who are more concerned with changing society and being politically active than they are with making vast sums of money. *But*,' he added emphatically,

159

'the sort of person who will cut back on food and dry cleaning budgets to go to fringe theatres or experimental dance groups.'

The team paused and reflected on the brown and gold *Yerba Sacra* poster, using it to help them visualize the future smoker. The image had taken care of the primary requirements. Now the creative media strategy had to take care of the secondary requirements.

Ted clasped his hands behind his neck and leaned back. 'People who, if they weren't smokers, would campaign against the tobacco industry.'

McKay snapped his fingers. 'That's it!'

'Smoking is the chink in their political armour,' Felicity added. 'Deep down they know they should campaign against it but it doesn't stop them from smoking. And when Dominion brings out a tobacco substitute, the response is positive. Whoopeee, here's a company capitulating to public demand and showing a little social concern at last!'

Ted chuckled approvingly. Nothing like a little negative positivism to evoke consumer response.

'People who will travel miles to see politically probing films. Fassbinder, Wertmuller, even if it means they can't afford the bus fare back,' said Tony.

'People who read *The Guardian*, the *Sunday Times*, *Time Out*, *New Society*, and at least we can advertise in the first three,' said Jonathan.

'I see them on Sundays at art galleries,' added Felicity, 'carrying young babies on their backs or wheeling two-year-olds in push chairs. Not just because they can't afford babysitters, which they can't, of course, but because they believe in exposing their kids to visual stimulation from birth.'

Sam Schenk, dreamily: 'When I designed the rough-textured freshly ploughed soil background for the pack, I kept thinking of this beautiful woman with long thick hair.' He looked up and appealed to the air, as if visualizing the image in the ceiling. 'She was wearing a handwoven material, not exactly a dress, and not exactly a caftan, something draped and in between. Perhaps she wove it herself. And she was pregnant.

Not coy or wearing a smock from *Mothercare*, but a quintessential woman. Mother Earth.'

Ted smiling: 'Whoever said pregancy wasn't a turn-on. Your Mother Earth slots in very nicely with the radical groups and Sunday art galleries.'

'Let's widen the image and call her "Ms. Earth" so everyone's included,' Tony McKay suggested, grinning at Felicity. 'Now what about Man Earth. Dark-brown suede jacket, well worn, had if for years. Possibly smokes a clay or corn pipe as well as strong cigarettes. Wears levi cords rather than jeans.'

The team threw in more suggestions.

'Home-made shoes. Recycled furniture. Everything strictly functional, but with good taste and sensitivity.'

'An eye for the unusual. They buy most of their clothes at rummage sales, shop at junk stores, scratch around demolition sites for old doors and make tables out of them.'

'They set up food co-operatives, bulk buy beans, rice, oil, whole wheat flour, and split peas. Whole food enthusiasts. Fits in well with the yerba bit, herbs and so on.

'They wear round, steel-rimmed specs instead of contact lenses. Put radical artists, actors and writers, and investigative journalists into your category of pressure groupniks and polytechnicites.'

'But remember Ms. and Man Earth transcend the classes and don't have much money. They're *not* radical chic. You'll have a working-class actor being what he is, mingling with a barefooted viola player who has abandoned a comfortable parental home in the suburbs to reshape a condemned house with friends.'

'Not petty bourgeois hard-ups about crossing sexual borders, but a strong sense of what is right and wrong in terms of human values and caring.'

'They start community newspapers on a shoestring, work for War on Want, Shelter, Friends of the Earth, Anti-Apartheid Movement, struggling publishing co-ops that churn out political and industrial exposés.'

'If they're not in art galleries on Sundays, they're at the

161

Other Cinema watching political documentaries about torture in Chile.'

'Most important. They're people who don't get sucked into the bourgeois mainstream when they leave college. If anything, they get more radical as they grow older. That gives us a range from seventeen to forty.'

Don't forget to include the people who make political documentaries, either as freelancers or for TV.'

'Basically these people are anti-establishment, anti-big business, anti-advertising.'

The evolving profiles stopped at that point. The team referred to their notes. A thoughtful silence filled the room. Sam leaned back in his chair. 'We can't fool these people. We knew that when we worked out the brand image.' Automatically, he reached for a sketch pad and whispered, 'Ms. Earth, Man Earth.'

'Earth people,' said copywriter Felicity, as if thinking aloud. 'Silly isn't it. Staring at us all the time.'

The team looked at her and smiled. It always took one person to articulate collective thought.

McKay looked dubious. 'Doubt if the Advertising Standards Authority will pass that. Thanks to ASH they made *Kensitas* drop the "You Get More Out of Life" tagline, received complaints about the country bread and wheat sheaves in *Embassy Mild* and made *Consulate* drop lines like "Where the air is clearer" and "Consulate gives you a breath of the country."' He paused and glanced at Ted.

Ted disagreed. 'I think we should have the guts to try it. I love Earth People. Have something milder on ice in case the ASA object.' He waited for reactions. 'I'm willing to bet the ASA will leave us a little rope here because it's tobacco substitute no one expects. We have a certain amount of educating to do. I leave that to your persuasive skills.'

The team was silent. They knew of Ted's eagerness to get as much as possible into their advertising before the government finally subjected tobacco to the limitations of the Medicines Act. The new *Denim* campaign kept just within the limits of the

162

voluntary restrictions on the advertising of heavy-tar brands. Low-tar, low-nicotine brands were allowed a little more leeway in what they could or couldn't imply in advertising because of the implied 'safer' cigarette. And Ted intended extending that with *Yerba Sacra*. He knew of the team's supreme efforts to say all in the logo and brand image, allowing graphics to deliver the punch. But there was no point in being timid in the copy. They all knew how long it took for government proposals to become law. Several new campaigns might roll happily into marketplace while Parliament dallied.

Ted also knew how frustrating it could be for a creative team to wheel something out as a fresh campaign only to have it neutered by government restrictions. But he was aware, too, of the media mileage to be made out of a controversial campaign. It stimulated curiosity and generated column inches in the newspapers. He smiled at Felicity. 'Go ahead with Earth People. It's terrific.'

Jonathan scribbled something down and frowned thoughtfully. 'Something you said earlier, Ted. The tobacco substitute nobody expects.'

'Drop the word tobacco,' warned research man Andy Pound.

'Fine. But the meaning holds,' Jonathan agreed.

Tony McKay: '*Yerba Sacra*. The one you didn't expect.'

Sam squeaked a felt tip pen across a sheet of paper and held up the suggested tagline. 'Too busy,' he said dismissively. 'The word "didn't" doesn't visualize well.' The pen squeaked out variations.

'I'm not so sure,' ventured Ted. 'I like the idea. It gets across the message that we're not trying to plug another fibroidal wonder. The low-tar cigarettes have been trying to overcome their lack of taste in ads. Smokers are convinced there's a connection between taste and safety. Puritanical thing almost. The safter the smoke the less you're likely to enjoy it.'

'But *Yerba Sacra's* ballsy.'

'You got it.'

'How about "The *taste* you didn't expect"?'

163

Various pens scratched away.

Ted got up. 'Play around with the Earth People and whatever inspires you about the expectancy thing. Try "good taste"—that couples well with everything you've been telling me about Earth People. Nothing chi-chi.' He ran his eye down the media schedule and glanced at his marketing executives. 'Someone said something about Earth People going to fringe theatres. Don't forget the pub theatres in our brewery division. They're always yakking for money. Maybe we could join forces in a promotion. Sponsor a few plays during the initial campaign. Hand out free packs. Call it *Yerba Sacra* Playhouse or something. I'll swan out now.' He turned at the door. 'Dig out a couple of radical playwrights, see if they can't come up with something for the launch. Let's finalize copy, visuals, and launch promotions Monday morning.'

15

Colette took one look at the warehouse and said. 'But this is impossible. I knew there were bomb sites in London. But I didn't know people *lived* on them.'

'Yes, I'm sorry,' Tessa said casually, squinting at the deserted factory opposite as if noticing it for the first time. 'I really should sweep up more often.'

Colette glanced at her and shook her head. She had visualized a neat mews house on a cobbled street. Only the rich could live like this with confidence.

Once inside she responded instantly to the inventiveness of the design, moving around silently to examine the joinery, and ask questions about the conversion.

The cats had arranged themselves along the windowseat, pressed against the warm glass. They glanced up at Colette. She was conscious of their scrutiny and kept a respectful distance.

Tessa placed a carafe of wine and two glasses on the wooden bar. Colette sat down opposite her on a barrel and was overcome with a sudden feeling of nostalgia. She began to talk about Paris, student friends with whom she had lost contact. 'I entomb myself in my work. Isolation. Ted has been my only human contact during this last year.'

'But no artist can work in such isolation.' Tessa remarked, pouring out the wine. 'What did you do for stimuli?'

'I looked within.'

'Jesus,' said Tessa. 'When I look within it's an exercise in self-punishment.'

Colette nodded. 'For the artist this can be very creative. Producing somehting from within your own energies is very pure.' She paused. 'To create something that is *yours*,' she stressed, 'quite untouched by the visual ephemera of the day.'

165

Tessa looked at her. 'That sounds terribly arid.'

Colette smiled. 'People are threatened when one opts out of the norm. My soul is in the Himalayas.'

'Oh yes, well, would the body in Islington care for more wine?'

'I embarrass you?'

Tessa shook her head and refilled their glasses. 'My own work is involved with the guts of life. People who can't make ends meet because they're old or disabled or forced to rot in prisons for political beliefs. I can't get too worked up about a soul in the Himalayas. I'm sorry. I didn't meant to be rude.'

The artist studied her thoughtfully. 'My work is involved with the guts of life too,' she said softly.

Tessa recalled the sculpted works with the raw centres staring like open wounds out of the polished and refined surfaces of wood and stone. 'A lot of people seemed upset at your exhibition,' she said, 'almost affronted by your new work.'

'That proved it did something to them. Disturbed them. Forced them to think beyound the decorative.' Colette got up and walked around. 'I need to do that to people. Every artist does.'

There was an urgency in her tone that startled Tessa. Colette had always seemed so passive, an object of great talent and beauty, but quite apolitical. She had never been with the artist before without Ted around.

Colette stood with her back to Tessa and gazed across the canal, hands pressed against the windowpane. 'Your view is one of despair,' she said, gesturing toward the deserted factory opposite. 'Why?'

Tessa sighed and slipped off the barrel. 'It's Dickens's London. The desperately poor once lived on whatever they could salvage from the raw sewage in the Thames and *that* canal.'

Colette turned around. 'But Tessa,' she said, 'that was over a hundred years ago! Why burden yourself with the *past*? Why blunt the instruments of the visionary in you?'

'Visionary? What visionary?' Tessa looked at her scorn-

166

fully. 'That's a luxury only the artist can afford.'

'So,' Colette replied with a smile. 'You sink to the popular rhetoric. You believe art is elitest and unnecessary. Why did you bother to come to my exhibition?'

Tessa didn't reply. She moved toward the windows and began to draw down the blinds, one by one. The stark, penetrating effect of the strong sunshine was immediately subdued.

The room became peaceful, cool. The lushness of the tall, leafy avacodo plants and trailing ivy was magnified by the muted light.

Law books and buff folders filled one side of the room. The other side was dominated by a heap of cushions, a rich assortment of silk paisley and Liberty prints in shades of crimson, green, and gold.

'No,' Colette said, shaking her head. 'No double standards. One view for politics? Another for sensuality? *That's* perversion.'

'Even for the visionary?'

Colette, angrily: 'More so for the visionary.'

'Very well then,' said Tessa, releasing the blinds. Each one rolled up with a quick snap. The room was flooded with light once more.

Brigid Anderson sat alone at the kitchen table. The current affairs programme on the TV facing her did little more than provide movement and noise in the empty room. She warmed her hands on a mug of instant coffee.

This evening was no different from any other. The children were in bed. Her husband was asleep. She had been on the go since 6 a.m. By the end of the day she was fragmented. Half an hour was all she asked for herself to glue her thoughts together.

The local priest had been around earlier in the month talking about death and hardship as if they were privileges. 'Our Lady has passed this burden to you and not to a weaker soul, Brigid Anderson, because she knows you have the strength to bear it.' Jimmy had overheard and shouted, 'Get that bleeding Jesus out of my house. Get him out!' The priest retreated as though he had seen a vision of mortal sin, and never returned.

Brigid had no time for the Church. There was a permanent engraving in her mind of her mother dying in labour to produce her fourteenth child, a Hail Mary on her lips imploring forgiveness from a priest hovering self-consciously over the bed, his eyes straying down toward the distended belly and open thighs.

Brigid felt very alone in London. The Irish weren't popular at the best of times. But since the start of the bombings, no Irishman or woman was safe anywhere. They were abused in public places. The police regarded them as fair game. They could be stopped and searched and held overnight in the police station at random. Anyone with an Irish accent, from the North or the South, was suspect. And God help the poor Irish bastard who found himself in a crowded pub when news of the latest bombing came over the TV.

Jimmy's family had never really accepted her. Even now they blamed his predicament on her, eyeing her suspiciously from his bedroom door whenever they visited. She bore the brunt of their anti-Irish scorn. When they were first married she was 'stupid and dirty'. Now they eyed the kitchen as though it doubled as a bomb factory.

The prospect of being at the mercy of the state frightened her. Soon as the youngest child started school she was going back to work. Anything. Scrub floors if necessary. As long as the council didn't turf them out of the flat.

Brigid stared at the TV screen for a few minutes, rose, and switched it off. It wasn't healthy to think too much. She couldn't afford the time, couldn't waste energy on her own fears. She was living for five people. She was one-fifth of the family and that was it.

She swilled out the mug and sloshed the coffee dregs down the sink before going in to see her husband. For the past day or so he'd barely been conscious of them, eyes opening now and then when she was in his room.

She had lived with his death ever since the day the doctors told them his cancer had gone too far to be operable, and he had five or six months left. But living with something, learning to adjust to it for the sake of the children, and filling up the day with practical things like shopping, meals, cleaning, laundry, was like marking time. Only in her deepest private thoughts did she go beyond that, admit things she could never discuss. Like the smell in Jimmy's room.

Why didn't someone warn her about the smell? Not even the district nurse when she came on her rounds, bustling in, bustling out. She couldn't compare the smell with anything else because there wasn't anything else like it. In the beginning it was by his bed, in his sheets when she washed them. Now it was in the passageway, by the front door. She scrubbed and sprayed, washed down the walls, opened the doors and windows, But it was still there. Now the children were noticing it, coming in from school, wrinkling their noses. And she hastened them into the kitchen to explain something even she didn't understand.

Tubes, Brigid thought, changing the urine bag. You began life attached to someone. You ended it attached to something.

Jimmy's breathing sounded brutal. The nurse had given him something to numb the pain but he wasn't conscious of anything now. Brigid looked down at his wasted yellow body. This wasn't the James Anderson who had courted and married her, loved her in his gruff, taciturn way. He'd been slim then. Dark. Nice brown eyes. Such a waste. Seeing him like this was like seeing him forty years on. As though their married life had raced on far and beyond for him. But had left her behind.

His sunken eyes made her very angry. She had felt pain, horror, even disgust before, but never anger. Not like this.

They'd been nothing all their lives. Born with nothing, expecting nothing. Now even death seemed an act of subservience.

He opened his eyes and stared at her, as if in shock. She stared back, unable to believe what she saw.

He was diminishing in front of her. The skin pulled tighter and tighter against his cheekbones, sucking in. Merciless. No time to spare.

She had lived with the moment for weeks. But now that it was here she could feel nothing but bitterness.

169

Death had never seemed poetic and beautiful to her. It was life's bailiff on his final call. Leering. Intruding. Degrading.

The face continued to stare at her, but there was no sight in the eyes. Yellow fluid began to pump rhythmically out of the mouth and nostrils.

Brigid watched the stain grow larger and larger on the sheet. When it was over, her husband's head seemed no bigger than a clenched fist.

No longer a man. From now on he would be a collection of components. One statistic among thousands.

16

Sam Schenk spread out the artwork for the various *Yerba Sacra* campaigns. There was to be one basic launch advertisement for the press to avoid diffusing the message, a different theme for street and underground posters. So far they were playing it relatively safe. But for the cinema commercials they went overboard. The combination was both provocative and informative.

For print media like *The Guardian* the team decided to play down the image, present it like an academic think piece. The full-page advertisements told the story of smoking, weaving in anecdotes from Indian mythology and the diaries of the first explorers who introduced the habit to Europe.

Felicity Klein had had a field day, poring over her notes, finally finding a satisfactory outlet for the intensive research of the past months. This was how things worked in her world. Months of work could end up in a couple of lines of copy and a snappy tagline. Or they could unfold and expand in a presentation rich with detail.

The tagline at the base read: 'You don't have to be an explorer to discover *Yerba Sacra.*'

It often happened in advertising that one campaign sparked off ideas for the follow-up. Tony McKay saw a direct and potentially exotic link between the explorer theme and the original consumer associations with the name yerba sacra. He referred to the charts. When the name was first thrown at test panels it had been described as 'Spanishy', capable of conjuring up images of distant lands. Future advertisements could capitalize on that, devote an entire theme to a mythical explorer, how he was first introduced to yerba sacra by an Indian chief, and how it was subsequently used in early trade. Actual facts would be respected as far as possible.

Initially it was important to introduce the product through association with the history of smoking. The team knew from the outset that they had to overcome a very serious problem. Because tobacco was habitually used as a generic term, any mass-produced alternative was described as a tobacco substitute or as synthetic tobacco. The object was to stop the public from thinking of *Yerba Sacra* as a tobacco, and start thinking of it as an independent smoking substance.

The purpose wasn't simply academic. It was aimed at cancelling out all the negatives associated primarily with tobacco. To succeed, *Yerba Sacra* had to arrive with a clean bill of health.

Street and underground posters would utilize the Earth People theme discussed and approved at the previous meeting. The artwork presented a group of the appropriate people sitting around in a relaxed circle on the floor. The tones and postures suggested an after dinner discussion.

The circle tied in neatly with the logo and the Indian sacred circle. Or it could equally imply that the group was just about to roll and share a joint. Except the faces were looking out of the poster as if to greet a new guest. That new guest was *Yerba Sacra*.

The tagline read: It's *Yerba Sacra!* The line at the base of the poster read: *The new smoke to greet the Earth People*. Thus both theme and message enforced brand positioning within the desired peer group.

It was generally agreed that the advertisement designed for the print media could be effectively alternated with the poster, for the subways. 'People actually *read* posters on the subways out of boredom,' Ted reminded them. The industry made prime use of London's undergrounds because the most frequent users were aged between fifteen and thirty-four.

The advertising team perceived their target group as principally under thirty-five, the time when smokers were more likely to switch brands. More specifically, the anti-establishment, possibly pot-smoking image of the Earth People was intended to catch the eye of the under twenty-fours, smokers and nonsmokers. The Earth People setting defined type rather than age. Clothing suggested suedes, corduroy, muslin natural weaves, timelessness and comfort rather than fly-by-night fashion.

Tony McKay stressed that the Earth People had to be regarded essentially as a pulse group. They moved within all age groups, like all political people. They were in the public eye a lot, their habits were noticed. 'No one notices a *Mace 8* smoker,' he added. 'But you notice Earth People in theatre foyers, at political meetings, on platforms, in demos. They're interviewed a lot by the media, and they're invariably smoking. That makes each one of them a natural advertisement for *Yerba Sacra*.'

The team murmured in agreement. The squat cigarette with its rough brownish wrapping and strong smell was bound to be noticed.

There was a reflective pause.

The team was aware of the peculiarly polarizing effect the anti-smoking controversy had had on the market during the past few years. The move to low-tar, low nicotine brands, had been partially offset by a backlash swing, especially among younger smokers, to strong-tasting, high-tar brands. *Gauloises* sales soared as a result, so did *Lucky Strike* and *Camel*. *Denim* was launched to capitalize on the growing trend.

Yerba Sacra was carefully aimed at swelling this market segment. The anti-establishment theme conveyed by the posters was seen as a plus. Low-tar brands, like the government health warning, was subconsciously seen by many smokers as a bureaucratic intrusion on their fun. It was important, from the start, to smother the impression that *Yerba Sacra* might be come lily livered, government directed compromise, some new low-tar brand.

Tony McKay turned his attention to Ted: '*Yerba Sacra* has to look as though it isn't part of Dominion.'

Ted agreed. 'It isn't anyway. It's from *my* new products factory.'

'That doesn't mean a thing to the world out there,' Sam Schenk interjected. 'We have to do more than prove this is a breakthrough. It has to look as though it's breaking away completely from company tradition, violently if necessary.' He pointed to the gold zigzag logo on a mock-up of the packet. 'The idea of lightning and eggs cracking conveys vibrant creativity. So let's go overboard with that in the cinema advertising.'

Like underground users, cinema audiences were predominantly youthful. Over eighty precent were aged between eighteen and thirty, making the medium highly appropriate for the launch.

Schenk encouraged the team to concentrate on the lower half of the age group, and to think in terms of people who were highly susceptible to innovative design. With the aid of very rough drawings, and much fist action, he demonstrated what he had in mind, raw ideas that would be shaped and refined by the team, and presented in a proper frame by frame storyboard prior to shooting.

Once more he referred back to Indian smoking cults. 'Something clicked last week when we were talking about Earth People,' he said. 'Remember when Ted told us about some Indian militant who was on trial for murder in America? And his friends among the defence witnesses all took their oaths on the sacred pipe? *Lot* of radical mileage there.'

The others agreed.

The designer delved into a file for a series of pages torn from successive editions of the *National Geographic*. 'Oglala Sioux tradition,' he explained. 'By pointing the sacred pipe skyward at dawn, they received an infusion of supernatural powers. Beautiful image, blood red sky, man meditating alone on hilltop. We couldn't get closer to the spiritual source of smoking if we tried.'

The fact that the yerba sacra plant wasn't used in such rituals didn't bother anyone. Schenk explained how the basic image could be utilized. The first frames would show the silhouette of a man on a hilltop, with the long pipe raised to the sky. Background colours would start off in a pinky haze, faintly mystical. 'No sound, except a slow drum beat, almost like a heartbeat. The silhouette will be our Earth Man, not distinctly

174

Indian or distinctly European, but primal man.'

The designer continued: 'We'll combine the mystical ritual with a speeded-up sunrise. The drums roll louder and louder, the sky gets redder and redder, the man evaporates in a transcendental haze. . . .' Schenk rose to his feet and raised a clenched fist in the air. Then, rotating it wildly, he brought it crashing down into his open palm. 'The sun, my friends,' he announced dramatically. 'A great ball of fire exploding and spinning out of the sky, to dissolve into, what else, a closeup shot of the packet!'

The team clapped spontaneously. Schenk acknowledged the applause and sat down.

'Phew,' said Felicity. 'You think we'll get it cleared? I mean, it's a pure drug trip, isn't it?'

'Ah,' said Schenk wisely, 'but we're not actually showing anyone *smoking*.'

'Drug trip my ass.' Ted interjected volubly. 'Most blatant piece of phallic and orgasmic symbolism I've seen anywhere. It's perfect. Let's go for it.' He paused and studied Schenk thoughtfully. 'You're an adman's dream,' he said approvingly. 'Way back in the 1870s, the tobacco manufacturers and retailers used to think like you. They used woodcuts of the ritual you just described on their invoice forms. Except they used a burning volanco instead of your sun.'

The team responded enthusiastically. They had achieved even more than they had hoped for in terms of subconsciously linking an ultramodern product with the past.

Tony McKay reached for the cost breakdown: 'We're within budget, too,' he said. 'The advertisement can be shot in a single location and the rest can be done in the studio. Words, Felicity, *words!*'

'Well,' she said, 'what else but "rising expectations"?'

The team started to laugh.

'Seriously,' she said, 'it links up well with the poster tagline, "The smoke to welcome,"etc., suggesting both expectation and surprise.'

McKay, deadpan: 'Why not simply "great expectations"—written in lower case of course, so Dickens doesn't sue us.'

'Go ahead,' Ted agreed. 'We're trying to convey an organic, wholesome product bursting out of the elements. We can't help it if the censors have dirty minds. Who do you have lined up for the drums?'

'My brother has a little act going in a Soho strip club,' Sam suggested hopefully.

Ted looked dubious. 'Line up several for me to hear, and include him too,' he added tactfully. He paused and tapped a pencil against the table. 'There might be a hit number in this. LP record or tape offers to boost sales when the brand goes national.' He removed a pocket calculator and began tapping out budgets. *Denim* had gone national with the help of a 'Go Dixie with *Denim*' campaign in the major university towns. A band was imported from New Orleans to do a whistlestop tour, and recorded live. The campaign had created a lively profit centre within the division. But Ted saw something a little more low-key for *Yerba Sacra*. Less noise and aimed at a more discerning ear. Nothing tacky.

He studied the figures on the calculator. 'We still have a little rope to play around with, and we can work some of the publicity budget into this. So get me the best drummers in London. It's worth it for the spinoffs later.'

McKay snapped his fingers. 'There's a fabulous black group playing at Ronnie Scott's right now. The drummer's fantastic. I'll personally talk to him.' He grinned. 'Terrific. That means the evening goes on expenses.'

'Bastard,' said Felicity. 'Why can't we all go?'

Ted rose. 'Why not? I owe it to you. I'll take the whole goddamn bunch of you. How about Friday night?'

The orderly stripped the sheet off the corpse on the dissecting table.

Tessa looked down at James Anderson's emaciated body. This wasn't her first autopsy. Normally she viewed the whole painstaking procedure with professional detachment and scientific interest. There was no point standing up in court and arguing a case unless she had made herself familiar, wherever possible, with the medical details.

But she seldom had to face someone on the slab she had actually met before death.

It would have been easier to watch the scalpel slit the skin from the sternum to the pubic bone if one hadn't actually visited the deceased's home within the past few weeks. She kept thinking about the gloomy Edwardian housing estate, the broken tiles on the kitchen wall. Fragments of the conversation with Brigid Anderson kept floating into her mind.

But the personality diminished as the skin was peeled back. Shears snipped through rib cartilage. The chest cavity was opened to expose the heart and lungs.

Albert Routledge, a consultant pathologist at one of London's leading teaching hospitals, had agreed to conduct the autopsy as part of his routine instruction of senior students.

He talked nonstop, dictating all the while to his secretary, alternately bullying and encouraging his students, and briefing Tessa as he went along.

A tight grey mass, like a belligerent fist, dominated the central area of Anderson's right lung. To enable them to make a closer examination Routledge removed both lungs and heart from the chest cavity and placed them on a separate dissecting table. Some of the students remained with the body to complete a detailed abdominal examination, and to find out if the cancer had spread.

'The location of the carcinoma made it inoperable,' Routledge said, 'because it pressed on the trachea.' Pausing, he explained to Tessa, 'The main inlet into the lung, Miss Courtland.'

One of the students glanced down and said. 'Just what we expected.'

There was an appalled hush.

Routledge rose from the dissecting table like a blacksmith from an anvil. '*We* Fairweather? Who, precisely, is the royal "we"?'

177

Fairweather flushed with embarrassment. 'I'm sorry sir,' he mumbled.

'Assume nothing, do you hear, nothing. If you would observe the number of wrong diagnoses made by those bloody fools in the wards you wouldn't make such inane remarks. The last epidermoid carcinoma they sent me was originally diagnosed as gastric ulcers.'

The students began to laugh nervously.

'I fail to see the humour,' Routledge snapped. He stood back, hands raised in the air. 'Very well Fairweather, I would like to observe your performance on the right lung. A step-by-step analysis for the benefit of Miss Courtland.'

Fairweather raised a long knife and prepared to make serial slices through the lung and the tumour. Tessa watched with alarm.

A careful cross-section was made. Sample blocks of tissues were taken from the tumour, the bronchial tubes on either side, and from different sections of the lung, for microscopic examination. 'The cells lining the bronchial tube change from one type into another in a smoker,' Fairweather explained. 'The altered cell is known as squamous, and this may appear normal, or may show precancerous changes.'

'So,' said Tessa, 'apart from the tumour itself, you may find cancerous cells in the surrounding tissue?'

Routledge took over. 'Not merely in the lung of course, but we may find smaller tumours or evidence of similarly cancerous cells in the liver, the adrenal glands, or the brain.' He glanced expectantly at the other students, who were still clustered around the abdomen.

The section of the lung Tessa proposed presenting in court was dutifully placed in formalin.

Routledge had already diagnosed the cancer type as 'small cell undifferentiated' from the appearance of the tumour. The diagnosis was later confirmed by the cytology tests. 'Referred to more commonly as "oat cell" carcinoma, Miss Courtland,' he explained, 'because of the oatlike appearance of the cells. I have been conducting autopsies for over thirty years and can recall

178

less than a handful of nonsmokers who have died from this particular carcinoma. Statistically, my own observations more or less match the national ratio. It's eight or nine to one. *Well,* ladies and gentlemen?' he said to the group that had been given the task of examining other organs for evidence of secondary characteristics.

'Spread to the liver, and kidneys' one of them announced.

The woman he addressed as 'Stephens' had slit the skull horizontally and was busily preparing to open it with a powered bone saw to expose the brain. Conversation froze the instant the saw got to work.

As soon as the excruciating noise subsided, Routledge returned Tessa's attention to the lungs. 'The idea that you can look at a pair of lungs and recognize a heavy smoker is myth Miss Courtland, sheer myth. Only the microscope can tell us that.'

Tessa studied the large, dark blue-gray mass, and the hard, gray, fibrous tumour. 'If the deceased started smoking something other than tobacco within the last eighteen months, could that have accelerated the cancerous growth?'

The pathologist touched the tumour thoughtfully. 'Are you trying to tell me he was on grass?'

The students looked up from their work in surprise.

Routledge waved the air dismissively. 'Don't take any notice of them. They think I was born yesterday. Grass couldn't do that to a lung, if that's what you wanted to know.'

'No,' said Tessa. 'This is a new material.' She explained yerba sacra to the silent and curious room, and discussed the smoking tests involving the deceased.

Routledge spoke generally about the synergistic effects of different substances on the body. 'The highest proportion of asbestos and uranium workers who contract industrial diseases are smokers,' he stressed. 'But pollution is only a contributory factor,' he added, 'not the principal cause of lung cancer, in spite of what the tobacco industry would have us believe.'

Stephens stood with her hands poised over the brain. 'Metastases, sir.'

179

'Ah,' said Routledge. 'A common partner of lung cancer, Miss Courtland. A patient can sometimes return home after a seemingly successful operation for the removal of the tumour in his lung. Within the month his family contacts the hospital because they believe he is going insane. Brain cancer.'

'But,' Tessa asked, 'is there any way of telling whether the *primary* tumour was caused by tobacco smoke, or the smoke of another material?'

The pathologist shook his head. 'We can only *relate* conclusions to the smoking habits of the deceased.'

Of all the details and facts that were thrown at her that day, Tessa concluded that: the yerba sacra tests were conducted on Anderson when his carcinoma was in its early, and as yet, undetectable stage: that the additional aggravation of the new smoking material *could* have accelerated the growth of the tumour and shortened his life; that by the time his predicament was diagnosed it was too far gone and too widely spread to be operable.

Most important of all, she discovered that, had the clinical team at Dominion been more observant and included X-rays in their routine checking of the human guinea pigs, Anderson's predicament might have been detected early enough to be operable.

It was around such evidence that she built her case.

Pip, the photographer assigned by *Vogue* to do an intimate portrait of Colette 'at home,' moved around her studio like an elegant weeping willow blowing softly in the breeze.

His long hair was parted in the middle and framed a gentle oval face, tawny eyes, and curling lashes. In a previous age it would have been said that his looks were wasted on a boy.

He wore a light-green suede sweater jacket with an elastic waist, that kept separating from a pair of close-fittings trousers. His tapering fingers wafted between a Pentax and a Hasselblad.

Colette had expected an art critic from the magazine's 'point of view' pages. She was startled to see Pip, an entourage of make-up ladies, and a girl in a clinging Jean Muir dress waiting

180

at the front door.

They spread themselves around the house, rifling through her wardrobe like prospective buyers, laying clothes out on the bed, passing them downstairs.

'We'll start down here, dolls,' Pip shouted from the studio, 'Marvellous vibes. Sloping skylight radiating natural light and energy, so we need good strong dramatic colours. Save the subdued tones for upstairs.'

The girl in the Jean Muir dived for Colette's flamingo-tinted dress and snapped her fingers for the make-up artist.

Colette protested. 'But I don't dress like that in my *studio*!'

No one took any notice. It was as though she wasn't there. Hands moved on her, removing garments, pulling them on, descreetly suggesting changes in underwear. 'Would you mind going without a bra,' said the Jean Muir girl. 'Matching tones please, Carol, and darken her skin.' She raised Colette's face to the light. 'Texture's beautiful but she'll look like chalk under the skylight.'

Colette was bewildered and annoyed, but gradually she allowed a certain artistic curiosity to overtake her. She became meek and subdued, a pair of eyes in the ceiling watching the bodies below. She held up her face for the layers of make-up, allowing them to reshape her mouth, shade her nose.

'Wonderful oriental eyes,' Pip murmured approvingly, gazing down into the Hasselblad. 'Shade the lids a bit more, lovey. Her cheeks are too pink in this light. The dress does it all.'

Colette lifted her face for the second round. The girl in the Jean Muir moved restlessly about the studio, dragging pedestals in or out of view, scraping the sofa along the floor. Her assistant came pattering downstairs with a sculpted vase from the sitting room.

'I like it,' said Pip. 'Put it beside her on the floor, teeny bit behind her, bit more to the right, back a bit. Super. Super. Can you position her hands, lovely, raised toward the skylight. That's it. Face slightly at an angle. Super.'

The Hasselblad clicked and was wound on. Pip kept up a

running commentary of orders and directional positions, breaking off only once to say distantly. 'I hear you're from Vietman. Marry a marine or something?'

Colette shook her head and started to open her mouth.

He waved the air impatiently. 'Don't move, doll. Could you lift your right leg slightly. Bit more so the material's stretched. One foot hooked around the other.' He looked up and walked over to her, running his hand along her thigh to position the pose exactly.

Meanwhile, the girl in the Jean Muir fired a series of questions at her. Birth, Education. What she did at the weekends. How she managed to combine her own career with that of her husband. Where she bought her clothes. What make-up she used.

The flamingo dress was peeled off and replaced with a frosted lilac silk organza creation. '*Definitely* sofa, Pip said. 'Lie full out, doll. Legs ever so slightly bent at the knees. One hand behind your head. Can you part that bodice a bit, naturalish, you know. Like you're asleep. Dress forms a lovely semicircle to the floor. *That's it.*'

He walked around her several times. 'Close your eyes and lift your head, just a little. Bit more. Nice.' He studied her thoughtfully. 'I want one breast to fall slightly to one side. Can you do that without looking as though you're about to roll off the seat? No. That's not quite it.' The photographer reached out for her breasts and moved them around like chessmen, releasing them to see how they fell. 'You're too firm,' he said irritably. 'I wanted a slightly floopy look, you know?'

Colette found herself apologizing.

Pip shook his head dismissively. 'Can't have everything, doll. You look great upright. I just wanted a more *languid* mood lying down.' He grinned suddenly, then squinted at her long fingers stroking the air. 'Carol, there seems to be a blemish or smudge or something up by her ear.'

The make-up girl clattered across the stone floor in her platform sandals, cotton wool posed for attack.

Make-up swiftly adjusted, the Pentax moved into view,

hovering about like a peeping tom, crouching below, moving to the front.

The team worked gradually through the house. Colette was alternately posed draped amongst the cushions on the lounge floor in her handpainted gypsy dress or poring over a huge sketch pad in the chamois jumpsuit. Finally they had her in black silk pyjamas, framed by the Georgian windows. She changed clothes a dozen times, obediently obliging with as many expressions. Bored to pensive. Provocative to coquettish.

The make-up woman moved around behind her, restyling the face to suit the selected pose.

When it was all over, she sat them down with a bottle of Black Tower and quietly excused herself.

She returned within a few minutes in an oatmeal smock, headscarf and goggles, carrying a bucket of water.

The *Vogue* people looked at one another, embarrassed.

Colette calmly reached into the photographer's bag, removed the rolls of film, and dropped them into the bucket one by one.

'*What the fucking hell,*' said Pip, rising angrily to his feet.

Colette held out her hand as though calming the sea. 'You have twelve different women in these films. Not one of them is me. You have not asked about my exhibition. If you came to record a sculptor in her studio, I am now ready for your cameras.'

17

'Honey, I *swear* I didn't know anything about it!'

'You mean Alun Hughes sets the whole thing up and doesn't say anything to you? What kind of an imbecile do you think I am?'

'Come on, Colette, be reasonable. There's obviously been a misunderstanding. Hughes doesn't even know anyone at *Vogue*.'

'So they spun his name out of thin air? He wanted this cosy *chez nous* story for you. Not for me. Not for my art, but for your image. I was a fool not to see this from the beginning.'

Ted stared at the mouthpiece.

'Meat. That's all I am.'

There was a hostile silence on the phone. Ted was genuinely baffled, but nothing he could say seemed to make the slightest bit of difference. 'Why don't you hammer this out with Alun?'

There was another long pause.

'What the hell,' she said, her voice suddenly more upset than angry. 'How would you feel if one of the art magazines came to do a photo essay on you as Colette Sable's husband?'

Ted swivelled around and gazed out at the Thames. 'I'm sorry,' he said tightly. I'll talk to Alun. Someone got their lines crossed. Come on, honey, you're bigger than this.'

The line hummed thoughtfully between them.

'Yes,' she said quietly. 'I am bigger than this. All of it.'

Ted frowned. His intercom was buzzing. He promised to speak to Hughes and quickly replaced the receiver.

He was expected downstairs at a press luncheon and had time only to make a hasty mental note to tackle Hughes about *Vogue* later. There were more important things to worry about

184

right now. Hughes and his team had spent the previous afternoon briefing him thoroughly, firing uncomfortable questions at him, trying to catch him off guard. The object was to prepare him for the press without making him seem like a briefed-up executive.

Outwardly he had to appear cool, informal, and not really part of the group bureaucracy at all. That wasn't very difficult for Ted.

Hughes had invited marketing and advertising writers from magazines and the dailies. Contrary to his own belief that Ted should be allowed to handle the meeting alone, the board insisted that he should be there too and quietly tape the entire procedure.

Before the group could start on the smoked salmon, Ted paced them quickly through the new campaign for *Denim*. There was an enthusiastic response to the cheeky feet theme. The message was lost on no one. The woman for *Media* ruffled her curly blond hair and stared at Ted. 'You can't deny this is aimed at young people,' she said crisply, 'in direct violation of the cigarette advertising code.'

'That's riduculous,' Ted replied dismissively. 'Those feet don't look particularly young to me. And the advertising standards authority hasn't raised any objection.'

'But we hear you're planning to issue a T-shirt imprinted with the feet,' the journalist persisted. 'That certainly suggests you're aiming at a youth market.'

Ted laughed at her. 'Everyone wears T-shirts. Not just young people. I see respectable middle-aged gentlemen out mowing their lawns on Sundays in T-shirts.'

She looked at him and smiled. 'One middle-aged gentleman and a few hundred kids. I thought you dealt with majorities, not exceptions.'

Ted smiled back. 'I can't stop you from using your imagination, Ms . . .'

'Jill Norstad.'

'Ms. Norstad.'

'Does the brand name go on the T-shirt too?'

'Sure.'

'With the government health warning?'

'Ms. Norstad, this is a T-shirt we're talking about. Not a cigarette pack.'

'That doesn't make any difference. The advertising code states very clearly that brand names used in isolation are regarded as advertisements for that brand, and must comply with the code.'

'Ms Norstad, what are you wearing?'

Everyone eyed her neatly pressed jeans and matelot top. She shrugged. 'Denim.'

'Then why aren't you carrying the government health warning?'

Jill flushed with annoyance and said nothing. In a perverse way, both she and Ted had made their point.

Other members of the press shifted restlessly, anxious to move on. A young man from the *Financial Times* launched into a pressing discussion on the *Catch* episode. 'Are you planning to withdraw the brand from the market?'

Ted shook his head. 'We've learned valuable lessons from that,' he said, emphasizing the positive. 'In any innovative marketing situation you must budget for your water tester. *Catch* has been like a prime researcher. It proved that the market wasn't quite ready for a synthetic.'

'Surely your prelaunch research would have told you that,' the young man persisted.

'Yes and no,' said Ted diplomatically. 'Remember, we're under great pressure from the government to produce more low-tar brands and a safe cigarette. We accept this as an inevitable market demand, and we're prepared to be accommodating. I'm not going to pretend *Catch* was a dazzling success. You can read the figures for yourselves. It's breaking even. But as the largest tobacco group in the world we felt it was our role to be the trailblazer with a safe cigarette, and to shoulder the consequences.'

Hughes smiled to himself. Presenting the group as a big-hearted paternalis institution would please Courtland no end.

'You use the term "safe" cigarette, Mr. Mallett,' said a tall reedy journalist from the *Sunday Times*. 'That implies your other brands aren't safe.'

Ted laughed good-humouredly. 'I believe someone from the media coined that term. And I myself prefer to avoid the word "synthetic".'

'That doesn't really answer the question,' said the *Financial Times*. 'If I'm correct, the "safe" label came out of your PR department.'

Alun Hughes shook his head. 'I believe it came originally from the Department of Health and Social Security.'

Jill Norstad: 'What the hell does it matter where it came from. *You're* using it. And that implies you accept the medical arguments against smoking.'

Alun Hughes answered quickly. 'We're not qualified to make medical judgements. We believe the medical arguments against smoking are inconclusive.'

'Then why are you using the term "safe"?'

'Because,' said Ted with studied patience, 'The government requires it of us.'

'So you believe the government is instilling unnecessary fear in the people?' said *The Times*.

'I think you should direct questions like that towards the D.H.S.S.' Ted suggested. 'We can sit here and throw polemics at one another all day.' He paused. 'I said earlier that I was reluctant to use the term "synthetic" because it instills negativism. Our research has proved that and we've used it as a guide for future product development.'

The press studied him with interest. The continuous search for tobacco substitutes conducted by all the large groups was no secret to anyone. But specifics about the unborn brands were left to speculation and intelligent guesswork.

Management Today picked up the implication of Ted's statement. 'You mean you're moving away from synthetics?'

Ted nodded.

Alun looked apprehensive. He understood Ted's need to direct the questions away from the medical issue, but a premature leak about *Yerba Sacra* could be a disaster. The object was to arouse curiosity, not provide facts.

The Times: 'If it's not a synthetic, then there are clearly two possibilities. A new way of processing tobacco to make the smoke less incidious. Or a swing in the opposite direction. A herbal cigarette, like that Honeyrose brand the health food shops are selling.'

Ted smiled. 'The truth lies roughly midway between the two.'

Alun's expression didn't change.

The press began firing questions at Ted. Did the company have a herbal cigarette up its sleeve or didn't it? Had it discovered a new processing method? Was this merely a curtain-raiser for the mass marketing of marijuana?'

Ted fielded the questions one by one, never losing ground, never appearing ruffled. Eventually he raised his hand. 'I will issue one statement and stick by it until the launch. It isn't tobacco. It isn't marijuana, and it isn't a sythetic. Beyond that I can say nothing for the moment.'

'So it must be a new herbal cigarette,' Norstad said dryly.

Ted shook his head. I'll stick by my statement. If you care to speculate, I can't stop you.'

Hughes cursed Mallett under his breath. He could visualize tomorrow's stories from the eager response in the room. *Damn* Ted. Trust him to give in to a momentary temptation. All the intensive briefing of the previous afternoon snuffed out in a few words. Soon as the first editions of *The Times* and *Financial Times* hit Fleet Street tonight the other dailies would reach for their phones. He'd be up the whole bloody night answering queries. Press office may as well put all other business aside tomorrow. The chairman was going to love this.

Ted was in his element. He had caught the imagination of the journalists in the room and enjoyed the feeling. They spoke his language, even adversaries like Jill Norstad. When they started reaching for glasses of wine and helping themselves to the buffet lunch, he regaled the gathering with stories of his early days on Madison Avenue with the *Heads Up* account.

Exaggerating his Southern accent and hunching his shoulders as though he were padded up on the football field, he made the group visualize him as he was ten years ago. hair shaved to the bone, promoting a men's shampoo. 'Why, when they spoke about a projected image, I thought they meant home movies.'

Alun Hughes watched the quipping and antics with a sinking heart. Wherever he could he attempted to redirect the conversation back to Dominion, but the group was enjoying the entertainment and simply wasn't interested. Mercifully, the call of early deadlines and afternoon appointments had the room evacuated before two-thirty.

Alun sat at one end, Ted at the other. For several long moments the two men stared at one another across the lunch debris and discarded press kits. Ted's jacket was slung over a chair arm, his hair was untidy and he'd had too much wine. But when he spoke, the quip-a-minute, dial-an-adman tone had gone. He rose slowly and put on his jacket. 'You conniving bastard Hughes. You two-bit back street hustler. *Vogue*. Colette. Using my wife and *her* work to promote me. *Me*. You try another cheap trick like that again and I'll invite the press in to watch me kick your miserable ass around the foyer.' He turned and left the room.

Daphne Courtland sat alone in her garden in the rain, sheltered by a golf umbrella. A pot of tea and a ham sandwich lay untouched by her side. Sparrows chirped at one another nearby, but soon tired of the local gossip and came hopping through the long thick grass looking for worms. The air was heady with the smell of honeysuckle and cherry blossom.

Daphne scanned the neat rows of young shoots in the vegetable beds, and the raspberry bushes winding away from her along taut lines of wire. But there was a vacancy in her eyes. She couldn't reach Tessa any more and, genuinely, couldn't understand why. Her daughter talked to her as though addressing someone across a crowded courtroom. Phone calls were minimal, abrupt. The girl was obsessed about something, but what?

Yesterday had been no different. She had been overjoyed to see the Daf rattling up the driveway. But Tessa was abstracted, rushed, not there to see her. 'Mother, you know all those old letters Stirling and Amy and her father exchanged during World War I. Do you mind if I go through them?'

Daphne, who had long urged her daughter to write Amy and Stirling's biography, responded eagerly to the request, hauling down shoe-boxes crammed with letters and papers from her bookshelves.

'Biography?' said Tessa distantly in response to her mother's query. She was kneeling on the carpet and systematically going through a semicircle of yellowing papers and flimsy newspaper cuttings. 'Some day. Maybe.'

'You know, dear, Amy won't rest until someone puts all this material together.'

Tessa nodded vaguely. 'Why don't you do it?'

'You know very well why. Amy wouldn't think I had the capability.'

Now her daughter was angry. 'Oh stop being so bloody self-denigrating all the time!'

Daphne hadn't replied. She sat in the rocking chair, hands in her lap, watching the copper head move to and fro amongst the papers, sorting, sifting, discarding.

'Between them,' Daphne continued, 'Stirling and Amy compressed a lot of economic history into their lives. The opposite extremes of course.' She laughed. 'You're the only one who can write about it, dear. It's your heritage.'

'Don't tell me what my heritage is. I'll interpret that for myself.'

'Tessa, have I said something to upset you?'

Tessa looked up and stared at her mother. The words *your father wanted a son* kept churning through her brain along with seemingly unrelated images from the autopsy. But even if she raised the subject she doubted her mother would understand. There was too much going on, too many tangled emotions. She shook her head. 'I'm working on a difficult brief.'

Daphne nodded. 'Are you looking for something in particular? Maybe I could help?'

Tessa answered quickly. 'No. I'll know when I find it. Thanks anyway.' She had in mind a letter, a few cuttings, a private message, something, anything from her grandparents' lives that could, decades later, prove incriminating to Dominion. She needed something to be able to throw their counsel off guard in court. She wasn't sure if she would find it, wasn't sure she knew precisely what it was she wanted. But she would know when she saw it.

Nearly two hours later, she found it. She sat back on her heels, read and reread two old cuttings and half a dozen letters, and carefully filed them between plastic folders to take back to London.

Then she excused herself under the pretext of making them some tea, but went instead to her father's bedroom and systematically raided his rolltop desk. He kept it carefully locked but she had known how to work the lock with a piece of wire since the age of eleven. He organized his desk like a general planning a campaign. Private diaries from the past five years were neatly filed in a drawer on the left. Current matters requiring attention were filed on the right. Family and business matters were kept strictly apart. Family in the bottom drawers. Business affairs in the top.

Knowing her father was spending less and less time at home, rarely returning except on weekends, she removed the diaries and a handful of papers. With the aid of paper clips she made a careful note of precisely where and how they were filed, and at what angles.

When Tessa returned to Daphne's room, her mother was so busy trying to stop the cats from shredding the papers with their claws, she hadn't noticed the time lapse.

Or at least it hadn't occurred to her until the following afternoon when she wondered again what Tessa might have been seeking.

She rose, returned to the house, and searched thoroughly and systematically through her parents' papers. In her neat, methodical way, Tessa had left markers in the relevant gaps.

Daphne smiled. Purposefully, she reached for the phone.

Tessa answered on the third ring.

Daphne chattily: Hello, my dear. I think I found what you were looking for, Amy's notes on the IRA.'

There was a puzzled silence. Tessa stared across to the window. 'Umm,' she said, 'actually I wasn't looking for that. But hold on to them, I'd like to see them.' Quick. Dismissive.

But Daphne didn't intend to let go. Her curiosity was aroused. 'Well, it's obvious you weren't interested in her notes on the women's movement, because they're intact, except for . . . some letters, and a report on her speech at the cigarette factory.' Daphne continued probing, fishing. 'Some of Stirling Harmer's papers are missing too.'

Tessa smiled. 'You're getting warmer.'

'I shall have to know sooner or later.' Daphne paused. 'It concerns Dominion, doesn't it, dear?' Light, almost frothy.

'Yes,' Tessa replied grimly. 'Are you going to run and tell the chairman?'

Daphne laughed into the mouthpiece. 'I don't speak to him much. I'm hardly likely to discuss you with him, am I now?'

A few silent moments passed between them. Tessa felt acutely conscious of Colette's presence. Colette's links with Dominion. But this wasn't the time to resolve that.

Daphne spoke into the silence: 'Will you phone me tomorrow?'

'Yes, Mother, of course. Are you alone?'

'No more so than I have been for nearly sixty years.'

Tessa stared at the pattern on the carpet. 'Good night, Mother,' she said.

'Good night, dear,' Daphne replied.

Tessa replaced the receiver.

Charles Courtland read and reread the stories in the first editions of *The Times* and the *Financial Times*, delivered hot from the presses to his flat in Cadogan Square.

The chairman wondered what had happened to the golden days of city journalism, when groups like Dominion could simply telephone the editors and threaten to withdraw all advertising unless a sensitive story was spiked.

Financial journalism had never been quite the same since the merger era of the sixties, when proposed takeovers were reported with the pizzazz of Hollywood divorce scandals. The era gave birth to a brash breed of business journalists. Young, flamboyantly dressed men and women who thought nothing of ringing him at two in the morning for a comment. God only knew how many times he'd had his number altered.

Old guard executives like him never fully adjusted to the change. He thought back nostalgically to the days when share performances were discussed over a leisurely club lunch with some impeccably dressed city correspondent. But nostalgia didn't prevent the chairman from appreciating the positive effects of bringing daily journalism closer to the business world and vice versea. And he recognized the value of modernizing the group image via public figures like Ted Mallett and his stable of restless new products.

Still, Ted had to be viewed within the context of Dominion, and *not* vice versa.

In short, the stories infuriated him.

Dominion to launch herbal cigarette.

The description of Ted as 'Dominion's outspoken product development manager' making a 'surprise announcement' at an informal press lunch, signified a momentary loss of control. And that bothered him more than anything. Ted had violated company policy.

Alun Hughes had dutifully prepared him for the worst. Courtland knew what was yet to come when the other papers picked up and elaborated on the story. From what he could see in the first edition, the FT had toned down Ted's antics. They concentrated on reporting his negative view of synthetic smoking materials, and the need to regain public confidence with an imaginative product. But *The Times* wrote, 'Mallett's Madison Avenue background in fast-moving consumer products, and his time with Dominion's subsidiary, Harmer Brands, made him a suitable choice when the group set up a new products division in

193

London some six years ago. But Mallett has never made a secret of his unpopularity amongst the more traditional members of the Dominion board. He is given to sudden bursts of unconventionality, like running through Covent Garden with his wife past live TV cameras during a Dominion-sponsored performance of the *Marriage of Figaro* earlier this year. The American director said yesterday, with characteristic bluntness, "Hell. I was imported from New York to hit the marketplace with a megaphone, not a harmonica. If they wanted a harmonica they should have hired Larry Adler." '

Courtland read the words and winced.

Both papers summed up the race for tobacco substitutes, the *Catch* experiment, the joint projects under way with the chemical combines, and the limited venture into herbal cigarettes by one or two distributors of health products. 'Dominion's move,' wrote the FT, 'places the group at the forefront of the "safe" cigarette league.'

When Courtland first heard about Mallett's indiscreet news leak, he had personally informed the rest of the executive committee, and called an urgent meeting for the following morning.

His chauffeur drove him to Dominion House early. Before the meeting, he sat alone at his desk and quietly read through the late editions of all the nationals, comparing and analysing their different approaches to the story. The response was generally enthusiastic, inquisitive. But this didn't alter his annoyance one bit.

For the first time since he fought for Mallett's appointment, he was beginning to have grave doubts about the man. The last few months has shown him a side of Ted he genuinely believed had been tamed and toned down. First there was that insane scene at Covent Garden. And now this. Ted's innovative talents were beginning to belittle Dominion tradition.

But Ted was not to be subdued when the chairman called him in to berate him before the other directors arrived.

'Charles, I can't believe you mean this,' he said, leaning over to switch on the video linking Courtland's office with the stock exchange, twirling the dial until he got Dominion's share price. It had moved up two points since the stock exchange opened.

'This is the greatest shot in the arm that's ever happened to the company,' Ted said, pacing the floor. 'Not even the formal launch could have this effect. It's the unexpected, the surprise announcement that sets everyone jumping. My marketing executives have been flooded with enquiries, just from a few newspaper reports.'

Courtland looked unimpressed. He stretched across the desk for his meerschaum.

'It's not only the health food stores who're jamming the lines,' added Ted. 'Head buyers from the supermarket chains have phoned in personal orders. Charles, I don't think you understand what this means!'

The chairman eyed Mallett over his pipe. 'It means you'll snuff out interest very quickly because you can't provide the goods for several months.'

'My God,' said Ted, turning away, hands on hips. 'Stimulating demand in advance is one of the key arts in marketing.' He didn't tell the chairman of the personal feud between himself and Alun Hughes that had sparked the whole thing off. But he believed in capitalizing on it now it was here.

'But it's contrary to company policy to fly product flags like this,' the chairman retorted icily. 'Good Lord, Ted. You hadn't even announced it to the trade. We don't do things like this.

'Then it's about time we did!' Ted faced him across the desk. I'm sick and tired of trying to create products for the 1980s like a gentlemen from some old-fashioned banking family. If Stirling Harmer operated like that in his time, Dominion Tobacco wouldn't be here today.'

The chairman raised his eyebrows. 'The hypothesis is irrelevant.'

'It damn well is not.'

The two men were silent.

Mallett had never made his hero-worship of Stirling Harmer a secret to anyone. But at no time since joining the

195

company did Ted find the contrast between Harmer's dynamism and present conservatism as marked as during the committee meeting following his confrontation with Courtland.

'Gentlemen,' he said, pounding a fist on the boardroom table. 'Britain has the highest record of new product failures in the world. Why? Because unlike the Japanese, the British don't indulge in the same excessive care and attention to detail. I could paper this boardroom with marketing opportunities missed because of myopia or a complete lethargy where experimentation is concerned.'

Members of the executive committee responded with hostility. But Ted hadn't finished.

'Apart from your worldwide reputation for Scotch, Jaguars, and faultless tailoring, most of your consumer goods take their marketing cue from America. Although Dominion is the world's largest tobacco combine, the fastest-selling cigarette brand is aggressively American. *Marlboro*. Have you ever stopped to ask yourselves why?'

'Ted,' the chairman interrupted. 'This has *nothing* to do with the story leak.'

The committee murmured in agreement.

Ted was on his feet. 'It has everything to do with it! We have to stop acting like old women with each new product launch. Playing things to the book. Being tentative. Coy. Lifting the hem of our skirts to Parliament and the press. Doing what the trade has been accustomed to for the last thirty years!'

Board members began to shift uncomfortably in their chairs. When Ted got going there was no stopping him.

'We failed with *Catch* because we were overcautious,' he continued. 'We trickled that brand onto the market like an apology for a cigarette. If we hadn't we could have weathered *any* criticism. *Yerba Sacra* is going to start at the top.' He cleared his throat. 'We have the market's ear, let's make use of it. I propose we bring the launch date forward.'

The boardroom remained silent.

The committee was still smarting from Ted's outburst.

Jolyon Williams, his face a mask of contempt, exchanged

glances with Alun Hughes.

Ted caught the look and paused. Alun had once been his staunch ally on the board. But after yesterday even that support had cooled. Alun didn't like other people messing up his strictly organized public relations schedule, turning the press office upside down. The personal clash was only a part of it.

Ted realized that he was totally alone. He picked up the nearest telephone and dialed the chairman's assistant, Henry Peach, to find out the latest share price. He replaced the receiver slowly. 'Gentlemen,' he said, 'the share price has risen by ten pence in the few hours since the stock exchange opened its doors. Ten pence!' He paused, addressing each one in turn. 'If this isn't why we are in business together, then will one of you explain what we are doing here?'

18

The midday editions of the evening papers carried the story on their front pages. 'The World at One' invited Ted in for a live interview, and he was also scheduled for a slot on the six o'clock TV news programme. One of the tabloids sent a photographer along to shoot him running down the steps of Dominion House.

Action on Smoking and Health, the antismoking pressure group, issued its usual guarded statement: 'We welcome any move that is made to reduce the harmful effects of smoking.' But as the product wasn't yet available for general examination, the ASH spokesman didn't elaborate.

The share price continued to rise through the day. The financial sections of two dailies decided to lead on the story for the following morning.

But some members of the Dominion executive committee retreated behind a wall of silence, stung and angered by Mallett's anti-British remarks. It was bad enough seeing him running the show. Jolyon Williams moved from office to office on the executive floor all day, rallying support, pandering, reviving old grievances to top the morning's outburst.

Outwardly, Courtland remained aloof. It wasn't his role to get excited by the day's happenings, or to indulge Williams's politics. But he felt a bitter sense of disappointment, not only in Ted, but in Alun Hughes as well. Indirectly he blamed his PR director for what had happened. 'You wanted Ted exposed to the media to restore public confidence in us Alun,' he said crisply. 'It's up to you to see this is handled responsibly by the press.

Wherever possible, telephone calls to Ted were rerouted to a thoroughly briefed team of press officers who read out pat company statements. 'No, a launch date hasn't been set. No, we are unable to give you a name. No, the chairman is not issuing a formal statement.'

But, inevitably, the occasional call slipped through. Ted's assistant, Manna Henderson was away from the office for two minutes during the afternoon, and he picked up the phone to hear the voice of an irate switchboard operator. 'Mr. Mallet, would you take this call please, sir. It's your wife and she says your private line has been busy all day.'

Ted smiled. 'Yes, of course. Put her through. Hi, honey!'

There was a brief pause. 'Actually, it's Jill Norstad from *Media*. It was the only way I could reach you.'

He laughed. He had liked the way she fired questions at him during the luncheon. The expression in her green eyes told him she knew exactly when he was bullshitting. The effect was disquieting, but he enjoyed it. There was something pleasingly crisp and orderly about the girl. He said, flirtatiously, 'I might have guessed it was you!'

The journalist was in no mood for a coy conversation. 'They want me to do a profile on you for this week's edition,' she said briskly. 'The copy has to be in by last night. Can you spare me ten minutes?' Dry, hurried, efficient.

Ted glanced at his watch. 'Why don't you hop in a cab and come on over?'

Norstad sounded exasperated. 'Because the cab ride would take thirty minutes' interviewing time. How did the board react to the news? What is your launch date? Is Kestner McKay handling the account along with *Denim*. What is your launch budget? Is this an exclusively British launch, or are there plans to do a simultaneous launch in America?'

Ted spent nearly twenty minutes dodging most of the questions, some more successfully than others. She was adept at trick questions. He tried to edge the conversation back to his own marketing expertise and switch from professional football into advertising. He could hear rapid typing on the other end of the phone.

'Fine,' she said, anxiously watching the second hand race around the clock. 'I'll flesh this out with the material from yesterday. Thanks.'

'Can't I buy you a drink after work?' asked Ted.

'No. Really. Thanks anyway. I have two stories to chase after this.'

But Ted wasn't going to be put off. He liked adversaries. 'How about Friday night? I'm taking Tony McKay and some of the agency people to Ronnie Scott's. Why don't you join us?'

There was a moment's silence. Her journalist's mind visualized a handful of stories, apart from the current topic. There was nothing like a group of advertising people unwinding after a busy week for catching up on agency gossip. 'Super,' she said briskly. 'What time are you meeting? Nine? Ten?'

Across the river, Tessa Courtland read the various news reports and telephoned the stock exchange. The news and the frenzied reponse had bolstered her decision to move there and then against Dominion.

Between them, she and Ciaran had gathered enough information against the company not to make the timing premature. She would prepare the writ straightaway. Normally a writ was a last-ditch stand following months of correspondence and fruitless meetings between opposing solicitors. But Tessa wasn't known for going by the book. In this case, she also knew her opponent. She was now more determined than ever to see Dominion in court.

Her prior reluctance to move so swiftly after Anderson's death was personal. Brigid Anderson had closed herself away, the funeral was scheduled within a few days. There had seemed no point in tampering with fresh wounds. But now, the news was doing that anyway.

She telephoned Ciaran at work. 'The writ will be ready for you tomorrow morning. Let me know exactly when you'll serve it on the company. I'll need to talk to my father about it of course.'

Ciaran whistled through his teeth. 'Anderson's hardly cold, Tessa.'

'Multiply him by a few hundred smoking-related deaths every day and pit your figures against Dominion's escalating share price,' she said angrily. 'I'm treating this like a murder case.'

Ciaran pursed his lips thoughtfully. He had wanted a test case, not a crusade. 'We don't have to go this far, you know,' he said gently. 'It would be enough to blow the whistle at this stage. A word in a few relevant ears in Fleet Street, some copies of the autopsy report, one or two statements from Anderson's mates. . . .'

'Are you asking me to back down?'

Ciaran smiled. 'I'm giving you the opportunity to make a graceful retreat.'

'Do you know what you are?' Tessa said bluntly.

'What?'

'A bloody scab.'

'Curb your peasant tongue, woman. I don't want a baptism by fire.'

Tessa ignored him. 'Does Brigid have any immediate financial worries?' she asked.

'Don't patronize her, Tessa.'

'I'm just being practical. She'll never know the source. Why don't you take her and the children over to Ireland after the funeral for a few weeks? I'll send you a cheque.'

Ciaran sighed. It would be wise to have the family out of London when news of the writ was made public, save them from a lot of prowling newsmen. And he hadn't seen Dublin for over a year. He could arrange to meet the families of some of his clients currently serving prison sentences in Britain. There was no emotional complication or loss of pride involved where Tessa's money was concerned. She made it sound like a public fund that was there for the cause. Quite unrelated to her personally. He accepted the offer.

'One last thing,' Tessa said briskly. 'I'd like you to set up a private meeting with George Samiou of ASH.'

Ted was too involved in his sudden and unexpected honeymoon with the media to notice that Colette's thoughts were distracted. She watched his reactions from the wings. She had lived through his frenzied highs and lows before, advancing or retreating where necessary. But this was different. She'd never seen him like this. She preferred to sit it out, not wanting to philosophize too deeply.

Tessa was capable of extremes and Colette needed extremes. She had once found that excitement in Ted, but he held no mystery for her any longer. She was saddened by the thought.

She uttered not one word of this to Tessa. It had nothing to do with the two of them. The subject of Ted and Colette remained upspoken between them.

There were many things about Tessa she would never know or change.

Tessa was finding that her idle thoughts were becoming equally absorbed with Colette.

She found the sculptor soothing, pleasingly mystical, but was afraid of expressing too much, too soon.

She had mentioned the pending court case in a few brusque sentences, knowing Colette would hear about it sooner of later.

Only a few months before Colette had listened to Ted expressing something of his own conflicts with Dominion.

'Between us,' she said, 'Dominion is taboo.'

'Why?' asked Tessa, 'Does Ted confide in you? About Dominion, I mean?'

'I am not Ted's conscience and neither will I be yours.'

Questioning her further would be pointless. So she conceded, reluctantly. If she confused the borders between love and law, she'd end up destroying both.

Tessa knew her father's reaction wouldn't be philisophical. But she had hoped to be able to discuss the matter on something of a professional footing. The least she expected was a reaction of some concern from the chairman.

He peered down in disbelief at the writ. Without even glancing at his daughter, he said: 'Am I to understand that this is the result of our clash in the Tabac Club?'

Tessa faced him across the desk in amazement. 'Do you

know so little about me that you think I would resort to my profession to resolve a family discord?'

'Discord? What discord? Good God, Tessa. I know we've had our little differences from time to time, but then what family hasn't, I ask you?' Courtland rose, ignoring the writ, and walked around the desk to the leather chair opposite her. 'I really can't take this seriously,' he said, sitting down.

Father and daughter studied one another.

Courtland was the first to speak: 'My father would have used his horsewhip on me if I had dared to cross him.'

Tessa looked away. 'Don't resort to that sort of argument with me,' she said casually. 'It didn't work when I was thirteen and it certainly doesn't now.'

'My dear girl. I'm talking about your *duty*!'

Tessa got up and walked across to the window. How long was it going to take to reach him? she wondered. She stared across the Thames. 'I am not here as your daughter,' she said slowly, 'but as a member of the Middle Temple. It would be morally indefensible if I continued to fight cases of criminal negligence in industry and chose to ignore those I discovered with Dominion.'

Courtland snorted dismissively. 'I'm certain the benchers at the Middle Temple would find this most irregular, if not unlawful.'

'The benchers are not the landlords of my conscience.'

'But Tessa, if there's something that angers or upsets you personally, why can't we iron it out between us like two civilized adults? I can't believe you intend pursuing this ridiculous farce. The case would be thrown out of court within hours.' Courtland reached across the desk for his briar pipe and began to fill it. His hands were shaking, but his daughter was facing away and didn't notice. He looked up at her back and the defiant set of her shoulders and glanced away quickly, concentrating on lighting his pipe. 'I don't wish to see you make a bloody fool of yourself in court,' he said curtly, searching for his lighter.

She turned away from the window. 'There's nothing more to discuss then, is there?'

'Nothing? But we haven't even begun. You still haven't told me why you are placing some tobacco worker you've never met and probably couldn't care less about over and above your family. The blood in your veins is the lifeblood of this company. Does that mean nothing to you, nothing at all?' Courtland spoke rapidly and angrily, gesturing in the air with his lighter.

Tessa reached for her coat. 'Why on earth should it? And even if it did, why should that oblige me to ignore criminal negligence? You are asking me to be a conspirator. Now, the benchers would find *that* unlawful.'

Courtland waved the air impatiently. 'Oh, do sit down, Tessa.' he said.

She obeyed, although there really didn't seem to be much point. She knew he was resorting to 'honour' and 'family tradition' simply because he was at a loss for any other form of argument. It was clearly quite inconceivable to him that a Harmer-Courtland should choose to challenge Dominion in public. The subject of the writ wasn't even discussed. Courtland flatly refused to see this as other than a personal attack on him.

Tessa attempted to direct the conversation towards the legal aspects of the case, but Courtland was rude and dismissive. It was almost as though he didn't believe a James Anderson had ever existed. As though he was just some figment of his daughter's revengeful imagination. 'This will destroy your mother. Finally push her over the edge. You know that, don't you?' he said viciously.

Recalling their recent telephone conversation, Tessa replied coolly, 'Mother already knows.'

'*God*,' he said, rising angrily out of the chair. He turned to face the wall and held his head in his hands. First Ted, and now this. 'You realize I'll have to offer my resignation to the board.'

'That's your decision,' she said quietly. 'But remember, none of this would have happened if you'd had a little more concern for the men on the shop floor.'

By the time Courtland turned around she had gone.

Courtland's offer of resignation was rejected by a large majority

204

on the board.

'Charles,' said deputy chairman Jolyon Williams loyally, 'you know your own daughter better than anyone. Our own solicitors couldn't have a more valuable client than the father of the opposition.'

The boardroom reverberated with shouts of 'Hear, hear.'

It gave Williams a perverse sense of satisfaction to be able to pit Courtland against his own family, to make that a condition of his remaining at the Dominion helm.

But Courtland missed the motive and was moved by the support. He had presented himself as a grieved and baffled father and gained immediate sympathy. Several board members could identify with him.

Only the younger members were a little sceptical. Initially, the impact of Tessa Courtland's move against the group far outweighed the actual content of the writ.

Ted, who was still riding a euphoric high, didn't even relate it to his own conspiratorial dealings with Lawrence in the research lab. His immediate reaction was to shrug the whole thing off as misguided radicalism. *Media* had profiled him that day, and the feature was uppermost in his mind. It had referred to him as 'Dominion's man with a megaphone,' and analyzed the herbal cigarette news against a flattering background of his American and British marketing successes. Jill Norstad used appropriate football imagery to talk about his ability to zigzag deftly between the advertising code and public criticism. Her feature was snide and cutting in parts. She described him as the executive who 'dresses like a *Lambert and Butler* advertisement,' talks like a '*Marlboro* cowboy,' and behaves as though he 'invented tobacco,' but concluded that anything was a refreshing change after the mountain of silence that had surrounded Dominion for years.

Ted didn't find the remarks hurtful. On the contrary.

The share price was still rising. Even if certain board members sniffed and looked away when he passed them in the corridors, Ted was convinced the publicity was the best thing to hit the company for years. Anyone who brought about change could expect resentment from the bureaucrats.

So, Courtland's surprise announcement didn't deflate him one bit. Like many members of the board, he saw the case as a family feud, but shared none of the sympathy expressed in the boardroom. He had seen Courtland in action against his daughter and was neither surprised nor alarmed at what Tessa had done.

At the same time, he sensed this was a good moment to square things with the chairman in public. He still felt rattled and annoyed about Courtland's reaction to the press leak. He was aware of the hostility towards him in the room. This was a good time to regain some ground with the board.

He took advantage of a reflective pause in the meeting to offer his own harsh judgement. 'Before we drown oursleves in tears, gentlemen, there is something we should consider.' Pointing an accusing finger at Charles Courtland, he said, 'How do we know that the chairman hasn't been discussing confidential company business with his daughter?'

There was a roar of disapproval. Courtland looked appalled. He stared at Ted for several long moments before answering. 'I believe the board is fully aware of which of us is capable of a public indiscretion.'

A loud consensus rose from the table.

But Ted wasn't thrown by the remark. He smiled slowly and said, 'The share performance will decide which of us has acted in the interest of the *company*, at a risk to his own popularity in this boardroom.' He paused, adding, 'Let the share price be the final judge between us, Charles.'

The board studied the two men uncomfortably. This was no longer simply a feud between Courtland and his daughter, but between Courtland and Mallett as well.

Suddenly, Mallett's and Courtland's traditional styles were in open and direct confrontation.

Where moments before personal sympathies had come down heavily in favor of Courtland, the mood of the board was beginning to shift. Even those board members who resented Ted's sudden catapult into the limelight were being forced to swallow their feelings. The issue was emerging clearly as one of personal feelings being weighed against the good of the company.

Alun Hughes hadn't felt much sympathy for the chairman from the start. Like Ted, he wondered if Courtland had unwittingly revealed snippets of classified material to his daughter. It was so easy to do that in a relaxed moment during a family weekend. Radicals like Tessa Courtland were never really off duty. It was possible her ear had caught the tail end of some after dinner remark casually uttered by Courtland over a glass of port.

No one was completely above suspicion as far as company security was concerned.

Alun caught Ted's eye. At least Mallett was forthright and open about everything, even his ruddy bunglings. The chairman could be overenigmatic at times.

Jolyon Williams didn't waver for a second. The prospect of seeing Courtland turn against Mallett, and vice versa, was immensely gratifying, an added bonus. His sandy moustache twitched with anticipation.

From behind his highly polished spectacles, financial director Paul Lombard reviewed the shifting expressions around the table, giving little hint of his own feelings. Like Courtland he shared strong family links with Dominion and had a great respect for company tradition. But there was an adventurous streak in him, too. Being the architect of Dominion's most recent and highly profitable acquisition policy, he was active in fields outside and beyond the strict confines of the tobacco world. That gave him something of an outsider's objectivity. He visualized Dominion's future in continued diversification away from the tobacco base. Like Mallett, he was inclined to judge controversial matters in terms of their profit value to the group. A director couldn't afford to be flabby. Personal sentiments had to be kept in their place.

There were times when he didn't altogether approve of Mallett's flamboyance, but Lombard liked Ted's business style and the way Ted consulted him, and Lombard was shrewd enough to respect the fact that 'new products' was one of the most profitable and tightly run divisions in the group. The current flurry in the stock exchange wouldn't last, of course, but it did indicate an immediate and encouraging public response to innovation within the industry. It confirmed his support of Ted's scheme for additional research facilities for young Dr. Lawrence.

Whatever the tobacco diehards on the board may have said about sticking to their guns and not giving into public pressure, he knew that no new tobacco product would ever have the same exhilarating effect on the stock exchange and the media as the leaked information on *Yerba Sacra*. So, in his own mind, he placed his support behind Mallett.

'Fitz' Fitzgerald felt differently. The director of overseas subsidiaries, tall, craggy, towering over the table like a massive cliff, had never approved of Ted's third world policy, believing his fellow director was politically naïve in that area.

He had felt personally slighted when Mallett ignored his advice concerning the cultivation of yerba sacra. So he stood behind the chairman and Jolyon Williams.

Conservative MP Nigel Swan, one of the nonexecutive members of the board, backed Mallett. Fellow Members of Parliament were responding enthusiastically to Dominion's willingness to keep searching for a successful tobacco substitute. And Mallett was the reason for that.

Research director Noel Sorensen, slack-mouthed, overweight, heavily tanned after two weeks with Dominion's subsidiaries in the West Indies, backed the chairman. Secretly, he didn't like the way Mallett had quietly rallied Lombard's and Hughes's support to set Dr. Lawrence up in a separate research project. If he was truly honest with himself, he knew he was jealous that Mallett, a nonscientist, had seen the opportunity, and he hadn't. But now, if the legal matter in hand was going to expose the research division and the labs to scrutiny, he wanted the chairman and deputy chairman behind him.

Other members of the board carefully weighed up the advantages and disadvantages, eyeing the faces of their colleagues for clues to their loyalty. Although a clear majority ended up backing Courtland, it was the minority with real clout in the group that eventually decided in favour of Mallett.

And this in spite of the writ's detailed accusation of criminal negligence taking place with the *Yerba Sacra* project. The involvement of the chairman's daughter caused everyone to view the writ itself with scepticism.

'She knows it would be pointless suing us on the basis of a so-called smoking-related death,' said Courtland. 'She knows well enough that not a single case of that kind has been heard in Britain, and that similar cases have been singularly unsuccessful in America. So she's cooked up this other charge.

'Noel,' he said, turning to the research director. 'Is it conveivable that this Stevenson fellow of Anderson or whatever he calls himself could possibly have had lung cancer during the consumer tests on yerba sacra in the laboratory?'

Sorensen affronted, shook his head. 'The idea is grotesque and preposterous. We conduct the most careful medical examinations on our volunteers. I haven't even heard of the man until now. What did you say his name was? George Anderson?'

'*James* Anderson,' Courtland said, reading the name slowly. 'Writ comes from his wife, Brigid Lucy Anderson.'

Sorensen shrugged. 'We must have dealt with dozens of volunteers. We can't be expected to know them all by name.' He was conscious of the board's attention.

Those members who had originally been dismissive of the writ, believing it would be resolved between Courtland and his daughter, leaned forward. The charge was ludicrous. But Sorensen looked uneasy. Why?

Jolyon Williams, who was head of the tobacco division as well as being deputy chairman, took command of the situation. He gestured toward Ted. 'This really isn't Dr. Sorensen's territory, it's *yours* Mallett, isn't it? Anything to do with *Yerba Sacra* is your domain.'

But Ted wasn't going to be thrown that easily by Williams. 'I leave the strictly technical side of my projects to experts like Dr. Sorensen and his excellent team, and I respect their recommendations,' he said, resorting to the formal and nodding toward the research director. 'There has never been any doubt in my mind that the research team has been other than dedicated and strictly mindful of how the required tests had to be carried out.'

A murmured agreement circulated the table. Sorensen acknowledged the praise.

Ted continued. 'If I didn't have the utmost faith in Dr. Sorensen's skills, I wouldn't have agreed to the establishment of the experimental project under one of his subordinates. Dr. Lawrence.'

Suddenly an image of the biochemist switching the mice with his pudgy fingers swung into view. Ted closed his eyes and bent his head. The room began to swirl around him.

He avoided the various pairs of eyes that were fixed on him by tapping out estimates and scribbling down a line of figures. 'Noel,' he said, studying the sheet of paper, 'the Tait Committee has cleared all the required tests on *Yerba Sacra*, hasn't it? I mean, they haven't come up with any special requests?'

The research director shook his head. 'The project passed all tests with flying colours.' He addressed the board. 'Members of the committee were most impressed with the care and attention to detail they observed in the lab,' he said emphatically.

Ted checked his figures. 'Well then, gentlemen,' he said, skilfully shifting the emphasis of the discussion, 'I propose we bring the launch even closer. We'll go into test market in London early this fall. We'll put production on double time. All it will mean is that we delay going national.'

Reactions ranging from surprise to outrage filled the boardroom.

The chairman tried to calm everyone down.

Jolyon Williams flushed with hostility. 'You must be mad, Mallett,' he said rudely. 'There's no saying how far the chairman's daughter will go to discredit the company. We could have a court case on our hands by the autumn. Your proposal is improper, cynical, and highly suspect.'

Several directors voiced their agreement. Only Alun

Hughes and Paul Lombard watched Mallett's face with curious interest.

Ted looked at Williams. 'You seem to be forgetting something, Williams,' he said pointedly. 'Way back in 1962 when I was still playing football, and you were managing director of the Mace Tobacco Company, you went ahead and launched *Mace Filter* in the same year the Royal College of Physicians issued their report, *Smoking and Health.*'

Williams rose angrily, but Ted waved away his objections. Those directors who were associated with the company at the time nodded in agreement. The launch was still regarded as something of a classic in tobacco marketing. *Mace Filter* was a heavily advertised, coupon-linked brand that hit the market like a rocket late in '62 and was brand leader with over twenty precent of the market under its belt by '65.

It was still regarded as an outstanding case study. There was a far more profound reason for it success than simply giving the consumer additional value for money via coupons at a time when smokers were battling against steep prices rises.

The RCP report, *Smoking and Health*, gave a hefty boost to the swing to filter tips, in the same way that the college's second report, *Smoking and Health Now*, of 1971, gave a boost to low-tar, low-nicotine brands, and the third report, *Smoking Or Health*, of 1977, boosted tobacco substitutes.

The logic that persuaded Williams and his team to go ahead with the planned launch of *Mace Filter* in the year of the first RCP report was a precise reflection of industry philosophy. First, spokesmen denounced the indictment against smoking by saying that the medical research was inadequate and that there was a growing body of evidence highlighting the pharmacological and psychological merits of smoking. Second, the industry was aware that at the time of the report the majority of ex-smokers had abandoned the habit for reasons of cost, not health. What better way to encompass all marketing factors than through a coupon-linked filter tip brand?

When the government woke up to the effect *Mace Filter* and subsequent coupon brands were having on the market and attempted to impose a coupon ban, the industry responded with fury. Statistics were wielded to show that ten thousand jobs were at stake. The chairman of a rival group used a unique twist of logic to explain that coupon brands actually kept consumption down. Banning coupons, he warned, would result in a lowering of prices that would inevitably increase cigarette consumption. The ban never came about.

The antismoking lobby didn't fall for the industry's unique interpretation of economics and was still battling for a coupon ban. But *Mace Filter* continued to hold its market position.

The modern tobacco business, as the tobacco diehards in the boardroom well knew, built its marketing policy around the chain reaction sparked off and consolidated by the political climate of the day. New brands reflected that policy. They brought their own defence with them. When the second RCP report boosted a flurry of low-tar, low-nicotine brands, the industry used this development to defend itself against further advertising restrictions. How can we inform the public properly about low-tar brands, they argued, if you insist on imposing advertising restrictions? Thus curbs on advertising were presented as being against the public interest.

A rival group launched *John Player Special* in a black packet in the same year that the report, *Smoking and Health Now*, was released. *Catch* was launched within months of the publication of *Smoking Or Health*. Meeting the tide of criticism with a new, confident brand was fast becoming an industry hallmark.

So Ted's proposal to hasten the *Yerba Sacra* launch to ride in on the tails of the court case made sound commercial sense. It would also exploit the current tide of goodwill generated by the new leak.

'It would show the smoking public that we have utmost confidence in the brand and aren't bothered by the pettiness of a law suit,' said Ted, addressing each board member by turn. 'We'll even go as far as saying in our advertisements that the brand was developed to reduce the health risk some medical authorities associate with smoking. Hell,' he said imploringly, 'if we *don't* launch it, now that the public has heard something about it, we imply hesitation, a loss of confidence in oursleves and our research.

The chairman listened, carefully noting the varied reactions circulating the table.

After a few reflective moments, he said, 'I had hoped my daughter and I might sort this out between us. At the worst I anticipated that we might settle out of court.

Ted raised his hand and glanced at Alun Hughes. 'Correct me if I'm wrong here, Alun. But wouldn't you advise us to avoid any action that might indicate a guilt complex? Sweeping the issue under the carpet, delaying the launch would do that. Right?'

Hughes nodded and looked at the chairman.

Courtland raised his eyebrows and took a deep breath. They were suggesting that Dominion take a dismissive view of the writ, treat it as an insignificant item. Well, that part could best be decided by their own legal advisors. But, use the writ as a reason for launching the brand? He turned to Jolyon Williams for a reaction.

Williams shrugged. 'Tobacco substitutes have nothing to do with me.' he said sourly.

Ted folded his arms on the table. 'Mr. Chairman,' he said, 'your daughter is trying to find mud in a cup of clear water. It's likely the media will dance to her tune for a while. We can't ignore that possibility. The only way we can prove there is no mud is to launch *Yerba Sacra* with a bang. Nothing tentative. No compromising anywhere.'

Courtland passed the matter over to the board. 'Gentlemen. Shall we take a vote on this? Those in favour of launching the brand in the autumn?'

A number of arms shot up.

'Those against?'

Jolyon Williams was the first to raise his hand.

The chairman counted the hands and looked across at Ted. 'Your proposal has been approved by two votes,' he said dubiously, silently wondering at the ability of the board to change allegiances so quickly.

The meeting broke up in near buoyancy. The men had found a constructive way out of a delicate situation by choosing a route familiar to the industry.

It was now time to select an appropriate legal committee and set the wheels in motion for a discreet internal inquiry into the content of the writ.

The chairman instructed the heads of the appropriate divisions to let it be known generally that anyone who contacted his daughter or her legal colleagues would be dismissed instantly.

19

Ultimately, the advertising team had decided to use the young drummer discovered by Tony McKay.

As the advertisements had to be finalized, media space reserved, and the commercial shot through the summer at breakneck speed, Ted offered appealing incentives to the team to readjust their holiday plans. The arrangements, and his obsessive personal involvement, kept him on an all-time high.

Only in moments of extreme weariness did he allow himself to face the reality of the problem. Uncertainty about whether or not the pending court case would expose his conspiracy with Lawrence left him alternately panic-stricken and coolly rational. He avoided discussing the matter with the biochemist, preferring to act as though the incident had never taken place. All incriminating evidence had been destroyed: mice, reports, everything. The research data had been cleared. What was there to worry about? If the unforeseen happened, hell, at least he'd go down at the height of the game. He'd played football like that and was damned if he was going to pussyfoot in business. This time he was going to hold on to the ball and run for the touchdown himself. He'd be remembered for the yardage covered even if the sweating meat on the field sacked him a foot from the line.

Of necessity, Ted forced himself to believe there was no possible way anyone could connect the results from the mice-painting experiments with the content of the law suit.

Lawrence had fiddled with only a small portion of the research. And perhaps, in retrospect, they had erred on the side of caution. Perhaps it hadn't been necessary at all.

During those moments when he wasn't completely immersed in *Yerba Sacra*, Ted had Jill Norstad to fill his thoughts. He shared a drunken tussle with her on the floor of her flat after the evening at Ronnie Scott's, and was excited to discover that her hostility quickly developed into sexual intensity. She was rude and snide about him in print, and he was determined to have her as a way of balancing things out. She wasn't the sort of woman he could conquer in the traditional sense. On the contrary. He was convinced she kept a notebook and pencil by her side all the time, ready to take advantage of any casual slip of the tongue. Starting an affair with her, yet being conscious the whole time of never allowing himself to be caught off guard, was a completely new challenge.

He was also enjoying her, and her enjoyment of him, immensely. There were moments with Jill when his body felt both exhilarating and exhilarated. He loved it when she would sprawl across his thighs with her body at a right angle to his, and love him with her hands, mouth, and breasts. The sensuous way she caressed him with her fingers reminded him swiftly, succinctly, of what it was that made him notice her during their first meeting at the press lunch. The way her fingers moved and looked when she handled a pen. A totally unselfconscious and totally arousing sight.

Jill didn't have Colette's coolness or sophistication but Colette didn't have Jill's knowledge of the agency world, and he needed that at the moment. There was something very gratifying about the was they could lie and talk to one another after they made love. They exchanged snippets of gossip about people they both knew, about disastrous campaigns, about the all-time classic campaigns, about a particular product's use of the media, and how they would vary it if given the account. It made Ted feel good. Jill was a sparring partner and he revelled in that.

Colette could see what was happening to Ted, but trying to stop him or slow him down was as senseless as trying to stop a whirlpool or a hurricane. He had to be allowed to run his course.

Their home life quickly adjusted to the new situation. Ted and Colette exchanged greetings and sentences on the stairs or in the sitting room like brother and sister. Polite, affectionate, but not really involved with one another. There was no tension. Communication was hurried, practical. 'We're out of coffee. Could you buy a couple of tins on the way home?' or, 'It's all right. I paid the electricity bill last week.'

With the warmer days, Ted was rising before six regularly and jogging to work, whether from his own home or Jill's. Colette ordered a new shipment of clay and spent a couple of days going at it like a boxer at a punchingbag. She began to spend more time with Tessa, using the mornings, when Tessa was at her chambers, to wander up and down the canal sketching Victorian bridges and ironwork, factory barges and the men who operated them.

When Ciaran returned to London with Brigid Anderson, Tessa began to construct the case with as much vigour and energy as Ted was putting into the *Yerba Sacra* launch.

Dominion kept silent. When news of the writ first broke, Alun Hughes issued a curt statement saying the charges were completely baseless. The chairman was unavailable for comment, and so were all the directors. Brigid Anderson wasn't around to give her story. The press wasn't aware of the involvement of the chairman's daughter because the name of the barrister was rarely, if ever, reported. If any legal advisor was sought for comment, it was usually the solicitor.

Tessa wanted it that way. She needed to avoid gossip columnists and speculative excesses in order to have the freedom and privacy to prepare for court. Barristers were a remote breed at the best of times. She couldn't avoid the inevitability of press discovery, but rather later than sooner. This was the summer silly season now. Fleet Street's senses were tuned to holiday plans, weekends by the sea. But she knew she was playing for time. *Private Eye* was bound to wake up to the news long before the case reached the Royal Courts of Justice.

Tessa had not spoken to her father since the day she left him facing the bookshelf in his office. Formalities were left to Ciaran and Dominion's solicitors. She had, however, taken the time to sit down with her mother and talk about it. But Daphne had barely responded. 'What you must do, you must do,' she

217

said with a shrug. 'Your father feels bitter and humiliated, but that's your father.' Then, standing up and smoothing down her skirt, Daphne had said, 'Have you seen the exquisite croci on the lawn?'

Yet for all her unpredictability and periods of distraction, Tessa found her mother remarkably saner than at any other time. It was as though the action had given her some new purpose.

Tessa knew that if the case was going to make any impact at all beyond the obvious family scandal, she couldn't depend solely on the medical arguments. The numerous suits brought against the industry in America had been structured around medical issues. To date, all had failed. For one very simple reason. The victim had chosen to smoke of his own free will. Cigarettes weren't prescribed.

Free will. The words rang hollow somehow. Anyone who understood the barest elements of mass advertising and promotion knew that. Free will was a malleable commodity like everything else.

But there had to be more than that. This wasn't simply an isolated death. It had to be viewed within the context of the morality of the industry.

And there she was on tricky ground. Any argument she raised was going to be assessed by the judge within the framework of her blood tie with the company. She couldn't escape that. So nothing could appear as a personal gripe. If it did, she would lose. She had to scale and skewer Dominion with an icy detachment. History was going to help her.

The medical issue was, of course, central to the case, and how she presented it was crucial. The more demonstrative evidence she could present the better. For once she regretted the absence of juries at cases like this. Convincing a lone judge could sometimes be infinitely more difficult than convincing a jury of twelve.

A jury was a useful barometer in court. A counsel could quickly sound them out just by reading their changing facial expressions. But judges were the epitome of the legal establishment. Most of them in the High Courts were elderly and their views were often deeply rooted. Their earliest experience of the lower classes was often in terms of nannies, house servants and gardeners. Some of them looked askance at socialism and militant trade unionism because it was a direct threat to the system of which they were a ruling part.

In a sense, Tessa knew, she would be on trial, along with Dominion. The judge would want to know that had driven her to such extremes. She was too old for this to be considered simply an act of rebellion, child against parent. She had to make their crime appear indefensible. Her own position had to be seen as a sincere act of conscience, bravely outweighing the family consequences. Convincing the judge was of paramount importance. At no time must she be seen as an abrasive radical exploiting the case for a well-publicized blow against the establishment. Instead Dominion had to be presented as an institution that 'simply wasn't playing cricket.' A shrewd portrayal of the facts would show how Dominion overstepped its paternalist role in society by taking advantage of an employee who had placed his trust in the company. Visualized in those patriarchal terms, the argument would be kept within the rules of the establishment. All Marxist arguments had to be avoided. This wasn't a company exploiting the workers. This was a landlord who hadn't taken sufficient time and care to heed the health and welfare of his serfs.

At all times, Tessa knew, she had to appear as the conscience, and not the enemy, of the establishment. She used this as a guideline in the selection of her medical witnesses. Appropriately authoritative voices would be called to support a solid presentation of demonstrative evidence.

During her first meeting with the young director of ASH. George Samiou, London-born son of Greek immigrants, she asked him to list the most eminent medical men in Britain who were involved in the antismoking issue. 'I want no radical junior hospital doctors,' she emphasized. 'I want the kings of the Royal College of Physicians, knighted academics, the most exalted men from within the medical establishment. I want impecabble accents and pedigrees.'

Samiou, nicknamed 'Socrates' by the tobacco industry, had no difficulty drawing up such a list. They agreed that he himself should be kept out of the front line of the case. For obvious political reasons, she shouldn't be seen siding with the enemy of the industry. But he would act as a principal consultant on the case, supplying facts, suggesting angles, acting as an important sounding board.

Samiou was loathed by the industry, a David to their Goliath. In a matter of a few years he had raised public and political consciousness on the antismoking issues, got the advertising code tightened, pestered sympathetic MPs to move on new legislative measures against the industry. He had also succeeded in stunting promotional campaigns that conflicted with the code and had had four new brands removed from test market on grounds of unsuitability.

The slight, dark-haired young man worked with Zenlike dedication, spent his limited spare time competing in chess championships and had few close friends.

He studied Britain's class structure and the ruling elements like an anthropologist might study a tribe of the fourth world, analyzing attitude, customs, and learning the language en route.

This was what really annoyed the executives of the tobacco industry. They couldn't dismiss him as some long-haired Trotskyite. He appeared at annual general meetings on the strength of his token share for the purpose of asking disquieting questions from the floor. He wore a freshly pressed three-piece suit, conservative tie, and had his hair neatly trimmed for the occasion. An eminent heart specialist or chest surgeon was often by his side.

Even so, meeting Tessa Courtland was a unique experience.

Earlier in the year, Charles Courtland had summoned him to the Dominion boardroom for a private 'man-to-man' chat prior to the annual general meeting. The chairman had been affable, confidential and called him 'George.' The purpose of the meeting was clear from the start. Courtland offered to answer any questions the ASH director might have prepared for the AGM, in an off-the-cuff open discussion. In short he was trying to offer the man from ASH twenty minutes of his own thoughts in exchange for a peaceful AGM. But Samiou didn't fall for the tactic. He politely refused the subtle *quid pro quo*. At the AGM he went ahead, asked his uncomfortable questions and enraged the shareholders.

All media reports of the company's AGMs carried items about the bantering between Samiou on the floor and the directors on the platform. Courtland would issue statements about Samiou's 'courtesy' and his 'regret' that they weren't fighting on the same side. And then, in a radio interview, when Samiou wasn't there to defend himself, would proceed to gut ASH as a group of 'misinformed do-gooders' who 'deliberately mislead the public with carefully selected facts that grossly distort the truth.'

Now, facing Courtland's daughter, George Samiou was both unsettled and curious. She looked and walked like her father, tall and purposeful. But she referred to her father curtly as 'the chairman,' and didn't find it necessary to explain her reasons for being on the case. Samiou didn't ask.

When she consulted him about suitable medical witnesses to put on the stand he nodded wisely. 'You would like the sort of gentlemen who might have attended the same type of school as the judge, and might conceivably meet him socially, at a club perhaps.'

'Yes,' said Tessa. 'Precisely. But not too uniform, mind. Add a dash of eccentricity somewhere along the line. Brilliant and establishment, but good and fruity, without being a buffoon. I believe in a little entertainment for the judge. Carefully selected, of course. Helps break the monotony and it provides a useful impact. Think about it.'

'Yes, madam,' said the man from ASH in all seriousness, licking the point of his pencil and scribbling down the order like the banquet manager of a large hotel.

Tessa smiled at him. Neither of them was giving too much away, but they were clearly on the same wavelength.

Ciaran was given the task of following leads chasing exhibits, researching details, preparing witnesses from amongst Anderson's friends, and boosting Brigid Anderson's morale.

It wasn't so much the fact of losing the great love of her life. Jimmy wasn't easy at the best of times. Nursing him could be hell. In some ways, he had had the easier share of the bargain. She was burned out, but she would cope. Although it stuck in her craw, she stoically accepted state aid as a temporary measure until she could find work and make suitable arrangements for the children. The important thing was to keep the family together.

It was her husband's subservience that had infuriated her. Lying there, accepting it all. Afraid of what Dominion might do to them if Ciaran took legal action on their behalf. Refusing to discuss it with her, saying she 'didn't bleeding understand' and, 'Ciaran and I will decide what's best for you and the children.'

If anything made her determined to stick with the case, it was to prove Jimmy wrong. For the first time since her marriage, she was making the decisions. Even if she made a mistake at least she would find that out for herself. But she had to do more than help *herself* if this case was going to mean anything.

20

Yerba Sacra was launched one Friday at the tail end of the silly season.

The court case opened at the Royal Courts of Justice eleven days later.

The coincidence was missed by no one, least of all the press.

Dominion made much of the Tait Committee approval of the brand. The committee head, Sir Heath Tait, former dean of medicine at Edinburgh University, appeared at the press launch to answer enquiries. For obvious legal reasons he chose not to comment on the forthcoming court case. He and members of the committee had reacted to the Anderson writ with alarm. Each one had gone over the research findings again with a fine-tooth comb. Was there anything they had overlooked? What about the results from the consumer tests? The animal tests? They held a series of meetings with research director Noel Sorensen and his team. But all tests had been carried out strictly according to the rules laid down by the Tait Committee and formally agreed to by the industry.

Still Tait wasn't happy. He had been approached by both sides to give evidence in court. This presented him with a dilemma. He was a careful man, concerned and conscious of doing the right thing. He was loyal to his committee, and had built up a sound working relationship with Noel Sorensen. His committee had cleared the product in all good faith. While the Anderson death was distressing, it had to be studied as a scientific incident, within the perspective of all available data. Even if he felt uneasy about the death, he would be unwise to make a hasty judgement based on an emotional reaction.

But to appear in court for Dominion would imply complicity, and his committee had to be seen in an independent light at all times. To appear for the plaintiff would imply misgivings. He resolved the dilemma by choosing to ignore the conclusions that might be drawn by the ill-informed. He was a man of science. His evidence would be the same if he appeared for the plaintiff or the defendant. So he agreed to appear for the plaintiff to establish his committee's independence of the industry.

Some years before he had stood out against a tobacco substitute launched into test market by one of the fibre giants without the committee's final clearance. He was angered at the time by the committee's inability to delay the launch. It had taken a stirring of the public and Parliament by ASH to have the brand removed for further research. When Dominion introduced *Catch* the committee had been genuinely impressed by the care and attention given to the product. And on that basis, they had developed a respect for the company that had carried over to *Yerba Sacra*.

But Tait well knew that science and friendly relationships didn't always mix. He was aware that some of the blame, if blame was to be found at Dominion, might inevitably fall on his committee. To back down at this stage would imply a lack of confidence. He must stand by their judgement.

Still, something niggled at him. He needed additional reassurance.

He glanced through the full-page advertisements for *Yerba Sacra* in *The Times*, *Financial Times*, *Daily Telegraph*, and *The Guardian*. The informative launch advertisements contained quotations from his committee. The quotations had been deftly written into the copy to suggest that the committee believed Dominion had made a great breakthrough in the search for a safer cigarette.

The committee hadn't said that at all, of course, but it was quietly implied, and it irked him somewhat.

ASH's tempering comments were contained in the accompanying news reports. George Samiou was quoted as saying: 'The public shouldn't get too excited. This must simply be regarded as another low-tar, low-nicotine brand.'

224

The former dean of medicine mulled over the reports and then placed the newspapers to one side. He stared thoughtfully at the telephone, reached for the receiver, and dialled the D.H.S.S.

Because it was the end of the silly season and the press was hungry for spicy news, the *Yerba Sacra* story made the front pages of two mass-circulation tabloids. It was discussed on successive radio news broadcasts throughout the day, and made TV news on both channels.

The Earth People campaign would break in the print media during the weekend preceding the court case. But the posters had already been pasted up at prime sites on the eve of the launch. Earth People sitting in a circle welcoming the new guest in the zany brown and gold packet faced the early morning rush hours at the exits of the busiest stations and undergrounds, and at key road junctions all over London.

The launch was preceded by lavish presentations to the trade and the introduction of various trade and salesmen's incentives. Tobacconists and retailers all over London made shelf and counter space for the neatly designed twelve packet display holders. Special introductory offers were made to the consumer via redeemable coupons offering a second packet at half price.

The brown and gold packet itself made a dazzling impact. The trade papers all carried large shots, and so did some of the dailies. The design had the desired effect and was stimulating publicity.

Supermarket chains agreed to give the brand additional shelf space for the launch week. Health food stores responded with enthusiasm. The response was more encouraging than anyone expected. Even Ted was surprised. Certainly the initial media impact enabled the new brand to weather some snide editorial comments about 'Dominion and the trade making hay'.

With the exception of a few sour comments from Jolyon Williams, the board was generally enthusiastic about the advertising and delighted with the response. It gave everyone a sense of buoyant security. The public seemed to be on Dominion's side, responding to the news of a 'safer' cigarette.

The subject of the forthcoming court case was treated with kid gloves by the press. Every word was carefully gone over by the newspapers' legal advisers to avoid any comment that might be considered prejudicial. The general feeling was one of wait and see.

When the news eventually leaked out about Tessa's involvement, that too had to be handled with care. The press baldly announced the plaintiff's counsel as 'Miss Tessa Harmer-Courtland', and then in the next sentence wrote 'Dominion chairman Sir Charles Courtland was unavailable for comment'. And if that wasn't enough of a hint, the business news sections of two dailies ran features on the origins of Dominion at the turn of the century, highlighting the Stirling Harmer story: 'The buccaneering red-haired American millionaire arrived unannounced in the offices of the Mace twins of Mace Tobacco with the historic words, "Hello, boys. Harmer from North Carolina. Come to buy your business".'

It wasn't difficult for the alert reader to draw the obvious conclusions.

Private Eye was the only paper to come straight out with the story. The *Eye* papered its walls with libel suits. One more wasn't going to make much difference. It had coined the term 'Tessa the Red' after the IRA trial, and made the current story sound like a medieval blood feud.

Courtland read the article and calmly dropped it into his wastepaper basket en route on the company screening room.

Tony McKay was running the *Yerba Sacra* advertisement for the executive board.

'Rather modern, isn't it?' said the chairman when the final frame was frozen on the screen before them. The packet shot loomed large over the punchline: GREAT EXPECTATIONS.

'That packet whizzing out of the sky looks like a Catherine Wheel on Guy Fawkes day,' sniffed Jolyon Williams. 'I didn't know we were in the fireworks business.'

Paul Lombard responded good-humouredly. 'I think it's positively pagan with that man standing on the hill, semi-naked one presumes. But my son and daughter would consider it "far out". So that's what counts I suppose.'

Tessa had advised Brigid Anderson and some of the witnesses she would call to the stand to acquaint themselves with court procedure well in advance. To take a bus to the Courts and slip in to any trial for half an hour or so. Anyone unaccustomed to the ritual and language of the courtroom could be too easily intimidated in the box. Counsels knew that and exploited the disadvantage.

Tessa had seen far too many potentially articulate witnesses crack under the whiplash of a cross examination. So she believed in grooming those who were unfamiliar with the system. Sometimes she subjected them to intensive grilling sessions to prepare them for the worst, throwing leading and trick questions at them, tying them up in knots, dismantling their evidence in front of them. Clients and witnesses often left these sessions wondering which side she represented. Later, they understood why she had trained them so thoroughly.

She told Brigid, 'They're going over your life and Jimmy's right now with a fine-tooth comb. If there is *anything* they can find, *anything* that will put you and your family in a bad light, they'll raise it in court to discredit you, to devalue you as a human being. So let's do a rerun of Jimmy's career, again. Did he ever clash with his boss? Any union troubles? Did he ever stage a walkout or anything like that? Come on, Brigid, *think*.'

It came as no surprise to Tessa that Sir Hamilton Crisp QC would be representing Dominion in court. Her father had obviously encouraged the choice. Crisp was a friend of his and the two men had recieved their knighthoods in the same list. Furthermore he knew there was no love lost between Crisp and his daughter. It was to his advantage to be represented by his daughter's social adversary.

'He has been clever enough to select a woman for his junior on the case,' said Ciaran. 'Diana Tonbridge. Her first degree was in biochemistry, so they'll probably do a little duet on your medical witnesses.'

Tessa nodded grimly. Diana Tonbridge was the daughter of a former cabinet minister who came from a large family of conservative politicians.

Ciaran was concerned on a more professional level. Weeks before, he had tried to persuade Tessa to have someone else with her on the case. 'Those two barristers you help to support, for the love of God. Why not make them work for *you* on this?'

But Tessa was adamant about tackling the brief single-handed.

'Arrogance,' Ciaran had snapped. 'Pride and arrogance.'

Tessa ignored him, but on the first morning of the case she began to have serious misgivings. This wasn't a normal attack of butterflies. She was accustomed to those. Now when she approached the Royal Courts of Justice, she felt sick with panic.

Like the PVC gas case, Tessa interpreted *Anderson v. Dominion* as a criminal case and had structured her arguments to that effect. If the case went against Dominion, the company could appeal to the Court of Appeal and thence to the House of Lords. So, winning a case like this was merely the first skirmish in a long battle with the establishment. The thought seemed more daunting today than it had at any other time in her career.

Tessa crossed the spacious mosaic floor of the entrance hall slowly, briefcase under one arm, wig and gown slung over her shoulder in a draw string bag.

She climbed the wide stone stairs leading up to a long line of courts in the Queen's Bench Division. Ciaran and Brigid were waiting for her, sitting together quietly under a stained glass window. The high stone arches and ecclesiastical atmosphere affected everyone. People waiting outside the courts talked in hushed tones, heads bent together conspiratorially.

Tessa gestured to them and turned toward the robing room at the far end of the black and white flagstone corridor. Several other barristers were there, but Tessa avoided eye contact with anyone. She needed privacy.

It was only when she stared at her image in the mirror that the curbed voice within began to shout in protest, refusing to be compromised any more. The gowned and wigged figures staring back at her slapped everything into perspective. She wasn't looking at herself, but at a woman garbed in the early eighteenth-century dress of a gentleman mourning the death of Queen Anne. No ordinary working man could dress like this. Only *gentlemen*. The symbolic implications struck her with a force. She was a walking embodiment of patriarchal tradition and the ruling class. An outward symbol of everything she despised. And at that precise moment, there was nothing she could do about it.

The ludicrous irony of it all suddenly made her laugh out loud. 'I wonder how many of us ever stop to see how silly we look. I mean, *really!*' she said to a dozen horrified faces. 'Doesn't it ever occur to any of you that the only other people wearing these bloody wigs are opera singers performing Mozart, or footmen at Buckingham Palace?'

'Miss Courtland appears to be under some strain,' one QC observed.

21

The irony of the *no smoking* notices in the courtroom was lost on no one. Least of all on the press and political sympathizers who crowded in en masse.

The unshakable traditions of the legal system were silently evoked by the rich wood panelling, worn leatherbound books lining shelves at the back, the antique clock firmly locked inside its case, and the carved coat of arms above the judge's chair. But the evocations stopped rudely when the eye hit the scuffed brown linoleum on the floor.

As counsel for the plaintiff, Tessa sat on the left side of the room. Sir Hamilton Crisp QC sat on the right, eye on the clock, florid face bulging over his starched wing collar and tabs. His junior, Diana Tonbridge sat behind him, wigged head bent studiously over a reference book. She was barely into her thirties and had been at the Bar just six years. This was the most important brief of her career and could establish her reputation. She was highly conscious of the opportunity and the growing public focus on the case.

The sight of two women in opposition stimulated the curiosity of the court. Set against one another in a heavily male-dominated occupation, women could sometimes be super-critical, rigorously attentive to detail, and scathing about the slightest show of stereotyped behavior. The court knew this and waited, intrigued.

Ciaran sat with Brigid Anderson in front of Tessa. Dominion's solicitor sat next to research director Noel Sorensen in front of Crisp. Becuase of the scientific nature of the case, it had been unanimously agreed that Sorensen should sit in for Dominion, the defendant.

A member of Alun Hughes's public relations team sat at the back next to the door, ready to rush to a phone if necessary.

Brigid looked suitably demure. If people came to court expecting to see a brow-beaten, timid widow, they were in for a disappointment. She showed signs of strain, but there was a grim determination in the set of her shoulders and the flecks of white paint clinging defiantly to her thick black hair.

She glanced over her shoulder, and her blue eyes widened with alarm. The court was crammed. People were still pressing through the swing doors and edging themselves into the tiered rows of the public gallery. Ciaran whispered a few reassuring words and told Tessa that her first witnesses had arrived.

Tessa smiled encouragingly at both of them and ran a quick eye over the various exhibits, neatly labelled and lined up on a table in front.

She had deliberately positioned a large grey plastic bin where it couldn't be missed by the press. It was the sort of bin used by teaching hospitals for storing human organs. Most of the people in the courtroom didn't know that of course, but their curiousity was aroused.

At thirty-three minutes past ten, the clerk of the court rose stiffly to announce the judge. The court scrambled dutifully to its feet.

Mr. Justice Blackford seated himself, wig carefully in place, red sash offering a suitably regal touch to the atmosphere. He was a man in his mid sixties, apple-cheeked, a little like a benign Santa Claus on the bench to all but those who knew him and the sharpness of his tongue. He eyed the crammed press and public galleries with disapproval.

The clerk sitting below the judge duly announced the case.

Tessa rose.

Blackford spent a few long moments carefully polishing his spectacles and holding them up to the light. He sat them on the bridge of his nose, folded his hands, and stared at Tessa.

Head held high, she stared back, wondering which of them would flinch first.

Eventually he said, 'Yes, Miss Courtland.'

The courtroom went very quiet.

Tessa placed her meticulously prepared notes to one side. The atmosphere in the room was now openly challenging, from the bench in front of her, and from the public gallery behind. She wanted to get her first witnesses heard in time to catch the deadlines of the early afternoon editions of the evening newspapers. Her introductory arguments were short and to the point.

'James Anderson was a trusting guinea pig,' she began, 'who, as the court will discover, was callously used by Dominion during the feverish commercial race to find a "safe" cigarette.' She continued: 'Medical witnesses will be called upon to testify that Anderson had lung cancer during the time he was used by the company to test a new tobacco substitute called yerba sacra.'

The public gallery reacted with alarm. Order had to be called before she could go on. 'Evidence will show that this is indeed possible, because a man can have lung cancer and not be aware of his predicament until it is too late. However, had Dominion, the defendant, been more attentive to the health of its participating guinea pigs, Anderson's predicament could have been detected sooner. It wasn't. We will seek to prove that the exposure to a new smoking substance compounded his predicament and hastened his untimely and undignified death.'

She paused and referred quickly to her notes. 'James Anderson was barely thirty-four when he died, leaving a widow and three young children under the age of eleven. He had been employed by Dominion for some eighteen years. During all this time he smoked one of the company's multitude of brands, *Mace 8*, made freely available to all employees. The sheer accessibility of the cigarettes helped contribute to the fact that he smoked heavily, between sixty and eighty a day.' She waited and studied Blackford's face thoughtfully. 'His smoking habits,' she continued, 'made him a suitable guinea pig for the company laboratories, and he became,' she said almost gently, 'as exploitable, and as expendable, as any lab mouse, dog, or cat.'

The public gallery murmured and rustled behind her, but she went on, 'Within a year of submitting himself to the research

232

programme, James Anderson came down with pneumonia. When this didn't clear, X-rays revealed a sizeable tumour in his right lung. Like any loyal, long-standing company employee, he told his boss about it, expecting support and compassion from the company. Did he get it?' she asked, glancing across at Noel Sorensen and shaking her head. 'All he got, as witnesses will show, was a brisk pat on the back, his pension contributions up to date, and his cards. Six months later he was dead.'

'But we are not here simply to examine some isolated death,' she added, folding her arms. 'We intend to show that Dominion is guilty of gross criminal negligence. The death of one young family man like James Anderson can tell us a lot about the immorality of the company when viewed within a political context.'

Tessa had been choosing her words with care and concern, not wanting to provoke the court or agitate the judge, but at this point she lost patience with her own measured arguments. 'James Anderson was an ordinary working man,' she repeated, raising her voice, 'and the guinea pigs were *all* ordinary working men, seeking to swell their wages in these inflationary days by a miserable twenty pounds a week. Not for luxuries, not for holidays, but, in Anderson's case, to buy winter coats and shoes for his family. No company executive offered himself for the test. He didn't need to. It was the men on the shop floor who came forward. It was James Anderson who ended up on the slab, not some manager or executive.'

The court responded with an angry roar. Order had to be called. Mr. Justice Blackford frowned disapprovingly. Suddenly Tessa's good intentions about playing down the class aspect of the case seemed unimportant. She was through with compromising. Ciaran was baffled and thrown by the sudden outburst. This wasn't Tessa's usual style at all.

Glancing at her notes, she quoted the industry's own statistics to show that the large majority of smokers in Britain were in the lower socio-economic groups, where the habit could be least afforded. Smoking-related deaths and diseases were subsequently higher within these groups. 'The Ministry of Health has estimated that bronchitis causes five times the number of deaths amongst working-class smokers than amongst the professional classes,' she said, adding, 'The Royal College of Physicians tells us that fifty million working days are lost per year through smoking-related diseases, disablements, and deaths.'

Softening her tone, she continued: 'Non-smokers may well be intolerant of such statistics. After all, no one forces the smoker to smoke. It is up to the individual, they argue, to choose between a packet of cigarettes and a few pounds of fresh fruit. But remember, the choice isn't always quite that simple, because we are talking about an *addiction*. We are talking about *the* most addictive product that can be bought over the counter. Alcoholism is a minor problem by comparison, so is drug addiction. According to the Department of Health, some two thousand people die from alcohol-realted causes each year, and a similar number die from drug overdose. These are the problems we think about first when we talk of addiction. Yet smoking kills *fifty thousand* individuals each year in Britain.'

The public and press galleries watched and listened, some curious, some cynical. This tall, serious-looking girl, with the formal gold-rimmed spectacles and red hair tied down neatly under her white wig, seemed every inch the concerned barrister. This was no heiress revolutionary denouncing her family in four letter words from the street. This was strictly controlled anger alternating with restraint.

They murmured in agreement when she damned the tobacco industry for stimulating and sustaining the nation's most serious addiction and health hazard.

Returning to the subject of *Yerba Sacra*, she warned the court against believing that the research for a 'safe' cigarette was a top priority with Dominion. Drawing freely on statistics she had lifted from her father's private diaries, and combining them with published figures, she whittled her arguments down to a brisk comparison between the *Yerba Sacra* budget and the year's promotional budget for the company's range of 'low- to high-tar' brands. 'The reserach and development of *Yerba Sacra* has cost the company some eight million pounds over the last four years, or an average of two millions a year. Yet this year alone, Dominion will spend approximately fifty million pounds to advertise and promote its other brands, in the press, magazines, cinema, posters, through coupons, sponsorship, and various promotional offers. Such priorities must be uppermost in our minds throughout the duration of this court case.'

She paused. 'It has taken one death to bring us into court to examine these priorities, and to question the validity of this so-called 'safe' cigarette. Medical witnesses will show that *Yerba Sacra* is as capable as tobacco of including malignant tumours in laboratory mice. The company advertisements would have us believe that this is a wholesome product. We're told its tars are less harmful than tobacco tars. But what we're not told is whether or not this new smoking substance is capable of *compounding* the effects of tobacco smoke. The death of James Anderson forces us to examine this possibility.'

Having drawn the court's attention to the key issues, the clinical tests, the company's priorities, the class aspects of smoking, and the synergistic effect of one substance on another, Tessa brought her introduction to a close.

As her first witness she called Sir Heath Tait to the stand. The court responded with surprise. Some days before, he had appeared at a press conference to discuss his committee's clearance of *Yerba Sacra*. Why was he opening the case for the plaintiff?

The head of the Tait Scientific Committee on Smoking and Health and former dean of medicine was a short man with a thatch of white hair. He entered the box looking concerned and uncomfortable. He had agreed to appear as a witness for the plaintiff becuase he believed this would establish his committee's independence. After listing his various qualifications and publications, he was ready to answer Tessa's questions.

'Sir Heath, could you describe the sort of clinical tests to which James Anderson was exposed during the research on *Yerba Sacra*.'

'Certainly. The subjects smoked anything from one to forty cigarettes a day. Half the test group smoked the *Yerba Sacra* cigarette. The remainder smoked cigarettes containing tobacco only. The purpose was to compare the clinical effects of the two smoking substances.'

'Was there a limit to the number of *Yerba Sacra* cigarettes smoked during the tests?'

'Oh yes, indeed, no more than forty a day.'

'But no doubt a company employee could have access to more.'

Crisp: 'My Lord, I must object to counsel's questions. Counsel is asking the witness for a supposition.'

Blackford: 'I agree, Sir Hamilton. Kindly reword your question, Miss Courtland.'

'Let me put it this way, Sir Heath. There would be nothing to prevent the test volunteers from smoking whatever they wished outside the laboratory, in their lunch hour, or at home. Am I right?'

'Yes, of course. We can only advise a limitation.'

'But unless you keep the volunteers locked up in cages like lab animals you can't enforce it, can you?'

'No.'

'What kind of tests were carried out on the volunteers?'

'Respiratory and cardiovascular function tests, to determine the physiological effects of the smoke.'

'I refer to the report outlining your recommendations, Sir Heath, in which you say the investigations should be carried out by research teams with proven clinical experience in this field. Why aren't you more specific?'

'I don't understand.'

'Why don't you insist on the presence of a certain number of physicians to oversee the tests?'

'We leave that to the company concerned. We can only make recommendations.'

'I see. And in this instance, the tests were carried out mainly by lab technicians, the company nurse, and an occasional peek by the company doctor. Did you consider that adequate?'

Tait held his ground. 'We found their methods to be most

professional and adequate.'

'Professional and adequate? But the choice of respiratory tests is left to their discretion, it it not?'

'Yes, again we can only recommend. We advise that the tests should include an examination of the function of the large and small airways. We also require details on cough frequency, sore throat, expectoration, and so on.'

'But do you require a chest X-ray?'

Tait looked agitated and shook his head. 'We leave details like that to the discretion of the company.'

'Did Dominion X-ray their volunteers?'

Tait: 'No.'

Tessa paused. 'Was it possible for one of those volunteers to be in the early stages of lung cancer?'

Crisp, acidly: 'My Lord, I must object. Counsel is leading the witness.'

Blackford: 'I agree with you, Sir Hamilton. I would ask you to rephrase the question, Miss Courtland.'

'Yes, my Lord,' said Tessa. 'Sir Heath, how would the clinicians involved in the lab tests be able to tell if a volunteer was suffering from a lung complaint?'

Tait shifted his position in the box. 'The cough frequency and sputum tests would quickly tell them if there was.'

'Would cancer in the early stage reveal itself in cough frequency or sputum tests?'

'No,' Tait sighed, resigned. 'Not necessarily.'

Tessa waited a moment to let this sink in. 'So,' she continued, 'was it possible for one of the volunteers to be suffering from lung cancer, be unaware of it, and for the clinicians not to recognize it because they did not X-ray him?'

'Possible,' said Tait, 'but highly improbable.'

Tessa wasn't going to let go. 'James Anderson died some eighteen months after he first volunteered himself for the tests. If he didn't have cancer *before* the tests, wouldn't you say that was a remarkably fast growth rate?' She waited, fully expecting to see an irate Crisp on his feet. But there wasn't a murmur from the QC.

237

Tait said: 'The normal growth rate for lung cancer is between three to four years. But the diagnostic problem is, as you say, extremely difficult. Symptoms don't normally present themselves until it is too late,' he added, addressing the bench. 'As a result, most patients die within a year of diagnosis.'

The public gallery shifted its attention momentarily toward Brigid Anderson. The widow sat without moving, head bowed.

Tessa went on: 'Could the yerba sacra tests have accelerated his death?'

'That's highly improbable.'

'But you don't discount the possibility.'

'I say it's improbable.'

'Sir Heath, there is sufficient evidence in other industries to show that one substance can have a synergistic effect on another in causing disease. Wouldn't it be possible for yerba sacra to compound the harmful effects of tobacco?'

Tait cleared his throat. 'We do study that possibility very closely,' he said reassuringly. 'In this case, we required a series of skin tests on mice, involving the application of tobacco tars, tobacco and yerba sacra combined, and yerba sacra on its own. Yerba sacra induced a consistently lower number of tumours on the average. We concluded that the material was far less harmful than tobacco.'

'But it did induce malignant tumours in the mice.'

'Yes.'

'So how can you be sure it won't induce malignant tumours in the human lung?'

'The tars used in the skin-painting experiments are by necessity enormously concentrated. No smoker would ever be exposed to such a concentration of tar.'

'But Sir Heath, the laboratory experiments must be indicative of something, otherwise they would be purposeless, pointless.'

'They're useful in comparative studies with tobacco.'

'So mice are used to determine which of the two substances, tobacco or yerba sacra is the lesser of two evils?'

Tait paused. 'Frankly, yes,' he said.

238

'And you've cleared a product that induced skin cancer in the lab.'

Tait: 'The purpose of the test was to evaluate a smoking material that would be less harmful than tobacco.'

'Less harmful, but not harm*less*.'

'That is correct.'

Tessa paused and studied the former dean of medicine thoughtfully. 'Sir Heath, would you clear an over-the-counter drug if it induced malignant tumours during laboratory tests?'

Crisp: 'My Lord, I must object. Counsel is asking the witness to hypothesize.'

Blackford: 'I don't agree with you, Sir Hamilton. Please answer the question Sir Heath.'

Tait: 'Possibly not.'

Tessa: 'And yet your committee clears a *cigarette* that is capable of inducing malignant tumours. Why?'

Tait: 'People will continue to smoke,' he said philosophically. 'It is our duty to reduce some of the risks.'

Tessa: 'By clearing a product that you know, we know, and the industry knows, is capable of inducing tumours?'

Tait: 'Yerba sacra tars are far less active than tobacco tars. We cleared the product on that basis.'

Tait began to look increasingly uncomfortable.

Tessa: 'Did you ever make spot checks on Dominion's research experiments? Did your team or any of its members ever arrive unannounced in the lab perhaps?'

'Good heavens, no.'

'So technicians and research scientists involved in the experiments were always fully prepared for you. And if results weren't working strictly according to plan, things could be rearranged slightly or speeded up to produce the desired results. And you would be none the wiser?'

Crisp scrambled angrily to his feet. 'My Lord, this is preposterous. Unless counsel can present incriminating evidence, she has no right to ask the witness to hypothesize.'

Blackford: 'I agree. The witness is not required to answer the question.'

Tessa conceded. She had made the point, cast doubt on the validity of the tests, and that was enough. She moved quickly to her next question. 'You cleared the tests on *Yerba Sacra,* didn't you, Sir Heath?'

'Yes. My team made a thorough investigation of the various tests required and was quite happy with the results.'

'But you have gone on record as saying that it could take ten or twenty years before you can observe the full effects of *Yerba Sacra* on the smoker.'

Tait reflected on this. 'That is a risk we have to take with the search for a safer cigarette. We attempt to make it as safe as possible, realizing all the time that we are dealing with experimental materials.'

'So companies might be marketing an unsafe cigarette in the search for a safe cigarette.'

'I wouldn't put it like that.'

'How would you put it?'

'I'd say we're doing the best we can in an imperfect world.'

Tessa allowed a moment of silence. 'You cleared *Yerba Sacra,* and it is now shouting at the public from the mountaintops. Do you have any doubts about the tests?'

'No.'

'No doubts at all? Not even on the basis of James Anderson's death?'

'No. I'm convinced that his death was not related to yerba sacra.'

Tessa stared up at him. 'Well then, Sir Heath, in spite of your convictions, would you tell the court why—only last week—you asked the Department of Health to set up some parallel test experiments under their own supervision?'

Tait flushed with embarrassment. That information was a classified government matter. 'This isn't unusual in science,' he said quickly, but his initial reaction gave him away.

The courtroom hummed in anticipation. The feeling of doubt and uncertainty in the air made everyone restless, agitated. Tessa thanked the witness and glanced expectantly at Dominion's counsel. Much to her surprise, Crisp rose and said,

240

'We do not intend to examine the witness now, but we reserve the right to recall Sir Heath Tait to the witness box.'

The ex-professor bowed to the judge, avoided Crisp's eyes, and left the box.

Tessa frowned. This wasn't like Crisp. She glanced at Dominion's research director, Noel Sorensen, but he didn't seem unduly perturbed either. Diana Tonbridge stared vacantly into space.

Tessa shrugged and called her next witness, the pathologist Albert Routledge. Physically he was a direct contrast to the slight, gentlemanly, scholarly Sir Heath Tait who preceded him. He took his oath in a booming voice and waited for Tessa's questions, large hands confidently resting on the edge of the witness box. He was wearing a double-breasted suit, closely tailored to reveal his muscular back and shoulders. He managed to exude the same authority in court that he did at the autopsy.

For the benefit of the court. Tessa asked him to list his various qualifications and the consultancies he had held up until his present position. The mention of various famous teaching hospitals made Mr. Justice Blackford sit forward with interest.

He reconstructed the autopsy, giving the layman's definition for every medical term used, and emphasizing the typical nature of the cancer, 'small-cell undifferentiated', found amongst the smokers who ended up in his morgue.

'James Anderson was a young man,' Tessa continued. 'Is it unusual to discover carcinoma of this type among smokers of his age?'

Routledge scratched his head. 'The majority of victims are in their fifties and sixties. But the younger a smoker takes up the habit, the more susceptible he is to the harmful effects. The younger the lung, the more vulnerable it is.'

'And from your detailed examinations of his lungs, how long would you say James Anderson had been smoking?'

'Between twenty and twenty-five years.'

Tessa paused and addressed the bench. 'My Lord, from the medical evidence the deceased would have been between the ages of nine and fourteen when he started to smoke. May I draw your attention to Exhibit C.' A signed statement written by James Anderson before his death was passed to the bench, and down to the opposition. In it, Anderson confirmed that he had started to smoke at the age of ten, and was hooked by the time he was twelve. Tessa read sections of the statement to the court before continuing. 'Mr. Routledge, James Anderson was used in various smoking tests, and was exposed to a new smoking substance between eighteen and twelve months prior to his death. What effect would this have had on him?'

Routledge cleared his throat. 'To begin with, Miss Courtland,' he said politely, 'the deceased would have been in the early stages of the carcinoma at that time. If the disease had been detected then, the malignant tumour *might* have been removed from his lung. But if, as you say, he was exposed to a new or additional smoking material, this would undoubtedly have compounded the damage already done to his lung.'

A murmur of concern rumbled through the court.

Tessa did not pursue the point. Instead she addressed the bench. 'My Lord, I believe it would be highly instructive to the court if we allowed Mr. Routledge to demonstrate his evidence. May I have Exhibit "A".'

A court official lifted the grey plastic bin off the exhibit table and passed it to her. The people in the public gallery craned forward.

Tessa stood sideways so that the bin was in full view of the press and public galleries. Twisting off the lid she reached inside and withdrew part of a human lung, vacuum-packed in a polythene bag like delicatessen wurst.

There was a loud gasp from the courtroom. Brigid Anderson glanced down.

The judge eyed the list of exhibits at his elbow and peered down from the bench.

Tessa raised the lung in the air and handed it to the official to pass to the pathologist in the witness box.

'Mr. Routledge, could you describe the exhibit for the benefit of the court?'

The pathologist held up the bag containing the blue-grey

242

object and said: 'I confirm that this is a cross-section through the right lung of the deceased James Anderson, removed by me during the course of the autopsy.' Pointing at a tight blob dominating the centre of the object, he continued: 'We determined the carcinoma was of the type known as small-cell undifferentiated, or oat cell.' Addressing the bench, he added, 'This is one of the two most typical of the smokers' cancers, my Lord, the other being the epidermoid carcinoma.'

Tessa: 'Could you explain to the court exactly what happens to the lungs during smoking?'

Routledge ran a finger down the polythene against the interior of the lung. 'The intake of smoke exposes the lining of the bronchial passages to various abrasive substances,' he explained. 'It's popularly believed that air pollution has this same effect, but this isn't altogether true. While pollutants are obviously harmful, they are largely inhaled through the nose and that acts as a mild filter. But cigarette smoke is largely inhaled through the mouth, and the mouth wasn't designed to be a filter.'

'Could you tell the court about the bronchial passages and the effect smoking has on them

'The bronchial passages of the lungs have a protective mechanism,' he stressed. 'The cells lining them secrete a mucus that collects foreign bodies—dust particles and so on. The mucus is then passed out of the bronchial tubes and the trachea by the action of the cilia. These are tiny, hairlike structures lining the inner surface of the respiratory passages which move at a rate of some nine hundred beats a minute. This movement ensures the expectoration of the mucus and anything carried with it.'

The pathologist paused and glanced toward the gallery. Pointing with his finger, he said, 'If someone should faint in a crowded gallery like that, the most sensible thing to do would be to pass the individual along the row and out of the door. This is how the cilia work. But,' he stressed, 'excess smoking actually immobilizes the cilia.' Pointing again toward the gallery he added, 'Imagine a sudden paralysis of the people in those rows.

243

It would take some time for the sick individual to find his way to the door. Thus the mucus builds up in the bronchus, causing the well-known "smoker's cough".'

The court listened intently as he explained, 'So excess smoking has a multiple effect on the lung. It destroys part of the body's natural filtering mechanism, thus exposing the lining of the bronchial tubes to toxic substances in the tobacco smoke. Tobacco tar contains several hundred compounds, and at least ten hydrocarbons, that produce cancer in animals—when painted on the skin of a mouse, for example. Other chemicals in the tar are called co-carcinogens, which means they act with one another to produce certain cancers.'

Hamilton Crisp rose. 'My Lord,' he said wearily, 'with due respect to Mr. Routledge, I don't see the relevance of this discussion. Witness is presenting as facts matters that are at present disputed amongst the medical profession.'

Justice Blackford dismissed the objection. 'Please go on, Mr. Routledge.'

The pathologist turned to the judge and held the exhibit aloft once more. 'My Lord, when it comes to the dissection of a lung and a close examination of the damaged tissue, there is no dispute. I believe it is essential for the court to understand such facts. If I didn't, I wouldn't waste my time here,' he added impatiently.

Tessa supressed a smile. 'Perhaps you could explain the relationship between smoking and damaged tissue,' she suggested.

Routledge said, 'The heavier the smoker the more vulnerable his lungs are. If the deceased was smoking between sixty and eighty cigarettes a day, as you said, then his lungs were in no state to be exposed to a new smoking substance.'

Tessa: 'If you had examined the deceased some two years ago, prior to the *Yerba Sacra* tests, would you have advised him against participating?'

Crisp, on his feet: 'I must object to counsel's question my Lord. A pathologist can hardly be expected to answer this.'

Blackford agreed with him.

Tessa, to Routledge: 'Then, as a simple family doctor, Mr. Routledge, leaving aside your specialization for the moment, what advice would you have given James Anderson?'

'If he was a heavy smoker, I would have advised him strongly against participating.'

'Thank you, Dr. Routledge.'

Mr. Justice Blackford unfolded his arms and eyed the QC. 'Well, Sir Hamilton?'

Crisp rose, bristling, hands on his hips, gown fanned out. 'Mr. Routledge, would it surprise you to learn that of the forty men who participated in the *Yerba Sacra* laboratory tests, thirty-nine are alive, hale and hearty?'

'They are very fortunate.'

'Fortunate?' Crisp cocked his head to one side. 'But conclusions are drawn from the majority in experiments. Or, at least, that is what your profession keeps telling us.'

Routledge agreed.

'So,' said Crisp, 'if some forty men between the ages of thirty and fifty choose unselfishly and of their own free will to offer their services for the advancement of science, and one dies, wouldn't you draw a conclusion from the thirty-nine?'

'Normally I would,' the pathologist admitted. 'But I have not had the opportunity to examine the thirty-nine, and hopefully I won't be obliged to meet them in my morgue.'

Crisp waved the air impatiently. 'If a minority of one succumbs to disease, that is an exception, and suggests other causes, does it not?'

'Like what?'

'Come now, Mr. Routledge. Surely you investigative scientific nature does not permit you so easily to accept the obvious? I know from some of your students that you are most intolerant of the glib diagnosis and that you take nothing for granted. What more can you tell us about the deceased?'

'Well, sir,' the pathologist said, scratching his head, 'if you have some two days to spare I could take you on a detailed tour, muscle by muscle, cell by cell.'

The court started to laugh.

Crisp was clearly annoyed but was not one to be thrown so easily. 'The death of one individual in a group of forty suggests a certain genetic predisposition does it not?'

'Certainly some individuals are more susceptible to disease then others,' said the pathologist. 'That is a biological fact.'

'The deceased lived in London all his life, and his childhood spanned the years before the Clean Air Act. Would that not have contributed to the state of his lungs?'

Routledge addressed the bench. 'Pollution is obviously an irritant. But the public can sometimes be misled into thinking it is the prime cause of lung cancer, and it isn't. Smoking is.'

'Ah,' said Crisp triumphantly, 'but you don't *exclude* the harmful effects of pollution?'

Routledge glanced thoughtfully at Tessa. 'It's instructive to be reminded of several factors here. Miss Courtland mentioned the severity of bronchitis earlier. The Royal College of Physicians and similar medical institutions have made a close study of this. Statistically speaking, it is smokers, predominantly, who are affected by smoke from the combustion of coal, and the dust from mining and other industries. In the United Kingdom, chronic bronchitis or emphysema is uncommon among nonsmokers, even in heavily polluted areas.' The pathologist paused briefly. 'Lung cancer among smokers is certainly higher in the city than it is in the country, however. One must guard against jumping to misleading conclusions on this issue. The city of Reykjavik, Iceland, has the purest air in Europe, but the incidence of lung cancer has increased dramatically with the increase in smoking. Icelanders took up smoking largely during the Second World War. So, the lung cancer death rate between 1951 and '59 was five times that of 1930 to 1940.'

Crisp persisted. 'But air pollution is indeed a *contributory* factor to disease?'

Routledge began to show signs of irritation. 'Yes, of course,' he said quickly.

Crisp, insistent: 'Thus, as a scientist you do *not* rule out the combined effects of various substances inhaled from the atmosphere. After all,' the QC said sarcastically, half turning toward the public gallery, 'the *nose* is quite unable to pick and choose between one pollutant and another.'

The courtroom found this amusing. Routledge did not. Towering over the box, he stared down at Crisp as though the QC was a bloody fool. Crisp waited until the court had settled down before dismissing the pathologist.

Tessa's next witness was Andrew Wynn, head of cancer research at University College Hospital, London, and a key witness suggested by George Samiou of ASH. He was built like an elegant poplar compared with the oaklike physique of Routledge, but both men had a way of commanding awe without even speaking. Wynn was wearing a formally cut dark-blue three-piece suit. A gold watch chain swung to and fro across his waistcoat as he climbed into the witness box to take the oath.

Tessa's opening question could not have been more direct. 'Professor Wynn, does smoking cause cancer?'

Wynn: 'Yes.'

Crisp: 'I must object my Lord. No one knows precisely *how* cancer is caused.'

Mr. Justice Blackford: 'Prefessor Wynn, perhaps you would tell us.'

Wynn, passing a hand over his neatly combed hair: 'My colleague Mr. Routledge has described some of the effects of smoking. A close examination of several autopsy studies on cigarette smokers shows extensive metaplastic changes in the bronchi. The severity of these changes is related to the number of cigarettes smoked, and can be precancerous. Thus, the changes are extensive in smokers with lung cancer, but are infrequent in nonsmokers, to take the two extremes. In ex-smokers we note the body's remarkable ability for recovery and a *regression* of precancerous changes.'

Tessa: 'So the susceptibility to cancer increases with the amount smoked?'

Wynn, courteous, talking like an archbishop delivering a sermon from the pulpit: 'Indeed yes.' He raised two bony hands in the air. 'A simple analogy perhaps,' he said, rubbing the fingers of his right hand vigorously on the back of his left. 'If I

247

continued to do this day after day, the friction would produce changes in the cells of my skin that could be precancerous.'

Turning toward Crisp, he said, 'Smoking causes a similar friction within the body. The cells will resist it for just so long, and then give up. The result is a change in the cellular structure.'

Tessa: 'My Lord, may I draw the court's attention to Exhibit B. For the cytology tests, we were obliged to enlarge the photomicrographs. Sections from the deceased's lungs were compared under the microscope with sections from the lungs of a nonsmoker. Perhaps Mr. Wynn would explain the differences for us.'

The court official was instructed to pass Exhibit B, a large envelope, to the witness box. Wynn removed the colour enlargements and held them up to the judge. 'The normal cell, my Lord, has a distinct orderliness about it, as you can see in the photograph on the left. But the cancerous cell is distorted with a visibly misshapen nucleus, as you will see in the photograph on the right. This sample was taken from the lung of the deceased, James Anderson.'

Wynn turned to show the photographs to Crisp, Tonbridge, and Noel Sorensen. 'The extent of the disorder visible in the nucleus determines whether the cell is cancerous, or precancerous.'

Neither Crisp nor Tonbridge reacted. Tessa was surprised. She expected a caustic objection from the opposition. The evidence was plainly incriminating but they didn't seem unduly bothered. She was unsettled by their silence. She waited until the court official took the photographs and replaced them in the envelope.

'Professor Wynn,' she continued, 'could you tell us something about the chemistry of smoke?'

'Smoke contains carcinogens and co-carcinogens and these, both singly and in conjunction with one another, activate cell changes. There is also another factor to consider, the *temperature* of the smoke when it is inhaled, and the possible side effects caused by this modified form of radiation.'

248

'And the combination of the physical and chemical effects of smoke can be seen in the lungs of *any* smoker, whether their death is directly attributed to smoking or not?'

'Yes, related of course to the amount smoked.'

'Professor, have you studies the results of the tests on yerba sacra as cleared by the Tait Committee?'

'I have.'

'And what is your conclusion?'

Wynn raised his head thoughtfully. 'On the basis of the tests the product appears to meet the necessary requirements. But as Sir Heath rightly pointed out, it may take ten or twenty years for us to be able to study the effects properly.'

'Do you believe the exposure to yerba sacra hastened James Anderson's death?'

'Undoubtedly.'

'Do you believe Dominion was negligent in allowing him to volunteer for the tests?'

Crisp: 'My Lord, with respect, I must object. Counsel is asking for an opinion.'

Blackford, irritably: 'I believe the question is relevant. Please continue, professor.'

Wynn: 'I speak now as a physician and in my capacity as head of cancer research at a teaching hospital. I believe Dominion was grossly negligent of its duty as a responsible public company, in allowing the deceased to take part in the tests.'

The court reacted noisily. It took several moments before the atmosphere settled down.

Tessa: 'Given that volunteers have to be used in the move toward producing a safer cigarette, how many cigarettes do you think they should be allowed to smoke a day?'

Wynn: 'Given that situation, I'd advise no more than twenty or twenty-five, but I understand forty is the limit.'

'And if the volunteer smoked up to forty test cigarettes, and forty of his own brand, would you consider that harmful?'

'I'd consider it gross. It's difficult to imagine the extent of this addiction.'

'Professor, is it possible for two identical experiments to be set up and produce different results?'

Wynn smiled. 'Yes, it is. This is one of the biggest headaches in medical research. One is required to draw conclusions from averages taken over successive experiments.'

Tessa: 'And have you recently done some research on tobacco and yerba sacra in your own laboratories?'

Crisp glanced up in surprise. He turned and exchanged words with Dominion's research director Noel Sorensen, who shrugged and shook his head.

Wynn: 'Yes, we have. Following the guidelines set down by Sir Heath Tait and his committee, we subjected the $C_{57}BL$ strain of mice to tobacco, to yerba sacra, and to the two substances combined.'

'Why did you choose the $C_{57}BL$ strain?'

'We deliberately selected a strain predominantly known for its resistance to the induction of lung tumours.'

'And what were the results?'

Wynn: 'The combination of tobacco and yerba sacra produced the greatest number of tumours.'

Crisp was on his feet instantly. 'I must object. The evidence from one limited test conducted within the past few months can hardly be weighed against the successive tests carried out by the Dominion research team over the past four years.'

Blackford: 'I shall reserve judgment on that until Professor Wynn has had the opportunity of telling us more about the tests. Miss Courtland.'

A large buff envelope containing the tabulated results, and photographs from the tests, were passed forward. She asked Wynn to elaborate.

The professor agreed that the tests were necessarily limited, but offered to demonstrate the evidence and the conclusions reached in his laboratory to the Dominion research team and their counsel.

The judge glanced toward the material. 'I agree that the defendant should be allowed to examine the evidence before we pursue it in court.' Turning toward Wynn, he asked, 'Conflicting evidence is by no means unusual in science, is it, professor?'

Wynn: 'No, my Lord, hence the importance of parrallel experiments supervised by different research bodies.' He went on to remind the court of various demonstrative examples. 'Some cancer victims swear by the drug Laetrile,' he said, 'but tests done by the Sloan-Kettering Institute of America on lab animals drew negative conclusions.' He raised the thalidomide case. 'The drug produced no adverse effects on pregnant dogs, cats, rats, monkeys, hamsters, and chickens. Only in baby *rabbits* did it produce deformities similar to those produced in the human child.' He added that lung disorders, cancer, and emphysema could be induced in dogs and baboons, and gave a list of references. 'Where tobacco is concerned we already know the effect on the body. It's a sad state of affairs that we have to keep on and on demonstrating this to ourselves in the laboratory.'

Tessa: 'But obviously industry is required to conduct animal experiments prior to launching a tobacco substitute.'

'Yes, but these are clearly limited, as the thalidomide experiments proved. Without extensive evidence from smokers studied over a number of years, animal experiments can only offer guidelines, indications, important though they may be. With any new product there must obviously be a certain margin of risk when it is exposed to the general public.'

'Do you believe Dominion is taking a chance by launching *Yerba Sacra* into the marketplace?'

'Yes, I do. But as Sir Heath Tait said, we do the best we can within an imperfect situation. Personally I don't believe there is such a thing as a safe cigarette. The safest cigarette is no cigarette.'

'Thank you, professor,' said Tessa. 'We might need to recall you later in the week when the defendant has had a chance to acquaint himself with your $C_{57}BL$ mice experiments.'

'By all means.' Wynn bowed graciously and removed his pincenez.

Diana Tonbridge got up to conduct the cross examination. 'Professor Wynn,' she began, haughty public school voice contrasting immediately with Tessa's more abrasive tones. 'If, as you believe, smoking causes such physiological damage, can you explain why the overwhelming majority of smokers suffer no ill effects from the habit?'

'Obviously some smokers are more susceptible to diseases than others. Some suffer from heart complaints, stomach ulcers, or emphysema, while others contract forms of carcinoma.'

'But the vast majority don't.'

'That is true.' He gestured toward the court. 'I could inject everyone in this courtroom with, say, a cold virus. But not all of them would succumb to it.'

Tonbridge smiled. 'Which proves that no one single factor causes disease.'

Wynn, staring down at her: 'One would need to qualify that. If a single factor is capable of activating others, then it outweighs the numeric difference.'

'Ah,' said Tonbridge, 'but if that "single factor" was bound up within the genetic mechanism of the individual, and not an external factor at all, that would merit serious study, wouldn't it?'

Wynn, staring vaguely into space: 'If you are referring to the *genetic* disposition of smokers to desease, to what particular piece of research are you referring?'

Tonbridge, snappily: 'I'm asking the questions, professor.' Turning toward the bench, she said, 'My Lord, the current antismoking hysteria has turned tobacco into the convenient whipping boy of the diagnostician. Regardless of how or why a smoker dies, doctors automatically link the cause to cigarettes. A smoker might suffer anything from epilepsy to bed wetting and that would somehow be twisted to implicate tobacco.'

The courtroom started to snigger.

Tessa felt Tonbridge's pettiness didn't even merit an objection.

Blackford wasn't amused. Neither was Wynn.

Tonbridge, quickly: 'Professor Wynn, do you discount the genetic predisposition of certain individuals to certain diseases?'

'I discount nothing, madam,' he said tightly. 'But the rise

in lung cancer deaths paralleled with the rise in smoking since the early 1920s suggests a causative and not a genetic hypothesis. I will say, however, that genetic and environmental factors may determine which smokers are most likely to develop cancer.'

'What causes lung cancer in a nonsmoker?'

'The inhalation of carcinogenic substances. The individual may have been exposed to an abnormal concentration of such substances, perhaps in an industrial environment.'

'So the label "smoker's cancer" is wholly misleading, because non-smokers die from the identical cancers.'

'That is true, but very, very few.'

'But if nonsmokers die from the same cancer, that can't conclusively indict smoking, can it?'

'Scientists tend to draw conclusions from majorities.'

'Yes,' said Tonbridge, taking a breath, and glancing up at the bench to make sure the point hit home. 'And the vast *majority* of smokers lead full and healthy lives. Thank you, professor, that is all.'

22

Tessa was worried. Things were too smooth, too easy. She knew the combined forces of Crisp and Tonbridge were capable of much more than they had revealed so far. Their conscious mediocrity unnerved her.

But when the court adjourned for lunch, she revealed none of her anxieties to Brigid and Ciaran. The three of them crossed Fleet Street in silence and walked toward Tessa's chambers, where tea and sandwiches awaited them.

The lunchtime editions of the *Evening Standard* and the *Evening News* carried potted versions of the earlier part of the morning's hearings on their front pages. Their headlines were similarly worded: DOCTORS ACCUSE DOMINION OF NEGLI-GENCE. WORKERS ENTICED TO BECOME HUMAN GUINEA PIGS. Brigid Anderson was described as a 'modestly dressed woman who sat with her head down while her counsel Miss Tessa Courtland, fished the deceased's lungs out of a plastic bin.' The *Standard* added pointedly: 'Dominion chairman, Sir Charles Courtland, was conspicuous by his absence.'

Two pages on, both newspapers carried large colour advertisements for *Yerba Sacra*.

Brigid stood by the leaded window next to Tessa's desk, idling through the newspapers. Tessa busied herself with plates and cups, sensing an acute need for the practical, the common-place.

'Jimmy was a nobody when he was alive,' Brigid said suddenly, not really addressing anyone in particular. 'To be a *somebody* his guts had to end up under a microscope. If everyone had given him as much attention when he first got ill as they did this morning, he'd still be here! Those syrupy doctors couldn't get him out of their hair fast enough when he was dying.'

Ciaran and Tessa exchanged glances. Ciaran reached out to her quickly. 'Brigid, love, I did warn you it would be upsetting. You didn't have to be in court today.'

She ignored him and reached for a cup of tea.

Tessa took refuge in a brisk, businesslike attitude. This was no time to allow emotions to spill over. 'Brigid,' she said, 'sit down and have something to eat. We're doing magnificently in court. The brutal part is over, and there are only one or two things we have to go through before this afternoon.'

Brigid sat down reluctantly.

Ciaran stood staring into space, untidy grey hair sticking out around his head, suit pockets bulging.

Tessa eyed the pair of them. 'Oh come on, you two! Think of the rumpus we're creating. We're shaping history with this case! Look at the number of people who crammed into the courtroom.'

Neither Brigid nor Ciaran said anything.

Tessa reached into a drawer and withdrew a half-empty bottle of Teacher's whisky and three sherry glasses, 'Jimmy wasn't involved in anything like selling cigarettes on the side, was he?' she asked almost casually, searching for loopholes, whisky bottle poised over the glasses.

'Jesus, son of Mary,' shouted Brigid. 'We've been over that two hundred times. How often do I have to say no, no, *no*. Jimmy was law-abiding to the point of *boredom*. He wouldn't even pick a daisy in the park!'

'All right,' Tessa said quickly, 'but they'll try and dig up something to cast a slur on his character. We have to be one hundred percent sure.'

Brigid turned on her. '*They'll* dig up something? What more does the court need? They've seen his lungs, they know how we live. What gives you the right to expose us to those leering faces in court? Who are you to talk about the working classes? If a director died you wouldn't show his lungs in public, would you now?'

Ciaran interceded hastily, 'Brigid, we've been through that. You agreed to it. We all know it wasn't very pleasant, but

255

then nothing about this case is pleasant.'

'To hell with you!' she shouted.

She walked out, and her angry footsteps resounded down the old narrow stairway.

'Leave her,' Tessa advised.

'But she might do something foolish.'

Tessa shook her head. 'She's right, you know.'

Ciaran glanced anxiously toward the door. 'She didn't mean it. She's full of steam, building up for months now. I shouldn't have let her come to court this morning. It's my fault.'

'Now who's patronizing her?'

Ciaran sighed and rubbed his head. 'Oh *Jesus*,' he said.

Tessa glanced out of the window. Brigid emerged from the building and walked slowly across the grass, heading toward the Embankment.

She filled two glasses with whisky and handed one to Ciaran. The plate of sandwiches lay untouched between them on the desk. 'This morning worries me,' she said, concentrating hard on the case.

'Why?' he asked distantly, still preoccupied with Brigid. 'Top medical brass, unchallengeable types. It's what you wanted.'

Tessa shook her head and reached for a cheese and pickle sandwich. 'No one's unchallengeable in Ham Crisp's book. You don't have to be a snivelling petrol pump attendant to be flayed by his tongue. He was just going through the paces this morning, biding time. Both he and Diana could have been a damn sight tougher on Routledge and Wynn.'

Ciaran shrugged.

'Ham's got something lurking in the wings,' she persisted. For all her dislike of the QC, she knew how deft, how agile he was at getting witnesses to contradict themselves. Even the most articulate and erudite could end up squirming and stuttering in the box.

Tessa mentally dismantled and rebuilt the case several times. If there was a loophole anywhere, she had to find it.

She got up impatiently. She had deliberately planned the

256

day to have the heavyweights in the morning and the light-weights in the afternoon. Now she needed to clear her mind.

'Let's go and find Brigid,' she suggested, a practical streak rising to the surface. She replaced the whisky and reached for a packet of peppermints.

The found Brigid sitting alone on a bench by the Embankment. She flatly refused to be taken home, saying that if she'd lived through the 'stink' of Jimmy's death, she could live through anything.

The three of them returned to court in silence. Tessa didn't want to leave things unresolved. This was hardly the moment for a personal clash. 'Brigid,' she said, concerned, 'we're all limited to doing what we can.'

Brigid stopped in her tracks and stared at Tessa in amazement. 'You understand *nothing!*'

'You're probably right,' Tessa replied stoically, much to Ciaran's surprise. 'But I'm as much a victim of all this as you are.' She turned on her heel. 'I'll meet you in court in ten minutes.'

Ted stared at the late afternoon editions of the *News* and the *Standard*. He couldn't help worrying. If he allowed his paranoia to run wild, and it was running wild, he saw this as some kind of retribution.

He swivelled around in his chair and sat with his feet propped against the window, gazing down at the Thames.

Just the week before, he'd had news from the Columbia and other reserves cultivating yerba sacra that they could expect a bumper crop. Their original contract with the Columbia reserve had been adjusted to accommodate the local land claim and involve more Indian farmers in the cultivation of yerba sacra. But Ted wasn't naïve enough to think the militance had been snuffed out by this action alone, masterminded by Art Templeton, their Washington lawyer. Reports had soon trick-led back about a murder of the taxi driver on the reserve, and the subsequent rounding up and arrest of young militants. If Templeton and his FBI buddies were involved, Ted didn't want to know about it.

He had enough to think about in London. He glanced at his diary and was surprised to see he had forgotten about a dinner date with Jill. Normally he looked forward to their times together. But tonight he couldn't face it. He dialled the *Media* number, and left a message to cancel the evening arrangement, saying he'd call her in the morning. She was aware of the court case and would understand. He was relieved to be involved with a woman who didn't need lengthy explanations at times of company crisis.

His attention returned to the newspaper reports lying in front of him. He was engulfed by a sense of hopelessness. There was a time when *Yerba Sacra* problems had been a great challenge. In some inexplicable way the setbacks had given him energy. But now, everything seemed too much for him. He was losing control and could only await the final reckoning.

In that moment Ted bitterly regretted not coming clean from the start about the mice switching. How long did he think he could get away with that? Again, it was all a matter of short-term thinking. He'd dealt with every issue as if it were a single football game. But business was one continuous game, not a series of different games, and the final score was about to be announced.

It was the overwhelming feeling of uncertainty that was getting to him more than the fear. Things were happening to *Yerba Sacra* and he was no longer running with the ball.

Sir Heath Tait had asked the Ministry of Health to set up new experiments. Witnesses discussed the shortcomings of animal experiments.

What did they prove and what didn't they prove? When a tobacco company was sued by the widow of a lung cancer victim in the States, the company's attorneys had refused to accept the value of animal experiments as evidence. But in the British court, constant references were being made to the induction of tumours and other disorders in mice, dogs, and baboons exposed to cigarette smoke. Ted knew the Dominion counsel could hardly dismiss animal experiments as invalid, because it

258

was largely on the basis of those experiments that *Yerba Sacra* had been cleared and launched into test market.

Ted leaned on his hands. He could sit it out and hope for the best. Leave everything to the persuasive wit of Hamilton Crisp and Noel Sorensen. But what then? What about the experiments now being set up at the D.H.S.S.?

Going on the basis of what the court heard that morning, it wasn't unusual for scientists to be faced with conflicting results from two identical sets of tests. They would either draw a conclusion from this, or go ahead and set up still more tests. The Ministry's tests might conflict with those carried out by Lawrence and the boys downstairs. Or, by some weird fluke, they might match the results. How the hell could anyone predict these things?

A vision crossed his mind of a team of men fitting a line of *Yerba Sacra* cigarettes into a smoking machine to condense the smoke into tar. And then another line of men standing by, carefully shaving the backs of a thousand mice. And a third line of men waiting to dab tar on the exposed skin.

Ted shuddered. He buzzed his assistant and asked her to get hold of the latest prices from the stock exchange. She came back within seconds. The price was down one penny.

He reached across the desk and connected himself with the chairman's office.

'Yes?' said Courtland wearily.

'Are you alone Charles?'

'I am, Ted. Could you do with a snifter?'

Ted sat up, surprised. Courtland never, ever drank before the day's work was done.

Within minutes he was sitting opposite the chairman. Courtland's desk was bare except for two gin-and-tonics. The crystal glasses cast two lonely shadows on the highly polished surface.

The men sat and looked at one another, each waiting for the other to speak.

Ted reached for his glass and rolled it between his hands.

Speaking slowly and quietly, he told the chairman about

his conspiracy with Dr. Lawrence to switch some mice in the lab. All the time he was talking it was as though he were listening to someone else. He wasn't acting out of panic. *Yerba Sacra* was being lauded all over London. There was nothing to say the court case would expose him. And he couldn't be sure that parallel experiments would prove anything either. So why was he doing this? Conscience? No. The fear of living under a threat of exposure. If he was going to be exposed, he'd damn well plan the timing himself.

The chairman listened. When Ted finished talking, he made no comment but reached toward his intercom. 'Henry, my boy. Would you send Dr. Lawrence up here straightaway? And I *mean* straightaway.'

Before the biochemist appeared, Courtland rose and removed the gin glasses, carrying them discreetly into the adjoining bathroom. By the time had had locked the drinks cabinet, the biochemist was announced.

Lawrence walked in. He nodded politely at Ted.

'Ah, Dr. Lawrence,' said Courtland gesturing toward a chair. 'Sir Heath Tait and members of his committee were most impressed by the new research you are conducting downstairs, testing tobacco substitutes and new filters on tumour-resistant strains of mice.'

'Thank you, sir.' said Lawrence.

'They said you should be encouraged as much as possible. That you may have the nucleus there of research that could be of prime importance to the entire industry one day.'

'Thank you, sir,' he repeated modestly.

'Now what's this I hear about mice switching?'

The biochemist sat perfectly still. 'Mice switching?' he asked, sounding puzzled. 'What do you mean, sir?'

'*Mean*, Lawrence?' The chairman raised his eyebrows. 'Mr. Mallett tells me you and he agreed to a little, shall we say, "adjustment" in the lab for the benefit of showing clean results to the Tait Committee. Is this, or is it not, correct?'

Lawrence's expression didn't change. 'Sir Charles,' he said, 'I do not make "adjustments," as you call them. That

260

would defeat the whole purpose of research.'

Ted turned on him. 'I've seen you switch mice between cages with my own eyes. What are you playing at?'

A look of undisguised amazement crossed Lawrence's face. 'What mice, and what cages, Mr. Mallett?'

'You moved the B whatever mice in with the B mice. You did it to create the impression of fewer tumours.'

Lawrence didn't flinch. 'B whatever mice, with the B mice. I'm not sure I understand which mice you are talking about Mr. Mallett.'

Courtland's eyes moved between the two men.

Lawrence appealed to him. 'Sir, I believe there is a serious misunderstanding here. I could find this deeply insulting, but I don't,' he said patiently. 'My colleagues and I are constantly battling to keep men who have no background zoology, physics, or chemistry, abreast of our work. I've learned to accept this kind of misunderstanding.' He smiled.

Ted got up and repeated his earlier disclosure. 'Charles, this man came to me a few months ago with a proposition. He told me that tars from tobacco and yerba sacra combined produced an excessive number of tumours on three out of four strains of mice. The fourth strain was peculiarly resistant to the tars. As all the mice looked the same, he suggested that this particular strain should be mixed in with the others. I gave him the go ahead and agreed to set him up in a special research project as a reward.'

Courtland scratched the side of his head thoughtfully. The sun moved from behind a cloud and cast long shadows on his desk. 'Well, Dr. Lawrence?' he said slowly.

The biochemist looked genuinely baffled and hurt, a man attempting to think back through the weeks of intensive research. 'I'm trying to determine the source of the misunderstanding, Sir Charles,' he said. 'You see, we don't *use* four strains of mice. The committee only requires us to use two.'

'You devious little swine!' said Mallett.

Courtland silenced him swiftly.

Lawrence spoke as though Ted wasn't in the room, carefully addressing the chairman direct.

Ted noticed the confusion lining Courtland's forehead. Did Charles believe Lawrence, a two-bit junior scientist, over him? 'Why the hell would I have set him up in the lab if it wasn't on a *quid pro quo* basis?' he said angrily. 'Can't you see through his act?'

The chairman looked embarrassed. 'Dr. Lawrence,' he said, 'would you wait outside for a few minutes?'

The biochemist rose obediently and left the room.

Courtland got up and exhaled loudly. 'Ted, these are very serious allegations.'

'You don't believe me, do you?' snapped Ted. 'Why would I invent something like this, why?'

Courtland rubbed his chin. 'We're all under some strain. Things tend to become magnified, exaggerated in our minds.'

'Oh my God. So now. I'm hallucinating. Is that it?'

'Ted,' he replied reassuringly, 'you have just brought a new product onto the market in an inhumanly short space of time. Six months or so before the planned launch. Now we're in the midst of this wretched court case.' He stopped and turned toward the window. The Thames was glistening in the sunlight. Office workers were rushing across the bridge, anxious to get home to spend a few hours in the luxury of their gardens or nearby parks before sunset. The chairman looked away. He had no reason to rush anywhere any more.

Ted sat down. Something inside of him wanted to tear the office apart, kick Lawrence out of a top story window. Something else muttered, why bother?

Courtland continued patiently. 'Unless you have proof to support your allegations, I suggest we forget that this ever happened.' He turned and added, 'I believe your reaction is perfectly understandable, Ted. You drive yourself in a way no master would drive a slave. Unrelenting. It's fearsome to watch. How can you keep things in perspective?' He laughed hollowly. 'Blasted court case is making paranoids out of all of us. You should see what runs through *my* imagination. *God*!'

Ted didn't reply. He had no proof, of course. He had fed

Lawrence's report to the shredder. Contact between them had been minimal and secretive.

The chairman glanced at his watch. 'Why don't you go away for a few days? Take the lovely Colette up to the Lake District. Delightful spot.'

Ted just looked at him. The lovely Colette? He hadn't seen her for days. He felt a sudden pang of regret. He needed to be with her again, and to talk to her. Salvaging his marriage was suddenly very important to him. But he needed to resolve things between them. Together they were strong enough to overcome a transitory lull in their relationship.

Courtland cut his nostalgic yearnings short. Steepling his fingers, he glanced thoughtfully toward the door. 'I suggest you apologize to young Lawrence, Ted. Whatever personal disagreement may or may not have passed between you is immaterial at this precise moment. We mustn't lose sight of the fact that he is one of the most brilliant young biochemists in our research division.'

When Ted didn't react, the chairman grew impatient. 'After your outburst,' he stressed, 'Lawrence could walk out of here today. Imagine the consequences. We're *years* ahead of our closest competitor in the tobacco substitute market, you know that.'

Ted shrugged.

The chairman paused and frowned. Didn't Ted realize the implications? 'If Lawrence leaves today,' he said slowly, 'there isn't a thing we could do to stop him. And the secrets of our multimillion-pound research programme go with him to BAT, Imperial, Rothmans, or whoever offers him the highest salary. So I strongly advise an apology.'

Without waiting for Ted to reply, Courtland leaned toward his intercom. 'Henry, would you ask Dr. Lawrence to join us?'

The BBC and London's commercial radio stations updated the 'human guinea pig' story throughout the day. BBC TV and Independent TV both carried clips of Brigid Anderson arriving at court that morning, head down, refusing to comment.

263

Thames TV's *Today* show featured interviews with two Labour Members of Parliament who were calling for a public enquiry and more government control over the use of human volunteers in industrial research.

But the most vivid comment on the day came in the late editions of the evening papers. A single column highlighted spot check reports of the sudden run on *Yerba Sacra* at tobacconists all over London. Photographs of tobacco kiosks on London's busy Piccadilly Circus, Oxford Circus, and High Holborn were published over captions like *We were sold out by three o'clock*, and *People are curious to see what all the fuss is about.*'

Ted's marketing executives cancelled their evening dates, rolled up their sleeves, and hit the road with the sales force to make late-night deliveries to keep up with the sudden demand. As Dominion owned most of the corner store tobacconists throughout London, the company was profiting twice from the unexpected rush of supplies. As a precaution, extra security guards were placed on the warehouses to watch over the stacks of huge dark-brown-and-gold cartons awaiting dispatch. Production went on triple time to make sure the warehouses didn't run dry. Vast machines were set in action around the clock to roll three thousand short, squat, *Yerba Sacra* cigarettes a minute.

The only people who were tearing their hair out at Dominion were the leaf men. If their stocks ran dry everything would grind to a halt until a fresh crop of yerba sacra could be harvested and cured in America.

Pocket calculators were quickly whisked out when it looked as though the six-month launch targets would be met in one month if demand kept up. Leaf, stock, production, and distribution figures were fed into the computer for purposes of establishing an emergency rationing plan to be swung into action at a moment's notice.

But all Ted could see were Dr. Lawrence's fat pudgy fingers darting in and out of mice cages.

After his session with the chairman and the biochemist, he drove straight home. Finding the house silent and empty, he put on the first record that touched his fingertips and turned it up full blast.

He hunted out two new bottles of *Jim Beam*, emptied a tray of ice into a jug, and flopped down on the cushions scattered around the lounge floor. When Colette didn't appear, he began to drink himself into a stupour.

Tessa read through the late newspaper reports and wondered at the perversity of mankind.

How was it possible for people to read reports of 'human guinea pig' experiments, and then rush out to try the product for themselves?

Tessa was startled to come across a photo of herself, Ciaran, and Brigid walking dejectedly across Fleet Street for the afternoon session in court. They were all so absorbed in their own thoughts they hadn't even noticed the photographer. The juxtapositon of the sombre trio with the frenzied reports from tobacconists all over London spoke volumes. And yet, the evidence of the day was solidly on her side. Or was it? Was she becoming so caught up in her own dialectic that she was losing sight of the case?

She went over and over the afternoon's hearings. Witnesses included Anderson's family doctor who confirmed he had treated the deceased for pneumonia and then sent him to a speicalist when the complaint didn't clear up. The doctor was harassed, afraid of being blamed, constantly reminding the court that Anderson was one of two thousand patients on his files. The inability of overworked GPs to cope properly with the demands of a crowded London borough were made painfully clear. The chest surgeon who had made the diagnosis followed him into the box. Here, too, the court was reminded of key factors that were to appear again and again in the case. First, the difficulty of diagnosing lung cancer until it was usually too late. Second, the five percent average survival rate. Third, the crying need for heavy smokers to have regular chest X-rays. And fourth, doctors' objections to the free cigarettes made available to tobacco industry employees.

A former Dominion employee and friend of Anderson's spoke of the 'eagerness' with which men on the shop floor offered themselves for the tests to pad out their weekly pay packets.

'And what if the volunteers started to cough or complain of sore throats from yerba sacra?'

The witness shrugged. 'They were told to leave off for a day or so, those that wanted to.'

'But they weren't told to drop out of the tests.'

'Oh no. In fact the company encouraged them to keep on, becuase they needed to be able to study the whole test group. You know, to see how many were affected by the test cigarette over a certain space of time. If any men dropped out, it would have ruined the project.'

'And did they grade the volunteers according to the amount they smoked?'

'Yes, heavy, medium, light. But the heavy smokers interested them most, because they were easier to measure.

'Are you a heavy smoker?'

'Yes.'

'So you were in the same test group as James Anderson.'

'Yes, I was.'

'Did the cigarettes affect you?'

'No, not really.'

'And Anderson?'

'Yes, he complained to me several times of a cough and difficulty with breathing.'

'But the company didn't advise him to stop?'

'No. That was left up to us. Jim carried on because he needed the money.'

When Ham Crisp rose to do the cross examination he tried to get the witness to admit he was 'griping' at the company becuase he had been laid off work. Dismissing the evidence as 'unreliable,' he added, 'if a man is foolish enough to continue with smoking tests when he has a cough and breathing problems, the defendant really can't be held responsible for his decision.'

Crisp had a point there, of course, Tessa deliberated. But when the QC tried to make out that Anderson was motivated by 'greed,' she objected noisily. 'My Lord, twenty pounds a week can hardly be called *"greed."* We all know how far twenty pounds goes these days.'

The day's hearings ran and reran through her mind. Earlier apprehensions about Crisp, and who or what he had waiting in the wings still nagged at her. Any junior barrister worth his salt could have done what Crisp and Diana Tonbridge did between them that day. The cross examinations were nothing but gestures. No startling trip questions. No attempt to back a witness up against the wall. Tessa always preferred the fiery to the lukewarm opposition, because then she knew exactly where she stood. But Crisp hadn't revealed his hand. She knew that Ciaran was bothered too.

Before she got home, Tessa stopped at a local newsagent, and asked them to deliver copies of all the dailies to her until further notice. Comparing and contrasting the treatment of the court case according to the political bias of the newspaper was going to be a very necessary dawn duty for the remainder of the case.

When Tessa arrived home, she was pleasantly surprised to find Colette there. Knowing of Colette's reluctance to become involved, she had more or less resigned herself to not seeing her at all during the court case. She suggested a picnic and Colette began to prepare it.

Tessa went to shower. Ten minutes later she reappeared in a pale-green cotton blouse and jeans.

They left the warehouse and strolled along the canal to the park. A couple of fishermen and two small boys lined the way, staring hopefully into the murky green water.

'Any fish who survives in this water,' said Colette, 'deserves to live.'

Tessa didn't reply. Colette didn't pursue the point. Recently even the simplest remark might be blown up into a political argument. She could understand it, but it was beginning to rattle her.

267

The evening was golden and heady with the sunset. They dawdled together along the canal bank, and the park was practically deserted when they reached it. A few old people sat alone on the benches drawing out the day.

The two women spread a rug and settled under a leafy oak tree near the water. 'I listened to the news,' Colette said, laying out the meal on white china.

'Yes,' Tessa said grimly, 'but the laugh's on me. People are rushing out to buy the brand.' She sipped some wine thoughtfully. 'No doubt there are devious, murky minds out there who will say I have done this deliberately to boost Dominion's sales.' She paused and added quickly, hurtfully, 'Ted must be pleased.'

'I don't know,' Colette replied airily. 'We haven't spoken for days.'

Tessa apologized. She was fighting *Dominion* in court, not Ted Mallett.

A duck waddled out of the water toward them, took one look at the food, and waddled away in disgust.

Tessa startled to giggle. A release.

Colette touched her face. 'Silly schoolgirl,' she said affectionately.

'Oh, I know. I'll be forty in three years, and there are times in court when I have to bunch up my toes to stop myself from giggling.' She stopped short. To hell with law. She reached back and began to loosen her hair, suddenly realizing she had forgotten to unpin it in her haste to get changed.

Colette reached over and helped her.

Tessa studied her profile. The two sat and ate silently together for several long moments. The sky gradually faded from gold to a soft grey tinged with pink. One by one, the old people rose wearily from the benches and ambled slowly and reluctantly out of the park.

Colette lay on her back and stared up at the heavy branches of the oak tree.

'Why don't you change your name?' Colette suggested, suddenly.

'The name I can change. The chromosomes I can't do anything about. Anyway, "Harmer" has similar associations.'

Colette laughed at her. 'You're so conventional. Whether it is your father's or your mother's surname, it's still a name passed down by the male line.'

'So from this day onward I shall be known as Tessa Sunflower.'

'Tiger Lily, please.'

'All right then, Tessa Tiger Lily it is. I'll make the necessary arrangements tomorrow. Now, what shall we do about your name?'

Colette started to wrap up the leftover food and fit it carefully into the basket. 'Sable? Ah, perhaps this isn't such a problem. It means "sand" in French.'

'But it's a masculine noun.'

'Maybe. But it's gentle and universal, for all. Think of your own name, Courtland. Court plus land. Authority. Tradition. The ruling class. With such a name, how can you ever be free?'

23

Ted sat up half the night until he finally fell into a drunken sleep on the sitting room carpet. He woke up in the early hours of the morning with his head in a pool of vomit. A hurricane had crossed the ocean from the Florida coast during the night and settled somewhere between his ears. God, he felt terrible. He tried to clear up the carpet but kept falling over. Eventually he gave up in disgust and spent half an hour under the shower.

Semi-revived, he forced himself to eat dry toast to soak up whatever was left of his stomach and sat hunched over a mug of black coffee. Fuck Courtland, he thought sourly. Humiliating me like that. He had half a mind to call Courtland's daughter and tell her about the mice switching. Why the hell not. It would all come out in time. How long was he going to sit around and wait for it to happen?

Yerba Sacra. An image of the dancing gold logo crept into his mind. Was it worth all this? To wake up in a pool of his own vomit like some street bum? To be humiliated in front of a scheming, two-bit Ph.D.

Why not offer himself in court as a conscience-stricken executive? Anything was better than the prospect of being unmasked, and not knowing exactly when it was going to happen. That was the kind of tension he couldn't handle.

He eyed the kitchen clock. 6.15 A.M. So what. The idea of contacting Courtland's daughter was crazy enough to be appealing, and the earlier the better if he was going to talk to her before court.

He went directly to the hall phone and leafed through his black book for Tessa's number. The various Courtland homes had unlisted numbers, but the chairman believed in giving all three to his senior executives in case he were needed in an emergency.

Ted sat cross-legged on the floor and reached for the receiver.

Tessa was never to know how close she came to receiving information that could have brought Dominion to its knees in court. She too rose early, needing distance between the night and the day's ordeal in court. She was in the shower and didn't even hear the phone.

Colette turned sleepily in the bed and groped toward the receiver. 'Hello?'

Ted froze.

'*Hello?*' she repeated.

The first time he wasn't so sure. The second time, he tried to tell himself he was imagining things. But with the third impatient 'hello' he knew who it was. He stared at the phone in disbelief and hung up quietly.

24

Three people joined the commuter rush on the trains into London that morning.

Their personal missions were all directly linked with Dominion, but there the similarity ended.

They did not know one another, nor were they ever likely to meet.

One was a member of Scotland Yard's Special Branch. Another was Augustus Blond, medical historian and former Nobel prize winner.

And the third was Daphne Harmer-Courtland. With copies of *The Times*, *Financial Times*, and *Daily Telegraph* neatly folded in a briefcase, she got off the train at Cannon Street, and walked to her broker's office in the Stock Exchange building on Throgmorton Street.

The receptionist in the bare, maroon-carpeted outer office was just lifting the cover off her IBM when Daphne walked in. 'Good morning, Lady Courtland,' she said politely. 'I'll tell Mr. Donovan you're here.'

Joseph Donovan opened his office door and greeted her warmly, arm extended. 'Do come in, Daphne. How lovely to see you.' Turning to the receptionist he said, 'Sally, would you make us some coffee?'

'Certainly, Mr. Donovan.'

It was only when the office door was again firmly closed that the receptionist raised her eyebrows in wonder. Lady Courtland wasn't exactly known for her sense of chic. But, a long, handpainted peasant dress? Brown sandals? At *her* age?

Daphne rummaged in her briefcase while Joseph Donovan watched with an amused eye.

Dear Daphne, he thought affectionately. She never

changed. He listened carefully to what she had to say, fingers tapping his lips contemplatively.

The relationship between a stockbroker and his long-standing clients was one of frankness and trust. They had known one another for nearly forty years. Donovan was just down from Oxford then and being trained under his father's watchful eye to succeed him in the family firm.

Donovan had inherited the task of looking after the Harmer Trust. Daphne had come into her share when she turned twenty-one.

Stirling Harmer had organized the Trust before his death to prevent his impulsive wife from spending all the money he made on pet causes. She was provided with a generous income during her lifetime, but the bulk of the invested capital went to Daphne, with half to be divided equally between her children when they turned twenty-one. That portion of the Trust inherited by Amy also passed automatically to Daphne on her mother's death and would eventually be passed on to Tessa.

The nature of the Trust was such that the capital couldn't be touched. But there were no limitations set down in the Trust concerning dividends. It was up to the recipients to deal with them as they wished.

So, when she had turned twenty-one Daphne made a quiet pledge on her father's memory. On each birthday following her twenty-first she re-invested part of her dividends in Dominion shares, under a different pseudonym each year. The gradual accumulation of thirty-seven fictitious shareholders represented a block of shares in the company worth nearly two million pounds on the current market.

During all the time he had handled the Harmer Trust, and Daphne's thirty-seven offspring, Donovan had respected her desire for secrecy. He knew of her adamant need to keep her private financial matters to herself.

The receptionist moved quietly into the office with a tray of coffee. She served them both and disappeared with a discreet smile.

Daphne pushed her cup to one side. She held the briefcase

open and eased out a bundle of share certificates. 'My father may have been uncouth,' she said, sliding them across the desk to her financial adviser, 'but few businessmen could compete with him. Creating business was a game that grew out of a game. Being a multimillionaire never changed him, Joseph.'

'No, my dear.'

'He was born with a loud voice and a salty tongue. He died with a loud voice and a salty tongue.'

'So one has been told.'

'He made mistakes,' said Daphne, nodding and reaching for her cup. 'But he softened with the years, and never lost contact with the ordinary man.'

A muted silence settled in the office. After a few moments Daphne continued, between sips: 'My father would not have wished to see a man die because of some laboratory experiment.'

The stockbroker shook his head wisely.

She leaned over and fanned the certificates in front of him like a deck of cards. 'So, dear Joseph. Each one of us thirty-seven shareholders would like you to sell our Dominion shares by way of a protest. This morning.'

Donovan didn't reply at once. He replaced his cup and studied the certificates thoughtfully. 'Re-investing the capital—' he began.

Daphne raised her hand. 'Perhaps the Bahamas,' she said distantly. 'It's time I left England, don't you think?'

An elderly gentleman in a shabby tweed suit and scuffed suede shoes peered myopically around the entrance to the Royal Courts of Justice.

The two men on security duty glanced suspiciously at the crumpled paper bag dangling from his hand.

One of them called out to the man, 'This way, please, sir, if you don't mind.'

The man turned and looked from left to right to see who was addressing him.

The official crossed the floor and clasped him firmly by the elbow. 'Over here, please, sir. Can't let you in until we examine

274

your shopping bag.'

The man seemed confused. 'Oh dear me,' he said quickly, 'I'm expected to give evidence, and I'm late as it is!'

'Yes, well, do you have any identity on you, sir?'

'No,' he said, looking flustered. 'You see, I left my wallet on the train. I had to walk over the bridge from Waterloo, and I'm most *dreadfully* late.'

The officials eyed the tufted grey head and snippets of tissue stuck to his chin and neck where he had nicked himself shaving. One official placed the bag firmly on the security table.

'Oh dear, this really is most distressing,' said the man. 'That's only my lunch,' he added. A packet of egg sandwiches and a flask of tea were carefully removed and examined.

'I'm Mr. Augustus Blond, and a Miss Courtland is expecting me to give evidence. She'll be so cross with me if I let her down,' he insisted, watching egg spill over the table.

Miss Courtland?' asked one of the officials. He glanced down at the daily case list. 'Would you mean Miss Courtland, sir, *Anderson v. Dominion?*'

'Ah yes!' said the man, 'you see, I—'

'Very well, sir.' The official studied him dubiously. 'My colleague will escort you upstairs.'

Ciaran was just on his way out of the courtroom to look for Blond, when the surgeon appeared in the corridor and entrusted the solicitor with his precious paper bag.

Blond was embarrassed, apologetic, and smoothed his hair down like a schoolboy about to see his headmaster.

Augustus Blond, Cambridge professor emeritus and a Nobel prize winner, was one of the few men in his profession to refuse a knighthood. Since his retirement, he had devoted himself entirely to his greatest love, medical history.

Former students fondly remembered his instructional sessions at the operating table when even a simple appendectomy was made to resemble an archaeological dig through the decades of surgical evolution. He had studied classical Greek, Arabic, and Chinese to be able to read ancient medical manuscripts for himself. He had performed surgery with acupuncture years before it became fashionable in the West, and looked askance at people who considered him a radical for doing it.

Mr. Justice Blackford eyed the shabby, shortsighted surgeon as he climbed the witness box to take his oath. The courtroom hummed with curiosity. Blond was the sort of person who spoke too softly, head bent conspiratorially toward the listener, everywhere but in the hushed atmosphere of a library. There, his voice would ring out loud and clear. There was nothing he loved more than an audience, or the chance to talk about medical history.

He had recently published a series of articles in a medical journal on the historic links between smoking and disease, which is why George Samiou of ASH proposed him as a useful witness for Tessa. He also provided the dash of eccentricity she always sought in at least one of her witnesses.

Tessa intended to use him to dispel the defendant's argument that the tobacco-cancer link was a recent medical hypothesis that hadn't been fully explored.

'Recent? Oh dear me, no,' said Blond, shaking his head. 'As far back at 1671, the Italian biologist Francesco Redi published an account of the lethal effects of what he termed the "oil of tobacco" and what we would describe as tar.' He paused, enjoying the attention of the court. 'Of course, one must recall that some two centuries before, when explorers first acquired the taste from the natives of the Americas, the courts of Europe were roused and excited by the religious and *medicinal* rituals associated with tobacco. One heard of how the Aztecs attempted to cure gout by rubbing themselves with tobacco leaf and lime. Others sniffed crushed leaf or infused it to cure anything from a cold to madness.' He laughed loudly and turned to the bench. 'In our own practical way, my Lord, we smoked to excess during the Great Plague of 1665 to ward off the disease.'

Ham Crisp and Diana Tonbridge sat forward with interest. But if they thought he was doing their work for them they soon changed their minds.

Tessa: 'When were the British first made aware of a possible link between tobacco and cancer?'

'Ah, one must go back to 1761, to a distinguished physician by the name of Dr. John Hill, formerly of St. Andrews University. He published a tract entitled *Cautions Against the Immoderate Use of Snuff.*' Blond paused. 'Hill discovered that snuff produced "swellings and excrescences" within the nostrils, and further described the "polypi" that developed from an excessive use of snuff.'

'Mr. Blond, could we move on to the nineteenth century,' Tessa suggested tactfully.

'Ah yes!' said the surgeon. '*The Lancet* published a somewhat searing indictment of smoking during 1857, which does not depart *too* far from what we know today. The paper described the inflammatory condition of the mucous membrane of the larynx, a short cough, hurried breathing and circulatory problems, all relating to smoking. Of course,' he added, 'that was the time, too, when doctors believed *consumption* was caused by smoking.'

The courtroom hummed in response.

'Doctors are never entirely wrong nor entirely right, my Lord,' said Blond, wagging a finger toward the bench, 'but it is important to regress to be able to trace the evolution of research, to see what was discarded—like the consumption theory—and what was furthered. Indeed, we can date the *modern* period of investigation into smoking from the turn of the century.'

Tessa: 'Could you tell us how?'

The surgeon nodded and cleared his throat. 'Statisticians noted an increase in lung cancer and started to make a conscious note of the relationship between smoking and various cancers and heart disease.' He contemplated this and added, 'We believe skin cancers were first produced in guinea pigs painted with tobacco tars early in this century.'

'Then,' said Tessa, glancing toward Sorensen, 'why is it we are led to believe the links between smoking and disease are so recent?'

'This is understandable,' Blond said, patting his grey tufted head, 'because we depend on retrospective studies on which to base our conclusions, such as the studies conducted in

Germany in the early thirties. The American journal *Science* of March 4, 1938, published some important tables relating smoking to shortened life expectancy, based on research done by Dr. Raymond Pearl of Johns Hopkins Medical School.'

'What response did Dr. Pearl get?'

The elderly surgeon smiled patiently. 'Alas,' he said, shaking his head, 'the major American newspapers, all of which carried considerable tobacco advertising, ignored his report.'

Crisp rose to his feet and said patronizingly, 'My Lord, with respect, I really must object. Unless the witness can support this comment, I suggest it is too biased to be accepted as evidence.'

Mr. Justice Blackford agreed and waved the air for the surgeon to continue. 'Please confine yourself to the *facts*, Mr. Blond.'

Blond was unperturbed. 'During the 1930s.' he went on, 'medical researchers became increasingly alarmed by, and more attentive to, the rise in lung cancer. Retrospective studies linking the rise with smoking were done in '43, '45, and '48, and throughout the fifties. Today, we can refer to over thirty retrospective studies done in some ten countries, with a concentration of prospective studies done in North America and Britain.' Turning the the bench he added, 'Our own Royal College of Physicians has published three reports on the subject within a span of some fifteen years.'

Tessa smiled at him and asked, finally, 'As a surgeon and medical historian, Mr. Blond, is there any doubt in your mind that smoking causes lung cancer?'

'Oh my goodness, no. None whatsoever!'

'Thank you, Mr. Blond,' she said, and sat down.

Mr. Justice Blackford studied the surgeon thoughtfully for a few moments and scribbled down some notes before nodding toward the opposition. 'Well, Sir Hamilton?'

Crisp rose, rustling papers and turning the leaves of various reference books. 'Very entertaining performance, Mr. Blond. But of course, you have been highly selective in the way you inflame the court's imagination.'

Blond surprised everyone by laughing at him, hands stretched out on either side of the witness box. It was certainly the sort of response that required no additional help from Tessa. Ciaran turned and winked at her broadly, and smiled reassuringly at Brigid.

Crisp cleared his throat haughtily. 'In your extensive research, Mr. Blond, you have no doubt come across the observations made by a distinguished London physician, one Sir Percival Pott, as early as 1775? He observed a high incidence of cancer among chimney sweeps, who, one might add, were non-smokers.'

Blond leaned over the box, peering through his thick spectacles at the QC. 'You are quite correct, sir, quite correct. But it was not cancer of the lung from which they suffered, but cancer of the *scrotum.*'

'We are aware of that,' Crisp added quickly. 'But counsel for the plaintiff would have us believe that direct friction is a principal cause of cancer.' The QC drew himself up, hands clasping his gown on either side, chin raised in the air. 'Are we to understand that chimney sweeps cleaned soot with their *scrota?*'

The court burst out laughing. Even the judge had to look down quickly, passing a hand across his face to hide his own reaction.

Far from being thrown or annoyed by the question, Blond joined in the laughter, literally wiping the tears away from his eyes. When the court was eventually called to order, he shook his finger at the QC as if to say, 'You naughty, naughty boy.'

'Friction in conjunction with other chemical factors causes cancer, sir,' he said. 'Excessive exposure to certain substances can affect the body in different ways, according to physiological vulnerabilities. Impurities or disorders can be carried around the body during the exchange of fluids and gases, and will squat, if you like the modern term, where the organ is most vulnerable and unable to evict the squatter. For example,' he added, 'the urine of smokers contains a higher concentration of carcinogenic substances than that of a *nonsmoker.*'

Crisp moved impatiently from one foot to the other.

'Thus,' continued the surgeon, undaunted, finger pointed toward the ceiling, 'a smoker might contract cancer of the *bladder* and not the lung.' He paused, scratching his head contemplatively. 'I am aware of the extraordinary contortions of the body exercised by the young, but,' he added, 'to my knowledge no one has yet been able to smoke a cigarette with his bladder.'

The court broke up a second time, more so now that the joke was on Crisp.

Blackford wasn't very amused. He glanced disapprovingly at the surgeon. 'Mr. Blond, would you confine yourself to evidence of a strictly scientific nature. Do you have any more questions, Sir Hamilton?

Crisp shook his head. 'Thank you, Mr. Blond,' he said curtly.

The doctor looked disappointed. He glanced expectantly toward Tessa.

She rose, smiling. 'Thank you very much for your time, Mr Blond.'

He bowed graciously and left the box, self-consciously touching the nick on his neck to make sure the piece of tissue paper was still in place.

The concept of 'trust' is unique in the City of London, financial hub of the universe.

It is the understatement of the square mile, and unquestioned bond linking the men behind the transactions that crisscross the institutions and the money market each second of the working week.

A gentleman's word is his bond.

Although the times were changing, and the men in the headlines were frequently those who came snapping out of nowhere to turn the modern art of 'asset stripping' into multi-million pound business empires, the traditions that built the City lingered on quietly. The insider didn't need to be told. He lived it. The outsider sensed it, was intrigued by it, but knew he could never really be part of it.

Both Joseph Donovan and Charles Courtland were true

blue insiders.

When Daphne left his office, the stockbroker sat quietly contemplating the share certificates. His duty was to serve his client, of course. But trust was an expansive word. The City lived by certain codes, and gentlemen were bound by honour to serve them above anything. This required no explanation. If you lived by the unwritten laws of the City you could exercise them among your peers with a minimum of words. A raised eyebrow at a meeting with your merchant banker. A quiet nod and a mysterious smile.

Donovan reached slowly for his telephone and dialled Dominion. The mention of his name had him connected to the chairman within seconds.

'Charles?'

'Joseph, how good of you to phone.'

'I hear some of your shareholders are a little distressed with the news of the day. Throgmorton Street promises some lively activity.'

Courtland was silent for a few moments. Reaching for a pad and pen he said casually, 'Oh really? Any idea of the dimensions of the activity?'

Donavan mentioned a six-figure amount.

Courtland scribbled it down without comment. 'Most thoughtful of you. A quiet word in the ear of your contact perhaps? Something that will distract him from pursuing his clients' wishes for an hour or so?'

'I'll do my best.'

'I'm indebted to you, Joseph.'

As soon as the two men had wished one another goodbye, Courtland buzzed his financial director, Paul Lombard.

Lombard joined the chairman immediately.

'One hour?' he said, when the chairman told him about the tipoff. 'When does Hamilton Crisp propose to drop his bombshell in court?'

Courtland checked his wristwatch. 'Early this afternoon, I believe. Why?'

Lombard smiled. 'Ask him to hold off until the last possible moment at the end of the day. Too late for the news to affect closing prices but early enough for it to be hot and crackling for the evening TV news, and to make the front pages of tomorrow's newspapers.'

The chairman frowned. 'Price could be at an all-time low by then.

'That's precisely what I want, Charles.' He rose and checked the time. He had precisely fifty-two minutes in which to alert some key corporate shareholders and pension funds.

25

When news of the *Yerba Sacra* launch was first leaked to the press, the Dominion share price rose to an all-time high. But day two of the court case witnessed its dramatic descent. A share price that seesawed dizzily within a matter of weeks was unsettling and disturbing, especially for the uninformed.

The stock market could be a temperamental beast. Passive and docile one minute. Leaping and baring its teeth the next. Prices were fickle and edgy. They reacted nervously to anything from political upheavel to a juicy divorce scandal. But it helped if you knew what was going on.

Dominion's small shareholders listened anxiously to the news. Those most angered by the diminishing share price sought a tangible outlet for their frustration, the Royal Courts of Justice. Political sympathizers picketing the courts to raise public awareness of the 'human guinea pig' case were startled when voices hurled abuse at them from passing cars: 'You fucking troublemakers. What the hell do you know about what's going on?'

Paul Lombard knew exactly what was going on.

So did some major corporate shareholders who were advised to sell out as soon as the price began to fall. Awareness of a possible chain reaction activated by an event, and reactions to that event, could only be exploited if the investor was certain of what was to follow. And knowledge of that certainty was the privilege of the few.

As the impact of the sale of Daphne's shares, and those of some corporate shareholders began to be felt the price reacted with alarm. The financial advisers of smaller shareholders hastily alerted their clients. Panic selling started before lunchtime and accelerated throughout the afternoon.

City editors who were planning their lead stories for the financial pages of the dailies, watched the Dominion price plummet on the videoscreens above their typewriters.

But everyone was baffled by the sudden movement of the smaller blocks of shares off the market an hour or so after the exchange opened that morning. Who was this mysterious group of shareholders who clubbed together to do a protest sell within five or ten minutes of one another? Financial journalists reached for their phones and began a steady round robin and verbal bullying of their contacts in the City. 'Oh, come on, Tom. I know it couldn't be X or Y. Look, don't come to me next time you want to know what so-and-so's up to. Twisting your arm? Who, me?' Or, 'I've heard A and B offloaded their Dominion shares today. Any ideas where they might be looking now? What? Oh, it *wasn't* A or B? God, that bloody fool got his lines crossed. So it's C and D. What's that? No, of course I didn't hear it from you.'

Down on the Dominion public relations floor, Alun Hughes ordered his most reassuring-sounding press officers to stick by the phones all day. Then he retreated quietly into his own office and closed the door. The chairman had briefed him, as much as was necessary to ensure that key members of the executive board were moving in time to the same piece of music.

Alun personally phoned a few key people on the home news pages of the nationals. He suggested it might be useful for them to have someone in court at the end of the day, and not just depend on the wire services. Most of the journalists reacted suspiciously to the PR director's suggestion. Those who didn't know him well ignored it, believing he was trying to save his own skin while the company fell down around his ears. 'Smooth as hell. forget it,' said one news editor dismissively, and turned back to the photographs on his desk. 'Mm. Nice one of the picketers. Who are they? Friends of Brigid Anderson? International socialists? Workers Revolutionary Party? Great. Why not crop that one close to the girl with the big tits?' he suggested, adding, 'Mask off the priest. No, wait, *save* the priest and kill the bloke with the stringy hair.'

284

One journalist who received word from Hughes was busily collating material for an in-depth feature to be kept on ice until the judge's decision. He dialled George Samiou at ASH. 'George? Thought you might be interested to hear that Alun Hughes is encouraging his buddies to be in court later this afternoon. No idea. He wouldn't say. But he wouldn't comment on the falling share price, either. Why don't you drop into the courtroom to see what all this is about? Phone me at home tonight.'

The tobacco controversy was hot news at the best of times. But, until the *Yerba Sacra* leak, the press had found the anti-smoking reports and the personalities involved far more news-worthy than anything the industry itself had leaked out.

Now all eyes were glued to the falling share price.

The Dominion executive committee was so caught up in the activities centred aroung the offices of the chairman and financial director that no one noticed Ted's absence.

When Colette returned home, she was surprised to find the front door unlocked.

She went in quickly, saw the mess on the lounge carpet, and found her husband hunched over the kitchen table.

'Ted, why?' she asked, eyeing the empty Jim Neam bottle lying next to the sink.

'Maybe I wanted to look like I feel inside,' he said tightly.

'You succeeded. Does it make you feel any better?' Short. Crisp. She put down her things and reached into a cupboard for a bucket.

He watched her run water into it. So cleaning up the carpet was more important to her than his feelings. Had their marriage sunk this low?

'Who were you with last night?' he asked.

'Who have you been with for the last *forty* nights?' she replied, wringing out a rag.

Ted, quietly: 'What does she use on you, Colette, an empty St. Michel bottle from the family estates?'

Colette turned slowly and looked at him. She dropped the cloth in the bucket and walked out.

Ted flung his coffee mug at the wall. 'God*damn* you, sit down while I'm talking to you!'

She ran upstairs and locked herself in the bedroom. Ted lurched after her. 'You enjoy making a fool of me, don't you? It's not enough to fight Courtlands at the office. I have to come home and find they've been in my bed!'

A *woman*, and a *Courtland*. Jesus, was there no end to what this family could do to him?

He had a wildly irrational urge to go up and beat hell out of her, but a lethargic cynicism began to take over. He walked down to the basement.

Her studio was practically bare. A few clay models stood around on pedestals.

Systematically, Ted hurled each on to the ground. The models burst into pieces around his feet.

He stepped over the bits and opened the door into the walled garden. Everything seemed so totally pointless.

'You were too much of a coward to kill *me*, weren't you?' said a quiet voice from the door.

Ted turned. Colette stood there, a large portfolio or work in one hand, and a canvas bag in the other.

He sank to the grass. 'I've been fucking a woman who makes me feel I know more than she does in bed. With you it was always the other way around.'

'Ah, I see,' she said, opening the bag and reaching into a cupboard for her chisels and tools. 'And yet you couldn't talk to me about it.'

'What's the point. It's happening now and it'll go on happening. And yet I loved you so much.'

Colette eyed the floor and said nothing.

'I'm going back to Paris,' she said, wondering at the calm in her voice.

'I don't care. I don't need fantasies like you any more.' He didn't move from the grass. The words were intended to wound. The exorcism was now complete.

Colette turned and walked sadly through the studio, grinding the bits of broken clay underfoot. It was time to cut herself adrift.

286

The flowerbeds leading up to the Courtlands' country house were ablaze with colour. Daphne cast a satisfied eye over the abundance as she drove back from the station after her meeting with Joseph Donovan.

It had been a good summer. The primulas, stocks, snap-dragons, and dahlias had never been better. The grass looked thick and lush.

Daphne reached inside the front door for her floppy straw hat and wandered through the garden to the field beyond. An old deck chair was left there from the day before.

The long, untamed grass rustled underfoot, bristling and alive with communities of ants, crickets, grasshoppers and field mice.

She sat with her back to the house, lifted her head and squinted at the sun. 'I've been naughty, haven't I?' she said aloud, chuckling like a small girl caught stealing chocolate. 'Charles will never know it's me, poor dear.' She paused, as if waiting for someone to reply. 'Nothing can break the company, Father, you know that. But I wanted the satisfaction of knowing I could *agitate* things for a day!'

Daphne rose and walked slowly toward the house. There were papers to get in order, reference books to sort out. She had done some preliminary work after Tessa had been down to go over Stirling and Amy's letters. Perhaps she could spend the next few months getting a rough outline of the biography together, then take it to the Bahamas for the winter.

She leaned down to pick a handful of lavender. Her thoughts turned to Tessa. All that material the girl took away with her, letters, clippings, notes. If she didn't remind her to return them soon she'd never see them again.

Tessa never got a chance to use the snippets from her grandparents' letters in court.

She read about the falling share price when the court adjourned for lunch, minutes after she had examined her last witness. The news didn't surprise her one bit, but the last person she suspected as the cause of it all was her own mother.

287

She excused herself from Ciaran and Brigid and walked down to the Embankment to be alone. Reviewing the case helped keep her mind off other things. She thought ahead to her final summing-up.

So far, the evidence against Dominion had been heavily medical. But she still felt the company was getting off too lightly. It would take more than her evidence in court to convince the uninformed that Dominion wasn't the benign, paternalistic institution it appeared to be. She was convinced Hamilton Crisp would use this image to spearhead his case. How wrong she was.

She intended to conclude by using the exchange of letters between her grandparents during World War I, to indicate Dominion's frenzied war efforts to keep pace with the increasing demands for their products, and keep the profits rolling.

The time had come for an intensive corporate audit. The steady chalking up of debts had gone on long enough. Society had come to collect.

But on that day, the only accounting to be done by Dominion was taking place in Paul Lombard's office. And society wasn't collecting. It was losing.

Small shareholders watched with horror as the price plummeted by the hour. Many hastily salvaged what was left of their pathetic savings, vowing never again to place their trust in a solidly respectable industrial group.

Others quickly arranged to withdraw their Dominion shares and put what was left of them out to pasture on fixed deposit until things settled down.

Only those who could afford the services of a stockbroker were alerted sooner and were able to take swift advantage of the share tip of the day.

The court case became even more of a focal point for abuse.

Shareholders too far from the scene to bellow four letter words at the pickets outside the court began to jam the lines of the afternoon phone-in programmes on London's radio stations.

Protected by the anonymity of the air, angry individuals

weren't slow about giving vent to their feelings. 'Look, I'm sorry about this bloke 'oo died,' said one blunt Cockney voice, 'and it's tough on 'is widow and children, but I've lost 'alf my bloody savings because of this court case. That barrister stands up and talks about the suffering of an "ordinary man". *We're* the ordinary men and women 'oo're suffering now! These bleeding liberals. Why don't they all eff off to Russia?'

Paul Lombard and the chairman were unavailable for comment.

But the host of one radio show managed to get Alun Hughes on the line, and asked him to broadcast a few words of advice. Hughes's voice, more liltingly Welsh over the air than in conversation, sounded calm and reassuring. 'This will blow over,' he said. 'Those of you who decide to hold on to your shares will be laughing in a few weeks. I know you find this difficult to believe now, but we're the same company in whom you placed your original trust.' Chuckling, he added knowingly, 'We've weathered worse than this.'

The radio host was more sceptical. 'A lot of shareholders are afraid they're being wiped out by what's happening. What's your advice to them. Mr. Hughes?'

'My advice is for them to hold on. Don't give in to the panic.'

'Have you sold your shares?'

'Good heavens, no,' said Alun amiably. 'And I have a wife and three children to support, so I take no chances with my personal investments.'

'But you're the company PR man. How can we expect you to be objective in all this?'

'You can't, of *course* you can't,' Hughes agreed. 'But let me say something. If I didn't believe in the company, and was as panicky as everyone else, do you think I'd be sitting here talking to you? I'd be out looking for another job.'

'But it's your word against the stock exchange at the moment. Who are the shareholders to believe?'

A moment's silence crackled over the air. Hughes came back sounding genuinely concerned. 'If I were outside in the street, I'd feel confused and angry too. I'd be the last person to listen to the words of a PR man.'

'Who would you listen to?'

'No one. I'd sit it out for a few days until the dust settled down.'

The host didn't sound very convinced. 'Well, thank you for talking to us.'

'My advise is for people to sit on their shares,' Alun said firmly.

'Thank you, Mr. Hughes.' The host dismissed him and switched through to a financial journalist who did a weekly TV show. The journalist advised those who had all their savings in Donimion to pull out. 'Those who can afford to gamble, stay in,' he said. He also gave some off-the-cuff advice on industries and companies to watch.

Charles Courtland retuned his radio, keeping one eye on the ticker tape machines in the outer office and the other on the videoscreen relaying price fluctuations from the stock exchange as they happened on the floor.

The chairman was a little envious of Paul Lombard's capability and flair for turning disadvantage into profit. Certainly that had become the unwritten motto of the industry in recent years. But it was sometimes alarming for the wary, like himself, to see the motto flung into action. Lombard was taking a chance, but he wasn't reckless or impulsive. His intricate knowledge of the company and his reputation within the City enabled him to keep a tight rein on what was happening. Of course, what they were doing wasn't strictly legal, tipping off corporate shareholders, involving them in a conscious plan to deflate and inflate the share price. But those involved were a closely knit group of insiders: men who had built up understanding and trust over the years. They obeyed the laws that observed their mutual interests and preserved the respected institutions. They could be counted on not to abuse this trust.

Paul Lombard appeared in the chairman's office, shirt sleeves casually rolled up. He smiled at the chairman's worried frown. 'New York will barely get through a morning's work by

290

the time Ham Crisp drops his bombshell in court this afternoon, Charles. So Wall Street will hardly feel a thing. Tomorrow it will arise from its sleep to see our recovery.'

Courtland nodded slowly, one ear on the radio. 'Wish we could tell the shareholders that,' he said, listening grimly to the complaints. 'By the way, has anyone seen Ted?'

Lombard was on his way out. 'Knowing Ted, he's probably jogging between our retail outlets personally delivering supplies.'

The chairman wasn't so sure. When he was alone, he removed his attention from videoscreen and radio for a few moments. He buzzed Ted's office, and dialled his home phone number. He got no response from either.

26

There comes a moment in every barrister's career when he or she is faced with a choice between throwing the book at the court, or introducing some extraneous element to spin the case into orbit.

The detailed and labourious presentation made by one barrister aimed at pricking social conscience and raising political consciousness can be dismantled in seconds, if the opposition succeeds in finding the Archilles heel in time.

When Hamilton Crisp rose to present his case, he removed a gold watch and chain from his waistcoat pocket and propped it against a book in front of him. His opening speech was impatient and terse. He had the knack of creating the impression that the case was a ridiculous waste of time, a personal act of revenge and greed. He spoke of his client as a model employer of some twenty thousand in offices and factories throughout Britain. 'And who is here today?' he asked, glancing around. 'Not the angry voice of the employees, but the whining voice of a single widow who has the callousness to exploit her husband's death for personal greed and gain.'

Brigid Anderson sat through the speech, expressionless, not really taking much in. Tessa had prepared her for Crisp's scythelike tongue. But Tessa hadn't altogether anticipated the extent of the attack. Crisp warned the court against being fooled by the 'deftness' with which the deceased and his widow were presented as 'pathetic victims,' and remarked on the 'devious political motives' that had brought the case to court.

Tessa read that as a personal attack. Without mentioning names, Crisp had cunningly directed the court's attention to her, appealing to the collective logic in the courtroom to examine the evidence in the light of what she hoped to gain from it in political terms.

The medical evidence was considered of minimal importance, a political convenience. The falling share price, not the rush on *Yerba Sacra* sales, was cited as being precisely what the plaintiff wanted. 'Her malicious search for revenge has so blinded her that she has no consideration for the possible repercussions. Hundreds of men could be laid off work. To pursue her own selfish interest, she has placed many of her late husband's workmates in a vulnerable position within the company.' Crisp paused, rustling the notes in his hand. 'If a plant should be closed down,' he added, pointing across at Brigid Anderson, 'the men will have the *plaintiff* to thank.'

Tessa stared, concerned, at the back of Brigid's head. Crisp was using the oldest trick in politics, rerouting blame away from the company, turning worker against worker.

Ciaran was scribbling furiously. He passed a note over his shoulder to Tessa: '*See Marx 1870. Ruling class maintains power by pitting English worker against Irish worker. Can't Crisp think up something more original than this?*'

She scribbled back: *Don't worry. He can't fight us on the medical thing. Make sure Brigid doesn't take this pathetic line too seriously.*

Ciaran took the note and nodded, turning to smile and wink reassuringly at Brigid.

During the adjournment for lunch, Tessa had received a message from George Samiou telling her about Alun Hughes's alerting the press. At the time she hadn't been unduly surprised, thinking that Alun was reacting normally to the falling share price. The company PR director just wanted to make sure some responsible journalists were there to take note of Crisp's opening speech. That was understandable. The morning newspapers had dutifully reflected the solid body of medical evidence from the previous day. Dominion emerged as something equivalent to a Nazi doctor carrying out gruesome experiments on Jews in the concentration camps. Counsel had to do something to save Dominion's corporate face.

Now she sensed the court's thoughtful reaction to what

Crisp was saying. The press leaned forward, eyes moving curiously between the QC and Brigid Anderson, not wanting to miss the plaintiff's response. The court's attention focused on the trio: barrister, solicitor, client. Sympathies were suspended. The gears shifting silently between heart and head.

As his first witness, Crisp called Dr. Noel Sorensen to the stand.

The research director took the oath in a strong, confident voice and listed his qualifications. He was a graduate of St. Mary's Hospital in London and had entered industry at a young age, believing this would offer him the best opportunities and facilities for research. He had worked for the tobacco industry for over twenty-five years, and had served on the Dominion executive board for the past ten years.

Dominion's extensive programme of research into tobacco substitutes had been carried out under his jurisdiction.

With great care, and in intricate detail, he described the various experiments that had been performed on *Yerba Sacra*.

Crisp asked: 'Were workers encouraged to offer themselves as volunteers?'

'Good heavens, no. We pinned notices on the boards of our factories and warehouses situated within a convenient travelling distance of the labs at Dominion House. The notices merely stated that volunteers were required after hours, and would be paid overtime for their services. Those interested were asked to sign their names and report to the clinician in charge. You see, it was up to *them* to decide if they wanted to do overtime in their own particular job, or to participate in tests. They could earn the same money both ways.'

Crisp: 'Were you able to get the required number of volunteers?'

Sorensen: 'We got *three times* the number we required.'

Crisp: 'And how did you make the selection?'

Sorensen: 'It was really fairly simple. We eliminated those who had the most travelling to do between factory and Dominion House, Dominion House and home.'

Crisp: 'Was physical fitness taken into consideration?'

Sorensen: 'Yes, it most certainly was. Our doctor conducted a thorough physical examination on each of the volunteers. Indeed, some ten were considered unsuitable and were told not to participate.'

Crisp: 'But James Anderson was considered fit enough to be included.'

Sorensen: 'Yes. The examinations that were carried out to determine the function of his lungs and heart showed a perfectly normal response.'

The court murmured its surprise.

Crisp: 'Exhibit J, my Lord. A copy of the company's medical report card on the deceased.'

The folder was passed to the bench and then down to Tessa.

Crisp: 'If the deceased hadn't been sufficiently fit to participate in the tests, would this have been revealed in the initial examination?'

Sorensen: 'Yes.' Addressing the bench, he said pointedly. 'The clinicians who examined him reported that he was a healthy young man.'

Crisp: 'If he was in the early stages of lung cancer, would they have detected it?'

Sorensen: 'If they had detected the *slightest* obstruction in his lungs, he would not have been allowed to participate in the tests.'

Crisp: 'Thank you, Dr. Sorensen. I have no further questions.'

Blackford: 'Well, Miss Courtland.'

Tessa rose, the report card in her hand. 'Did you examine any of the volunteers personally, Dr. Sorensen?'

Sorensen: 'No.'

Tessa: 'So,' she said, waving the card in the air, 'you take this at face value.'

Sorensen: 'I respect the judgement of my colleagues.'

Tessa: 'And your "colleague" in this case, is, I see, a state registered nurse. Not a doctor at all!'

Sorensen: 'Miss Barnes has been with us for a number of

years. I have implicit faith in her capabilities as an examining nurse.'

Tessa: 'Nevertheless, she is not a qualified doctor.'

Sorensen, irritably: 'She is qualified for this particular job. If she hadn't been, the Tait Committee would not have accepted her examinations.'

Tessa: 'Why didn't you require chest X-rays?'

Sorensen: 'The committee didn't require them.'

Tessa: 'I'm not asking you to speak for the committee, Dr. Sorensen. I'm asking *you*.'

Sorensen: 'We didn't believe chest X-rays were necessary.'

Tessa: 'We being, in this instance, a nurse?'

Sorensen: 'No, the team of clinicians involved.'

Tessa: 'But I see no mention of a team on this card. Simply the nurse's signature.'

Sorensen: 'The volunteers were under the close supervision of the entire team.'

Tessa: But you admit you didn't examine them personally.'

Sorensen: 'No.'

Tessa: 'So you weren't in a positon to check the clinicians' findings for yourself.'

Sorensen, drawing himself up: 'As research director I am obliged to delegate the bulk of the actual experiments to my highly qualified team.'

Tessa: 'In this case we are talking about the opinion of one nurse.' Turning to the bench she said, 'You will recall the evidence supplied by the expert medical witnesses, my Lord, as to the state of the deceased's lungs. Had a chest X-ray been required by the defendant, his life might have been saved. Instead we have the evidence of "one" nurse.'

Sorensen, annoyed: 'I'm a qualified medical doctor. If I was in any doubt whatsoever about the examinations conducted by the team on the volunteers, I would have requested a further examination.'

Tessa: 'But you couldn't do that without seeing them for yourself.'

Sorensen, sarcastically: 'I can read medical reports, you know.'

Tessa: 'I've no doubt. But then you must be required to read dozens of charts and tables and lab reports and research findings that come to you from the various divisions within your department.'

Sorensen: 'That is correct.'

Tessa: 'So you can't possibly get around to checking them all personally. Tell me, doctor. In medical school, were you taught to accept the diagnosis of a ward nurse?'

Sorensen faltered. 'Diagnosis was frequently a matter of discussion between a dcotor and nurse.'

Tessa: 'That wasn't my question. A dialogue between the doctor and nurse suggests they are both personally familiar with the patient. Had the doctor not examined the patient, would he accept the nurse's diagnosis?'

Sorensen hesitated. To say no would be to wipe out his evidence. To say yes would make idiots out of medical practitioners. He decided on the latter, with some visible embarrassment.

Tessa, looking toward the bench: 'Dr. Sorensen, are you asking the court to accept the evidence of a nurse over that of the medical specialists who have appeared here?'

Sorensen: 'I believe that much of their evidence was hearsay.'

Tessa: 'I'm not asking for your opinion.'

Sorensen: 'Well then, I can't answer the question.'

Mr. Justice Blackford, annoyed: 'The witness is obliged to answer the question.'

Sorensen: 'My Lord. I believe the medical specialists were biased and prejudiced.'

Tessa: 'In that case, you would prefer to accept the opinion of a company nurse over the "biased and prejudiced" opinions of a consultant pathologist, and the head of cancer research from leading teaching hospitals?'

Sorensen was trapped in a corner and he knew it. But he wanted to get out of the witness box as quickly as possible. 'Yes,' he said with confidence.

The court expressed disbelief.

Tessa smiled and shook her head. 'I have no further questions.'

The research director squared his shoulders and left the box, returning to his seat next to the company solicitor. He knew it wasn't what one said, but the way one said it that counted. Sufficient confidence backed by medical qualifications could give necessary weight to any evidence. After all, he was the research director of the world's largest tobacco combine.

As his next witness, Crisp call Mr. John Knutford, consultant surgeon from a regional teaching hospital.

Crisp: 'Mr. Knutford, have you examined the various clinical and medical records of James Anderson?'

Knutford: 'I have.'

Crisp: 'Can you say with reasonable medical certainty that cigarette smoking is *the* cause of lung cancer?'

Knutford: 'No.'

Crisp: 'Can you say with reasonable medical certainty that cigarette smoking is *a* cause of lung cancer?'

Knutford: 'No.'

Crisp: 'Is it a generally accepted medical fact in the medical community that cigarette smoking is a cause of lung cancer?'

Knutford: 'No, it is not.'

Crisp: 'Can you say with medical certainty whether or not James Anderson's lung cancer was caused by prolonged or excessive cigarette smoking?'

Knutford: 'No, I cannot. My opinion is that cigarette smoking does not cause cancer of the lung. I base this opinion on my personal clinical experience.'

Crisp: 'Have you operated on non-smokers who contracted lung cancer?'

Knutford: 'I have seen a number of non-smokers who died of carcinomas identical to that of James Anderson, the deceased.' Pausing, he added, 'I take into consideration the very large number of heavy smokers who never develop lung cancer. One must, of course, widen one's observations to include the family. One can encounter a number of very old males in a family in which the incidence of cancer is relatively frequent.'

Crisp: 'And on my instruction, did you make an examination of the Anderson family?'

Knutford: 'Yes, his paternal grandfather and maternal great grandfather and one uncle all died of cancer.'

Crisp: 'Thank you, Mr. Knutford.'

Tessa rose for the cross examination, sensing the restlessness in court and the frequency with which Crisp kept referring to his watch. During the brief pause, three men and one woman tiptoed in quietly and slid into the press gallery. Tessa half turned and caught George Samiou's eye at the back of the public gallery. The courtroom was packed.

She turned to the surgeon. 'Mr. Knutford, are you speaking for yourself, or do you represent some official medical body?'

Knutford, brightly: 'I speak for myself.'

'And whàt, in your singular opinion, causes lung cancer?'

'No one knows the cause. It is a biological phenomenon that no one fully understands.'

'Do you understand it?'

'No.'

'So you admit that you neither know the cause nor understand it.'

Knutford looked at her uncertainly. 'That is correct.'

Tessa: 'Yet with so much admitted ambiguity in your own mind, you can say for sure that smoking *doesn't* cause lung cancer. How is that?'

Knutford: 'That is my clinical opinion, based on several thousand cases which I have examined personally.'

'But if you are unable to say what causes cancer, how can you say what *doesn't* cause it?'

'I don't believe smoking causes it.'

'But you don't know what does cause it.'

'No.'

'Then, you can't know what doesn't cause it, can you Mr. Knutford,' she said kindly. 'Now, you mentioned a number of non-smokers who, in your *singular* opinion, died of the same carcinoma as James Anderson.'

'Yes.'

'What was the ratio of smokers to non-smokers.'

Knutford, slowly: 'Roughly seventy-five to twenty-five.'

'Seventy-five smokers to twenty-five non-smokers.'

'Yes.'

'Wouldn't you call that a majority?'

'Not necessarily.'

'Oh? What figures constitute a majority in your mind?'

'As scientist we are taught to view each case individually, and not to draw glib conclusions from ratios.'

'I see. If a hospital caught fire and seventy-five people died and twenty-five people were saved, wouldn't you say a majority had died in the fire?'

'Yes, of course.'

'Well then, at least we can agree on which is the larger sum. Mr. Knutford, seventy-five or twenty-five. I ask you again, if the ratio of smokers to non-smokers suffering from small-cell undifferentiated carcinoma is seventy-five to twenty-five, the smokers are in the majority, are they not?'

'Yes, but it's unwise—'

'Thank you, Mr. Knutford. In the words of leading counsel, we are concerned with basing our conclusions on the evidence of majorities in this case. That it all.'

The surgeon looked bewildered and annoyed. He knew he had made himself look foolish and there was nothing he could do about it.

He vacated the stand and walked straight out of the courtroom.

Crisp glanced at his watch and turned to peer toward the door.

People in the courtroom half rose in anticipation, twisting in their seats to catch a glimpse of who or whatever was the object of the QC'a gaze.

Tessa turned too. Crisp hadn't seemed unduly put out by her dismissal of Knutford. No startling revelations had been supplied by his first two witnesses. Diana Tonbridge had sat throughout with a buttoned mouth. Crisp was made of better stuff then this. Her eyes flickered around the packed courtroom and the full press gallery. Today they weren't there to see her in action. What then was the source of this buzzing curiosity?

Justice Blackford looked impatiently toward the QC. 'Sir Hamilton, what is the reason for this delay?'

'My Lord,' he said graciously, 'my next witness appears to have been delayed. With you permission, I would like to recall the plaintiff.'

Brigid Anderson rose, head held high, shoulders straight and firm.

Tessa watched her anxiously. She had put Brigid in the witness box only briefly that morning, not wanting to ask her anything that might be twisted during Crisp's cross examination. The only evidence she was required to give concerned Anderson's smoking habits, the date on which he first complained of chest pains, his physical condition during the time of the tests, and anything he may have said to her about the effect they were having on him, the date of the visit of the family doctor, the specialist, and the brief time in hospital before his death.

The exchange of questions and answers merely supplied some necessary chronological information. Tessa didn't require her to offer any opinions or elaborate physical descriptions, believing that should be left to the medical experts. Nor was she going to use Brigid to sway the sympathy of the court. The facts would either do that or they wouldn't. Instead, the court saw a slight woman with large, sad, eyes, controlled, giving away no undue emotion.

When Tessa's examination was over, Crisp, responding to the chairman's request for a delay, had risen and announced that he had no questions for the plaintiff at that moment, but he requested permission to recall her to the box.

His first two witnesses had merely been time-fillers. Now he was ready to deal the blow he believed would bring the case to a swift close.

Brigid Anderson faced him squarely, hands firmly gripping the witness box on either side. The court was now given the opportunity of studying her in the box for the second time that day.

'Mrs. Anderson,' Crisp began, hands on hips, body swaying. 'You were in Ireland recently, I believe?'

'Yes,' she said, clear voice ringing through the court.

Crisp: 'And why did you go there?'

Tessa, quickly: 'My Lord, I must object. The question is quite irrelevant. My client is not required to account for her whereabouts.'

Justice Blackford studied Brigid Anderson thoughtfully for a few seconds and dismissed Tessa's objection. 'The plaintiff will please answer the question,' he said firmly.

Brigid: 'I needed to be with my family in Dublin,' she said bluntly. 'And I thought it best for the children to be with my sister.'

'Best for whom?' Crisp asked pointedly, 'the children or you?'

'For them, or course,' she replied. 'It was difficult for them, living through their father's illness and death. I wanted them to go away from where it happened, and to be out of London during this case.'

'You wanted them out of the way for a while, so *you* could pursue a fresh start. They crowded *your* freedom, did they not? It was a matter of convenience leaving them with your sister, wasn't it?'

Tessa, angered: '*Objection*. These personal taunts are insulting and irrelevant.'

Blackford: 'Please make your point, Sir Hamilton.'

Crisp, again consulting his watch: 'I'm leading to it, my Lord. The plaintiff's counsel would have us believe that her client has been left destitute by early widowhood. A trip to Ireland can be very expensive. Who paid for it, Mrs. Anderson?'

Brigid glanced down at Ciaran. 'I . . . Mr. McGann lent me some money.'

Crisp peered over at the solicitor, taking in every inch of his shabby linen suit. Ciaran ran a hand self-consciously through his long grey hair.

302

Exercising all her professional control, Tessa rose and asked permission to approach the bench. The judge granted it. Crisp also moved forward, smiling.

'My Lord,' she said, 'let me save time for us all. I asked my client's solicitor to take her and the children to Ireland. *I* sent an anonymous cheque. My client does not know of this, and I see no purpose in Sir Hamilton's attempts to embarrass her unnecessarily. This was a private matter.'

The judge looked shocked. 'Miss Courtland, it is contrary to the ethics of the profession for counsel to become *privately* involved with a client. I consider this highly irregular.' However,' he said, turning to Crisp, 'I see no value in your line of questioning, Sir Hamilton. You will please withdraw the question.' He sat back and dismissed them both with a wave of the hand.

Tessa avoided Ciaran's eye as she returned to her seat. She was to blame, but something far more serious than that bothered her. How the hell did Crisp find out? The cheque had been made out to Ciaran's firm for professional services. There was nothing unusual in that. He was carrying out certain investigations on her behalf. Their phone conversation . . . not a bug, surely. Jesus, to be tripped up by something so innocent and casual. Judges didn't like it when a barrister went beyond the call of duty. There was no such thing as an impulsive humanitarian gesture in the curtly professional relationship between counsel and client. It reeked of collusion, even bribery.

Crisp had found her Achilles heel. But it wasn't enough. Brigid Anderson had one, too.

'Mrs. Anderson,' he continued, one eye on the door. 'Who did you meet when you were in Dublin?'

'Meet? I was with my family.'

Crisp chuckled: 'Come now, Mrs. Anderson, we're all adults. Your husband had been ill for a number of months. Weren't you eager for male company?'

Tessa: 'My Lord, I object most strongly to counsel's line of questioning. We are here to determine the content of James Anderson's lungs, not the content of his widow's character!'

Blackford overruled her, saying they were there to examine all factors pertaining to the case. '*Well*, Sir Hamilton?' he asked impatiently.

'My Lord, with your permission.' Turning toward Brigid, Crisp asked, 'Did you or did you not spend several days—and several nights—with a lover?'

'No,' she said fiercely.

'Did you, or did you not become the mistress of one Shamus Liam O'Neal, a member of the Irish Republican Army who has been wanted for questioning by the Special Branch in connection with successive acts of sabotage in Britain?'

'*No!*' she shouted.

Crisp remained cool. 'May I remind you, you are under oath, Mrs. Anderson!'

Tessa, angrily: 'Objection! My Lord, these questions are insulting and irrevelant.'

Crisp: 'Indeed, they are not. Nothing that endangers the security of the nation can be considered irrelevant in *any* case that is heard before a British court.'

The courtroom responded loudly. Booing and hissing from the left. Anger and concern from the right.

Blackford reacted with alarm. When a muffled calm had been restored to the gallery, the judge said acidly, 'The next person who creates disorder in this courtroom shall be arrested and charged accordingly.' Turning toward Crisp, he added in the same tone of voice, 'Sir Hamilton, if you have any evidence of these allegations I suggest you present it now.'

Crisp bowed politely. 'With pleasure, my Lord. With your permission I call Shamus Liam O'Neal.'

The doors opened at the back to reveal a young man, grey and lined with exhaustion, handcuffed on either side to members of the Special Branch. The trio moved slowly toward the front of the court.

The press was dumbfounded. O'Neal had been on the wanted list for months. How on earth had the Special Branch managed to keep his arrest quiet? Those nearest the door slipped out quickly to phone the scoop through to their news editor.

A flood of abuse from the witness box quickly diverted attention away from O'Neal. 'You filthy swine!' Brigid screamed at Crisp. 'You'll do anything to keep the Irish in hell. You'll even watch our *beds!*'

Shouts of support burst out of the public gallery. A sea of clenched fists shot in the air. Screams of 'sexism,' 'racism,' and 'establishment bastards' drowned the clerk's futile attempts to be heard.

The judge ordered the court to be cleared. He sat rigidly still until the stamping and shouting subsided with the last person to leave the room.

Tessa rose: 'My Lord, I request time alone with my client.'

Blackford's gaze moved from Brigid down to O'Neal standing handcuffed between the two Special Branch men. He glanced toward Crisp, and then finally at Tessa. 'Miss Courtland, under the circumstances I am obliged to deny you that request until leading counsel has completed his cross-examination.' With a wave of his hand, he said, 'Please continue, Sir Hamilton.'

Tessa remained on her feet: 'My Lord, I must insist on my client's right to consult me in the light of the extraneous evidence that has been brought against her.'

Blackford began to lose patience: 'Miss Courtland, these provocations have gone too far. If the plaintiff cannot control herself properly in court, she cannot expect us to interrupt the cross examination on her behalf. Please *continue*, Sir Hamilton.'

Crisp: 'Thank you, my Lord, With your permission I would like to read a written confession from Shamus Liam O'Neal concerning the plaintiff.'

'No!' Brigid shouted from the box. *'No!'*

Tessa, quickly: 'My Lord, I must insist on my client's right to consult me in private. Leading counsel is introducing material that is clearly irrelevant to the case. My client is *not* on trial in this court.'

Blackford dismissed her coldly. 'Please *continue*, Sir Hamilton.'

Tessa refused to back down.

The judge gazed toward the tiers of the now deserted public gallery. He spoke with such control that his tone was almost gentle. 'Miss Courtland, we are in this courtroom to hear *all* the facts pertaining to this case, as you yourself reminded us yesterday when the matter of the deceased's lung was raised. Am I to understand that you wish to deny the same measure of freedom to Sir Hamilton and Miss Tonbridge?'

Blackford knew exactly where to hit home. The quiet way in which he placed a stress on the single word 'freedom' was aimed to strike Tessa at the core of her political beliefs. The onus was now on her. The small group in the court knew that.

But Tessa wasn't one to be thrown so easily. This wasn't the first time a judge had tried to use her politics to challenge her as a barrister.

She allowed a few moments to lapse. The group in the courtroom waited patiently.

'My Lord,' she said, smiling softly, 'we are all equally concerned with the facts, and with freedom, and with the rights of the individual before the law.' Glancing toward the opposition, she added, 'I do not begrudge leading counsel's right to pursue his argument, and I believe neither he, nor you, will deny *me* the right to consult with my client at this point.'

The ball was back in Blackford's court. Both he and Tessa knew exactly what they were doing. But they both shared a stubborn streak. He studied her. She had a right to interrupt the cross examination to have time with her client. But he had already denied her that right. As Mr. Justice Blackford, he wasn't going to back down on his word. He was a judge, and no junior barrister, no young woman, was going to have an edge over him.

He felt the eyes of the court on him. Brigid Anderson in the box, angry, defiant. The Special Branch men, on duty, expressionless. O'Neal, waiting. Hamilton Crisp, rustling impatiently. Miss Tonbridge with her silly pointed face. And Tessa. He resented her strength.

'Miss Courtland,' he said, unable to meet her gaze, 'you may have time with you client when leading counsel has completed the cross examination.' Turning to Crisp he said emphatically, 'I ask you again, Sir Hamilton, to continue.'

Tessa's eyes never left his face for a minute as she sat down. He avoided the expression of disgust.

Crisp's tone was almost sympathetic. Everyone in the courtroom was aware of the momentary challenge and the intensity that had passed silently between Blackford and Tessa. It made everyone feel uncomfortable. But Crisp's words soon refocused attention on the glaring issue of Brigid Anderson and Shamus O'Neal.

'My Lord,' the QC began, 'with your permission, I will summarize the contents of the confession signed by Shamus Liam O'Neal.' He cleared his throat. 'During June of this year, Mr. O'Neal and the plaintiff, Brigid Lucy Anderson, spent some three weeks with one another, during which time they became involved in an active sexual relationship. The plaintiff was a willing participant and the relationship elevated her usefulness to the Irish Republican Army.'

Tessa continued to stare at the judge, to his increasing discomfort.

Crisp dampened his finger and turned over the page. 'Anderson was sent back to the United Kingdom with the specific purpose of recruiting Irish women in selected boroughs of London, and organizing them in illegal activities involving political action and sabotage.' He paused, and glanced toward Tessa and Ciaran. 'My Lord, this mockery of a case was part of a deliberate plan to deal a blow at the establishment of which my client is a leading member. It was also a cunning way of gaining substantial funds to further the IRA's aims to sustain and perpetuate panic and disorder in Britain, via systematic acts of sabotage.'

The QC then asked a court official to hand copies of the confession to Blackford, Tessa, and Ciaran. 'My Lord,' he concluded, 'this case is nothing but a trumped up political front, a new and insidious form of sabotage directed against the leading institutions of Britain.'

Tessa rose angrily. '*Objection*! Unless leading counsel can present concrete proof beyond the testimony of one man to support these allegations I suggest he drop this cunning ploy and return to the facts of the case. My client is *not* on trial. It is both despicable and unlawful to confront her with extraneous material while denying her the right to consult me.'

Blackford, angrily: 'Sit down, Miss Courtland. I do not believe this matter is in any way extraneous. I consider it a grave abuse of the judical system when a case is found to be politically motivated.'

Tessa: 'My Lord, may I ask if Mr. O'Neal has legal representation?'

O'Neal, white-faced, shook his head. Brigid stared down at him from the box but he avoided her eyes.

'Then,' Tessa snapped, 'I question the validity of this alleged confession. Are we to understand that Mr. O'Neal has been denied the right to see a solicitor since his arrest?'

Crisp: 'I must object. Mr. O'Neal is here as a witness for the respondent. The subject of his legal representation is irrelevant.'

Tessa: 'It most certainly is not. An alleged confession extracted under circumstances in which Mr. O'Neal was denied legal representation cannot be accepted as evidence in this case.'

Brigid remained very quiet throughout the exchange. Her eyes moved from one side to the other, resting occasionally on O'Neal's bowed head.

The angry words and legal arguments echoed noisily throughout the near-empty room. The clerk of the court and the officials waited passively.

Ciaran listened to Tessa's deft attempts to invalidate Crisp's evidence, but sensed the futility of it all. He and Tessa had fought a case on behalf of the IRA less than a year before. And here they were again, fighting for the rights of a woman who *happened* to be Irish. Who wouldn't use this against them?

Suddenly Brigid Anderson raised both arms in the air and shouted, '*Stop!*'

Blackford looked at her in amazement. 'Mrs. Anderson, you will oblige us by not interrupting.'

'Why?' she shouted back. 'Am I being charged with something?'

Tessa: 'My client has a legal right to know her rights, my Lord.'

Brigid: 'I know damn well where I stand! How can I expect justice in a British court? You're filthy rotten swine, all of you. This isn't a just court!'

Blackford: '*Be quiet*, Mrs. Anderson.

Brigid: 'I will not be quiet. I will not be silenced any longer.'

Blackford: 'Unless you control yourself, I shall have you forcibly removed from this courtroom.'

'*I'm as good as removed now*,' she shouted back from the box.

Crisp: 'My Lord, are we to understand from the plaintiff that she no longer pursues the claim she has brought against my client?'

Tessa: 'My Lord, my client cannot be expected to continue like this without consulting me.'

Brigid: 'Why? Do you think I'm incapable of talking for myself? The Dominion company can go to *hell* and take you with it.'

Tessa: 'My Lord, I must insist on an adjournment.'

Blackford didn't answer immediately. He felt enraged, used, and deceived by what had taken place. His fleeting moment of admiration for Tessa was dead.

Turning toward the witness box, the judge asked, slowly, 'Mrs. Anderson, is Mr. O'Neal your lover?'

Brigid said nothing.

Blackford repeated the question.

Again, she refused to answer.

He asked her a third time.

She folded her hands in front of her and refused to budge.

'Very well', he said, adjusting his position, 'you leave me no choice. You have *deliberately* sought to obstruct justice by your behaviour,' Turning toward Tessa he said, 'We will adjourn for precisely thirty minutes, Miss Courtland. This will give you ample time to advise your client of her rights.'

The court rose. Blackford turned abruptly and left the room. Ciaran gestured to Brigid. Tessa led them quickly out of the doors and as far away from the atmosphere of the court as was possible, to a small office at the end of the corridor.

Ciaran surprised Tessa by turning on Brigid. 'Why the hell didn't you tell me about O'Neal?'

Tessa tried to silence him, but Brigid interrupted, angry blue eyes moving between her legal advisers. 'But I'd told no one, *no one!*'

'*Oh Jesus,*' he said swiftly and turned away.

Tessa glanced at her watch. 'We have twenty-seven minutes and cannot afford anger. Not now. Please.'

There was so little time, and yet for a few moments, not one of them could say anything.

Eventually Tessa spoke, quietly and gently. 'Brigid I respect your need for privacy, political or personal. It would have been easier if Ciaran and I had known because we would have been better prepared. Not for our sakes, but for *your* sake. But we didn't and I can't blame you.' She meant that genuinely. Brigid had perjured herself from the witness box, which was precisely what Crisp had counted on to cast doubt on the validity of the entire case.

The QC had aimed at rousing the judge's anger and at completely minimizing the medical evidence. He had succeeded.

Between them, Tessa and Ciaran advised Brigid of the legal position in which she stood and what she should do. Ciaran was still smarting from the revelations in court, and Tessa sensed a hint of jealousy in his reaction. She herself responded to the delicate personal and legal matters confronting the three of them by being gentle and calm.

'Brigid,' she said firmly, 'I want you to understand that what happened in court this afternoon presents two separate legal issues. Crisp was using a tactic with which every barrister and solicitor in Britain is familiar. Do you think I haven't done that myself? It simply means he *knows* he can't beat us on the

310

medical issue. He is indirectly telling us he has no case and must resort to your private life to bring us down. Whatever happens, I want this case to continue. If we lose it, we appeal, and we go on appealing right up to the House or Lords.'

Brigid laughed in her face. 'You're a patronizing cow with your fine silky words, the House of Lords, indeed. Jimmy's soul has been ridiculed enough with his body in bits before the court. Let him rest and let *me* get on with my own life.'

Ciaran said nothing.

'I understand,' said Tessa, recognizing Brigid's need to give vent to her feelings. 'But I'd strongly advise—'

'*Advise?*' Brigid stared at her. 'I don't need advice from any fucking Courtland!'

Ciaran turned. 'You need legal advice,' he said cuttingly. 'You can't handle this on your own.'

'I can't? Who says so?' Brigid got up and folded her arms. She stared at them both. Solicitor, angry, hurt, dishevelled. Barrister, gowned, wigged, grave, concerned. Glancing at her watch, she said, 'The vultures are waiting for us. I *instruct* you,' she added clearly and coldly, 'to bring this ugly Dominion case to an end. I want no more of it. I want to start my own life. Now. This minute!' With that, she turned toward the door.

Protestations from Ciaran and Tessa did nothing to change her mind. She saw the issue with painful clarity. She knew exactly what she wanted and the entire Bar couldn't have dissuaded her.

The three of them returned to the courtroom in silence. Ciaran, bitter and reproachful. Tessa, overwhelmed by an appalling sense of futility. O'Neal was still standing between the Special Branch men. Crisp and Diana Tonbridge waited quietly. Dr. Sorensen and Dominion's solicitor sat side by side without talking.

The judge returned to his chair when the thirty minutes were up and instructed that the press be recalled.

Eight reporters duly trooped in looking curious and agitated and lined up along the tiers of the press gallery.

Tessa rose. This wasn't the moment for longwinded

311

rhetoric. Surprised at her own matter-of-fact tone, she simply informed the judge that her client wished to withdraw the claim against Dominion.

Blackford's gaze moved between client and counsel. When Tessa finished, he asked the plaintiff to rise. His own role in the case was by no means over, because of Brigid's behaviour in the witness box that afternoon. 'I hold you in contempt of court, he told her crossly, 'and request that you be held in custody.

Tessa and Ciaran had predicted that this would happen and had warned Brigid accordingly. So no one was surprised when the judge instructed the tipstaff to make the necessary arrest. Both Tessa and Ciaran knew that the contempt charge would provide the Special Branch with an excuse to interrogate her.

Everyone in the courtroom knew this. But Blackford was determined not to drop the issue.

The press had come to the courtroom that day expecting to see a mighty tobacco combine brought to its knees. Instead they were being told that the case was politically motivated by 'sinister terrorist forces' who wished to exploit a man's death as a 'front' and utilize whatever damages were awarded to sustain a 'reign of terror' in the streets of Britain.

The case had set a 'serious precedent' said Blackford, a 'new and insidious' form of sabotage aimed at disrupting and twisting the course of justice for political ends.

Finally, Blackford directed his outrage against Tessa. He accused her of being an accomplice and of debasing the honour and dignity of the Bar. He urged that immediate disciplinary action be brought against her by the Benchers of the Middle Temple.

Tessa raised her eyebrows and glanced thoughtfully toward the scribbling pens in the press gallery. How many of you will see through all this? she wondered.

There wasn't a murmur from anyone as Shamus and Brigid were duly led from the courtroom. The judge made his exit without saying another word.

A lot of vigorous handshaking and smiling passed between Sir Hamilton Crisp, Dr. Noel Sorensen, Miss Diana Tonbridge, and Dominion's solicitor.

Tessa and Ciaran waited behind until the courtroom emptied itself. They sat without speaking and stared at the bench.

'A banana republic would find this farcical,' said Tessa. 'Blackford's personal prejudices would get a junior *barrister* disbarred. How the hell does he know if she did more than simply *sleep* with O'Neal?'

Ciaran looked at her cynically. 'Just holding hands with O'Neal would make her an immediate security risk.'

'Come on,' she said, gathering her papers together. 'No point wasting any more energy. It's our own damned fault for not realizing something like this might happen. The guinea pig issue goes on whether Brigid likes it or not. Let's get a press conference together with George Samiou. I'll nail Blackford on TV if necessary.'

Ciaran rose. 'That will really give the Benchers something to dance about. Do you want to get yourself disbarred?'

Tessa looked at him in amazement. 'Ciaran, I don't care,' she said. 'If that's the only way I can make my point, it would be an honour.'

27

Ted watched the six o'clock news and laughed so hard he rolled off the bed onto the floor.

The phone had been unplugged all day. After Colette had gone he had lain on the grass in a heap of self-pity until a voice shouted from a neighbouring window, 'Are you dead or alive down there?' He had picked himself up, embarrassed and gone inside, crunching clay under-foot.

He took another long hot shower and collapsed on the bed where he dozed off and on for the rest of the day. In his waking moments, his eye travelled the room, studying the open cupboard doors. Colette had left most of her things behind. Clothes hung over a neat row of shoes. She was never one for clutter, not even in the bathroom, so it was difficult to tell exactly what was missing. Except for her.

The sight of intimate objects belonging to someone who has gone has a curious effect on the one left behind. Initially the objects cause pain, memories. The possessions haven't changed. Only the associations are different. Then they begin to irritate. By mid afternoon he had hauled out several large suitcases and begun throwing in anything and everything he could see that belonged to her. Shoes and bottles of perfume were flung on top of evening dresses and slammed out of sight.

Then he took the suitcases downstairs and left them in the hall. To hell with her. If it had been anyone else they might have sorted things out in time. But a woman, and a *Courtland!* Stirling Harmer's grand-daughter!

Which was why the news of the dynamited court case struck him as so damn funny.

He picked himself up off the carpet and spreadeagled across the bed. When the TV news moved on to a different item,

314

he leaned over and switched it off.

One Courtland had lost. Another Courtland had won.

And the chairman's little act with Lawrence the day before had been played out with the full knowledge of what was about to happen in court. No wonder Charles hadn't taken him very seriously.

Ted lay back and sighed, staring at the ceiling. The house felt large and empty around him. Perhaps he'd put the goddamn house on the market and find himself a snazzy penthouse in a new apartment block overlooking Hyde Park. Make up for some of the bachelorhood football had prevented him from enjoying. Fill his nights with Jill Norstad and whomsoever crossed his horizon.

Dominion? Hell.

He felt himself drifting back to sleep.

Tessa was interviewed live on *News at Ten*.

Shamus O'Neal's arrest and dramatic appearance in court dominated the headlines.

Tessa stressed that her client had been denied the right to consult her before being formally linked with O'Neal. 'Unfortunately the press was excluded from the main part of the charade,' she said. 'O'Neal didn't utter a word, and his alleged confession was handed out by the counsel for Dominion. Does the current state of emergency give the defendant's counsel in a civil case the right to become a prosecutor? No, it does not. Both Shamus O'Neal and Brigid Anderson are innocent until proved guilty. What we saw today was a gross perversion of justice.'

The reporter smiled. 'Miss Courtland, the public could accuse you of sour grapes,' she said.

'Let them,' she replied. 'I can only hope for support from those people who are better acquainted with the law then either Mr. Justice Blackford or Sir Hamilton Crisp appeared to be today.'

'Your own involvement in this case has caused a great deal of speculation. Why did you accept the brief?'

'If I fight criminal negligence in one industry, morally I

315

can't ignore it in another because of family connections.'

'But this case has gone beyond the limits of criminal negligence. The alleged IRA involvement has possibly lost you a great deal of public sympathy.'

The reporter then turned to two MPs, one for Tessa, one against. Her supporter was setting the wheels in motion for a public enquiry into the use of human guinea pigs within Dominion. 'The cases of James Anderson and Brigid Anderson are two separate issues. The public musn't be conned into confusing them. The medical evidence still stands against Dominion.'

The opposing MP pooh-poohed this as a ploy. 'On the contrary,' he said, 'the public has been conned into believing Brigid Anderson was a poor bereaved widow, when all the time she was plotting to blow up innocent people. This case has opened our eyes.'

'Let's concentrate on the facts and not get carried away by prejudice,' said the other MP.

Off camera, Tessa listened. She knew the odds weighed heavily against her, but that wasn't going to make her back down. The case had raised issues that had be be kept alive. When the interviewer returned to her for a concluding statement, she said, 'The *Anderson v. Dominion* case forces us to question the inflated power of the courts and the power of certain multinationals to exploit this. I'll risk being disbarred to keep these issues in the public eye.'

Her opponent quipped: 'The public has the right to question *your* suspect political motivations.'

Her supporter retaliated: 'The public has the right to know which side is politically motivated. Dominion or Miss Courtland and Brigid Anderson.'

Tessa drove home from the studio wondering how long it would be before the wrath of the Middle Temple's Benchers fell upon her. She didn't intend to hold back now. Her refusal to let the issues die, and the fact of her financing Brigid Anderson's passage to Ireland certainly placed a question mark over her future career at the Bar. Given the way the law could jump this way or that under the emergency regulations, she could even face a conspiracy charge. She felt calm, purified, and resigned to what might or might not happen to her.

Ciaran was waiting for her in the warehouse, busily switching the TV from Thames to the BBC for the late night news. 'Brigid's spending the night in Holloway prison,' he said grimly. 'They'll not let me see her until tomorrow.'

The personal edge seemed to have gone from his voice when he mentioned Brigid. Tessa decided it was tactful not to probe his feelings at that moment. Maybe later in the week they would discuss it when emotions weren't quite so raw.

'Hmm,' she said, deciding to concentrate on the case. 'I still don't believe a word of this crappy confession, but I'm sure the Special Branch is having a field day with her. All leering and snide about her affair with O'Neal. *That's* what she's being judged on primarily.'

Tessa stood with her back to Ciaran and busied herself around the sink.

He studied the TV screen for a few minutes, then frowned and glanced around the warehouse. The sketchbooks had gone. 'Where's Colette?'

'Col . . . ? Oh, she's gone back to Paris.'

'For good?'

She shrugged and reached into the fridge for some cold beer.

'Do you want to talk about it?' Ciaran asked.

She shook her head, sensing he was as aware as she was of the need for their personal lives to remain private for a while at least. All she said was, 'If I hadn't been so wrapped up in her and so obsessed with conquering Dominion. I might have predicted Crisp's move.' he paused. 'Damnit, it was staring us in the face. Dominion probably had Brigid under surveillance from the day the writ was served and I should have known that. Crisp only involved Diana Tonbridge to creat the impression he was going to blind us with science. Poor girl was hardly on her feet. It all seems so *obvious* now.'

Ciaran sighed and accepted the beer.

'It's just that, oh hell . . .' Tessa continued. 'Brigid seemed so *apolitical* until this afternoon.'

Ciaran looked away and gazed across the canal. 'When are you going to stop being to bloody naïve? A person doesn't have to argue Stalinism versus Maoism with you to be considered political, do they?'

Tessa studied him thoughtfully. 'Are you trying to tell me I've been deliberately used?'

'I'm trying to tell you that you have to stop thinking you have the exclusive political edge on every brief you handle. Stop being so *patronizing!*' He paused, head down. 'Brigid won, don't you see? *You* lost, and you're left footing the bill. She'll become a *cause célèbre* of the women's movement. The radical and sexual prejudices of the courts have been sharply dramatized. They'll have Joan Baez singing 'We Shall Overcome' outside Holloway prison, next.'

Tessa sat down and said nothing. She couldn't view the case in such cynical terms. Brigid's martyrdom for the cause was a bare reward for winding up in a London prison, with her children stuck in Dublin. And it's all my fault, she thought bitterly. She was so concerned with using the Anderson case to denounce Dominion, that she had missed the obvious. What am I? she asked herself. A tobacco heiress playing chess with radicalism.

The late night news was announced on TV. She got up and switched it off. 'You know, I, ah . . . . before all this happened, I was seriously thinking of leaving the Bar anyway, giving up my inheritance and changing my name.'

'Mmm,' he said tightly. 'The ultimate Tolstoyian solution. Honestly Tessa. When you're not being patronizing you're being impossibly romantic. What were you going to do then? Rush off to Mozambique to work on a Marxist commune?'

'No—actually I was going to offer my services at the local law centre.'

'With your accent and attitudes? Don't make me laugh!'

'Now who's being patronizing? Who got me involved with Brigid Anderson in the first place?'

He looked at her, thinking back to the evening he had

deliberated about involving her. He had specifically wanted her because of the publicity she could generate. He also needed to diminish the image he was acquiring as an 'IRA solicitor' and wanted the experience of a big test case in a different political arena. The Dominion issue seemed ideal. Hot. Topical. But there they were, right back where they'd started.

'I think I'd better go,' he said, 'busy day tomorrow.'

'Tell Brigid I'll probably see her in Holloway prison if they slap a conspiracy charge on me,' she said dryly.

'Well, at least you can afford the best legal minds in London, can't you?'

'So can Brigid,' she snapped. 'I got her into this mess, and I'll pay through the nose to get her out of it.'

'That's what it comes down to in the end, doesn't it?' he snapped back. 'The power of influence and money. What makes you think she'll accept it?'

'Jesus, you're sour. There's no humanity or fight left in you, is there Ciaran?'

He shook his untidy gray head, crumpled the empty beer can and dropped it in the wastepaper basket. 'As Brigid said, you understand *nothing*.'

Without saying another word, he turned and left the warehouse.

Tessa sat propped against the cushions for a long time after he left.

She understood only too well

But there was no point living in a state of permanent self-condemnation. Discipline and disbarment would liberate her from one aspect of the system. But Dominion was the quintessence of that system. How long could she go on living off its dividends?

Long enough to see Brigid Anderson and herself through the present crisis, at least.

And what then?

Tessa rose gloomily and began to turn off the lights. Enough was enough for one day. Denouncing her inheritance would be like committing hara-kiri. She only lived off a small portion of it anyway.

Disbarred, she thought, climbing the stairs to her bed-room, I can at least be a constant source of embarrassment to the legal establishment.

Dominion's share price started to rise sharply an hour after the stock exchange opened its doors the next morning.

Observers credited the quick recovery to the news that had dominated the evening's broadcasts and the morning papers.

Those few corporate shareholders tipped off by Paul Lombard were now able to buy back at rock bottom prices, securing huge profits from their sales of the previous day. Again, the small shareholder who had sold, lost out, because by the time he realized what was happening, the buying price was again much higher than the sale price he'd received the day before.

The Dominion executive committee was bristling with good humour and self-praise. Paul Lombard was the man of the day. Even Jolyon Williams entered into the spirit, although he couldn't quite hide his jealousy. He no longer considered Ted Mallett a threat, but now there was Lombard to consider as a likely replacement for Charles in a few years. Apart from the current flurry under the spotlight, Lombard had the advantage of being 'family.'

Charles Courtland accepted much of the praise as though he had won the case himself. He still couldn't bring himself to phone his daughter and commiserate. It was up to Tessa to contact *him* and apologize.

And where was Ted in all this?

He kept himself aloof, arriving at Dominion House in a pair of jeans and an open-necked shirt just before midday. He called his assistant into his office and dictated a short letter of resignation. She was upset but didn't seem surprised. 'All this is so messy,' she said philosophically. 'I don't blame you.'

Ted smiled and quickly cleared his desk. She returned with the letter. He signed it, exchanged a brisk goodbye with her, no different from that of any normal working day, and made sure the passage was clear before leaving.

He was relieved that none of the board members had seen

320

him. He didn't feel like talking to anyone.

Re-emerging into the clear day, Ted wove his way through a group of picketers. They crowded the car park and steps, placards aloft: STOP HUMAN GUINEA PIG EXPERIMENTS: BOYCOTT YERBA SACRA: THE TRIAL GOES ON. Other picketers could be seen heading toward the building, placards waving in the gentle breeze from the Thames.

Ted, too, knew this was only the beginning, and he wasn't going to hang around to see the subject picked apart, bit by bit. What was he going to do? Hell. Sell the house, use some of the proceeds to buy into Tony McKay's advertising agency and join him as a partner? Maybe. Although, maybe not for a while. He needed to forget about *Yerba Sacra* and *Denim*. He'd already achieved more than most marketing and admen achieved in a lifetime. What more was there to do? What more did he need to prove?

Yerba Sacra. Was it only a product?

It didn't really matter what he did now. The publicity resulting from his resignation was bound to inspire some kind of offer. Even it if didn't, he certainly had enough to set up something on his own. A marketing consultancy perhaps. Nothing longwinded. He could become an itinerent trouble-shooter. Charge a hefty fee to hop around from industry to industry solving internal marketing problems. The idea appealed to him. It meant he could move on without the administrative worries of trying to make his creative ideas and solutions actually work long-term. Wouldn't cost him much to set it up.

He was at the bridge. Picketers passed by him on either side. No one stopped to look at him with his unshaven chin and spiky hair.

He paused when he was halfway across and leaned on the wall, gazing down the full length of the Thames.

He didn't see Charles Courtland's silver Rolls drive by. And Courtland didn't stop to take a second look at the husky man in jeans, quietly enjoying the river view.

MP Nigel Swan sat next to him on the back seat. 'Hamilton

Crisp was brilliant, Charles, quite brilliant,' he said. 'Pity the man didn't enter politics. We could do with someone like him on the front bench.'

'Hmm,' Courtland agreed, only half listening to the chatter.

Swan patted his knee. 'You're not worried about this dragging on, are you Charles?'

'A bit,' the chairman admitted, touching Ted's resignation letter buried in his pocket. He was annoyed with Ted for letting him down, for not even talking it over with him. He felt slighted. It was the worst possible time for Ted to walk out. *Yerba Sacra* was in turmoil. Who on God's earth did Ted think would sort it out? Oh well, he decided. Jolyon Williams would just have to step in. The company man. Dull and boringly dependable, but perhaps his image would be useful right now. It would counterbalance all the noise and flamboyance that had turned *Yerba Sacra* into nothing short of a circus.

If they were in for an enquiry, Jolyon Williams was the best man available. He could be counted on to say and do the proper thing at the proper time.

Nigel Swan was a little more flippant about the enquiry. 'Don't worry! We'll find a way to muzzle it somehow. Anyway Charles, you know how long enquiries take. By the time this one is resolved, no one will care any more.'

The chairman nodded.

The Rolls swept by.

Ted turned and continued across the bridge.